THE BODY *Spoken*

Also by Janice Deaner

Where Blue Begins

THE BODY *Spoken*

JANICE DEANER

A DUTTON BOOK

DUTTON
Published by the Penguin Group
Penguin Putnam Inc., 375 Hudson Street, New York, New York 10014, U.S.A.
Penguin Books Ltd, 27 Wrights Lane, London W8 5TZ, England
Penguin Books Australia Ltd, Ringwood, Victoria, Australia
Penguin Books Canada Ltd, 10 Alcorn Avenue, Toronto, Ontario, Canada M4V 3B2
Penguin Books (N.Z.) Ltd, 182–190 Wairau Road, Auckland 10, New Zealand

Penguin Books Ltd, Registered Offices:
Harmondsworth, Middlesex, England

First published by Dutton, an imprint of Dutton NAL, a member of Penguin Putnam Inc.

First Printing, March, 1999
10   9   8   7   6   5   4   3   2   1

LIBRARY OF CONGRESS CATALOGING-IN-PUBLICATION DATA:

Deaner, Janice.
    The body spoken / Janice Deaner.
      p.   cm.
    ISBN 0-525-94414-1 (acid-free paper)
    I. Title.
    PS3554.E1743B64   1998
    813'.54—dc21   98-14818
                                                                                 CIP

Printed in the United States of America
Set in Palatino
Designed by Leonard Telesca

PUBLISHER'S NOTE
This is a work of fiction. Names, characters, places, and incidents either are the products of the author's imagination or are used fictitiously, and any resemblance to actual persons, living or dead, events, or locales is entirely coincidental.

THE BODY *Spoken*

P L A I N S

1

*S*he told him she'd been living as a man for five years. When he asked her why, she looked straight into his eyes and said it was much too long a story. He complained that she shouldn't have told him that much if she wasn't prepared to tell him the rest, but they were strangers on a train, and a remark like that could only get him so far.

The Amtrak train had been crowded when it left Penn Station and everyone had to share a seat. It was she who sat next to him, not the other way around, and it was she who uttered the first word that ever passed between them. She said a few things before she announced that she had been living as a man, but nothing of any consequence. She made conversation, like how hot the weather was now that it was August, how the train was crowded for a weekday, and how the prospect of leaving New York behind was like a breath of fresh air.

It was when he'd asked her her name that she'd stumbled. He first saw the confusion in her eyes, then heard it in her voice.

My name, she said. I was, well. Oscar Lourde—

She stopped speaking and looked at him helplessly, as if she were lost. Then she said it:

I've been living as a man for five years.

She said it, as if to explain herself, as if she were trying to tell him, *I don't know my name anymore. I haven't lived as myself for so long.* He would have liked to have known more, but he could tell she had never meant to say that much, that it had just slipped out the way provocative things sometimes do between strangers. She apologized for it and then put a finger to her lips.

When the train sped through the heat-stroked backyards of a small Pennsylvania town, she uttered another thing. She'd been watching out the window for a long time when she turned to him and confessed, I just took a cab to Penn Station, bought a ticket to Los Angeles, and without a phone call or a fax to anyone, I left my life in ruins.

She smiled and looked away, and it was hard to tell if she was serious or not, but the words *in ruins* echoed inside him.

In the afternoon she retreated to her sleeping quarters, where he stopped in to see her a few hours later. She had a first-class deluxe bedroom, for which he knew she'd paid a great deal of money. Certainly more than he had paid for his standard bedroom, which came with a small cotlike bed and nothing more. Hers had a private bath and a window, and if you paid a little extra money (she did), you could have white cotton sheets and a red velvet drape that could be closed to cordon off the bedroom from the tiny sitting room.

It's the closest I can get to the past, she said.

And she was interested in the past. She was interested in putting the present behind her, even if it was just for a week. She wanted to escape it one last time before there was no escaping it anymore. She wanted to pretend she belonged to a time when certain things didn't exist, like Formica countertops and plastic chairs, when there weren't fax machines or internets or terrorists. A time when dames were dames and men were men, she said and smiled.

He wasn't so much interested in the past as he was in knowing what lay beyond the present. He was interested in becoming someone he wasn't now; he wanted a whole other way of thinking to emerge inside his mind, so he could see the world in a completely different way, to think different thoughts than the ones he always thought now. That's why he'd done what he'd done, he told himself.

At the thought of it, guilt surged through him, a few images flooding his mind—broken dishes, the overturned table, the shredded curtains. He tried to thrust them out. It had all been a part of creating a rupture, he told himself. That's why he'd done what he'd done, he reasoned—he'd broken with his life so brutally to change himself. Then he'd climbed onto the train, to borrow time, to reckon with what he'd done, to see if in his act, which had been so unreasonable, he could become someone else, or discover another piece of himself perhaps, a piece lost to him or at least invisible. He told himself this was true, but he couldn't be certain.

He went looking for her and found her in her room. She looked happy, in the corner, tucked away, amid the white cotton sheets and red velvet curtains. He stayed no longer than fifteen minutes. She was reading, he could see. When he left, he closed the door behind him and walked a few steps down the corridor before he remembered the book he'd left on a small table next to her bed. He knocked quietly and opened the door—it'd just been seconds since he'd closed it—and found her sitting cross-legged on her bed, her eyes closed, her hands palm-down on her knees. He thought perhaps she was praying, but he didn't ask. When night fell, he came by and found her eating her dinner, while she was reading a book and watching the string of towns, like pearls on a strand, slip through her fingers.

They met a few hours later in the passenger car. They sat for a while in the darkness, talking occasionally, her voice easy and soft like talcum. It was late when she finally invited him into her room. It was awkward at first, he didn't know where to put himself, until finally he stretched himself out on her bed and crossed his long legs. She sat next to him, her back against the wall, her knees drawn up like an adolescent girl's, her hands motioning up and down when she talked, as if they were shadows of her words. She gestured for everything, and her voice was low and excitable. She made sound effects and spoke in accents, and used expressions, like *smoking up a storm*, that amused him. He tried to pinpoint her accent, but he couldn't. He wondered if she had tampered with it over the years.

While she talked, he squinted his eyes and tried to imagine her as a man; she had short, dark hair, a long, pale neck, and green eyes. He wondered what she had done to change her face, how she had worn her cropped hair, how she'd carried herself. She was fairly tall and was by no means a tiny woman, but still she was a woman: the curves were in the right places, the sway of her hips, the movement of her hands were just right.

She wore a long white skirt with a slit up the side, and her lips and fingernails were painted red. He thought she was beautiful, although she laughed when he said it. But it was true; her mouth was full, her cheekbones high and delicate. She looked glamorous, he said. In fact he worried that she might be a bit out of his league, but at the same time it attracted him immensely. He even told her, joking, that he thought she might be too glamorous for him. She said it was the red lipstick and the red fingernail polish, which she hadn't worn in five years. She told him it was the strangest thing when she caught sight of her hands and saw those ten red tips and when she was in the bathroom and her face appeared in the mirror, red-lipped.

Because you lived as a man? he asked.

Yes, she said.

He asked her again to tell him why.

It's too long a story, she said.

But we have nearly four days on the train.

It's not so much the length, she said.

She gave him a look which he took to mean that it was the depth of it that she found too long.

Could I at least ask you a question? he said, and when she nodded, he asked the question that had distracted him, and which he now felt embarrassed to ask.

Genitally speaking, are you a man or a woman?

She thought it was very funny and repeated it back to him on and off all night. *Genitally speaking*—she'd insert it where she could. It was the first time he'd really heard her laugh hard, and after he'd heard her, he tried to arrange for it again and again. It was a worthwhile sound, he told her, productive and abundant.

Later that night, when they were lying side by side on her bed, she said, I've always wanted to take a train across the country and meet someone I've never met before and will never see again and make up a story about myself. Make up the whole thing.

Have you ever? he asked.

She turned to him and smiled.

No, never, she said.

Are the things you've told me so far true? he asked.

I've told you almost nothing, she said. We've talked about impersonal things mostly and we've laughed.

Except, he said, that you told me you lived as a man for five years.

Yes, except that, she said.

Then she looked at him, at the bruised look on his face, bruised from being shut out, and said, I'm sorry I told you. I shouldn't have. It just slipped out. It even surprised me when I said it.

Her face lost its life and suddenly she looked as bleak as anyone had ever looked, as if she'd seen whole crops fail, laid husbands to rest, placed stillborn babies in pine caskets. He knew then that she'd lived through something. He recognized that face, the downturned eyes, the slack corners of the mouth when you were caught grieving—he'd seen that same expression on his own face many mornings in the mirror while shaving.

It was when she took her sweater off after the air conditioner had failed that he was sure of it. She had two long knife scars on her right arm, one long and jagged, thick as a twig, the other fat and shaped like a horseshoe. He noticed she did nothing to conceal them, as if she were proud of them. He couldn't take his eyes off them.

What happened? he said.

A steak knife, she said.

Who did it?

My ex-husband.

But that's all she would say.

She wouldn't tell him her name, either. She said it was enough that she'd told him the name she had used as a man.

Are you running from something? he asked.

Not running, she said. I'm taking a train away from it. One must travel away from a ruin to gain the distance necessary to see it for what it is, and then to cut oneself from it. I've told you. She paused and smiled. My life lies behind me in ruins.

He thought she meant it, but even so she was conscious of the drama she created and seemed amused by it.

What kind of ruins? he asked, playing along.

She smiled again and touched a finger to his lip.

Denied specifics, he formed images in his mind, images of her bed, swathed in white cotton, unmade, a rose silk slip, like the one she had, flung across it, images of Limoges dishes in the sink, of a faucet dripping over them, of a window open and a white curtain fluttering and sailing while a telephone rang and an answering machine picked up, time after time. A lover. A husband.

But "in ruins" was all she'd give him.

When she lay down on her back, he did the same and turned his head toward her.

What will we call each other? he wanted to know.

We don't need to call one another. We're on a train.

I could call you Oscar Lourde, he said.

He watched the sadness creep back into her eyes, the corners of her mouth draw down. He could see that there was some age on her. She was somewhere in her thirties, thirty-two, thirty-three, he guessed.

Don't call me that, she said.

And he knew she meant it. She turned over on her side, putting her back to him.

He waited a few moments before he asked her, What if I was going to write a story about you and me, what would I call us? He said it playfully, to win her back.

The man and the woman, she said. That's what we are. The *man* and the *woman* on the train, she said, drawing it out with mock seriousness. Like in one of those pretentious Swedish films, darling, with the subtitles you can't read.

He played along, flicking his cigarette with bored nonchalance, and asked, Will it always be so?

She looked over her shoulder, a bit of her face, a portion of her eye showing, playing at being a woman.

I don't know, she said.

He liked that about her, that she never pretended to know anything. In the short time he'd known her, she had never assumed an authority on any subject other than herself. She understood that life had a way, a way of moving that was all its own, without reason, without care, that life had a way of subverting all expectations. And she understood it fully, without bitterness. Perhaps better than he.

When he asked her what she'd done for a living, she said, I'd rather not say.

Why? What does it matter? he asked, a trace of annoyance in his voice.

It doesn't, she said. It doesn't matter either way, but this is my ride across the country, and that's how I want it. You have a choice—be with me on the train, or don't be, but this is how I want my train ride to be.

So he wouldn't know her name, or what she'd done for a living. But she ended up telling him other things that night. And he found himself collecting the things she told him, as if they were the pieces of a jigsaw puzzle that someone had flung out a window— a jigsaw puzzle that once pieced together would answer some question that burned inside his body like a cellar light that never went off, that would rearrange the pattern of his thinking, until he thought differently, until he wasn't the same man who'd climbed on the train. He hated to admit it but he needed something from her. He wanted to know what the rupture in her life had been, the one that had caused her to live as a man. But mostly he wanted to know what she'd learned: had she returned as someone else, as someone completely different?

What it was they did in her room the next night, as the gentle hills of Ohio swept past the window, was hard for him to categorize. They made things up, like what they would do if this happened, or if that happened, or the way it should have been or the way they meant it to have been. He tried to remember the next morning, to connect all the stories, but he couldn't. When he tried to place her, to form her in his mind, there was nothing there. No real facts, just random, floating topics, connected to nothing. The world in her room was white cotton sheets and red velvet drapes (a world he didn't know) and a window through which they watched the countryside pass—the farmlands of Ohio and Indiana as they stretched out endlessly, the fields rolling and darkened under the glow of the moon; the tall grasses and the delicate tips of wheat shining faintly as they bent in the wind. He couldn't exactly remember what they'd said. Sometimes they said nothing at all, just lay there lulled by the constant *tha-thunk* of the train, their skin touching. By the time he got back to his room in the morning, their words were already gone, like air.

When he washed up in the public bathroom, he looked in the mirror and saw fear in his blue eyes. He was stooped over, his height and broad shoulders too great for the small room. He pushed his straight brown hair from his eyes and splashed water on his face. As his long fingers moved across the well-defined planes of his cheekbones, he remembered her words *in ruins*. It was true, he thought, he'd left his own life in ruins.

The passages of his bronchial tubes began to constrict in an asthmatic spasm. He'd had asthma since he was a small boy; it was debilitating then, now it was inconvenient. He gasped for air and reached into his pants pocket for the inhaler. After he put it to his mouth, he took a deep breath, and relief came within moments. He thought perhaps it was the small cramped space of the bathroom which had brought on the attack, as if it were too much like the oxygen tent he used to lie under countless times as a boy. He remembered its sickly vapors and his mother's face wavering outside the plastic as if she were underwater, her hand constantly touching his legs, his arms, his chest. How he'd longed to get away from her, but he'd been so thin and weak. He stuffed the inhaler deep into the dark of his pocket, as if it were a piece of thought he wanted to suppress.

Fear surged through him at the thought that perhaps his act and his flight onto this train were not radical acts, that they were not part of some grand personal quest. What if they were something else altogether, something more drab, more mundane, something simply banal? He told himself, no, it was not this way, that these fears were merely evidence of repression, of an internal policing the culture had imposed on every man to keep him from his darkest impulses, to keep him civil. No, he was justified—by doing what he did, by breaking violently from his life, by climbing on this train, he was breaking this policing. It had to be done. There could be no discovery while being repressed, while being censored, while being pinioned beneath convention. It was death to anything creative. *Whoever looks into himself as into vast space, and carries galaxies within himself, also knows how irregular all galaxies are; they lead into the chaos and labyrinth of existence.* This stilled him.

The sun was beginning to rise on the last of the Indiana farmlands when he found her in one of the passenger cars. He had walked down the aisle in his long, even gait, and had stopped just short of her seat, where he watched as she sat with her legs tucked beneath her, a gray scarf wound around her neck, while she looked out the window. He quietly slipped into the seat next to her. When she felt his presence she turned and smiled.

Why don't you ask me what I do? he began. But he wasn't the least bit interested in telling her. He was just curious about her mind—a woman's mind that didn't care what he did.

I've heard too many life stories, she said.

Like whose? he asked.

Many.

Like whose? he insisted.

People like you, she said seriously. People like the people on this train. People from the country, people from the city, happy people, sad people, old people. She paused. Men on Death Row.

He hadn't expected her to say this. He could tell that she meant it. Even so, he could see that she was aware of how provocative it was.

Now he wanted to know about these men on Death Row; but he was afraid that if he asked her too pointedly, he would scare her away, so he spoke carefully. How did you happen to hear the life stories of men on Death Row?

But he had sounded too eager, had pressed too hard, and she closed down. It gave him hope, though, because things leaked out of her like that. He figured it was only a matter of time. If he was silent enough, if he slowed himself down, like a cat, watching, she would give herself away. Before they reached L.A., he would know her.

He wondered if he had unconsciously linked knowing her with knowing himself. He didn't understand it, yet it felt that way in his mind now. He'd gotten on the train with the idea of becoming someone else and somehow she had been woven into it, this woman who'd lived as a man, who'd known men on Death Row. Why her? he thought. Of all the people on the train, why had this woman sat down next to him?

He spent some of the early evening alone in the cafe car, a place that looked and smelled like a moving McDonald's, and over cups of coffee and cigarettes he read a battered paperback he'd picked up and then a *Newsweek* he found laying around. He thought about the dark-skinned man from Kenya in the *Newsweek* photograph who was standing in the middle of the road, dressed in the traditional skirt, a spear in one hand, a cellular phone in the other. An image like that in an American magazine: at one time it was new and had brought with it a certain way of thinking, but it was nothing new anymore. He wondered what would replace it, what would appear next as new, and where it would lead thought. He was most interested in this.

He wondered too if she was an example of what was new— this woman who'd lived as a man and who was so wearied of it, was now dozing in a first-class bedroom, complete with red velvet curtains and white cotton sheets, seeking the past, wanting nothing more than to shut out the reality he was most in search of? What was it she knew?

He looked up at the young men who'd gathered at the next table in the cafe car to play a game of cards. Their heads were shaven and across the youthful muscles of their upper arms and over the sinews of their forearms tattoos careened. What they thought was subversive had already been absorbed by the culture, he thought. He'd seen Calvin Klein ads featuring tattooed flesh and shaven heads roar past on New York buses. It was nothing new anymore, yet he could see in their postures, in their language, in their carved flesh their need to be free from convention. Some part of him longed to join them, but their way was already a relic. He turned away from them, from their cruel laughter, and wondered how long it would take before their thoughts were no longer their own, before their bodies and souls were utterly lost to them.

He heard in his mind now the words, *You have to be a man.* The words that had so enraged him, the words of someone who had no idea what it meant to be a man. Yet why did they ring in his mind now? Why were they lodged there like a piece of glass? Was it the cut of truth, or was it another example of the culture, of its incessant voice to be this, to be that, to be good, now so internalized it enslaved him?

He lit a cigarette and snuffed out the match between his thumb and forefinger. She didn't know about him, and she wouldn't, he decided. It was good that she didn't ask where he'd been or where he'd come from or what he did, or even his name. He'd spent years racing from women's questions, their need to know. Yet he'd wanted her to ask him, wanted her to hang over his shoulder while he tried to sleep on his side, prying into him with her eyes. I need to talk, he wanted her to say. But she didn't. He wondered if she was being aloof to bring him to her.

When he left the cafe car, he found her sitting in one of the passenger cars. He sat down next to her, and when he caught himself hanging over her shoulder, asking, Did you ever sleep with a woman, when you were a man? he imagined he was being like a woman.

I was never a man, she said, bitingly. I only lived as one.

Okay, he said. Did you ever sleep with a woman when you lived as a man?

When he heard himself ask this, he remembered almost perfectly a night when a lover had hung over his shoulder while he was trying to sleep and had asked, How many women have you slept with besides me? He felt foolish now that she wouldn't answer him; he remembered how stupid he thought his lover's question was. He told himself not to push it, to let it go, but he heard his voice asking again.

Did you?

It doesn't matter, she said.

I know it doesn't, but I'd like to know.

The words his lover had used, he remembered.

No, she finally said. I didn't. Not really.

Once the train began to wind its way through Nebraska, he found her sitting mesmerized, watching out the window as the flat green prairies reached back miles to meet the horizon and the expansive blue sky. He had wanted to be near her, and had walked slowly through all the cars, looking in every seat, searching for her. He found her transfixed, her nose three inches from the glass window, as the tumbleweeds and windmills paraded past.

I've never been through Nebraska, she said.

No?

It's beautiful, she said. The grasslands are like blowing horizons. The windmills against the half-cloudy skies are like prayers, like hands folded in prayer.

Her face softened and her eyes filled with light. When she lowered her eyes, he knew she had given something away. She was poetic, he thought, romantic.

When he looked out the window again, he saw the grasses and the windmills as if he'd never seen them before. He wondered how she could get away with saying something like this, though—it was corny, yet she'd said it truthfully, in a way few people could, and that impressed him.

When they had a two-hour stopover in Conklin, Nebraska, she found out from an elderly couple inside the train station that the best restaurant in town was the Linklaen House. They walked through the deserted town in the evening heat, down two blocks of red-brick buildings with storefronts that now stood cut out against the starry night sky.

The Linklaen House was on the corner. They climbed the stairs and walked through bright red doors into an extremely elegant dining room. There was carved wood everywhere, the deepest tones of black and brown mahogany. The white linen tablecloths were a bit tattered and moth-eaten, but in the hazy light, it was barely noticeable. The linen was stiff, and he saw her feel it for its quality. He watched her eyes as they moved across everything, lovingly; the silver candlesticks and platters, the chandelier above them, the crystal gleaming muted under dust, the rug under their feet worn, but beautiful in its deep red.

Time has stopped here, she said.

She ordered rice and vegetables and a bottle of red wine. She ate exactly half of the rice and vegetables and asked for the other half to be packed up for her. He ordered veal and drank the greater portion of the wine. She had only one glass, but he was sure it was responsible for loosening her tongue; when they went back to her room, aboard the train, she told him something.

Inside her room it was hot and stifling. The train had stood in the station for two hours without any air conditioning. He took off his shirt, and she took off her blouse and revealed a white, sleeveless T-shirt underneath. He noticed her breasts, he couldn't help it—the T-shirt was tight and he could see through it. He wasn't quite sure why he hadn't noticed them before, but now that he could see them, he was aroused by their roundness. Her breasts weren't huge, but they were full. He couldn't help imagining his hands on them. He wondered what she'd done with them when she'd lived as a man.

How did you conceal your breasts? he asked.

I bound them, she said.

How?

What do you mean, how? I bound them.

Tell me the details, he said.

So she pantomimed binding her breasts, saying that she had used a long strip of a particular kind of elastic, like an Ace bandage, but stronger, and that she had wound it around and around her torso. He watched, fascinated.

Was it comfortable? he asked.

Yes, she said.

But not now?

No, not now.

When was the last time they were bound? he asked.

Two weeks ago.

This surprised him. Her living as a woman was very new then, he thought. He sensed then the thinness of her skin, the fragility, and understood he would need to respect it.

Where is the elastic band now? he asked quietly.

At the end of my bed.

He couldn't get it out of his mind—the idea of her unbinding her breasts and flinging that elastic band across her unmade bed of white cotton. He could imagine her breasts, warm and unbound, as she fell backward into the whiteness.

Where were you when you first bound them? he asked.

You can't be serious?

Oh, but I am, he said.

She sighed, and said, All right. I was next to my bed, in my apartment in New York. I had found the elastic in an old trunk I was looking through. Is this the kind of thing you want to know?

Yes, he said.

It was very hot, not so unlike tonight. A night in July, or it could have been August. A man had just left, and something drew me to the trunk, my father's trunk, and it was in there that I found the elastic. When I looked down at the elastic, I understood I was to bind myself with it, though I can't explain how I knew this exactly. I walked over to my bed. I lay the elastic on the pillow then took off my shirt and flung it down at the end of the mattress. I unhooked my bra and dropped it in the wastebasket. Then I picked up the elastic and began to wrap it around and around my chest. A faint smile played on her lips. Am I being specific enough?

Yes, he said. Please go on.

After I was finished, I put on a white T-shirt and looked in the mirror. I was transfixed by my reflection, as I had already cut off my hair, and now I could see that I looked like a man. Well, more like a teenage boy.

Like Oscar Lourde? he said.

Yes, she said, like Oscar Lourde.

He watched the way her breasts rose and fell under the white T-shirt, swelling a bit when she took in air. He had the urge to pull off the shirt, to unclasp her bra, to unbind her breasts completely, to let them breathe.

He reached out and touched the scars on her arm instead. The long, twiggish one first, the fat horseshoe one next. She didn't mind. He sensed that she even liked it, but when he tried to run his tongue down the scar, she said no.

Why not? he said.

We aren't that for each other.

But why can't we be? he said.

Because we don't know each other.

That's not my fault, he said. I've been trying to know you ever since we got on the train.

She looked at him for a moment. He looked left out, and he saw her eyes open to his need.

I know, she said. I'm sorry. Then she spoke quietly and said shyly, I've forgotten how to be a woman. Then she touched his face with her fingers.

He wasn't sure what she meant him to feel.

After a long pause, he tried again to run his tongue down her long scar, and this time she held quiet. He started up near her shoulder and ran his tongue down through the fine blond hairs, over the hot blue veins, to the hollow of her elbow, where he tasted her flesh and rolled it around in his mouth, down to her slender wrist, where the scar ended abruptly. He took her fingers into his mouth and sucked them, and when he looked up at her, he could see her eyes were closed and a tear rolled down her cheek.

He knew then the skin covering who else she had become was thin, like tissue.

After a few hours they parted. She wanted to read some, she said, and he understood that she wanted to be alone. He didn't go to her room later. He found it ridiculous that he should feel this way, but he wanted her to come to him. He lay on his cot, on his back, his hands behind his head. He felt he was stalking her in some odd, benign way, but stalking her nonetheless, and he wasn't the type to stalk women. They generally stalked him. He lay there listening for her, lulled by the rhythm of the train, content to be inside its ribcage, waiting for her.

He couldn't help but wonder why this experience had await-ed him on the train and not some other. Why a woman on a train who had lived as a man, and not a murderer or an adulteress or an ordinary man. Was it just random, a matter of chance, or was there something more at work? He told himself it was simply random, the chance of events, but he wondered if something in the psyche, the part that yearned for freedom, had the power to order circumstances, to bring about a certain collision, and then look purely random. Had he and the woman on the train been drawn to one another by something inexplicable, something one could never know or see, something completely beyond reason? He didn't know, but he understood that all else had ceased to exist to him. He was going to uncover her, to split her open, to take what he needed. There was nothing else to be done.

When she came, she opened the door and peered in at him.

Here you are, she said. Her face was flushed; her short hair, mussed. You don't want to be with me?

He found himself answering in a way that surprised him; it was so transparent.

You're toying with me, he said.

It came out of his mouth before he could stop it, but it was the truth.

She stared at him for a few moments, searching his eyes, but said nothing.

He hitched himself up on his elbow.

The first thing you tell me is that you lived as a man until recently, he said, and then you won't tell me why. I can't know anything about you, and I'm not to tell you anything about myself, no names, nothing, and yet you let me touch you. You are playing some game, some weird man-and-woman-on-the-train game, and frankly, I don't want to play.

We *are* on a train, she said, trying to make a joke.

It had gone past that, he knew it and she knew it, but there was no saying it yet. Something else had to be said first.

I don't care, he said at last. It doesn't matter. We could be alone in an igloo and I would still have trouble with this arrangement. You're toying with me, and I don't like it.

She took a deep breath, then closed her eyes and thought for a moment. You're right, she said. Of course, I'm sorry. She paused, then moved closer to him. What can I do to keep you? she asked quietly.

He held still, and looked at her.

You could tell me about yourself, he said.

It's a long story, she said again, and I don't like to tell it much.

Yes, so you say. But tell it one more time and then never again, he said.

Their eyes locked, and hers gave way first.

All right. I'll tell you about what happened when I was fifteen years old. But after that, it's over—the telling.

Why when you were fifteen? he asked. Why can't you tell me about why you lived as a man?

I can't tell you that without telling you everything that came before it. It would make no sense, and anyway I am only offering this one story.

Then, after you tell me this story, then what? he asked.

You'll probably want to tell me something about yourself.

You make it sound so awful, he said, and suddenly he was aware that he felt like a small boy clamoring to show his mother his coloring.

That's my offer, she said. Take it or leave it.

So they left his berth, and he followed behind her, through the gray darkness of the second-class slumber coach, down its skinny, narrow aisles clogged with half-dressed people, to the wider, well-lit hallway of the deluxe first-class coach, where there was a door she opened with a key. They walked in, and after they settled themselves behind the red velvet drapes, he noticed how different the air in her room was from the air in his. It was the scent of her perfume, her rose night slip discarded at the foot of the bed, her German clock ticking evenly.

She pushed her skirt up past her knees. Her skin was so pale, her calves so slender, the ankles as delicate as any he'd ever seen.

Is this really going to be true, he said, or is it going to be the story you make up on a train?

She smiled, and he looked straight into her eyes and noticed the distance, as if she lived ten or fifteen miles behind them. He longed for such distance. How had she gotten it? he wondered again.

Are you ready? she asked.

Yes, he said.

All right, she began. My mother had visions sometimes and prayed three hours a day. I think that is the best place to start.

Okay, he said.

2

*S*he was dark-haired and red-lipped, and her name was Bo. She was a great beauty, and my father said glamour accompanied her like a silent, devoted servant. His name was Benjamin Lourde, but we all called him Lourde. He was a big man, tall and muscular, with brown curly hair and gray eyes, and he disappeared in green work pants and a white T-shirt every morning to our attic, where he sat on a mattress from nine until five and wrote plays, never making enough money to take care of a wife and four children. The truth was, he never made a dime.

In 1972 we were eating cornflakes for lunch and scrambled eggs for dinner, and Bo and Lourde were screaming at each other every night in their room, my sister Zellie and my brother, Oscar, and I cranking up our cheap Montgomery Ward stereo, throwing Led Zeppelin or Grand Funk Railroad between them and us. Then one hot, dusky evening in June Bo disappeared down the road we were living on, dressed in a pair of Oscar's bell-bottom jeans, walking with her hands clenched behind her back, the sun waiting for her to get to Ross Yeager's farm before it sank out of sight. We thought she was going to tell him how poor we were, like in the Depression days, then ask for some milk or eggs, maybe a chicken, things were that bad. But Bo wasn't interested in food. She wanted to know how to make alcohol.

Ross Yeager was thrilled that a beautiful woman would want anything from him, and considered it a great honor to sweat in the back room of our kitchen for the three nights it took him and Bo to put together this thing, this slate-gray, hulking shame. And when it stood on its own, spitting and breathing, Bo left in the middle of the day with an old, rare quilt from India slung over her arm, and came back in Ross Yeager's truck with a bunch of antique tables and chairs and old pictures and a black upright piano. Lourde wouldn't have anything to do with it, so the rest of us got stuck the whole hot June night pulling sofas and chairs out of Bo's living room, hauling them upstairs to our spare bedroom, then going back downstairs to arrange and rearrange Bo's newly acquired tables and chairs in the empty space. Red-lipped, Bo moved languidly among the furniture, her long movie-star dress trailing after her, while our little sister, Frieda, ran from one table to the other, sitting at them all, watching the piano as if it might play. Bo kept tipping her head from one side to the other, trying to see it all through other eyes, until she finally saw what she wanted to see—something none of us saw—the parlor of a 1920s speakeasy. Where we saw a jumble of old tables and chairs grouped in our living room, Bo saw something far more promising. She always did.

A manila-colored liquor license turned up on the dining-room table a week later, which cost her plenty, she admitted, and since she could scarcely afford the fee, the still in the back room was put into motion making booze, which Ross Yeager said was as good as any he'd ever tasted. We all tasted it, but none of us knew if it was any good or not. We'd never tasted moonshine, and that's what it was, despite what Bo said, despite the fact that prohibition was ancient history. It was moonshine, stuff that Ross Yeager, now in his seventies, could remember his grandfather making back in the twenties. None of us knew the first thing about moonshine either, not to mention starting a latter-day speakeasy, Bo included. She grew up rich in New York City drinking cognac, so where she got the idea, none of us knew. Zellie said it was just Bo's variation on the hippie back-to-the-earth theme, her way of baking her own bread or preserving peaches, but finally I thought Bo simply longed to be more interesting. Her mother, Georgia, had been a doctor in New York City who had died in a prison at the age of fifty-five, jailed for performing countless illegal abortions in the back room of her Park Avenue apartment. Perhaps Bo had wanted to top her or at least come out even. But who knew? Maybe by making a still Bo was trying to shame Lourde, show him she was more of a man. I tried not to think about it, it seemed so strange, making a still in the 1970s, but you couldn't tell Bo anything. She got an idea into her head and that was it.

We were living in a small town, about forty-five minutes outside of Syracuse, a town named Morrisville, a nothing sort of town, a crotch between two hills really, a town with a population of two thousand and a stoplight and a two-year college which brought in a modicum of drugs and student antiwar demonstrations—enough to keep us from utter desolation. Bo and Lourde moved us there when we were still babies. They took Bo's inheritance (money from her mother's illegal abortion practice) after they'd graduated from Syracuse University and bought a huge old Victorian house, surrounded by wheat fields and pine woods, and turned it into the house where Lourde was to become a playwright and Bo was to raise us, and in the end, the house from which Lourde's plays were to make the jump from Salt City Playhouse to Broadway. But of course they didn't, and Bo's inheritance ran out, and the screaming came to two people who normally waged their wars in silence. Only once before had I ever heard them argue. When I was ten I listened, terrified, from my bed, as they yelled at one another down in the kitchen. Bo said I needed to see a psychiatrist, she thought I was emotionally disturbed, but Lourde screamed no, over his dead body would I ever see a psychiatrist, and that was the end of it, though I never forgot it. It always stood out in my memory, as if in some stark, final way it defined my childhood.

What Bo made that June night in our living room was named Bo's Place. It was just supposed to get us over our rough spot, but when Bo hired a black man named Coleman to play the piano the college kids started coming, and Bo and Lourde's friends from their old Syracuse days came, and when they told their friends who told their friends, pretty soon Lourde and Oscar were out hacking down the sunflower garden, turning it into a parking lot. After a few months all kinds of people were coming—college students from Colgate and Morrisville and Cazenovia, old people who remembered speakeasies, black people who followed Coleman wherever he played, Italians and Jews from Syracuse, and an old Russian man named Mr. Antonovsky. For a while it was the hippest place around, one of the first theme bars to come along, before "theme" was something that could be manufactured, a place where people wore what they wanted to wear—everything from flapper dresses to halter tops and bell bottoms—and "did their own thing," which often meant reading poems or singing a little folk music up on a stage Bo had made.

Supposedly no one knew Bo made the alcohol herself, but she spent hours disguising the taste anyway, mixing up all kinds of concoctions in the back room, which she stored on shelves in old glass milk bottles she found in a dusty corner in an antique store. She took great care at night to keep the kitchen door closed so that no one went near the back room where that hulking monster of gray metal and glass spit and breathed booze and the contents of those milk bottles stood waiting to hide the taste. We were all sworn to secrecy, and though I can't vouch for my older sister, Zellie, or my older brother, Oscar, I never told a soul.

It was the secrecy which ended up winning Lourde over to Bo's enterprise. Lourde relished secrets—not all secrets, only secrets of a particular kind: the sort where he could inflict some sort of evil, of which the person was completely ignorant, and more importantly, where he could go not only undiscovered, but unsuspected as well. Once, for example, he ordered a dog whistle from England, he hated the next-door neighbor's dog so much; it barked while he was trying to write, and it gave him great pleasure to blow that whistle from the attic window and then to watch the dog writhe on the lawn below, the neighbors completely baffled as to what was tormenting it. Then, when he was mowing the grass or something, he would talk to the neighbors about their dog's affliction, trying to guess what it might be, as if he had no idea, and at the dinner table he would recount the story, convulsing in laughter.

So Bo's secret became his pleasure—it appealed to him to hand a person a drink made from an illegal still concealed in the back room of his kitchen that cost him two cents to make, when the person thought they were paying two or three dollars for regular bar liquor, especially considering there were a lot of people in town Lourde didn't like. And while they stood there and drank this counterfeit drink, he amused himself by telling them dirty jokes, as if they were all friends.

It didn't really matter anyway about the drinks, because no one came for the drinks; they came because Bo was exotic and classy in her long, trailing movie-star dresses and red lipstick, and this place was the cool place to go, a speakeasy in the middle of a small, dead nowhere town, in the early 1970s, when there was no romance left, when Vietnam was still raging, when people were struggling to get jobs, lining up in front of gas stations in small, compact Japanese cars, hoping to get a little gas. It was a refuge: the lovely fringe lamps, the old pictures, Coleman playing ragtime on the piano, people spilling out French windows onto porches with wheat fields blowing in the distance, bent by the wind.

We all worked at Bo's Place. Lourde ran the bar and told dirty jokes I tried never to hear, Oscar made the booze, and Zellie and I raced back and forth waiting tables. Frieda was much younger than us and spent her time going from one lap to another. It made for a long night, especially after a whole day in school and then two hours of homework at the kitchen table under Bo's watchful pale-blue eyes, but it had to be done. None of us wanted the screaming anymore. It was better to be tired, and it did end, after one o'clock in the morning when everyone left and Lourde and Bo went upstairs while Zellie, Oscar, and I finished cleaning up. If they went at it, whoever heard the bed first said, "Here we go again," and no matter what we were doing, the three of us piled into the kitchen and waited it out, glad they were loving again. If we weren't too tired, Oscar and I slipped on some old boxing gloves and killed the time by dancing around the kitchen, jabbing and throwing haymakers, while Zellie rolled her eyes and tried to read a magazine. It was all nice in a way, and when I sank into my bed at night, I thought about how lucky we were, how good it all was, especially after the hard times we'd gone through, and I tried to forget about the hideous assemblage in the back room, which had never seemed right, but which had rescued us, there was no denying it.

Then something happened, something flukish, something scarcely believable that marked my life forever. I was fifteen. I don't know how old Mr. Antonovsky was, in his seventies somewhere. He was an old Russian man who'd come to the United

States to live near his grand-niece, Patty Baker, a woman who'd never been to Russia and knew next to nothing about it. He bought a house downtown sandwiched between hers and the fire station, and to earn money he rented out his back rooms to college students.

He came to Bo's a lot and sat alone, always in the front corner near the window, the tumor on the crown of his head turned mercifully towards the wall while he drank and watched the six o'clock news on the bar television. He was a large man and that tumor was the size of an Idaho potato, white and misshapen, and though no one ever said it, you could almost see it metastasizing under his bald head, sending out shoots of lethal hopelessness, like the runners of a wild strawberry. He so hated the thought of anyone seeing it that when he walked to the bathroom, he went around the whole room with the tumor turned towards the wall.

"Bring me a drink, please, Miss Hemy. I am waiting long time now," was about all he ever said. The rest of the time he just sat there like a big, stoking furnace, silent in that loud way that let you know his mind was never at rest. Lourde, who nicknamed everyone he didn't like, referred to him as Mr. Assholnovsky. None of us knew much about Mr. Antonovsky, especially about what he'd done in Russia, and if you asked him, it was the same thing as asking him about his tumor. He recoiled. The only opinion we ever knew Mr. Antonovsky to have was about black people. He insisted on calling them "colored" or "Negro," and on occasion "nigger," although he did seem to understand that it was offensive, and whenever the news covered a story about the Black Panthers or black power, Mr. Antonovsky could hardly contain himself. It was fine to see Vietnam being blown to shreds, but if one of the Chicago Seven bombed a house, Mr. Antonovsky couldn't bear it. He hated black people, especially Coleman, our piano player. He loved the jazz music Coleman played, but Coleman Mr. Antonovsky could not stand.

It was nothing for Mr. Antonovsky to say, "Is such a nice place, why you let colored man play piano?" and for that reason it became nothing for Coleman to say, "This song is for my *good* friend Mr. Anton," in the softest, sweetest, most exaggeratedly homosexual voice, after which he played a love song, caressing the keys seductively as if Mr. Antonovsky's skin lay beneath them, all the while flashing Mr. Antonovsky a white toothy smile, which drove Mr. Antonovsky to the brink. Appalled, he would slap the table and say, "What, that grin! Looks like idiot, like grinning idiot."

Their mutual hatred became part of Bo's Place, a situation we became so accustomed to we didn't notice it anymore, indistinguishable from anything else, like the click from the revolving fans above or the drone of the TV above the bar or the smell of the booze. I think Lourde even relished it. Mr. Antonovsky would let it drop that he didn't like coloreds, and Coleman would turn up at Mr. Antonovsky's table, bending over, looking from under the cliff of his brow, saying in a sugary voice, "Mastah, could I gits you a drink? It no trouble. I fetch it, Mastah. I plays you sometin lif up yur spirits." Then, the smile came, the brilliant white idiot grin, which night after night Coleman perfected, and when Mr. Antonovsky pushed him away, Coleman jumped back, crying out, "Oh, Mastah, forgives me! Forgives a poor crazy nigger like me," until Mr. Antonovsky, on the verge of hysteria, would yell, "EICH, STOP THIS! I AM PAYING CUSTOMER. MR. LOURDE. MR. LOURDE."

And there were days, because Oscar and Zellie dared me to, that I walked over to Mr. Antonovsky's table and in all my foolishness leaned close to him and whispered, "What would you think if I told you I was going to marry the darkest, blackest African, the very blackest, like Coleman?" And there were times when I told Mr. Antonovsky that I was hopelessly, madly, passionately in love with Coleman, because Oscar and Zellie wanted to see the look on his face, to hear him gasp, "Eich, don't say such thing! It could happen, and you be sorry. You have children— *baboon* children, and you see, is no good." I knew when I said these things it wasn't right, but I said them anyway.

Then one night Mr. Antonovsky, feeling raw and abused by Coleman's incessant "niggering," fell apart and screamed out in Bo's Place during a hot, crowded night, the hottest perhaps, the most crowded: "You are nothing but nigger! NIGGER, NIGGER, NIGGER. Dirty, filthy nigger. You belong with pigs in sty. Now go from me. You are not worthy to stand in my presence, you ugly, ugly . . . *baboon.*"

Bo's Place froze, and though no one spoke, you could feel the raw pulse beating in everyone's throat. You didn't say "nigger," not anymore, not in the 1970s, not even in this small town, not since the civil rights movement, not since Martin Luther King, Jr., not since any of that, and if you absolutely had to say it, then it had to be in a whisper in some back room, certainly not in front of a crowd, much less a crowd with black people in it. But Mr. Antonovsky was a stranger in this strange mixed-up country, and he had gone and said it, and now, with no shame he shifted his eyes from Coleman to his drink and then slowly swiveled his neck towards the window as if Coleman no longer existed. Coleman just turned and walked away, and I felt my part in it, like it was a sharp stick jabbing my ribs, the way I'd helped to set Mr. Antonovsky and Coleman apart.

The worst came when Coleman sat down at the piano a few nights later wearing a thin white elastic band strapped to his head. No one thought twice about it. It looked like he was wearing it to keep the sweat from running down his face, but when he turned to the audience and said, "This song is for my old pal Mr. Anton," I knew he was going to get Mr. Antonovsky back. It was a saucy love song he played with exaggerated hand motions, licking his lips, glancing at Mr. Antonovsky and Mr. Antonovsky only, as if there were no one else in the room. Mr. Antonovsky twisted in damp misery, barking out orders to me, "Miss Hemy, please, I am best customer, I am waiting too long now," until three songs later Coleman turned and revealed what was on the other side of his head—a large, pale potato. Underneath that elastic band was a fat white potato, the exact size and location of Mr. Antonovsky's tumor. There was one large, collective gasp from me and Zellie, Oscar, Bo, and Lourde, from all of our regular customers, who knew about this hot debate between Coleman and Mr. Antonovsky, an invasive stabbing gasp, followed not by Coleman's fluid laughter, but by a moan, a wounded moan, which came from deep inside of Mr. Antonovsky, a moan that sounded as if it had been forming for a century. When Coleman was certain that Mr. Antonovsky had had a good look at the potato, he simply repositioned himself on the piano bench and turned his head, revolving the potato out of sight.

I thought Lourde might fall on the floor laughing, and though Bo ran over to comfort Mr. Antonovsky, Mr. Antonovsky never forgot Coleman's insult, and as the August nights melted together in the heat, the hatred mixed in, an indistinguishable thread that stitched these hot, crowded evenings together. Then, in the midst of it all, the still, with its metal nerves, overheated and blew up; hot and overused, it exploded during the eleven o'clock news.

The blast knocked out most of the French windows and up-ended half the tables, throwing a few people halfway across the room. Every glass in the place fell and shattered in tinkling unison, as if it were the last sustained note in a deadly symphony. Oscar careened out of the back room, his pant leg on fire, and Lourde tackled him, overturning the tub of ice Frieda had been chipping away at all evening. People staggered to their feet, stampeding out to the porches, as if the ground underfoot were trembling, women screamed, more glasses fell to the floor, and the shrill sound of Frieda's cry soared above it all. Mr. Antonovsky clenched the table, his knuckles turning white, as if something like this had happened to him before and he were only reliving it now. I thought about helping him out, helping him heft his weight up, but I saw Coleman running across the room towards me in long strides, his face carved with worry, his arms outstretched. Within moments he pulled my head to his chest, as if to hide me from the spectacle, and I forgot about Mr. Antonovsky, forgot about helping him up, until I heard his voice, loud, distinct: "TAKE YOUR BABOON HANDS OFF HER!" In shock, Coleman and I turned, and we both watched as Mr. Antonovsky rose from the table, a whale breaching the water, and moved quickly toward us, his huge hands reaching and tightening around Coleman's neck, all the pressure of his wretched youth, his sodden adult loneliness, his ruined health applied to this squeeze. Coleman gasped and struggled, slamming Mr. Antonovsky's hulking body with the hooks and cuts he'd learned in a gym, but it wasn't enough to shake Mr. Antonovsky's grip. It wasn't that the old man didn't feel the blows, they just didn't weaken him. His long suffered anger was bigger than Coleman's fists, bigger than his own pain, bigger than everything.

He was going to kill Coleman, that was all there was to it.

Zellie screamed "LOURDE!" at the top of her lungs, but there was no way he could hear her. Fire was consuming the back room, and he and a whole mob of men were trying to put it out. Bo had rushed Oscar outside in the grass and was tearing his pant leg off, her long black dress ripped halfway off of her, her black hair wildly disarrayed. The other people were out on the lawn, in shock. There was no one in that room to help, and when Zellie's screams failed to produce a single soul, her eyes fell on me.

"HEMY!" she yelled, "GET THE GUN!"

Blood pounded in my ears.

"GET IT!" Zellie cried. She was holding on to Frieda, screaming into her ear, the two of us knowing it was only a matter of seconds before Coleman had nothing left.

I don't know how I got to the back of the bar, or how I ended up with Lourde's gun in my hand, but there I was, feeling its cold weight in the palm of my hand, while Zellie yelled, "Shoot him. *Shoot him!*"

I heard a gurgle bubble up from Coleman's throat and saw the whites of his eyes pop. It was his death rattle. I knew it with utter certainty, and then came Zellie's voice again, desperate, hoarse, a command that seemed to issue from a place bigger than Zellie. "GODDAMN IT, HEMY, SHOOT HIM!"

I pointed the gun at Mr. Antonovsky, I shut my eyes, and then I squeezed the trigger. The sound of that gun I will never forget. It was the sound that ended my life as I had known it thus far, the sound of Mr. Antonovsky's scream beginning something entirely new, the scream low and baritonal, unforgettable to a fifteen-year-old girl who had never heard a man so much as moan. I opened my eyes and saw Coleman laying sprawled on the broken glass, gasping for air, Mr. Antonovsky on his back, his legs and arms splayed wide like he was in the open position of a jumping jack, shards of glass stuck to him everywhere, like some bizarre Liberace costume. Blood had accumulated in a pool underneath him, but what was worse was his scream—husky and low and manly. It was this, the maleness of his pain, that was unendurable.

Mr. Antonovsky's eyes shifted and fell on me, and suddenly I felt the enormity of my act. I had shot him. I had shot a man. I had shot Mr. Antonovsky. Then everything sped up, and I could hardly breathe. People were running, screaming, Mr. Antonovsky's moan quickening. The sheriff, pot-bellied and nervous, and his loping deputy broke through the crowd of gaping people wedged in the blown-out windows, and looked from Mr. Antonovsky lying on the blood-soaked floor, over to me with Lourde's gun. It slipped from my fingers, and the next thing I felt was the pressure of hands, of many hands, whose I don't know. Suddenly I was being ushered away rapidly, forcefully, the crowd parting, a pair of hands under my armpits, my feet not always touching the ground. I was dragged through the living room, through the foyer, Zellie's voice at my ear, as if it drove this retreat. "She had to do it! Mr. Antonovsky was *killing* Coleman!" The word "killing" like a shot of adrenaline.

I was dragged past Oscar. He reached out to touch me, but hands pushed him away, as if I were now completely off limits. They pulled me through the hallway, and I heard the sound of sirens, saw the lights whorling, slapping across the walls. I was dragged up the stairs to the second floor and hauled down the corridor, my knees scraping against the wood, Zellie following, her voice growing more desperate. "She had to do it! Coleman . . . he would have been killed!" That word again, like a knife stuck in my brain.

Then I was thrown on my bed, and Zellie was pulled from my side. She struggled to keep hold of my hand so long I felt the bones of my fingers slip from their place. Then the door slammed shut, the light was cut immediately, and the darkness raced at me like wild horses. All I could hear was the distant clatter of footsteps, as if everyone were running away from me.

I became aware of my beating heart, of the pulse that ticked from every pressure point inside me, of the throb I had become. I felt my perspective being wrenched and shifted, as if a hand shot out of the darkness, plunged into my mind, and thrust my brain sideways. All of a sudden I saw my life in a wholly different way, an unfortunate way, a way that was flooded now in unbearable light, as if all the time prior to this moment it had taken place in the deepest darkness, as if until now I had never been conscious of it or of the darkness or of any consciousness or light. But I had shot a man. My sister had said "Shoot him" and I had picked up a gun and shot him. How could I have? No one else would have, they'd have found someone else to do it for them—someone like me. Suddenly I became aware of these long-suppressed memories, things I'd done, strange, unforgivable things that turned up in this blasting light, as if they were a circus act ripping into a tent with whips and chains, the sun gaping through the hole. All told, it was four pairs of bell bottoms and six T-shirts I stole from Mrs. Connell, whose store I cleaned on Saturdays, shoving them, one by one, week by week, into the hole along with the vacuum-cleaner bag, picking them up in the trash cans outside once I had my paycheck. Then it was calling up this sad and unfortunate girl, and in a deep voice pretending I was a man named Steve who had seen her from afar and had fallen in love with her. A dozen times I dialed her number, and she came to me in the bathroom at school all trembling and aching, to tell me about this man named Steve who loved her and to ask my advice. And then it was Oscar slipping into my bed with every rainstorm since I was ten years old, and holding on to me in my terror of thunder and lightning, me growing older, year after year, until I began to secretly relish every moment of it, shot full of thrill from the weight of his body against mine, the only trace of him in the morning, the intoxicating smell of his hair on my pillow and a warm spot near my hip, which I pressed my lips against.

I felt his fingertips on my eyelids. I opened my eyes and found him staring down at me, his silence impenetrable, as if something horrible pinned his tongue down. His lips moved, but nothing came out; then, awkwardly, he smiled. It was the uneasiness of his smile that made me remember Mr. Antonovsky.

"Oscar," I said, my dinner stirring in the back of my throat.

His fingertips landed lightly on my face, gently moving across my cheekbones, the bridge of my nose.

"How's Mr. Antonovsky?"

I watched Oscar's Adam's apple ride up his throat like a Ping-Pong ball. "Hemy." He took my hand and squeezed it, as if to give me a shot of strength. "I don't know how to tell you this."

Panic swarmed inside me. "I killed him."

"No, you didn't kill him." He paused for a very long time. "You shot him in the . . . *groin*."

"The *groin*?" I said. Such a strange word, a strange place to shoot a man, an unheard-of place, a terrible, unspeakable place.

"Yes," he said.

"What, his groin?"

"His . . . you know," Oscar whispered, not wanting to say it.

"Shot if off?" I struggled to say. "His whole . . . ?" I tried not to see it in my mind, but there it lay, severed at the root, on a plate my mind had conjured.

"I don't think the whole thing," Oscar whispered. "I think only half," and the sodden lump of pink flesh on my mind's plate shrank. I thought at least it wasn't all of it, yet when I considered it further, I knew it would never be any good anymore; half or all, it was useless now.

A long cry escaped from me, and Oscar shushed me, his fingers working my face, as if they could mold my emotion. He gave up on it moments later, as if touch wasn't good enough, and began to kiss my cheeks, my forehead, to speak my name on a breath of air so pressed I felt my throat constrict. My grief fell away like clothes unfastened, and I began to kiss him back, his eyes, his cheeks, his nose, and when our lips met, I felt something happen inside my chest that I could never have imagined—a young, wild horse let loose inside, kicking at my ribs, stepping into my stomach, slapping up against my heart, writhing and teeming with temper, awkwardly shimmying to break loose of my bones, my tendons, my ligaments, all that webbed me together, and yet I contained it; I used it like fuel. He's my brother, I thought, but it was in the tiniest letters, "He's my brother," stuffed into the back closet of my mind, a small pinprick of pain, a mosquito's nuisance. I forgot everything and became all lips and tongue and slamming heart, hungry for a taste of male flesh, for the scent, the touch, the breath of a man. And together we became something else, became like two racing cars speeding down a hill without any brakes, vaguely aware of the possibility of ending up ruined against a telephone pole, but unable to stop it.

The door flew open and Zellie stormed in, Oscar disengaging

himself immediately, jackknifing to his feet, the two of us study-
ing Zellie for any indication that she had seen us. She went straight
for the lamp next to my bed and pulled the chain.

"Get up, Hemy," she said. "We've got to go to Coleman's for
the night." I swallowed in relief. She had no idea what she'd just
broken up, but the thought of it made me weak, filled me with
writhing shame.

"Come on," she said, whacking my legs. "Coleman's waiting."
It seemed the more grievous a situation, the more Zellie rose
to it, something inside of her secretly loving calamities because
while everyone else was decimated, Zellie could stride up and
take command.

"Where's Bo and Lourde?"

"They're in jail," Zellie said matter-of-factly, as if they were at
the movies.

"They're in jail?"

"Yes, they are," she said, rifling through my dresser for clothes.
"And Mr. Antonovsky is in the hospital." She opened one of my
suitcases and dropped an armful of my clothes inside. "You shot
his dick off, you know." She snapped the suitcase shut and looked
over at me. "Come on. We've got to go."

I stared at her for a moment, conscious of her colossal nerve.

"You told me to shoot him. I shot him because you told me to,
Zellie."

"I didn't tell you to shoot his dick off," she countered. She
picked up my suitcase.

"You told me to shoot him, Zellie. I would never have even
thought of it if you hadn't said it."

"What was I supposed to say—'Shoot him, Hemy, but don't
shoot his dick off'?"

"Fuck you, Zellie." I grabbed the suitcase out of her hand and
lurched out of the room, my heart pounding, the blood rising to
my face. She'd spent her life living on top of me; I'd always been
on the bottom, trying to eke out a life beneath her, wanting, plotting, to beat her at something, to finally stand on the rumpled
heap of her defeated form and stick the flag of my success straight
into her guts. I heard Oscar running behind me. "Don't worry

about Mr. Antonovsky. I doubt he ever has a chance to use it anyway." Then came Zellie's laugh and Oscar's breath behind me, and I thought, What's wrong with me? I want to impale my sister and make love to my brother, and now I've shot a man.

3

She stopped speaking. They lay next to one another on their backs. She rolled onto her side, propping herself on an elbow, and looked out the window at the passing fields, at the blowing grasses dim and shadowlike in the blackness. He turned his head and watched her stillness. He admired the curve of her back underneath the thin cotton blouse that stuck to her in the heat. He reached out and touched her long, pale neck with his fingers.

Her voice came then.

Was that what you were looking for? she said.

Yes, he answered. But am I supposed to believe you?

She rolled onto her stomach and peered seductively through the crook of her elbow. Why would I tell you something I didn't want you to believe?

It's odd, he said.

I know. It certainly is, she said.

It sounds like something that would have happened in the thirties, he said to her.

She turned onto her back and stared up at the ceiling.

Everyone always said that about Bo—that it seemed she was from another time.

He turned his head toward her. Did you really shoot Mr. Antonovsky's dick off?

She looked at him and said, Yes.

Of all the things that she had told him, he thought, this was the most fantastic. He remembered the story of Pierre Rivière, a nineteenth-century man who'd shot his mother and his sisters to free his father from bondage. Had it been a similar impulse? Had

Mr. Antonovsky been a substitute for her father? Shoot off the male member to protect the mother from enslavement?

Do you think it was purely a random act? he asked her.

She looked at him with new interest in her eyes.

As a girl I assumed it was.

But as a woman, he said.

She smiled.

She was smart not to answer, he thought.

Your name is Hemy Lourde? he asked.

Yes.

And when you lived as a man you took your brother's name?

Yes.

You loved him?

The way her eyes moved from the white cotton sheets up to his eyes told him yes, that she did, greatly. The mention of her brother took some of the light out of her eyes. Grief chased it away. He knew better than to ask why she'd taken his name. But somehow he was thrilled by her story—the incestuous relations with her brother, the fact that at fifteen she'd shot a man. He wondered how it all connected to her later binding and to her living as a man. It all had to do with the body, he thought, with sexuality. He wondered about his own body then, about his own sexuality, and what part, if any, they played in his circumstances.

Why didn't your father stop Bo from making a still? he said.

Because Lourde wanted to write plays, and Bo wanted him to write them.

She must have loved him, he said.

She paused. She feared him. She said it strongly, as if to leave no doubt.

Did you also?

Perhaps more, she said. She didn't turn away. Instead her eyes blazed, staring straight into his.

He pulled a cigarette out of his pocket and lit it, then dropped the match into a Coke can he was using as an ashtray.

She looked at his mouth and then reached over and traced it gently with the tip of her finger.

Your mouth is beautiful, she said.

He kissed her finger.

She took her hand away, but her eyes stayed on his mouth.

Tell me the rest, he said.

It shouldn't be so important to you, she said.

She rolled onto her back and turned her head towards him.

I am no one to you.

She smiled, and when she looked into his eyes, he knew that her words were untrue, that she didn't believe them any more than he did.

He flicked his ashes into the Coke can and took a deep drag off his cigarette, exhaling slowly. You'll tell me, though?

She smiled. All right, I'll tell you the rest, she said, and then we'll talk about nothing. Okay?

He looked forward to that last hour when they would talk about nothing, long after midnight when they were dusty with sleep and their hands might touch each other, when he could think only of her body and of his and what they might do.

She stirred and settled herself, and before a minute passed he sensed that her thoughts had turned. He waited for her to speak, as if there were something in her words for him.

4

I was taken up to the police station, where I sat between Zellie and Oscar, squinting in the fluorescent light, handling the sheriff's questions as if they were wounded birds dropped into my lap. "What would make a fifteen-year-old girl shoot a man?" the sheriff asked me. The light in his eyes betrayed how much the idea interested him. I said, "Mr. Antonovsky was killing Coleman, and Zellie told me to shoot him, and since no one was around, it seemed that if I didn't do something Coleman would be killed, so I pulled the trigger." The deputy, all gangly legs and unruly hair, stared at me, crossing his arms over his chest, his face twisting into seriousness, as if this were all quite important, crime-wise, and required the utmost consideration. "Do you do everything people ask you to do?" he asked, his eyes whirling in the centers, where I could almost see images flickering on the underside of his eyelids, images of him crouched on his knees in the front seat of his patrol car, asking me to give him a blow job.

"I don't know," I said.

They both stared, the silence moving between us all, a fragile, bony thing no one wanted to hold, until the sheriff finally asked me what I had to say for myself, as if there were some statement I could give to sum it all up. The words "I shot a man" ran through my mind. Shotaman. It could have been someone's last name, I thought. Mr. and Mrs. Shotaman. Hello, this is the Shotamans' residence. No, I'm sorry, Mr. and Mrs. Shotaman aren't home at the moment. Could I take a message? Yes, thank you, this is Mr. Ikissed Mybrother. I'm an Eskimo calling from Alaska. Please have Mr. Shotaman return my call, will you?

I finally told the sheriff, "It's a crying shame," which so amused

Oscar and Zellie that they laughed about it all the way to Coleman's house, saying "It's a crying shame" every chance they got.
It helped to keep me from thinking of what it was that was such
a crying shame, but in the silence that followed, it all began to
settle in my mind—the shooting, that is, that I'd shot a man.

Bo and Lourde were held in the Wampsville County Jail, a two-
story gray brick building, so unaccustomed to real crime that there
were no barbed wire or gates to speak of, you just parked your
car in the parking lot and walked in. Coleman drove us over there
every day and waited outside with Frieda while Zellie, Oscar, and
I crowded around the glass window and talked first to Lourde,
then to Bo, who were just about the only prisoners who weren't
doing time for drugs. I stood between Oscar and Zellie, thinking how strange it was that you could just go along as part of a
family having a fine time, and then a still your mother shouldn't
have made but did make blows up, and because a black piano
player and a fat white man hate each other, you end up standing
in your living-room-turned-bar with your father's gun in your
hand, shooting the white man in the groin, and then there you
were in jail talking to your mother and father behind reinforced
glass.

Bo said stranger things had happened, mentioning the Man-
son murders, and in the same breath told me she wanted me to
visit Mr. Antonovsky to apologize, although I refused. It was
bad enough we lived in the same town, forget about sitting in his
living room mentioning the injured member delicately, or worse
yet not mentioning it at all, pretending that it was something
else, an arm, a leg, an ear. No, I refused, and on Bo's further in-
sistence I wrote him a letter of apology which quickly became
such a tangled, crippled thing that Lourde finally wrote it for
me. "Dear Mr. Antonovsky, Not a day goes by that I don't think
of you. Your misfortune has become my own. I suffer the deepest regrets. There are no words strong enough to convey the depth
of my sorrow. I long for your forgiveness. Sincerely, Miss Hemy."

The whole time Bo and Lourde were in jail, we stayed with
Coleman in a town named Peterboro, about five miles deeper
into the country than Morrisville, in a small white house on whose
living-room floor I slept pressed between Zellie and Oscar for a

week straight. Neither Oscar nor I mentioned what had happened in my bedroom, although a look kept slipping back and forth between us, hot and longing and always accompanied by guilt. When we boxed out in Coleman's backyard I wanted to bring it up, but I couldn't get myself to mention it, not in the midst of Coleman's mother's weeping willows and lilac bushes, in the quiet that had gathered back there, not with the sound of Oscar's breath and mine mixing again. I kept it to myself, this gnawing, constant realization that I'd shot a man and while he was being rushed to the hospital, where was I but up in my bed making out with my brother. It was a shame that when horrible things like this happened, a notch wasn't cut into the back of your neck so you could reach around and touch it, to keep track of all the times you quit one life and began another, because that's exactly how I felt, like I'd quit my old life and had started another.

Within the week, Bo was let out of jail, pleading all the way out of the cell and the front doors and into the summer air, in her sunglasses and red lipstick, that she be kept and Lourde let free, as the still was really her idea, but no one listened to her. "Lourde is the man," she explained to us, "and just as a woman is not allowed any greatness, she is not allowed any sins, either." On the drive back to Morrisville, she reminded us that far worse things had happened on the day we had our explosion. "Like American planes accidentally bombing a Cambodian village and accidentally killing four thousand people," she said. "Just remember that. What we had was a tiny explosion in a small town. That's all."

When she got to Morrisville, she held her head high, even when we rode through town and all the people on the street stopped and stared at us passing, a station wagon full of trouble. We were infamous now, the infamous Lourdes, the parents land in jail and the daughter shoots a Russian man, never mind where. There was no way to live something like that down in a town as small as Morrisville.

"They're never going to forget this," Zellie said, as we watched them all staring at us. Bo loosened the gray silk scarf at her neck and said, "No, I don't suppose they will, but what do they know?" I looked at Bo then, she looked at me, and without a word, I

knew I would have traded her; I would have rather made the
still and been arrested and thrown in jail like she had been, rather
than to have shot a Russian man, you know where.

A hole in the middle of the kitchen floor faced us when we
got home, a hole where the still had landed when it exploded.
Bo slid an easy chair over it and told us to go on living as if it
weren't there. The living room was strewn with blackened debris that floated calf-high in dark, stagnant waters. All the tables
and chairs were upended and had been vandalized in our absence, legs and arms scattered about the room, words scrawled
on the walls in childish letters, GOD'S WRATH HATH DESCENDETH,
SINNERS REPENT, and YE REAP WHAT YE SOW, as if a Sunday-school
class had taken a field trip to Bo's place to see firsthand where
sin led.

Oscar and I had trouble not stealing glances at one another
across the black water or across the armloads of debris Bo made
us cart out to the back field to burn. I tried my best to forget
about it, especially when we stared through the flames of a great
bonfire and Oscar said, "We can't, Hemy," and I nodded, but
later in my room I couldn't stop thinking about the look in his
eyes, which had said, "Let's anyway."

The fire smoldered for days out in the field and was finally
put out by a late-night thunderstorm, which brought Oscar to
my bed. In the sound of rain against half-opened windows, of
wind at the curtains, we lay for a long time, not saying anything,
just breathing.

I wasn't sure how, but our lips met again, and within moments
the world we lived in, the world of Bo's Place and trees and fields
that gave way to hills, was lost and became something else—
two young bodies longing, eyes big and open, staring, curious
and amazed, hands loping drunkenly, unsure but driven. Voices
in my mind called out, Hey, hey, hey, he's your brother, in a variety of grave tones, none of which dissuaded me, because when
he took my hand and placed my fingers on the elastic waistband
of his underwear, I slipped my hand past it, holding my breath,
not knowing what I would find, afraid that it would be awful,
excited that it would be great. Hard, the skin silken velvet, unbearably soft, it was the most thrilling thing I'd ever touched. My

fingertips moved over the heartbreaking skin, stopping on a pulsing vein, my hand tightening around it, holding it, pushing it
against my belly, which hurt with a longing that unfolded inside
me like a rose. I imagined telling the man I might someday marry,
I lost my virginity to my brother, and Oscar telling some breathless,
beautiful girl, *My first girl was my sister.* It was ruined then, and I
took my hand back. Our eyes did not cut away like they might
have, but rather stayed engaged, as if we were searching for something, a clue, the reason for our longing. "I love you," he said. He
mouthed these words, and I mouthed them back, as if in depriv-
ing them of our voices the words weren't exactly true, not in the
real sense, not like love words spoken between real lovers, such
as we could never be, as if in the end it was the only language
for brothers and sisters.

We both fell back on our pillows and blinked violently up at a
ceiling crisscrossed with light. He took my hand and whispered
in the faintest, powdery voice, "I'll stay until the storm is over."
"I'm not afraid of storms anymore," I said back in a voice that
was stripped of everything save breath. He laughed, and I laughed
because he was laughing, and he laughed harder because I was
trying so hard not to laugh loudly. Then we stopped and lay there
quietly, no longer possessed of each other, no longer laughing,
now drained of it all, uncertain which way things should go, as
if there were any protocol for a brother and sister who'd crossed
the line.

His voice came again, barely a voice, less than a whisper, a
sound between a voice and silence which you could only hear if
you really listened: *If you don't see me for a while, it's not because of
you.* I suddenly felt a fear I hadn't felt a moment ago, had not even
considered—that he was going away. I had desperate thoughts
of feigning migraines or locking doors or begging him not to
vanish, but something deep inside told me not to say a word, to
nod my head and smile, as if I understood. Then it was over. He
squeezed my hand and he was gone, and I was left with it.

I woke up the next morning and wondered if I was no good.

When I rode my bike downtown for the first time, I was
hailed by a group of boys standing out in front of Sautter's

Diner: "Hey there, Half-Dick Hemy." I pedaled past on my bike, my heart a mess, feeling huge, like Godzilla, with no place to hide. I retreated to my bedroom for a few weeks, asking my girl-friends Louise and Hillary to forgo swimming at Eaton Brook or hanging out at Sautter's, to sit in my hot, sodden room while I waited for people to forget about me and Mr. Antonovsky.

"They're never going to forget," Zellie said. "It's too unfor-gettable, Hemy. Who's ever going to forget that?"

But Louise Van Sant and Hillary Holden were kinder. They said they thought it was possible for people to forget, and were content to sit with me in my soggy room during the days, listen-ing to Joni Mitchell and Neil Young, and to walk with me on the country roads at night. It excited them to be my guards, usher-ing me to and from under cover of night, making certain during the day that I was neither seen nor heard. I did my best to enter-tain them with my dramatic and moving readings of the stories in *True Confessions*—Mindy and Brandon lying wet and sandy along the California coast, Katherine and Aubrey up in the hot widow's peak of Katherine's father's mansion on Cape Cod. And when they went off to get me something from the store, they did it with a certain trace of mystery, looking over their shoulders every so often, whisking in and out of the grocery store, keeping whatever item they'd gotten for me under tight seal. They never spoke of me either. When asked by the boys, "Hey, where's Half-Dick?" they'd said, "She's out of the country." Then, at night, they'd turn up at my back door and escort me down the country roads, glancing around all the while like a couple of devoted se-cret service agents. It became a game—to fan out into the night and go absolutely unseen, to fade into the darkness without the slightest trace, to not be glimpsed by so much as a passing car.

What Oscar did was run. He left on his bike in the morning and came home late, after dark. We hardly spoke. Instead, we exchanged sulky, sheepish glances across the living room or in the hallway or on the stairs, he avoiding me, me trailing after him hurt and banished. When I couldn't stand it anymore, I knocked on his door late one night in August and found him typ-ing on an old typewriter Lourde had given him. I wanted desperately to see what he was typing, as if his words could answer my questions, soothe my nerves, but he wouldn't let me. He said only that it had something to do with what had happened between us, which was on his mind all the time, certainly he wasn't taking it lightly, and could I accept that we loved each other, just loved each other, not like two toothless hillbillies from the mountains, because that was what he was worried about. He didn't want to be like those people in *Deliverance*. No, he wanted to make sure that what we had done was not like anything they'd done. I told him I was worried about the same thing, about being white trash from the Appalachians, breeding with my brothers, but that no, it wasn't like that. I admitted that I felt stricken or maybe it was shattered or maybe it wasn't that grave at all, maybe I just felt displaced. The whole thing with Mr. Antonovsky and this thing with him, and now the bar was closed and Bo was not herself and Lourde was in jail. I guessed anyone would have felt displaced, and it would seem otherwise if we boxed again, like we used to before it all fell to such pieces. So he smiled, and we walked down the stairs, past Bo and Zellie as they hunched over the table adding figures, and walked out into the back field with our boxing gloves dangling from our shoulders, not saying anything, me thinking I'd gotten my brother back. The two of us boxed out in the wheat, in the light of the moon, laughing and throwing haymakers, like old times, me aware of a new glint in his eye, aware of that same glint in mine, conscious of its power, and glad that underneath all of its trouble and confusion we were still brother and sister and could box like hell out in the back field.

Lourde lost twelve pounds, and every day after we visited him in jail Bo sank into quiet misery on our drive back and took to her bed when we got home, sitting cross-legged like an Indian chief, praying, her eyes pressed lightly shut like ricepaper shades over bright windows. One afternoon we actually saw Lourde sitting in his jail cell, on his bunk, his legs hanging down listlessly, an image that never once left me, an image which caused Bo to suffer even more. Something about it thrilled me, and I wondered in the dark of my room late at night if it weren't all his fault, if somehow, through some silent, unseen means, he had compelled it all. But Bo took it literally that it was all her fault, and once we found her stretched out on the wooden floor in her bedroom, face down, her arms extended in the shape of a cross, the way she'd told us she prayed during the five years her mother had been in the Manhattan prison for performing illegal abortions in the back room of her Park Avenue apartment. Zellie called it the jail prayer, but Bo said it was the most serious prayer position, there was none more serious, it was to be used only in the most dire circumstances. She even stopped wearing red lipstick and dresses, and wore instead Lourde's khaki pants doubled over at the waist and his white T-shirts, as if that would bring him back. She believed so completely that it was her fault Lourde was in jail and harassed the poor lawyer so much to get him out that he finally told her what she needed was not a lawyer but a miracle worker.

When Happy showed up in our kitchen a few weeks later, I'm afraid Bo's mind put these two things together—Happy and miracle worker. I never knew for sure if Happy contacted Bo, or if it was the other way around, but there he was in our kitchen, sitting in the overstuffed armchair that covered the hole in our floor, one leg crossed over the other, wearing a dark suit with an open white shirt, a gold necklace hanging in the V where a tie normally fell, his dark hair thick and curly and rounded into a relaxed Afro. He was from Syracuse, a regular patron of Bo's Place, the spiffy one Zellie had a crush on. He was about thirty-four and handsome in that rugged, pit-faced sort of way, the one who came to Bo's Place with all the beautiful women in miniskirts and tight shirts, the one who rarely said anything.

We didn't hear what he and Bo talked about in the kitchen those four nights he came over, because she closed the door and told us to make ourselves scarce, but we had a feeling it wasn't good, that what she was plotting in our kitchen was ruinous. She wasn't the kind of woman you could back into a corner,—no matter, she found a way out. The only thing we knew was that a week after Happy appeared in our kitchen, Lourde was let out of the Wampsville County Jail, and within hours of Lourde's return Happy was in our kitchen again, the whole conversation between him and Lourde and Bo not lasting more than three minutes. While Happy sat down at the kitchen table, Bo and Lourde stood across from him, as if they were applying for a job, and a shadow came and hovered above that table as if Happy had the power of a cloud before the sun. When he asked Zellie, Oscar, and me to leave the room, Lourde nodded for us to go, and Bo pushed Frieda after us, the four of us drifting out to the living room, where we stood in the blackened, damp mess, straining to hear what they said, glancing at each other nervously, Frieda twirling around us, unaware that something terribly wrong was happening.

After Happy left, Bo and Lourde disappeared to the wheat field just beyond our backyard, where Zellie and I could just barely make them out from Zellie's bedroom window, the two of us watching their bobbing heads in the dark field, as if they were a pair of buoys rocking on a turbulent sea. Only two words came back to us, the words Lourde spoke harshest, the words "devil" and "forever," until near the end when Bo screamed the truth of it and her words were ferried back to us by the wind: "I love you, goddamn you, that's why." We heard no more, just the blur of angry voices, and watched helplessly as they drifted farther back in the wheat field, until Zellie finally gave up and slammed the window closed.

"If you hadn't shot Mr. Antonovsky's dick off, this never would have happened," she said, falling back on the bed.

"The still blew up anyway," I argued.

"If you hadn't shot Mr. Antonovsky's dick off, the police would never have come."

"The firemen had to come."

"They're not the police," Zellie asserted. "It was the police, Hemy, not the firemen who shut down Bo's place and arrested them."

"Fuck you, Zellie," was what I said.

A couple of workmen turned up the next morning in a big pickup truck with every kind of tool imaginable, and for a week straight they repaired our house, replaced all the windows, re-did the floors, painted, sprayed, spackled, and trimmed, and in-stalled two new stills with meters in the back room off the kitchen. I asked Bo why she didn't just buy alcohol instead of bothering with the stills, considering that people didn't make stills anymore, considering the first one had blown up and landed her in jail. "I can't get a liquor license now," she said.

"Happy can't get you one?"

"He says no."

She pushed her fingers through her short, dark hair and glanced out the window, a faraway look settling into her eyes. She looked beautiful just then, red-lipped and pale-skinned, her neck long and thin, her waist slender in the long black dress she wore.

It was never the same in Bo's Place after that. We had more customers and Coleman played the piano, Bo was still classy and exotic, Lourde poured the drinks and told even dirtier jokes, Zellie and I still waited on the tables, Oscar made the booze, and Frieda still went from one lap to another, but underneath it all was strain. Bo and Happy argued constantly in the back room, Happy demanding more money, Bo not wanting to give it to him. "He says he brings in most of the customers and he deserves more, and Bo says that wasn't the deal, he's not getting it," Oscar told me and Zellie, because it was Oscar who floated between Bo and Happy, Oscar who took the blows from both sides, Oscar who soothed Happy, who paved his path to Bo when a path needed to be paved, because Lourde couldn't stand to be in the same room with Happy, and there was no one else to do it. Happy liked Oscar too, perhaps more than just liked him, though no one would say, instead all of us watched silently as he invited Oscar to his table where all the beautiful women sat and then never said a word to the women, just talked to Oscar, looked at Oscar, smiled at Oscar. When I asked Oscar if he liked it he said, "Hell, no, but if that's what Happy wants me to do, that's what I have to do, Hemy. You don't say no to guys like Happy."

Lourde wouldn't forgive Bo for having gotten involved with a man like Happy. It drove him mad to be run by this pock-faced man. Bo said to ignore Lourde when he talked about killing Happy, but then he went so far as to buy a rifle, which he practiced shooting out in the field, to Bo's horror, and his jokes got filthier to annoy Happy. One night Lourde told an especially bad one about a teenage girl who had to give her father a blow job to get a prom dress, but I didn't hear it all, nor did I see exactly what happened between him and Happy—I raced away from the joke, from all the tension it caused, slipping outside to the porch, where, from the window, I saw Happy slam his fist down on the table. I watched Lourde leave the living room in a rage, and when I went back inside, Bo was laughing to cover it up. Bo tried to smooth Happy over, telling him that Lourde was really quite refined, he just had a small penchant for the vulgar, but Happy didn't care, he'd heard enough, he said.

After this, Lourde wouldn't leave it alone—every chance he got he brought up the subject of Bo's Puke-Faced Thug, pointing out that for a woman who knew things, she should have known better than to get involved with him. "You'd be hovering in a jail cell if it weren't for that thug," Bo would say, but she knew what Lourde was talking about. Bo knew things. She knew things that no one else knew, and she was always right about what she knew, so why she didn't know about Happy, Lourde would never understand. She foretold a flood in 1968 when the creek overflowed its banks and ruined fifteen houses. She knew when Lourde's father died two hours before his sister Bella called with the news. She predicted that our neighbors would have three baby girls, and they did. She looked at children and knew what they would do with their lives, and she even told us that Zellie would be a painter and Oscar would live in a different world from the one he now lived in. So why couldn't she have predicted Happy? Lourde wanted to know, but Bo said she just hadn't seen this thing with Happy, and if Bo didn't see a thing or she wasn't sure, she didn't say anything about it, not until she was absolutely positive.

That's why it terrified me when she touched my arm in the still, hot darkness of our living room one night and told me what she knew about me. Her dark, curly hair looked wild, the long navy dress hung loose on her, she'd lost so much weight, and a cigarette burned between her fingers. They were crazy words, what she said, but once Bo told you something you were stuck with it. She never spoke anything that didn't come true, and for that reason we believed Bo, we believed every last word she ever told us. Her fingertips drifted across my cheek now. "Hemy," she whispered, "I didn't make it very far in this life. I was supposed to, but I didn't. I was stopped just when I started." Two of her teardrops fell on my arm, warm and salty, long overdue. "I felt it pass me and there was nothing I could do about it. You will do it, Hemy."

"What will I do?"

"You have a great destiny ahead of you, Hemy."

"What?" I said.

"You will change the course of history."

There was a blast inside my chest, as if some small, white-uniformed man stood in the breathing room between my lungs and threw a switch.

"I don't want to."

"You will, Hemy." She spoke rapidly. "Later, when you're older, it will come to you." She brushed the hair out of my eyes. "Okay?"

"Maybe you've got it mixed up, Bo."

"No." She shook her head firmly. "No, I don't. It was because of Mr. Antonovsky that I know."

"I don't want anything to be because of him," I said. Mr. Antonovsky was my shame, the disgrace of my life, my stigma. To hear his name made me cringe, to see him in the streets made me shiver. In the darkness of my room I considered taking my life because of him. Please, you have no idea, let nothing be because of Mr. Antonovsky, nothing, not one thing, not one single, solitary thing.

Tears fell from my eyes, and the next thing I knew Bo was pulling me into the car and driving recklessly through the blackness to Eaton Brook. I glanced at her across the darkness, the word "desperate" surfacing in my mind, Bo desperate, like in 1966 when she ran for congresswoman after she had gotten it into her head that she was a politician, and had lost. She had stopped praying then, and after three months Lourde had to put her in a mental institution in Syracuse, she'd gotten so bad. I remembered when he came home and said, "Bo has to pray three hours a day just to be like normal people," and a cold pang hit my heart when I realized she'd stopped praying again. The day Happy had entered our lives, she'd quit.

I glanced at her again. Her black hair was thin and wispy, her red lipstick smeared. She was a rosebud at its last point of beauty, smoking another Old Gold from Lourde's pack, one more in a countless stream of Old Golds. She'd substituted smoking for praying, and now the cigarette was trembling between her fingers.

It scared me that one person could take up smoking and quit praying and the walls you felt were so faraway and sturdy were suddenly up so close you realized they were hovering things, flimsier than you could have imagined.

Bo swerved into the dirt drive of Eaton Brook and slammed to a stop near a small cliff, which hung like a prominent brow over the lake, and towed me up to the edge, me wrapped in her white robe, which flapped around me like the spastic wings of some wounded angel. She brought us here at the end of every summer after the dandelions had gone to seed, and it was here that we participated in Bo's religion, if she had any.

"Let him go, Hemy! Let Mr. Antonovsky go!" she yelled above the wind. Her fingers dug deep into my arm, and I stood there, her silk robe slapping against my back, knowing that she was crazy, but lofting the yellow dandelions she had thrust into my hand nonetheless, repeating after her, "These are all the thoughts which have lingered in my mind and kept me from peace," while the dandelion heads fluttered apart, the tiny spores caught up by the wind. I invoked the incantation, screaming like an idiot, "Go, all of you,—go, all of you,—go, all of you," until it sounded like some obscure Hindu chant: *goaluvu, goaluvu, goaluvu.* Perhaps it was the night or Bo's ragged voice or the strangeness of my life, but I felt Mr. Antonovsky wad himself deeper into my heart, and I knew I could no more toss him to the breeze than I could part with my own skin, but I kept this fact to myself and climbed into the car with Bo, which she drove one-handed back to Morrisville, her right arm slung across my shoulders, a heavy anchor in the darkness. Even in the blackness you could see that something possessed her.

I waited awhile and then I asked her. "Bo, how come you aren't praying anymore?"

"I've got to get back to it," she said, glancing at me. I was breathing through my mouth, staring at her with wide-open eyes. She reached over and patted my knee. "Don't worry, Hemy, I'm not going to go nuts. I've got ten years of praying behind me."

I wanted to believe her, so I did.

Then the silence pushed the words up from the bottom of my thoughts where they wouldn't lay straight, the impossible words: *How am I supposed to change the course of history, Bo?* At a bend in the road, a point of utter darkness, the words had slipped from my mouth one after the other, and there I was, after having said them, a clod, ungainly, sitting in Bo's car, with skinny bare legs, shivering inside of a white silk robe.

"I don't know exactly. It will come to you in time," Bo said, and I was relieved not to be told the exact circumstances, to have it left dark and murky, as if then I could possibly miss the signs and go down the wrong path, avoiding it altogether. I was content to forget about it, to leave it in the future, as far down the road as possible, but as soon as I closed my bedroom door behind me and lay down on my bed, I had the uneasy feeling that the walls I had found to be flimsier and closer than I had ever imagined were even more insubstantial than that. They were less than flimsy, matterless actually, intangible, more concept than anything. There was no such thing as walls. I knew firsthand that a night could come like a murderess and involve you further in a plot you were following and didn't really know you were following until later. Then suddenly the sense that made up your days and nights vanished like an exhaled breath, and your eyes were entirely new and would never see even the smallest thing, like your bed and the curtains that fluttered across it, the same way again.

I wondered what I would do, what my destiny would be. I thought of Oscar and Mr. Antonovsky, of their weight on me like two barbells pressed heavy against my soul, of what someone would see if they opened me up—guilt piled on top of thrill. I could never tell anyone about Oscar, never, but one night in soft slippers I drifted upstairs to the top floor where Lourde wrote his plays, a place I almost never went, I was frightened up there as if it were a cellar and not an attic bathed in light, but there was no one else to tell my fear—that I had killed Mr. Antonovsky. Lourde assured me that a man was more than his genitals, the mention of genitals between us so queasy to me, but even so his words didn't soothe the jagged, saw-toothed guilt inside me.

No, it still gnawed at me, prodding me to do something, as if there was something I could do, some action I could take, like burning candles in a Catholic church, or throwing money into coffers for the poor. I needed something to give, something to do, an act, a gesture, and in the dark, vaporous air of my room, I struggled against tormenting images of taking Mr. Antonovsky strings of German sausages or packs of Oscar Meyer wieners, and then late one night I seized upon an idea that came to me from nowhere, it seemed—I would learn to play the jazz piano for him, he loved jazz music so much.

B R U S H   L A N D S

5

She turned her head and watched out the window as the Wyoming night passed. The sky was clear and the moon illuminated the tumbleweed, dusty and broken, and the stone-brown, bloated mountains. The vegetation was sparse and scrawny, the land itself spacious, but filled with such broken-down things, like one of God's hidden back rooms.

He touched her bare, pale neck, ran a few circles with his finger, near her ear.

Was Happy in the Mafia? he asked.

Her eyes never left the window. When she took in a deep breath of air, he watched her breasts rise and fall beneath her thin, cotton blouse.

I don't know, she said. Perhaps. I never found out.

He wanted to ask her if she'd changed the course of history yet or if she was still building towards it or in the midst of it, but he didn't. It seemed it might be disrespectful. But it interested him, the idea of changing the course of history; not necessarily the bloodshed, the oppressed throwing off the oppressor, but how shifting the course of history could prompt ideas to change, to create an unexplainable twist that would cause a whole culture to think differently, even just one man. Was it all random, or was there some progress in it all? He doubted it, but it interested him that Bo had equated the two—great destiny with changing the course of history—and that she had chosen a daughter rather than a son to do it.

Why do you think your mother made the still? he asked.

She turned and looked at him. His question interested her.

Maybe she was afraid that she would be boring otherwise,

she said carefully. Or maybe she built something primitive, some-thing faulty, something that would explode.

What did she want to blow up? he asked.

Maybe she merely wanted to blow something open.

Her eyes never left his.

Like what? he said.

But she wouldn't say.

She fell silent, and they both watched out the window. Even in the dark they could see the rough edges of the land, the ripped-ness, as if a crude hand had reached down and torn it away.

She turned to him and said, This is the last of the story. After this, there is no more.

He brushed the hair from her forehead and said, Okay. But he knew it wasn't true. He didn't know how, but he would find out the rest.

She looked up at the ceiling again, and after the train whistle sounded she spoke.

6

*B*o's Place got bigger and more well known, and we finally had the money to quit eating cornflakes for lunch and scrambled eggs for dinner. Bo and Happy fought all the time, but we all more or less got used to it and started to think of him as the unfortunate family member everyone wanted to disown but couldn't. Bo smoked like a truck driver and her hair got wispier and crazier looking and her movie-star dresses hung loosely on her tall, thin form, but like she promised, she didn't go nuts, and we all appreciated that. Lourde wrote two plays and sent them off to a couple of New York agents, both of them coming back so fast, he was sure they hadn't read a word. The rejections made him drink and stay drunk for weeks, and the drunker he got, the more he talked about killing Happy, elaborating, in detail, what he would do with Happy's dead body, his favorite idea being to leave it out in the field where it would be picked apart, piece by piece, by vultures. "And I wouldn't feel the least bit of guilt either. Not the least," he would always say.

Bo told us to just ignore Lourde, but one night he said something to Zellie and me which I found hard to ignore. He looked at us at the dinner table and said, "If either of you are playing Hide the Wienie with any of the boys, I don't want you sitting at my dinner table." Zellie threw her fork down in digust, I stared down at my plate, speechless, while Bo made a lot of noise passing everyone more mashed potatoes. Zellie pointed to this as proof that we were witnessing the dissolution of two lives, and Oscar said we should take it as a lesson that dissolution was the way of life, the natural course of things, that to pretend otherwise was a lie.

I understood dissolution and didn't want any more of it, and fearing that it would come to Oscar and me if we touched, we kept ourselves from it. We had a few close calls when Lourde knocked down a wall in the living room and Bo assigned the two of us to clean up the mess, and there we were carting a lot of things down to the cellar where it was warm and dark and private. We didn't do anything, but at nights in the sweat of my glowing want and guilt, I lay in my bed and searched the interior of my chest, trying to root out the terrible attraction, as if I could capture it like a wild dog running through the unpaved streets of my heart.

Then, finally, I went down to Mr. Antonovsky's house one hot summer day to give him what I had decided to give him. I knocked on his screen door with timid knuckles, my heart whipping like a sheet in the breeze. A television rattled inside, that and a fan, but nothing more, no footsteps, no voices, no stirring inside of any sort. Mr. Antonovsky just materialized behind that screen door without a sound. "Miss Hemy," he said, genuinely surprised to see me, and very quickly, as if he didn't want to lose a moment, he pushed the door open and moved out of my way.

His living room wore a darkness as if it were perpetually shrouded. I stopped breathing through my nose the minute I stepped inside and looked around for something light, something to buoy me up in this dark, acrid place, and suddenly he was pointing to a chair, a cream-colored winged-back chair whose arms were filthy with his sweat. I slipped into the chair lightly, trying not to touch it, while he eased himself down into a darker sister chair, his hands falling into his lap like two thick slabs of steak. I tried to keep my eyes from wandering down there, but I wasn't entirely successful.

The room was quiet and airless, as if it had been mummified and tucked away in some dark drawer, and I could hear the heartbeat of a few mantel clocks and the distant bass sound of a rock band coming from the students' rooms in the back. But in the air between me and Mr. Antonovsky there was only silence, squeamish, time-slowing silence.

My fingers pulled at each other in my lap, my voice barely

marring the quiet. "I wanted to tell you how sorry I am for what happened," I finally said.

"No need. Your letter says very well," he answered. His folded hands shifted on top of his lap.

"I wanted to tell you in person. I feel very bad about it."

"Is not important," he said. He cleared his huge throat. "Is nothing more than water hose now."

I sat there blinking. "Still," I said. *Still.*

"Is not so bad," he said, leaning forward slightly, conspiratorially, as if he were going to tell me a secret. "You want to see?" he said. The blood in my body fell like a waterfall to my feet. "No," I said, and he smiled, drifting back in his chair. "You always make joke on Mr. Antonovsky. Now Mr. Antonovsky make joke on you." Then, a bone-dry, rusty laugh ground out of him.

I didn't think it was funny, but I fixed my mouth in a smile, and since there was no easy way to break my news to him, I just said it straight out: "I learned to play the jazz piano for you." He looked amused and said, "Play then," and with his huge hand waving towards the piano, he paved my shaky passage over to a black upright, where I situated myself on the piano bench, and without any introduction launched into a Scott Joplin song Coleman had taught me. There was nothing, no reaction, just his lined, stoic face, where trouble brewed behind his eyes, but somewhere in the midst of it, his index finger began to tap on the sodden arm of his chair, and continued to tap through my second song and through my third. When I finally finished it stopped and made a slow sojourn to his wet eyes. "That was nicest thing done for me in many years," he said.

I found myself pushing back the piano bench, rising to my feet, walking towards him, grateful for the power of his response, I had expected so much less. I stopped by a dark side table strewn with Russian newspapers and opened my mouth, and words came out that promised him I would come and play for him whenever he liked, and I wished as soon as I spoke them that I could breathe them back in.

"You come Wednesday nights at eight o'clock," he said.

I nodded, although I felt the flight in my feet, in my thighs, the ache in my knees, as if they longed to bend and unbend in my race away from Mr. Antonovsky. It was all I could do to stand there. Then Mr. Antonovsky insisted that I have a cup of Russian tea, despite the fact that it was sweltering and sweat was beading up on us like a rash of blisters, and I couldn't find the nerve to object. I'd shot him. There was nothing to talk about besides that, and since we couldn't mention it, not again, we sat there like two hot, mute people, raising our cups to our lips, our eyes meeting briefly once or twice, until it finally became so unbearable that Mr. Antonovsky pointed to one of the black-and-white photographs hanging on his wall and said, "This was my brother and his wife." I nodded and was going to remark about how handsome they were when Mr. Antonovsky said, "Two months after picture taken, both dead." I withered and Mr. Antonovsky pointed to another photograph of an older man and his wife sitting at a kitchen table, saying, "Was teacher and his lovely wife. We make many films together." He paused here before adding, "Both dead no more than year later. These two," he said, pointing to another young, eager couple, "dead no more than three weeks." I had to avert my eyes from this eerie cemetery of the wall, there was nothing else to do.

But every Wednesday at eight, I turned up in Mr. Antonovsky's living room and played the piano for him, and then stayed for an hour afterwards, sipping his Russian tea and listening to his life story, which he parceled out in small packets of sadness. It turned out to be the most gruesome yet riveting sequence of events I'd ever heard, and I couldn't help but listen with the sort of rapt attention one gives a good murder mystery. He'd lost his whole family in 1917, when he was just sixteen years old. He'd watched his mother and father shot to death on a cobblestone street, not far from where they lived. "They fell forward on stone, their heads cracking like nuts. This sound I never forget," he said. His brother was lost under the hooves of a wild rush of horses; his sister was raped in her bedroom and then summarily shot. He had witnessed all but the trampling of his brother. I wondered if his tumor was an addition to his brain, like an extra room, added to house all the grief.

It wasn't more than a month before Mr. Antonovsky became the most exotic person I had ever met, his life, populated with counts and countesses, Bolsheviks and revolutions, began to inhabit my mind, bit by bit cutting through the thick-skinned walls of isolation in my small-town mind. I honestly grew to like him and found that I could say just about anything to him. Nothing shocked him anymore, Stalin had taken all shock away, he said, and so I told him many things, things that you wouldn't ordinarily imagine telling a seventy-year-old man from Russia, in 1973, when it was nothing for a girl my age to smoke pot or drop acid or sleep with her boyfriend.

Then, somewhere along the line, fat rumors began to circulate about Half-Dick Hemy and what she was doing over at Mr. Antonovsky's house playing the piano every Wednesday night. They were saying I went over to Mr. Antonovsky's house and did things to his stump, rubbed it, sucked it, massaged it, washed it, nursed it, held it, cuddled it, and stuck it inside. There was even talk that I had secretly married him. I wanted to hold a public meeting and invite the whole town so that I could tell them the truth, Mr. Antonovsky vouching for it, but Bo said it would never work. Instead she taught me to bear up, to walk down the street, past all the bold eyes hooded with carnal thoughts, holding my neck high, not the least downcast, with eyes that looked straight into theirs and told them that I was ashamed of nothing.

7

He lay on his side, she on her back. Her face was turned towards him, and he stared at her deeply, descending for a moment into her pale green eyes. He noticed how dark her pupils were, how swallowing, and he moved away.

Is this the truth? he asked suspiciously. What you've just told me?

She smiled.

I'm just to believe you? he asked.

She nodded, but there was something mischievous in her eyes.

You could be toying with me, he said. You toyed with me once. Why should I assume that you're not toying with me now?

You'll just have to trust me, she said. She pushed her fingers through her short dark hair and smiled.

Why don't you show me some sort of identification or something? he said. A driver's license or a credit card?

She laughed, and he propped himself up on his elbow.

Why are you laughing?

You said you wanted to hear something about me, she said, so I told you something. We did not discuss my having to prove myself after I told the story. I did not agree to that, and I do not feel inclined to prove anything to you.

All right, he said.

She turned and looked out the window at an almost pitch-black Wyoming night. The train's headlights illuminated the stitches of tracks that cut across the cracked land, scarred with brush.

I want to get off the train when it stops tonight, she said. I want to walk out on the land. It's not good enough just to see it from the window. Why don't you come? We'll just stay the night and catch another train tomorrow.

When the train pulled into the small station at Laredo, he said, All right, and followed her off. After they got their bags, she asked a few people inside which hotel in Laredo was the oldest and grandest, and they told her it was called the Maclarean on Giant Street. So they went there.

When he stood in his room, it reminded him of an old woman's, the way the dark, heavy furniture imposed and the yards of drapes hung fixed, but the way she rearranged hers took the oppressiveness away. She pushed the drapes back and flipped the dark comforter over, revealing its white cotton back. She put away all the unsightly table dressings and replaced them with a tortoiseshell hair brush, an ivory hand mirror, a few bottles of perfumes, and two yellow-white candles. He liked watching her walk slowly around the room in her bare feet as she performed these small acts, her hips swaying under her long gray skirt. She looked glamorous, her lips red, a white silk scarf loose at her neck, her skirt slit up the front to her thigh.

They went out into the night and walked through the small, darkened town, where plastic crouched on top of grimy steel— McDonald's and Busy Bees piggybacked on factories, a few diners here and there, hanging on to the edges, like vestigial structures. She said she found it depressing, a basin filled with grime and steel and broken families, with the Saw Tooth Mountains clamoring up around it. They were both relieved to get back to the hotel, to the decaying elegance. She wasn't much interested in the town, she said. It was the land she wanted, the land she wanted to walk over. They would go out tomorrow in the light of morning and walk over it.

She invited him into her room and lit the yellow white candles. He stretched out on the bed and watched as she walked across the room in her long rose-colored slip. He liked the way it clung to her hips, the way the right strap fell off her shoulder; he liked the way her breasts moved beneath the satin as she quietly lay down next to him. She put her hands behind her head, and while she watched the ceiling fan above them, she talked about finding the kind of road that went on forever. She spoke low, and while he listened he tried to imagine what she had looked like when she'd lived as a man. He couldn't get this from his mind somehow.

When she was done talking, he asked her, If you were still living as a man and had met me on the train, how would you have acted?

I don't know. She shrugged.

What if I'd asked you a question?

I would have answered you.

Could I ask you a question and you answer like—

No, she said. I didn't live as a man for your amusement.

She sat up, and he turned on his side.

Then why did you live as a man? he asked.

It was a transition, she said.

What kind of a transition?

A modern one, she said.

How? he wanted to know.

She looked at him, at his curiosity, and he could see it amused her. Stop, she said, and poked him in the side. He grabbed hold of her hand and laughed, but it embarrassed him to be so insistent. It was one thing to discover her. It was another to be discovered.

She reached for his pack of cigarettes and shook one out. She took it between her fingers and put it in her mouth.

I once smoked three packs a day, she said. She pretended to take a drag, then exhaled slowly.

He slipped the cigarette from her fingers and sought her eyes.

Come on, tell me why you lived as a man, he said.

Her long arms and legs moved slowly and gracefully as she curled around a pillow.

I've been very gracious, she said. I've told you a great deal, and I did not bargain on telling you any more. Can't you respect that?

Yes, I can, but now I wish you hadn't told me anything. It was almost better that way. Now, you've teased me with it.

I can't win, she said. If I don't tell you, I'm toying with you. If I tell you, I'm teasing you.

Why did you tell me at all? he asked.

She smiled and lowered her eyes. When she looked up, she said, I didn't want to lose you.

He touched the side of her face and stared straight into her clean eyes. Then he lay his long fingers on the back of her pale neck and drew her towards him, pressing his lips against hers. She pushed the pillow out of the way, and he pulled her towards him, feeling the satin of her slip beneath his fingers. It started out slowly; he slid his tongue into her mouth and pulled it back, but then the kiss went out of control and transformed into a deep, passionate kiss, much deeper and passionate on her side than on his. It came so quickly that it scared him. *Hungry for a taste of male flesh, for the scent, the touch, the breath of a man*—he remembered the words she'd used. They inflamed him, and yet he feared he could not match her passion. He pulled away and stared into her eyes. They were deep, like warm, open windows with great rooms behind them—rooms, he feared, where one might be swallowed.

Sadness slowly filled her eyes, and quietly she turned over on her side away from him. He wanted to ask what had happened, why she had turned away. Now that she was gone, his fear had dissipated, and he felt inflamed once again. He wanted her mouth back, the greed of her lips, the passion of her breath, the swallowing. Is that why she pulled away, because she knew it would make him want her?

The curve from her hip to her waist was alluring under the satin slip. He lay his hand there and began to kiss the soft, short hairs at the nape of her neck, the delicate bones of her spine. When she held still, he kissed the small of her back, the hollows under her shoulders, then her neck again, but when he tried to turn her over, her voice came.

That's all I can give now.

He didn't understand, and when she fell asleep on her side with her back to him, he was left alone to wonder what had happened. He had turned his back on a lot of women. He had left them alone just like she had left him, and he understood now how they must have wondered if they'd done something wrong or distasteful. He remembered a few of them had cried softly into pillows, a few had paced in the dark while he slept, vaguely aware of them. He had felt himself detached, as if they had nothing to do with him, as if they were possessed by some hysterical strain of female gene that no one—no man anyway—could account for.

He lay there now with her back to him, his hands behind his head, and watched the fan revolve around and the drapes breathe like lungs. The room felt large to him, like a box too big to fill, and it was so quiet he could hear his own breath. It was he who kept the night company now, he thought, along with a thousand women, and it cut him.

He began to feel uncomfortable, as if his need to know her might bring him great pain. He found himself wishing that it had been another experience that had awaited him on the train and not this one. Why had it been her, this woman who'd lived as a man? He felt a small crack in his composure, as if perhaps the break he'd sought to create in himself was only now just beginning. The idea flooded him with fear, but he understood that if one was looking to become someone else entirely, it would not come without a price. Nothing was ever gotten easily, so he agreed to it, to feel whatever it was the experience brought, to feel like a woman, if that was what it took, though he had not bargained for it, nor was it anything he would have ever chosen.

When only just a moment ago the room had seemed too large, he now sensed it closing in on him. He felt the confines of the oxygen tent, the memory of his mother standing over him, unnerving, the feel of her hands running over his flesh, sickening. He found it difficult to breathe now. He felt his bronchial tubes constrict, a strange reaction his body had always chosen, over which he had no conscious control. It angered him that it should seize him now. He searched his pants pocket for the inhaler, and turned away from her when he took the adrenaline into his lungs. It took only a few moments before it took effect, and after that he lay awake all night, like a woman.

In the morning, she asked him to leave her alone for an hour. He knew she'd sit on her bed with her eyes closed, her hands on her knees. He wanted to ask her what it did for her, but it seemed too private.

He found a small diner on Giant Street, where, among a group of working-class men, he sat at the counter and drank three cups of coffee and smoked five cigarettes. He thought about their kiss last night and felt sickened at the thought of how much he had feared the force of her mouth. What did he think would happen? he asked himself, but he had no answer.

He met her back in her room, and they packed their suitcases before they walked out to see the land. They found the road she wanted, the kind that seemed to go on forever, and they wandered down it. It was a dusty road with little in sight but the blue sky and the scraggly land, unbroken by civilization, except for the telephone poles and a billboard advertising Kool cigarettes.

She wore a long beige skirt and a white cotton blouse and straw hat. He had on his tan trousers and a white T-shirt. If it hadn't been for the sunglasses he wore, he thought, he might have felt faint in all that sun and glare. It was scorching hot, the heat lines entrancing, the sky like blue topping on a desert pie.

She hardly spoke, and when he asked her why, she said, I don't have anything to say.

She had no fear of the silence. He liked that about her, he liked that she left the silence alone.

He followed by her side much of the way, aware of the quiet, of what made up the silence—the rhythmic slap of their feet on the asphalt, the occasional cry of a bird in the air, the cha-cha rattle of unseen, seething insects, the sound of their combined breath.

She stopped at one point and said, I'm going to walk out there.

I'll wait for you here, he said.

Somehow he knew she wanted to go alone.

He watched with great attention as she moved away, watched her hips as they moved beneath her skirt. She looked every bit a woman, he thought again, but when she pulled her skirt up over her knees to climb a small knoll, he couldn't help but notice how muscular her thighs were. He would never have guessed, her ankles were so delicate.

He didn't give it much thought, but it occurred to him that perhaps she'd taken steroids or hormones, testosterone even, when she'd lived as a man. He remembered that she'd never really answered his question: Genitally speaking, are you a man?

He watched her walk out a good distance. Then she stopped and stood with her back to him, gazing out across the land pocked and cracked with fever. She looked somehow to be part of it, pale-skinned and dressed in beige and white. She could have been a product of this land, its fruit, its soft white offering, born of the burned, sparse earth, as if it had struggled and struggled and collected all its waters and fluids and light and had made her.

He watched as she knelt on the craggy earth, while the sun beat down on her, a few blackbirds circling overhead. He some-how knew that it appealed to her to kneel out in the middle of nowhere, looking back at the life she'd left behind in New York, in ruins. He wondered what ran through her mind just then, the train of thought of a woman who'd lived as a man for five years. Why had she done it? he wondered. Was it so awful to be a woman?

It startled him when he realized that he had never quite imag-ined a woman's thoughts. They had always seemed to him so chaotic that he'd avoided them. So why should he be so inter-ested in hers? He wondered if he would have cared at all had she not lived as a man. The thought that she had become linked to his knowing himself made him suddenly uncomfortable. What could he possibly want from her? Her eyes, her *seeing*, as if his were tired and wasted? But he couldn't say.

When she finally got up and walked towards him, he felt as if she had become a stranger again, as if during her walk on the land, she'd become mysterious again, unknowable. It disturbed him down in his guts, and he knew he was going to have to press her to find out the rest.

They didn't speak much as they walked back to the dusty lit-tle town, although he found himself wanting to know how she'd liked her walk on the land, what she'd gotten from it, but she didn't offer a comment. She walked with her back straight, her eyes straight ahead, as if she were under its spell. They sat down at a cafe, and before the land could slip from their thoughts, he asked, What did you get from the land?

It's very wounded, was all she would say.

He fixed his eyes on the scars on her arm, the long twiggish one, the fat horseshoe-shaped one. He recalled the time he'd run his tongue down the long one, and he remembered again how she'd never answered his question: Genitally speaking, are you a man?

When they walked back to the train station he said, I want to know the rest of your life.

Didn't I tell you enough to keep you? she said, putting her arm through his. They walked past all the storefronts, carrying their suitcases.

I want to know more, he said.

He had to hear the rest of the story. He needed her to bring the story around to the moment where she was lying on a bed with him in a first-class bedroom on a train. There was no other way.

Why does it mean so much to you? she asked.

I don't know, he said. And it was true, he didn't really know.

He walked a few steps in silence.

Once I was reading a book in the woods, he said, and I accidentally left it there. When it was night, I wanted that book so bad, to find out what happened next, that I walked five miles in the pitch dark through the woods to get it.

If you can, it's best not to care about anything too much, she said.

When he looked in her eyes, he saw the distance again, and he envied her.

Well, I do, he said. I do, Hemy.

Her name on his breath stopped her. She quit walking and stood stock still and stared at him.

All right, she finally said. I'll go on. I'll tell you the next part, but it won't be fun. Didn't you like it better when we laughed?

Yes, he said, but this is important.

Nothing is important, she said, especially not my story. She started walking again. I certainly don't want you to think I'm telling it because I think it's important.

Then why are you telling it? For the first time it occurred to him that she had her own reasons for telling her story, reasons that had nothing to do with him.

I've gone and gotten attached to you, she said, and now I have to have you in my room with me. She paused and gave him a suggestive look. And I'm afraid if I don't tell you this story, I'll lose control and ravage you.

She laughed, and he worried that she knew he was afraid he couldn't return her passion.

Lose control any time you want, he said nervously.

Then he laughed and she gave him that look again, that look that he worried said, You couldn't hold your own. But he knew this reason was not the true reason she was telling him her story. She was telling him for another reason altogether, one perhaps she was not even aware of, although he doubted that. He thought instead that she knew exactly why she was telling him her story, that she knew something beyond his own understanding, and he did not fail to notice how much it unnerved him.

When they were in her room (a similar first-class bedroom on another train) lying side by side on her bed, her legs resting on his, he felt better. The white cotton sheets, the red velvet drapes, and the window through which the rugged Wyoming land passed gave him comfort. She took his hand, and he was grateful for her presence, for her pleasant room, and for her story, which he hoped would help him reckon with everything.

There's no easy way to tell this next part, she said. I would leave it out if I could, but it would be like telling the story of a cow that went to slaughter and leaving out the part about the slaughter.

She loosened the gray scarf at her neck and touched a finger to her eye to still an itch.

All right, he said.

It's not fun, she said.

Yes, I understand.

8

About a year after I'd shot Mr. Antonovsky, in July, I was in his living room playing a jazz song on his piano when the fire alarm went off. The fire station was right next to his house, so we heard the alarm and all the commotion like it was happening in his living room.

"I don't dare think of what goes on," Mr. Antonovsky said.

I shrugged, and the two of us listened to the sound of all the fire trucks and all the ambulances racing out of the fire station, the sum of them all outlining the enormity of whatever was happening. It was so disturbing that I stopped playing the piano, and we skipped ahead to drinking our tea. I thought Mr. Antonovsky would forgo his story of death and torture at the hands of Stalin, there was such chaos out in the night, but he didn't. He stopped long enough to say, "Still it amazes me how indifferent is this God of ours," but he went on with Stalin, with the slogging of rocks, the smashing of lives, the shattering of souls, and outside the sound of the sirens, of hell brewing, underscored his story like a soundtrack.

It was only a matter of time before I lost track of the sirens, of whatever catastrophe had been let loose, and gave myself up entirely to Mr. Antonovsky's latest installment: his wife carted away in the middle of the night to one of Stalin's work camps, never to be seen or heard from again, Mr. Antonovsky discovering through a vast secret network the details of her death—a bludgeoning with a rock after her refusal to sleep with one of the trusties in the camp. I would think of this every day. Without fail, the idea of concentration camps, of Mrs. Antonovsky fighting off the trusties, would come to me in some form every single day of my life from this moment on, always accompanied by the question: How did any of them survive?

And when I left Mr. Antonovsky's just after nine and rode my bike through the balmy night, barely hearing the sirens, it was this—Mrs. Antonovsky's bludgeoning that consumed me—the blow to the back of the head, the look on her face, the thud to the ground, her last breath. I was considering how they'd disposed of her when I saw the huge flames, the ladder work of fire trucks silhouetted against it, the whirling lights from ambulances and police cars, slapping across the fields and hills.

It took a moment for me to realize that this burning house was mine, and once I did I became all pulse and slamming heart, riding my bike down the last stretch of road, my legs like rubbery pistons, what I remember glued together in a horrible conglomerate of memory: ragged, wheezing breath; brutish pound of heart; the scream of sirens and people; lights whirling in the darkness, like things let loose in the wild. I don't remember how I got to the house or what I did with my bike (I never saw it again), but I remember running across the lawn, past at least ten firemen who were positioned in front of the flames like soldiers. Someone yelled "There she is!" and pointed to me as if I were some scrawny, runaway dog, and I started to run, as if there were somewhere to run, until one of the volunteer firemen caught me by the wrist, and then dispensed with all civility and swung me over his shoulder. I thrashed and kicked and cried out, as if what was really happening were just between me and this man swinging me over his shoulder in a way that was far too intimate, as if the horror of the scene were contained in my breasts bouncing against his back, my belly plastered against his shoulder, my pubic bone knocking against his chest, as if it were really me against him, and the burning house in the background were just some flickering backdrop for our sticky exchange of sweat and spit and breath.

He dropped me into the front seat of someone's Toyota and left me, and when I tried to get out I discovered the doors were locked. There was no one in the car either, no one to offer me the slightest explanation. I may as well have been an ape in the zoo. I called for Bo and Lourde, for Zellie and Frieda, but mostly for Oscar, my voice reminding me of a howling wolf, it sounded so alone. Then a blowzy, gray-haired woman shoved into the front seat next to me, and dropped her flabby arm over my shoulder, pulled me into her surplus flesh. She told me her name, Gussy Keys, and then moments later another woman pressed inside the car, pushing against me, a short, hard-breathing woman, who started the car. Then she drove us away, and Gussy Keys breathed the words, "Your house was bombed," while the hard-breathing woman squeezed my hand tightly.

They took me to Hamilton Hospital and pulled me down a few darkened corridors to an office where they helped me into a chair. Curtains were lowered, and Gussy Keys pulled an ottoman up to my knees and hunched over in her lap, taking my hands into hers, saying in the vaguest whisper, "Your father lost his life in the explosion."

"Lourde?" I said. Gussy Keys nodded and hunched closer to me, taking my hands so deep into hers, it seemed they had pockets. "Your mother was rushed to Crouse Memorial in Syracuse. She's in the intensive care unit," she said.

I stared at her for a moment, this big slab of a woman, and then shoved my fingers deep into my ears. She and that hard-breathing woman tried to take them out, but I fought so hard to keep them in they finally gave up and instead escorted me down a half-darkened hallway. They took me to a little green hospital room with a small white bed and linoleum floors, and the hard-breathing one said, "We're going to undress you," while I stood in the middle of the room and let them, I didn't know what else to do. They couldn't get my blouse off because my fingers were in my ears, and I only agreed to take them out when Gussy Keys promised not to say any more. "Not another word," she said, making a motion with her hand, as if she were turning the key to her lips.

I crawled under the covers Gussy Keys held up for me and heard the hard-breathing woman whisper "Good luck," as if I were some pain-in-the-ass case, and when my head touched the pillow, Gussy put a pill on my tongue and told me that it would make my night easier. I swallowed the pill and waited for the ease, while Gussy applied cold compresses to my forehead and stroked my face with the smooth-tipped fingers of the old. Once someone came in and told her she had a phone call and she said, "Tell them it will have to wait. I can't leave this girl." The person said she'd watch me while Gussy took the call, but Gussy said, "Whoever it is will have to wait. I won't leave this girl."

I lay in the quiet, breathing in the same air as Gussy Keys, aware that at some level my soul was intimately wrapped up with hers, as if she were lending me hers for the night, the way you might lend someone a blanket or a pillow or even a hand. I thought about Lourde losing his life in the explosion, and then the network that usually worked so well jammed up, and I started thinking about something else altogether, like the black shoes Gussy Keys wore, and how it happened that a person who was once a girl like me could ever reach a point where black orthopedic shoes were acceptable.

I went over and over all the things in the room, outlining them, as if my eyes were pencils, going from the curved edge of the bed where the white sheet was perfectly tucked in, to the black TV attached to the wall, to the gray metal cabinet, to the inside where they'd hung the pair of hip-hugger bell bottoms I'd stolen from Mrs. Connell's clothing shop, and my suede pocketbook with the fringe. I went over and over the purse, outlining it twice, three times, while I thought about what was inside. I went back to the edge of the bed and began outlining it again, going from it to the television on the wall, and then over to the gray cabinet with my clothes inside, and after I thought of everything that was in my purse, I added Gussy's hand. I watched it as she picked the white washcloth out of the bowl of cold water, wrung it out with one clenched fist, and washed my face, first my forehead, then my cheeks, then my chin and neck. I thought she was a machine, until my eyes accidentally met hers, and I knew then she was no more a machine than I was, her eyes the eyes of something greater than I had ever seen, something vital and living that had merely rented this worn-out slab of a body of hers. It seemed we were like two living beings, blinking silently from the prison ships of the bodies we were hopelessly incarcerated in, with only eyes to signal with, to bear our testimony to life.

I don't know when it was during the night, but at some point my mind turned over like a slumbering body, and I wondered what had happened to Zellie and Frieda, what had happened to Oscar, the questions passing through my mind, incessantly, like waves coming forward, reaching a peak, then crashing. "My sister Zellie?" I asked, and immediately Gussy dropped the white washcloth into the basin of water and took my hand into both of hers, placed them against her cheek, and hunched close to me. "She's in the intensive care unit in Crouse Memorial," she said carefully.

"My baby sister, Frieda?" I breathed, Gussy pressing her lips to the back of my hand, pressing it against her cheek again, coming even closer, her mouth almost to my ear. "She was trapped behind debris and they couldn't get to her until she was already too badly burned." My breath left me like it leaves a balloon, quickly and all at once, and for a moment my lungs lay inside my chest, stung. Gussy Keys pressed her lips to my forehead, and I don't know why, but I looked straight into her eyes and I told her that I loved Oscar. "I love him more than anyone in this world," I said, so that she would know what kind of love I was talking about. She squeezed my hand and nodded, and then pressed her lips to my ear and whispered, "They never found him. They think he was too close to the bomb." She touched her warm putty lips to my cheek and then to my forehead. "Once the fire's out they will look for his remains."

She gave me another pill, and a moment later, another.

When the drug wore off, my eyes popped open, the sleep stolen from me like a blanket on a freezing cold night. Gussy's worn-out face appeared above me, and I remembered what she'd told me before the drug had the decency to take me away. The thought of it, like a barbed anchor, plunged into my stomach and sank, a weight so heavy it dragged my stomach to an unfamiliar depth. Could I have another one of those pills? I asked Gussy, but she said no, that it wasn't good to take another one, and I almost begged her, but had the sense not to. She put a breakfast tray in front of me before she said any more about my family, but when I couldn't eat a single forkful, she started again. She did it with the softest of voices and those bony, powdery fingers touching my skin, but still.

Bo was in a coma, she said. The doctors thought she might be blind, but they wouldn't know for sure until she woke up, if she did, and she gave me the impression that I shouldn't count on it. Zellie wasn't exactly in a coma, I was told, but she wasn't exactly conscious either. She had been impaled by the leg of a table, though no one could say how that happened. The leg had gone straight through her on the diagonal, hitting part of her spinal column, her stomach, and her liver. The doctors believed she would live, but they couldn't say in what condition.

A minute passed in silence, Gussy's eyes stuck to my face, mine wandering the walls, imagining table legs impaling Zellie, Bo lying in a coma, though I couldn't quite imagine it, the words taking over my thoughts, words that had never once meant anything to me: "impaling" and "coma." The question I finally asked, "Who bombed my house?," was answered with the greatest delicacy. "No one knows for sure, but there was talk that it might have been someone from the Baptist church in Morrisville." I tried to imagine one of the Baptists sneaking into my house in the middle of the night to plant a bomb, but I couldn't. They wouldn't even let their pasty-white children go to the movies in big downtown Morrisville because there might have been a little sex in them.

Gussy said she would take me to Syracuse to see Bo and Zellie in an hour, but in the meantime she had to run her social-work rounds at the hospital. When she popped in on me ten minutes later, to make sure I hadn't hanged myself with the sheets or slit my wrists, I imagined, I said, "What should I do?" She looked sad that she was in such a hurry when the question was so fundamental, but she answered me anyway. "Nothing."

I hardly moved. I imagined this was how people felt when they were slowly freezing to death out in a blizzard. I'd heard it was rather painless. They just sort of slowed down, little by little, their movements becoming less and less, while molecule by molecule they froze, until there weren't any molecules left to freeze. Their thoughts slowed down in direct proportion, until minutes would go by before their mind conjured up the next word. The only thing was, I could feel my other self throbbing and stinging miles away, like a half-severed toe beneath wads of cloth.

When we got up to Crouse Memorial, Gussy suggested that I go to Bo's room first. While she waited outside, I walked into Bo's room and crept up to her bed and stared down at her. She looked dead. Her chest barely rose and barely fell under the white sheet. Her head was capped in white gauze that also covered her eyes. Two clear plastic tubes ran up her nostrils, and a small, plastic spout poked out of her head just behind her ear, draining something yellow into a plastic bag. Her hands were wrapped in white gauze, and little burn patches, shiny with ointment, dotted her arms like died-out campfires. Two machines stood on either side of her, appropriating her with black plastic cords. One read her brain, the other her heart. They both made a windy breathing sound, mechanical, but rhythmic, as if they were more alive than Bo was.

I carefully peeled back the sheet to see the rest of her. Her right shin looked flayed, and her whole thigh was a marbled mass of black and blue. A skinny plastic tube ran out from between her legs, yellow with piss. Jesus, Bo, I said. I couldn't believe she'd ever flapped around me in her silk gowns, chainsmoking, all nerves, talking a mile a minute, telling me I was going to change the course of history, and now here she was nearly dead. Where did all of it go? All that bustling and worry about who was going to wear what, and should the tablecloths be white or checked, and what should Oscar study at college, and were we spoiling Frieda too much, all the concern for the lives of that household that now lay charred and lifeless? You couldn't tell me it just vanished, just poof, gone, like none of it ever mattered.

I pulled the sheet up to Bo's chin and sank backwards in the chair. My eyes felt scalded, as if they were two peeled grapes left out in a noon sun. I didn't know what to do, so I took one of her gauzed hands and put it up against my cheek. I tried to feel her presence, but I sensed nothing from her. "Bo, are you in there?" I whispered into her ear. "If you are, squeeze my hand or nod your head." I waited a few minutes. Nothing. I leaned forward again, closer this time, and raised my voice slightly. "Bo, are you in there? If you are, squeeze my hand or nod your head. Anything." I waited again. Nothing. The next time, I touched my lips to Bo's gauzed-over ear and said, "BO, DO YOU HEAR ME?"

Gussy poked her head in the room. "Hemy," she said, "your mother's in a coma."

I looked at her and then at Bo. My eyes stung, they felt so dry.

After that, I didn't say a word, but I thought, You should have known better. It would have been different if she'd been a squeeze-toy woman, all breath and capriciousness, spending money left and right on dresses, primping in mirrors constantly, hanging on to a man's arm day and night, tottering on heels, her mind filled with nothing but possessions. But that wasn't Bo. She prayed three hours a day and had visions sometimes. Her life spoke for itself, didn't it, spoke of a few good dresses and flat shoes, of hanging on to Lourde's arm for closeness, of having a mind filled with ideas and hopes; this was not a woman who made stills. So why did she make one? That's what I wanted to know, and when no answer came, I sat with my hands empty and upturned, my eyes cast upwards.

Someone should have prepared me for the sight of Zellie. Her face was so badly swollen I didn't recognize her, swollen like something left too long in the water. The colors, yellow and purple mainly, swam in the swollenness like colors do on oil. She was strapped into a bed that rotated every fifteen seconds, a bed you might think belonged to the future, a space-age bed, all angular and stainless steel, a machine that clicked and had feedback and output panels that were lit up in red. At first she faced the ceiling, then the motor kicked in and the whole bed shifted and she faced the right wall for fifteen seconds. It moved again and she faced the floor. When I came in she was on her side, facing the door. Her eyes were closed, but I could see them moving back and forth under her eyelids as if she were watching a dream. I sat down in the chair and waited while the bed went through its cycle of turning towards the floor, the left wall, and then up again. When it came back around, Zellie's eyes were open.

"Zellie?" I said.

Her eyes landed on me, but they didn't fix or register anything, as if she could see me but didn't have the slightest idea who I was. I stared at that bloated, purple-yellow face, those zombie-dead eyes, until the bed rotated her to the side and then down, out of my sight, and I had a thought, a thought I couldn't avoid:

I don't love her right. It seemed a pity I should have this thought, of all times to have it, just when she needed to be loved completely, unconditionally, but she'd been mean to me most of my life, there was no getting around that. She'd tried to make me look like an ass whenever she had the chance, calling me Ed for emotionally disturbed, when I was ten until I was fifteen because she'd heard Bo tell Lourde I needed to see a psychiatrist. Then, in front of Bo's customers, pointing me out, saying, "Yeah, there she is, the girl who shot off Mr. Antonovsky's dick," or "Look who's coming, Duke Ellington and his jazz piano," when I was learning to play the piano for Mr. Antonovsky. But the bed came back around and there was her face, all ruined and grotesque, and I laid into myself for having those thoughts when she was so broken up, instead remembering how she'd carried Frieda everywhere until Frieda was almost four years old, caring for her more than Bo did some days, the two of them all loving and touching, and me on the outside, boxing with Oscar. It was just that they didn't love me the same, the two of them, together all the time, inseparable. "Please," I said, "I'm sorry for thinking anything bad."

When the nurse came in, I told her that Zellie's eyes were open.

"She opens them quite a bit," the nurse said, "but she doesn't recognize anything."

The nurse stopped the bed from rotating and undid the straps that kept Zellie from falling out. I watched as she pulled the sheet down and opened Zellie's gown. Where there was once seamless white flesh, there was now a mess of gauze and bandages binding her torso. They were matted with blood and yellow ooze, and a gash ran out from underneath them, as if it had a will of its own, and crossed her breast like a grisly red road. The part of me that had once wanted to stick the flag of my success into her guts was appalled.

"I have to change these," the nurse said. "You don't want to see."

I left the room and sat down on a steel chair outside the door. I heard the radio across the hall playing "Tie a Yellow Ribbon Round the Ole Oak Tree," and I thought, Oh God, they're playing Tony Orlando and Dawn at my mother's coma. I tried to keep my mind from leaping into the future, it felt so bottomless and black, like a wrecked ship sinking into the dark, cold soul of the ocean.

"I lost my whole family," I told Gussy during our drive home.

"Oh, you don't know," she said. "It's too early to tell yet."

I didn't really believe her. I'd seen them.

When we got to Gussy's house, I excused myself and went up to the room Gussy had made up for me. By the time I heard her down the hall washing up for bed, my eyes burned so much, I had to spit on my fingers and touch them to my eyeballs. Then I lay there stone still on my back, my arms down by my sides, my eyes pinned to the ceiling, my mind racing, repelling the bursts of terror and pain that came up from below. Bo in a coma, Zellie a zombie, I recited the facts over and over, Lourde lost his life, Frieda too, sometimes listed rhythmically, sometimes to a tune. Your life is never going to be the same again, Zellie and Bo might die, you might be left alone. Fear surging up like a geyser, and then a quick placating, Maybe they'll live, they might, and Oscar might come back. But they might not, maybe Oscar's gone, and the doors opened again and let out a bolt of pain, a hot blast. What if they all die and I'm left? I winced, bit my lips, hung on to Gussy's mattress, hands like knobs, and told myself, It's okay if you lose your family, it will make you stronger, you can take it. Another blast, Your life is ruined, and I pinched my eyes shut and felt it rock me, roll me over, bully me. Oh God, how is this fair?

In the morning, Gussy drove me to Morrisville so I could see my house and collect the things that could be salvaged. When we got there, she pulled into the drive and shut the car off. The two of us sat in the silence, looking at it, at the blown-out windows, at the wood charred black like a piece of toast, at the lawn strewn with bits and pieces of tables and chairs, of clothing and shoes. Considering how big the fire was, I thought the house would be a heap of smoldering ash, but it was still standing, blackened and proud, though soaking wet.

"You want me to come in with you?" Gussy asked.

I shook my head.

I walked across the lawn, stepping over the wet, blackened

debris, and made my way up the front porch steps, my legs shaking, my mind saying, You don't do this to someone, take their family, burn their house down. The living room was empty of the bits and pieces of tables and chairs I thought it would be so strewn with, the back room empty of the sight of stills, no metal, no meters, nothing, only two black, sooty circles on the floor as evidence. The rooms were blackened sockets, the dark spaces where a tooth wasn't anymore, as if the things either had burned away in the fire or had been carted off.

I looked around for Gussy. She had gotten out of the car and was sitting on the porch waiting for me. I told her I was going upstairs. When she worried that it wasn't safe, I said I'd test every step I took, but I didn't. I just walked up the stairs and down the hallway and figured if I fell through, what did I care.

I went into my room first and found my bed collapsed, the mattress gutted by fire, no trace, not even a shred of sheet or blanket. My cheap little stereo was melted, along with my record albums—Neil Young, Cat Stevens, Led Zeppelin, the Beatles. All of them, a mass of melted black plastic. Words started through my mind then, words that felt manufactured, attached to nothing, barked out of some loudspeaker, like a running commentary, as if there were a tour guide sitting up in the front of my brain, explaining everything. This is where you grew up. In this room. You've cried in here. You've laughed in here. This is the bed Oscar first lay in with you. I felt a wave of nausea pass through me, and I wanted to quit, to avoid the rest, it stretched ahead of me so long and black and ugly. I just wanted to sink to my knees and quit, and stood there blinking in the morning light.

I went across the hall to Oscar's room and opened the door slowly. When I saw his boxing gloves hanging over the bedpost, half blackened and melted, my hands started to shake, and I remembered clearly the last time I'd seen him. He was typing at his desk, a play, and he'd asked me not to tell Lourde. I promised him that I would never tell a soul, no one. The memory shot through my mind and was followed quickly by the realization that he was gone, that all he had said was finished now, wiped out forever. I ran across the wooden floor, over to the window, as if I could get away from it, the constant pumping realization, He's gone, he's gone, he's gone, like a full, vital heartbeat. My breath left me then, and my head throbbed as if it amplified my heart, and the half-burned curtain I grabbed to keep myself standing came crashing down. I sank to the floor like a sail and told myself, You don't know if it's true.

Gussy's voice floated up those stairs. "Are you all right?"

"Yes," I said. I looked down at myself, fallen with legs splayed, covered with black soot, wanting to hold my hands out to show someone, "See what happened."

"Did you find anything?" Gussy called up. I could see her standing down on the lawn in her big white sandals and blue seersucker dress.

I latched on to the idea of finding things, grabbed hold of it like there was something to be gotten from touching and taking these burned things, like there was progress in it, as if in doing it I would move from this point to the end of it, because that's what I wanted, to be at the end of it, looking back from a sure, safe place. So I got up, I moved again, I had a job—to find everything I could find. I combed through all the possessions in Oscar's room, poked into every inch of it, half looking for him, half looking for anything that had something to do with him. I took everything that wasn't completely burned or ruined. Anything that I could identify, I kept. I hauled out wet clothes, half-burned pillows, shoes, books, notebooks, and his small typewriter, unusable now with keys that had melted together. I carted them downstairs and Gussy raved about them all.

We searched the kitchen and found flasks and pots and pans, books, cracked white bowls, and Lourde's gun, which I discovered behind the door and didn't mention to Gussy. I slipped it inside Oscar's typewriter and never said a word. I felt giddy, as if there were joy in finding these things, and then it came out of my mouth, in one small sentence, the truth of my lightness. "Maybe Oscar's still alive," I said while we were putting everything out on the porch. The words had been running through my mind, in the background like the lines of a song. Gussy looked up at me. "Ah, sweetie," she said, "they found his remains."

I lost all interest in finding anything more and wanted to leave, to hide in the dark folds of sleep in Gussy's upstairs room, but she told me to go up to the attic and take Lourde's manuscripts out of his trunk. So I walked up to his writing room with an anchor in my heart and stood in the quiet, surveying the mess of burned and blackened things, the mattress where he wrote soaking wet, his last page lying in a puddle, the ink blurred almost beyond recognition. I picked it up and struggled to see what he'd written, to know what were his last thoughts, and managed to read the words . . . *it is better to fall into the hands of a murderer than into the dreams of a woman in heat.*

It stunned me to think that these were Lourde's last words.

"What are you doing?" Gussy called up to me.

I was sitting there breathing, shocked by the quiet, by how utterly untouched it was.

My skin turned to goose flesh when I looked down and found the darkened remains of a family photograph on the floor by my foot. You could see me and Oscar and a little piece of Bo and Zellie. The rest was burned away. As if something not quite made of bone and blood had passed through me, I looked around the room to see if anything had changed and found that only my consciousness had changed. I was aware of being there, of squatting in disaster, of the water up over my shoes, of being tapped on the shoulder without being touched and made to pick up a shard of a photograph that would mean something to me.

I wanted to believe it had been left to me by God. Gussy said it had probably just happened that way, who knew why, but I took it as a sign from God that Oscar was still alive, that Bo and Zellie would live. When I showed people the photograph and told them what I thought, their eyes softened in pity. They couldn't believe in anything they couldn't see or touch. They'd forgotten that what was most real in this life was what they could never see and never touch. You knew it was there because it touched you. I had never once had that thought myself, but when I reached down and picked that piece of photograph out of the ruins, I sensed there was something greater than me, hovering always, waiting until a person stopped fighting and consented.

I went back to my house the next two days, once with Gussy Keys, once with Louise and Hillary, who smoked and watched me, occasionally exchanging dire looks which I interpreted as agreement that I was to be pitied. "Hemy," they'd say after a while, "Oscar's not here. They took what they could find of him to the funeral parlor." I denied that I was looking for him, although I was. I knew I wasn't going to find him whole and intact, standing in one of the corners, but I was hoping that I'd find something of him, a piece of proof that he'd been blown up like they'd said. Not an arm or a leg, just a piece of his shirt or his hair or his shoe, because I didn't believe he was really gone.

I carted all the stuff I'd found to Gussy's and what was wet I laid out on the back lawn to dry. I kept myself busy with the other things, turning my room at Gussy's into a Lourde family museum, with me the sole curator and only visitor. The words to these things kept me going, kept me from sinking to my knees in the middle of my room: Put Bo's pots and pans on the rocking chair. Put Lourde's book next to it. Get all of Lourde's and Bo's things and put them all on the rocking chair. Fix them nice, Lourde's on one side, Bo's on the other. . . . When I was all done, I didn't know what to do, so I took Oscar's boxing gloves and wore them like a necklace.

Then I lay up in Gussy's upstairs bedroom for two days, smoking Old Gold cigarettes and watching the sun creep across the summer sky and disappear, leaving a night sky, a vast black sheath, pinpricked with light. I listened to the heartbeat of the field outside, to the *lub-dub* of the crickets, and lay there carefully as if I had dozens of eggs inside me perched on all different kinds of ledges. And though I wasn't immune to them, I got used to the words that said Lourde had died and Frieda had died, that Bo and Zellie were half-gone, that Oscar might not be found.

I made it through those days and nights, I don't know how, and was amazed each morning when I opened my eyes and heard the quiet. I knew then that the struggle took place only inside of me; the rest, the whole world, was unfazed.

What got me the most about the memorial preparations was the casket they had for Oscar. I understood that there should be one for Lourde and one for Frieda, but why for Oscar, a whole casket for his remains, a black lacquer one with gold trim, as long as Lourde's?

"What's in it?" I asked Hank Lester when I went down to the funeral parlor to plan the service. He was a squat, nervous man with large patches of red eczema hidden under his starched white shirt, a man who at fifty-five still lived with his mother. He excused himself, and when he didn't come back, I walked over to Oscar's casket and tried to open it. It was locked, so I hunted around and found a wrought-iron poker. I took it back to the room where Oscar's casket stood, and in full view I tried to pry it open, gouging the lacquer in the process, panting from the effort, determined to open that casket, like a cat seeking entrance to a birdcage. When Hank Lester came into the room and caught me, he nearly died.

"STOP!" he cried, lurching over to me. "You can't open that!" He stopped buffing the part where the poker had scratched the shiny lacquer long enough to look at me.

"I'd like to see," I said. "I don't believe he's in there."

For a moment Hank Lester shook, and then he compressed his lips and stared at me, his eyes melting the way Louise's and Hillary's had when they'd watched me paw through the ashes looking for Oscar. "It's not anything to see," he said quietly.

"What's in there?"

"Nothing recognizable."

"Then how do you know it's Oscar?"

"The dental records," he finally said.

"So his jaw is in there?" I couldn't find the words to express it, but I wanted to tell Hank Lester that if Oscar's jaw was in there, I wanted it. Hank Lester never admitted whether Oscar's jaw was in there or not. He just put his arm around me and steered me past the caskets and into his office, where he sat me down in a chair and brought me a glass of cold water. I looked down at the water and saw a reflection of my mouth, huge and fishy, and told myself that as soon as this was all over I could jump off a bridge. I just had to get through this next part, to give Lourde and Frieda a memorial service, and when it was over, I could go up to the hospital and leave Bo and Zellie a rose and a note that said I couldn't wait any longer, just in case they ever woke up. It was just too much to ask a person, I would write.

I spent the whole memorial service semihidden under a black veil Mr. Antonovsky had lent me, dodging everyone's looks of pity. Mr. Antonovsky and Gussy Keys sat on either side of me and kept me from slipping from the pew to the floor, while Louise and Hillary sat behind me, every now and then their small shaky hands landing on my shoulders like hummingbirds.

I was distracted from concentrating on the memorial service because of the minister, the Reverend Scott Packard, a cliché-ridden hypocrite with sagging jowls and a measly heart, a minister who betrayed the confidence of his profession, and in all his shabbiness told Hillary's father what poor Hillary had confessed in tears in the private sanctuary of the church—that she had made love to a boy in the backseat of his car. Quite a few times during the service I wanted to stop him from butchering the memory of my family, because his heart and soul were so cut off from his mind, from the part of him that formed sentences and spoke. He could have inserted anyone's name into the rot he spoke about Frieda, about Lourde: *Frieda, a young, innocent girl. . . . Benjamin Lourde, a good man, a man who will be missed, a man who meant a great deal to us all.* I was embarrassed in front of Lourde, he was a playwright, he deserved something better. I should have known, I should have written something myself and stood up there in front of everyone, timid and broken, and spoken something true. I apologized to them in my mind, Forgive me, Frieda, Forgive me, Lourde, and then found myself cursing Bo. Thanks a fucking lot, Bo. Thanks for leaving me to do this myself.

When it came time for Oscar's eulogy, I couldn't listen anymore. It was so unbearable I plugged my ears halfway through it and listened to myself breathe. I admitted that it was possible that I just couldn't face the fact that Oscar's remains were really in the casket simply because it was too great a thing to face. I had succumbed to the fear and faced it and thought myself a fool, but regardless of all the evidence to the contrary, I often felt I knew he was still alive. I went crazy with knowing, though, hunting it down, stalking it, trying to hold it in one place so I could look at it, touch it, turn it, press against it, asking was it really knowing, did I really know, or was I fooling myself? It'd slip from my fingers and I'd have to search for it again, the knowing, finding it again, and in my grief and frenzy I'd try to capture it again, to turn it into something concrete, evidence, and just when it felt like I knew, it slipped away again, and I was left with not knowing if I knew.

I couldn't face the cemetery either. The wind blew my hair across my eyes and I did nothing to push it away. I didn't look and I didn't listen either, until they lowered Oscar's casket. When they did, I looked up and thought how I was going to have to come back and dig it up. It seemed a waste, considering it was right here and could easily be opened, and the whole time they were lowering it, I had to stifle the urge to yell, "Hey, wait a minute!"

I spent the rest of the week visiting Bo and Zellie. I watched them from a chair, Bo breathing, Zellie flipping over and over in that bed, my eyes as dry and stinging as the Sahara, my mind torn from end to end, as if a bunch of thugs had come in and ransacked it. There was no getting away from it either. I wanted to reach up, take it off my neck and set it on the bedside table, where I could heave up and turn my back on it.

At night I sat up in my room, rocking in Gussy Keys's rocking chair, embroidering peace signs, small as teardrops, on the sleeves of my blue jean shirt, half listening to Helen Reddy singing "I Am Woman" over the radio, while I thought about killing myself. It was endless, the ways in which you could do it. When Gussy went to bed, I touched razor blades to the inside of my wrist. I held handfuls of sleeping pills in one hand and glasses of water in the other, and late some nights, I walked a mile out of town to a highway where semis barreled past. I hated Bo for ever making a still, and I hated Lourde for being so incapable of making a living that Bo even thought to make one. Then I hated myself for surviving and for surviving because I had shot Mr. Antonovsky and was away playing the piano for him to make amends. And when I heard Zellie's voice saying, "It's all your fault, Hemy. If you hadn't shot Mr. Antonovsky's dick off in the first place, this never would have happened," I hated her too.

"Thanks a fucking lot," I said to them. "Thanks a fucking lot for leaving me here by myself."

9

$\mathcal{S}$he sat up and wiped her forehead with the corner of the white cotton sheet. The back of her pale neck was beaded with sweat, her cotton blouse stuck to her back.

This must be true, he said. He dropped his cigarette into the Coke can and heard it extinguish.

She turned and looked at him, motes of grief in her eyes.

Why? she asked.

Her voice was worn and low, her neck bent.

You are shaken, I can see, he said. He turned on his side towards her and watched her carefully. She had had the experience of breaking violently from her life, like the one he had tried to create when he climbed onto the train. He so envied this break, envied her for standing there saying "Thanks a fucking lot for leaving me here by myself," envied the fact that she had been opened to the unthinkable. He wished for this effacement, for what followed it.

Then other thoughts raced to him: the implications of a woman's still, blowing apart a family, killing a husband who had last written the words: *It is better to fall into the hands of a murderer than into the dreams of a woman in heat.* But what were the implications? He wondered if they could be stretched to include everyone, as if Bo and Lourde had not been isolated characters, but rather were representatives of man and woman, as if this event had significance to the whole world, as if in the explosion, in the silence that followed, lay some truth about man and woman. It scared him to think of it; he understood the words Lourde had written down—he'd felt them himself. But he couldn't think of that now.

What was it like? he asked quietly, as if she could tell him something.

It was suffering, she said.

Only suffering?

She did not answer.

You fell apart completely?

Yes, of course.

Tears came to her eyes and she pushed them away. There, are you satisfied? she said. Is this what you wanted? To see me cry? The woman who lived as a man?

No, he said, but privately he knew it was true.

He reached up and laid his hand on her shoulder. I'm sorry, he said.

She pushed her eyes into her kneecaps to stanch the tears.

I'm sorry you lost your family, and I'm sorry I wanted you to tell me, and I'm sorry too that I did want to see you cry.

She wiped her face with the palms of her hands, and then without a word she slipped past the red velvet curtains, into the sitting room. He pushed back the curtains and looked at her. Her hair was damp and her neck bent as she tucked her white cotton blouse into her skirt.

I need a drink of water, she said.

I'll get it for you, he said.

No, I need air.

So he followed her down the ribbon-thin aisles, his stride long and even, through three cars, to the cafe car, where she quietly drank a bottle of Evian water. How strange she looked in this cafe car, he thought, her wanting the past, sitting now at this plastic-topped table, rap music playing on someone's boom box nearby. There was some part of her that didn't belong and never would, some part of her that was detached, as if she were of another world, one lost, or at least one unknown to him. He reached across the table and touched her forearm with his long, tapered fingers. She looked up at him and smiled, and an image came into his mind, a strange image of prison cells, of men sitting on small cots, their heads bent, their hands dangling listlessly.

How do you know men on Death Row? he asked her.

His question surprised her, and when her eyes blinked rapidly, he knew that he'd touched something vital. Had she been on Death Row? He tossed the hair from his eyes.

Was Oscar Lourde a man on Death Row? he asked pointedly, as if he were cross-examining someone accused.

She looked him straight in the eye and stared at him deeply, as if she were trying to see past his skin, past his bones, to his soul.

Who are you? she asked.

He laughed nervously and shifted his eyes away. He sensed she could see her way clear to that naked place every person wanted to hide, and it unnerved him.

Now *you* want to know? he said, playing at being flippant.

Yes, she said. I'm beginning to worry that with every word I utter, I am losing something, while you are gaining.

He smiled coyly, touching his thumb to his lip, but she rose from the table like a flame and left the cafe car. By the time he got to his feet and brushed past a line of people who had formed near the doorway, she was gone. He went back to her room, but she wasn't there. He could tell by the way the white cotton sheets lay that she hadn't been back. A panic rose inside him, and his heart began to beat fast, until he reasoned that there was no place for her to disappear on a moving train.

He went methodically from car to car, looking for her. He walked quickly, turning his head from side to side as he searched the aisles. When he didn't find her in any of the seats, he began checking the smoking lounges, until he finally found her in the last one. She was sitting in a battered red vinyl chair, in front of a window she'd cracked open, her feet up, watching the Wyoming night slip past.

When she heard the door open, she glanced over her shoulder, as if she were expecting him. Her eyes were full of want, and he didn't begin to understand.

He pulled another red vinyl chair up next to hers and sat down quietly. He propped his long legs up on the metal window ledge and watched the last of Wyoming pass by. Even in the darkness he could see the scraggly brush land giving way to the white sands of Utah.

We're almost to the desert, he said.

I know, she answered quietly.

He shook out a cigarette, struck a match, and lit it. They both watched as the blue-gray smoke raced wildly out the window. Neither of them spoke for what felt to him like a long time. They fell into the rhythm of the train, rocking to and fro as if they were being cradled. She rested her head on the back of the red vinyl chair and closed her eyes, while he smoked another cigarette, and the little faucet next to them drooled water and hissed.

When it seemed all the dust between them had settled, he spoke.

Who bombed your house?

She didn't so much as open her eyes. Who do you think?

Happy, he said.

Good guess.

But she didn't say any more, and he knew he was going to have to ask her again, ask her to keep going, because he wanted to know, but he held quiet and waited to see what she would say. He swore he would not speak until she had spoken, even if it stretched into hours. While she sat with her head against the vinyl chair, her eyes closed, he smoked quietly, watching the brush land lose itself to the desert.

It was nearly fifteen minutes before she said anything.

What is your name? she finally asked.

When he didn't answer, she opened her eyes and looked at him.

Why does it matter? he said, the way she always said it.

It doesn't. It's just that you know mine now.

So? he said.

You're right, she said. It doesn't matter. Have your name.

When she closed her eyes again and rested her head against the back of the red vinyl chair, he smiled to himself. "Have your name," she'd said, and he felt he was gaining, that he was winning, but then he wondered why it mattered to him. He swore again that he wouldn't speak another word until she spoke, but he wasn't able to hold quiet this time. Not more than ten minutes passed before he heard his voice.

So did Happy bomb your house? he said.

She opened her eyes and looked at him. What?

I want to know who bombed your house.

She thought about it for a long time and then said, My first inclination is to tell you to go pester someone else.

What is your second inclination? he said coyly.

I could give way to it, consent to it, to you, she said.

Will you? He smiled and pressed his thumb against his lower lip and then slowly into his mouth.

She looked at him carefully, for a long time. She saw clear through him, he thought, to his need.

She took her feet from the windowsill and sat up. All right, she said. I will. He didn't know why she'd decided to consent to it, though he remembered what she'd said before: *I sensed there was something greater than me, hovering always, waiting until a person stopped fighting and consented.* He wondered if this had anything to do with it, but there seemed no way to ask.

She rose from the chair and left the smoking lounge, threading her way through the cars, down the aisles, back to her room. He followed her, watching the slit of her skirt ride up and down her strong calves.

Once they were lying side by side in the white cotton and red velvet, he felt better. He pushed off his boots, let them drop to the floor, and turned on his side towards her, his right arm stretching across her pillow. She lay next to him, her breath slow and even.

She watched out the window for a long time, not speaking, watching the white sand of the desert pass, while he touched her pale neck with the tip of his finger.

We're in the desert now, she said.

He looked out the window and could see the white sands stretching for miles, like an ocean, wavy with details of shadow and light.

Utah, he said.

She turned her head and looked at him.

I'll tell you who bombed my house and how it worked out, she said, and then I'm going to sleep, and in the morning I'm going to get off the train in the desert and stay the night.

Do you want me to come with you? he asked.

Yes, she said.

Thank you, he said.

She took hold of his hand again and began speaking boldly, hotly even.

10

I don't know when it was exactly, but somewhere along the line Happy's name began to surface in my mind, quietly at first, but consistently, like the fin of a shark in bloody waters, until I slowly began to realize that he had bombed my house and destroyed my family over a few percentage points Bo wouldn't give him. I don't know why it took so long for me to realize it, it was there from the start and made such perfect sense, but once it surfaced in my mind, it did so with such clarity that from that moment on there was never a doubt in my mind.

It pulled me from Gussy's bed, where I'd spent many days and nights, seething and smoking, sweat-soaked and broken, and took me to Morrisville, where I walked from the police station, to the fire station, to the people's houses who were in Bo's Place the night the bomb exploded. I showed up in front of them with nothing, showed up skinny and pale, curly hair and beanpole legs, and opened my mouth and talked, asked more questions than anyone wanted to answer. I told them everything I knew and remembered about Happy and the bomb. I walked back and forth along Route 20, in a pair of Indian sandals, wearing the ripped-up pair of blue jeans and peasant blouse I'd worn the night my house burned, my fringe leather bag hanging from my shoulder. And I went from one to the other all day long, sometimes into the early evening, and talked, then argued until my jaw hurt and my mouth dried out.

When I first told the police that it was Happy, I discovered they weren't calling it a bombing anymore. They were calling it an explosion. "Your mother's illegal stills exploded," they said, but I distinctly remembered hearing Gussy Keys say "Your house was bombed" when we rode together in the front seat of a car the night my house burned. When I asked her about it, she said that was what she'd heard the firemen say, and she was even good enough to tell the police what she'd told me, but afterwards they said, "We thought so, but after further investigation we realized that your mother's stills had exploded."

The firemen claimed they had never considered the possibility that it was a bombing and had never used the word in connection with the explosion. I asked them, "Then why did the police say at first that they thought it was a bombing, and then decided it was an explosion?" They said they had never told the police it was a bombing. When I went back to the police and told them what the firemen had said, the police took back what they had said earlier and now gave me what became their official line: "We never called it a bombing. That was just a rumor."

After that I approached the people who were in Bo's Place that night, or the families, in the case of death, and with a shaky-new voice, I told them that Happy had bombed my house. Many of them were angry at me, as if it was my fault that they or someone in their family had gone to Bo's Place to begin with. Some of them said that they didn't know Bo had illegal stills in the back that could explode and threatened to sue me, some told me to forget it, I was just a skinny little girl, no one would listen to me, others looked at me with sloppy pity in their eyes, and one of them, a middle-aged, churchgoing man named Spike Harris, took me aside and whispered, "You'd better watch yourself, talking about this Happy character."

At night, I lay up in my bedroom at Gussy's and hatched something with claws and spine and spitting anger. I became tense-veined and pulsing, on red alert, with eyes open, hands knotted, mind ticking: Don't fuck with me. There is no fairness, not even in this small, white-churched, green-lawned town, no fairness at all. Never was, never will be, get used to it. These people, they are cardboard, interested in their own asses, won't any of them stick their neck out for you. Don't expect anything, not even that the sun will come up the next morning. There is no law, only Happy's law, the law that got Lourde out of prison early, the law that helped Bo set up another business and protected her from shutdown. Something that crouched down low in my guts and had never spoken before spoke now: Fight, girl, fight like hell, like a pit-bulled, matadored prick. This voice was a new voice, raw-edged and daring, and it said: Get the fuck out of my way—you took my family, I'll take you.

I made Louise sit down on the bed up in my room while I walked back and forth across the worn floors, all breath and sweat and fervor, pounding the dresser with my fist, listing the facts over and over and over again, coming to the same conclusion every time: Happy did it, who else could it have been, there was no one else.

I lay up in Gussy's bed at nights, nerve and gut strung together on bone, lay there clench-jawed and smoking, watching myself in combat boots, imagining shaving my head bald, wearing sleeveless shirts, and tattooing my arms with pictures of bombs.

"You know, you've really changed," Louise said.

"You lose your whole family in a bombing, you aren't the same."

"You didn't lose your whole family," she said. "Bo and Zellie are still alive."

"You call that alive?"

In the three weeks I'd been visiting them, Bo hadn't so much as moved a muscle, and though Zellie did open her eyes, they remained as dull and blank as those of a fish. I tried to tell Louise what that did to a person, just sitting there, helpless to stop the flipping, the shallow, deathlike breathing, waiting, while time flew and passed them by, without the slightest bit of progress—no spark in the eye, no raised hand. I tried to explain the fingers that descended and dug deep into your guts while you were sitting there hoping, half expecting a miracle, and the cold voice that uttered: What are you, crazy? Nothing is going to happen. And then taking the bus back to a place you couldn't call home and lying awake in a bed that wasn't yours, wanting in a way that was relentless and unforgiving, chewed up by the unfairness, the lousy cruelty.

But Louise was right. I had changed. You lose your whole family, you don't feel like you've got anything else to lose.

"You can't say that for the rest of your life," Louise said. "Every time something happens you can't say, 'Well, I lost my whole family and so that's why I'm this way.' "

Somehow I heard Louise's mother in Louise's words. I could just see the bone-thin woman stirring her meat-and-potato stew, saying, "That girl can't be bringing that up every time something happens. It's unfortunate and all, but she can't be doing and saying what she wants and then using the loss of her family as an excuse." That's why when the time came, I didn't move in with the Van Sants, like they asked me to. Something told me Mrs. Van Sant's tolerance was puny, as bony as she was, wafer thin. So, it was into the room Mr. Antonovsky offered, the room at the back of his house, that I carried a borrowed suitcase filled with a few donated clothes and all the artifacts I had recovered from the ruins of my house. He said he had lost his whole family at my age and felt he understood, and it was true. He did. Unlike Louise and Louise's mother, Mr. Antonovsky understood perfectly, he understood my hatred, my seething anger, my burning sense of injustice, understood it completely, shared it even, as if it were his. My Happy was his Stalin, and together we passed whole evenings in his living room, wrecking the silence, outlining the politics of evil hour upon hour, becoming such compatriots in suffering and loss that I completely forgot about Mr. Antonovsky's dick. I understood what he meant when he had told me not so long ago, "Is nothing now. Is nothing more than water hose." You lose your whole family because of some evil bastard's whim, losing half a dick is nothing.

His room up at the top of the stairs became my home. I lay up there for hours on top of the bed, my hands folded on my stomach, reminding myself over and over and over again about what I had lost, telling myself time after time that all I owned in the world stood now on the desk, hung in the closet, and lay in the dresser drawers, repeating like a credo that I had one real, true enemy in this world, all the hatred and loathing in my skinny body racing to a point in my heart, as if the name Happy were etched into it.

It was when I envisioned Happy sitting somewhere eating his lunch, yukking it up with his pals, completely oblivious of the fact that he'd taken the lives of a whole family, leaving one skinny girl behind, that I came to know madness. In those moments, I touched it, pressed up against it, came to recognize, somewhere deep inside myself, the murderess. I possessed now the darkest interior. I was filled with the most evil thoughts, thoughts that had been denied to me before, thoughts filled with hatred. I felt released from all strictures, thrust outside of life now, of the world that functioned as if these things did not happen, as if Happy were never in anyone's backyard; I had been cast out of the world of tables set for dinner, filled with plates of well-cooked food eaten under warm lights, the world of clean-smelling clothes and white bed linen. Where I stood, it appeared wholly different—the world was dark and vicious, chaotic and irrational, full of hatred and anger, a terrifying place and now it lay inside of me. Had you cut me open, you would have found "Happy" tattooed on the inside of my veins, etched in black across my heart. I hated that man, loathed him utterly, wanted nothing more than his ruin, which I plotted every chance I got. There was no person more evil to me, no person more in need of capital punishment. Every night I grew a little bigger in my bed at Mr. Antonovsky's house, a little more grizzled, more whiskered. I saw myself walking down road after road in a pair of army boots, smoking Lourde's Old Golds, my jaw square, my mouth unsmiling, my eyes fixed straight ahead, no bullshit, a person to reckon with.

I lay up in my bedroom at Mr. Antonovsky's for weeks, praying that Happy would mess with someone who wouldn't think twice about snuffing him out. I was partial to the idea that someone would break down his bedroom door, catch him in mid-stroke fucking one of his big-breasted women, and before he could take another breath, gun him down in a spray of bullets. I would have been satisfied if he just got mowed down by a bus or a Mack truck. I didn't even mind the idea of him not dying, just so long as he was profoundly maimed, like the man in *Johnny Got His Gun*, who lost his arms and his legs and had to seriously consider sideshow work in the circus.

When I told Louise all of this, she said I was getting stranger and stranger by the day. I didn't know how to tell her that it wasn't so much strangeness she perceived as it was distance, that

I couldn't articulate what had taken me away, except to say that I had a healthy respect for the unseen, whorling powers in the world, over which I had absolutely no control.

"We're like ants, Louise, and as ants we live in this world where people with big feet walk wherever the hell they want. And because we're just ants, we can't ever predict where these feet will land. And there isn't anything we can do about it. So when you begin to realize how easily you can be picked off, you start to feel grateful when you are allowed to go in and out of your ant-hill, hauling your loads, without getting stepped on."

"But we're not ants, Hemy," Louise said. "We're those walking people with the big feet."

I let it go.

At first what I proposed to Louise was just finding Happy. "But you can't just find him and then stare at him," Louise said. I wanted to find him and stare at him so he would know that I knew. I thought about asking him, too, telling him that I knew what he had done, until I realized that I would be leaving myself wide open to getting offed. In fact, when I thought it through, even staring at him was too risky, considering he'd blown up a whole house and a whole family. It would be nothing but a light chore to get rid of a grief-stricken sixteen-year-old.

"I think there's only one thing I can really do," I finally said to Louise.

"What?"

"Kill him."

I don't know how I managed to rope Louise into my plan of killing Happy. She said she thought she must have become addicted to me, because she certainly didn't think I should kill him. When we'd talk about it, she'd sometimes slap her face and say, "I can't believe we're sitting here talking about killing a man." I'd remind her that he wasn't a man. "He's a devil," I said, echoing the word Lourde had spoken out in the back field the night our fate was sealed.

"Maybe there's another way to handle it," Louise said.

"Like how?"

"Maybe you could take it to the Supreme Court or something."

"With what? There is no physical evidence of a bomb. There

is no physical evidence of the stills. Everything I heard Happy say is hearsay, and besides, it's not like Bo was an innocent person. She was running illegal stills, Louise. When you operate outside the law like that, this is what you get."

"It will ruin your life, though," she said.

I told her it was already ruined.

"You could start over again, Hemy. Killing him won't get you anywhere."

I said it would bring me peace.

"You're crazy," she said.

I smiled. It was my new identity. The crazy Hemy Lourde.

When Louise balked at the last minute, I took her to the cemetery and presented her with the three grave sites, and then dragged her up to Crouse Memorial, where the two of us sat, first in Bo's room, watching her breathe, then in Zellie's, watching that bed flip over and over again, so Louise could feel for herself the helplessness in watching time fly and pass them over, without the slightest bit of progress.

"I see what you mean," she said.

It took a little doing, but we found out that Happy lived at 124 Onondaga Avenue and hung out at a club called Rocky's just three blocks from the Syracuse Hotel. I decided we should wait for him across the street from his house, and when he came home late at night, I would shoot him with Lourde's gun, the same gun I had used to shoot Mr. Antonovsky, the gun I had found in the ruins. Louise was with me when I took it out of the top drawer of my dresser in Mr. Antonovsky's room and slipped it, barrel down, into my fringed leather bag, wedging it between a wallet and a big bottle of aspirin. It was slightly charred, but there were still three bullets inside.

Louise was terrified, and all the way up on the Greyhound bus she tried to talk me out of it, but I was firm about it, one-minded. It was hard to explain to her that you couldn't lie up in a bed like a bug on a stick pin, writhing and thrashing forever, that at some point you had to take some action or the whole thing would twist you, make a mess of your heart and liver, wreck you, steal your life, your breath, strangle you. Why should he breathe when I couldn't? I said.

The bus dropped us off at the Greyhound station, and while we waited for one of the inner-city buses to pick us up, Louise said, "What are we going to do after you shoot him, Hemy?" It was a game by now, this conversation, and it always began with this question.

"Run like hell," I said.

Louise thought about it, and after pausing the requisite number of moments, I said, "What's the worst thing that could happen?"

"We could get caught and sent to jail." Above all else, Louise feared jail. She feared it more than getting shot.

"First of all," I told her, "you won't go to jail. You won't be the one who shoots him. The worst they could pin on you is accomplice, and I promise that if we get caught, I will say that you were trying to prevent me from doing this. They won't put you in jail. They'll only put me in jail."

The bus dropped us off on Grant Street, two blocks from Onondaga Avenue, and in total silence Louise and I walked those two blocks to Happy's house, Louise shaking, me with imaginary combat boots, thick-necked and pop-veined, a gunman with a job, Don't anyone fuck with me, do you hear? When we stopped, it was across the street from a squat red brick building with three black letters, 124, outlined in gold. It may as well have said "Happy lives here" for all the fear I felt. I hadn't expected the fear either. I had expected the hatred to override it, had expected steel in my backbone, and prayed now for the courage, because I'd come all this way and didn't want to get back on the bus a skinny teenage girl. I wanted to go back the gunman.

So we sat down on the stoop across from Happy's house and waited for Happy to come home so I could shoot him. We waited for two hours on the cold concrete steps, shifting every few minutes, talking, watching for him, looking into every car, truck, and face that passed us. There were all kinds out that night—old men in gray slacks walking boxer dogs, teenage girls edging down the sidewalk in hip-hugger bell bottoms, smoking cigarettes, half hiding behind their long, smooth bangs, vans driving by filled with long-haired young men and women who sang loudly to Pink Floyd and passed joints back and forth, blowing smoke out the windows, black boys with Afros and tight pants drifting by talking black power, shooting Louise and me dirty looks, we were so hopelessly white.

Then finally a taxi pulled up in front of Happy's house. Suddenly the gun had to be taken up and my nerves had to be straightened out, so I stuck my elbow into Louise's side to quiet her, but right away she started breathing noisily. "Louise," I said, and slipped the gun out of my purse and laid it in my lap while I waited for the cab door to click open, waited for that horrid being to emerge. As I took the gun into my hand and started to position it, Louise tugged on my arm and broke down. "Don't do it, Hemy," she cried. "It's not worth it. Please don't."

I jabbed her with my elbow. "Louise, be quiet."

Happy emerged from the cab with a big-breasted woman in tow, and when I pictured him writhing in bed with her, completely oblivious of the fact that he'd wiped out a whole family and left behind a trembling girl, I raised the gun, aimed it at his heart, and pulled the trigger. The gun dry-snapped, but Louise screamed anyway, Happy and his big-breasted woman wheeling around, staring across the street where Louise and I were sitting on the porch as if we were just a couple of teenage girls. I could have repositioned the gun and pulled the trigger again and again and again until I hit into one of the chambers that held the bullets, but I didn't. Something broke inside me, like a thin blister covering a well of warm, salty water, and I dropped the gun into my purse.

After a few moments, Louise and I rose up and stumbled away. I was breathing hard, my hands shaking, the sound of a gun in my ears marking off my life again, though it hadn't made much of a sound. But I had pulled the trigger. For the second time in my life, I'd aimed a gun and pulled a trigger, and all the way home Louise kept asking, "What if one of the bullets had been in the chamber, Hemy?"

"But it wasn't," I said back, because that was the truth.

"Yeah, but still, if it had been you would have shot him. You would have. You would have shot him, Hemy." She looked at me in the hazy light of the bus, half in admiration, half in horror, and said, "Don't you see that? If the bullet had been in the chamber, you would have shot him."

I tried to explain to Louise that right after I pulled the trigger and Happy was still waltzing down the sidewalk with his high-heeled woman tucked under his arm, I had a moment of perfect clarity. I saw in my mind images of holes, of blackness, of things going down, of dissolution, and in that split second I understood that killing Happy would do nothing to repair the hole that was rent in me, that it would merely rend another, which would rend another and another and another, until there was nothing left. I couldn't explain myself beyond that, but suddenly something inside me opened like a door into the air, and I dropped my head in Louise's lap and wept loudly, like an unstrung violin. Poor Louise patted the side of my face, the sound of my weeping so disturbing that it finally brought people to our seat, and Louise had to tell them, "She lost almost her whole family in a bombing," and then hands, I don't know whose, reached over the seat and touched my hair, my face, my shoulder, briefly, but softly, cooed words following, hushed, sibilant, and necessary.

11

She stopped talking and turned her head towards him. He was lying on his side, his arm draped across her waist, watching her intently.

Do you want me to go on? she said.

Yes, of course.

But you're crying, she said. She reached over and wiped the tears from his face with her thumbs.

He didn't know why he was crying. He felt confused. He had been excited by the idea of her shooting Happy, of her exacting her own brand of justice, outside of the law. It would have been so perfect, but chance had had it another way, and instead of the bullet being in one chamber, it had been in another. And she had found, not justice, but something else, something about which he didn't know what to think.

Why didn't you want to rend another hole? he asked her quietly.

It was uninteresting, she said.

How was the alternative more interesting—going away unsatisfied?

Something else besides rending holes could happen, she said.

Something good?

No, just something else. Something I didn't know.

An existential choice? he said.

She smiled.

Did you feel morally superior?

No, she said. I pulled the trigger.

It impressed him that she hadn't felt morally superior, that she wasn't relieved that she hadn't shot Happy so as to be good. He felt then that he could trust her more.

Why are you crying? she asked, softly brushing the tears from his cheeks.

The image of the girl Hemy crying in Louise's lap after losing everything came to him.

It's very sad, he said.

Their eyes caught, and it was she who leaned in close this time and kissed his mouth. She did it so boldly and with such relish that it stole his breath. Then she pulled away and stared into his eyes, as if to dare him. He lunged back, greedy, his mouth sliding over hers, his tongue slipping inside. He pulled her to his chest and pressed himself against her, as if his whole body were erect and ready. He wanted his strength, his show of force to impress her, to fill her with fear and desire, as she had filled him the night before; but she pushed back with equal force and pulled him to her with such power in her arms that he found himself wondering again, was she man or woman? It became difficult to engage in this potent kiss with strange images turning in his mind—images of women's bodies surgically changed to men's, of small, grotesque appendages, sewn on. The thought so disturbed him, he finally broke the kiss.

You never answered my question, he whispered.

What question? she whispered back.

Genitally speaking, are you a man or a woman?

She stared into his eyes a moment, then tipped her head back and laughed. He felt foolish, but her laugh was so lavish he forgot.

When she settled down, she found his eyes, then took his hand and placed it between her legs, where through the cotton weave of her skirt he felt the unrelieved smoothness of her pelvic bone, the flesh of her lips, the split. She smiled and reached down and touched him between his legs. Through his khaki pants, she felt him stiffen, and when he was fully hard, she took her hand back.

I guess you're a man, she said.

You weren't sure?

She laughed when she looked at him and saw the pain in his eyes, the small defeat that came when a manhood, any manhood, was questioned.

She kissed his lips sweetly and whispered, What would you have done if you'd felt between my legs and found a penis?

I wouldn't lie in here with you anymore.

Would you still care to hear my story? she asked.

Yes, I would, but in the cafe car.

She fell back on the pillow laughing, her white throat exposed, her laugh loud and deep. He loved the sound of her laugh and touched his lips to her throat.

Tell me more of your story, he whispered. It was becoming uncomfortable to him, her telling this story, but still he wanted to know more.

She looked at her German clock and frowned.

It's getting late. Do you think I should keep going?

Yes, please, he said.

Where was I?

Crying like an unstrung violin in Louise's lap, he said.

Oh, yes.

He turned on his side and watched her mouth form the first word, her knees tapping lightly together, as if they were the engine to the whole thing.

12

$\mathcal{T}$he next thing I knew Zellie woke up. A nurse from Crouse Memorial called to tell me, and with a clattery heart I took the first bus up to Syracuse, thinking how strange it was that Zellie had come back. I would never have thought it possible, I'd given up hope, but then a horrible thought came into my mind, the sort of thought you are loath to admit, the sort of thought you wish you could thrust back. Why Zellie? Why, out of Lourde, Bo, Oscar, and Frieda, was Zellie spared? Before I could stop myself, I wished it had been someone other than Zellie who'd survived, anyone but Zellie, she was my least favorite. It shook me up too, the idea that I might not be alone anymore. I had pulled solitude around me like a shawl, had drawn into myself, had gathered the strength that was deep in the pit of a being when it was utterly, entirely alone. It was now sacred space around me, four feet deep, six feet tall, an armor, a shield, it was all I had, and I feared Zellie's wakening would puncture it and blow it all away.

When I walked into the intensive care unit, the nurses crowded around me, the word "miracle" suddenly on everyone's lips: It's a miracle, she's a miracle, we've witnessed a miracle. "Does she know?" I whispered, and their faces lost all expression, the word "miracle" suddenly dropped, as if it had been crushed under the weight of our knowing, one of them finally answering, "We didn't tell her that much." They'd only had the nerve to tell her that her mother's still had exploded and that she'd been impaled by a table leg. "I see," I said to them. "So I'm supposed to tell her the rest," and when they nodded, I saw my mission stretch out before me, long and scarred and ugly. When the nurses saw me balk, their arms fluttered up and landed on my shoulders, and they whispered that I was the only one to do the job, that I was an amazing girl, with enormous strength, they'd seen it themselves, none of which alleviated the dread.

Zellie was asleep when I went into her room, so time sat in my lap and watched my fingers pull at each other, as I considered how I was going to tell her that she'd lost her father, her sister, her brother, and most likely her mother, that I was the only one who had survived, her least favorite, our feelings toward each other being mutual. I watched her bed flip and realized I had gotten used to the bed, to the strange figure who lay strapped to it as being my sister. I had grown accustomed to my room at Mr. Antonovsky's, to the fact that I was alone and that all I had in the world filled one suitcase, but I couldn't get used to the whole of the loss, the collective one. It still lay inside my chest, my heart bound, as if part of it had been amputated.

When Zellie's eyes opened and fell on me, something queer and slippery passed through me. How many times her eyes had landed on me before, glazed and glassy, recognizing nothing; but now, so strange, Zellie turned up behind them.

I said, "Hello, Zellie. How are you feeling?" I didn't mean to, but I spoke to her as if she were half my age.

"They told me Bo's still blew up, and a table leg went through me," she said.

I hadn't expected her to bring it up right off like that, as if she should have mentioned the weather first, or God knows what, but of course what else could possibly be on her mind?

"Is it true?" she asked.

"It is true except that Bo's stills didn't blow up," I said. "Happy bombed them because Bo wouldn't give him any more of the money he was trying to extort."

The bed rotated Zellie out of my sight, and I heard her voice, clear and sure. "I doubt that. He wouldn't do something like that. He wasn't the type."

"Oscar said he was the kind of guy you didn't say no to." I closed my mouth, and silence fell between us, the only sound now the clean click of the bed's motor.

"What happened to Bo?" Zellie said when she came back around.

I looked into her eyes and noticed that they were missing a certain strength of light, a light that was directly connected to her spirit, which had once been so alive and haughty, however much I didn't like it, and now seemed dimmed, weakened, perhaps even extinguished altogether.

"She's in a coma, down the hall."

The bed rotated again and took her away, and my stomach contracted as if I had eaten poison.

"Lourde?" she asked.

I wanted to get up and leave the room and tell the nurses they had to tell her, that it was the worst thing I'd ever had to do, tell a person strapped in a flipping bed that her whole family was dead.

"Lourde is dead?" she breathed.

I waited until she came back around and then nodded.

"What about Oscar and Frieda?"

I looked into her stark, unblinking eyes and nodded once for Oscar, another time for Frieda.

A moment passed in stunned silence, and then Zellie opened her mouth, and I thought she was forming a word, but instead of a word, a low, wounded scream slid out of her in one long, rich, unbroken string. I tried to grab her hand, but the bed rotated her out of reach, and the scream continued, as if it were stuck in her throat, like a needle in a record groove. "Zellie!" I yelled, but there were no words, and that bed, it kept flipping, and her scream, like a siren, relentless, undone, without apology.

A nurse raced into the room, her rubber-soled shoes squealing across the floor.

"What happened?" she asked.

"I told her."

A few more nurses rushed into the room, one of them flipping the switch to Zellie's bed, another one unstrapping Zellie, scooping her up and pulling her gown from her withered white bottom, while a third one readied a syringe and jabbed the needle into this paucity of flesh, Zellie's scream ceasing within moments, her eyes lolling in her sockets, her eyelids fluttering like two sheets in a distant breeze. The nurse held her and whispered solacing shushes in her ear, until Zellie went slack, her stick-thin body barely a weight in the nurse's arms, the nurse easing her down to the bed, where Zellie's gown fell open, and I saw her wound again—a tight, festering hole just under her ribcage, a few jagged lines radiating from it, like cracks in her skin, as if a wrecking ball had slammed into her.

It took Zellie a long time to accept her bad fortune. She fought it hard, like an unbroken colt fights everything, and there was no one besides myself and a humpbacked old social worker named Shirley Comstock to fight her back. Every day after school I took the three o'clock bus up to Syracuse and walked down the familiar hallways of Crouse Memorial, three rights, then a left, fifteen floors up on the elevator, a left, then another right, nodding to all the nurses, the backs of my bell bottoms dragging on their floors, dread forming in my stomach like a rising dough, because whether I wanted to or not, I was on my way to visit a raging flame. I sat down in the chair next to her flipping bed, which they had begun to shut off for an hour at a time, but you couldn't call that progress. I sat there with no hope of speaking, no hope of being heard. No, everything was black, nothing was going to get better, it was all over, and I sat and listened because what else was there for me to do, I had been spared.

"And I don't know why you were spared either," she always said. "It's not like you're the least bit special."

She loathed God for sparing me, for everything actually, but mostly for that, and no longer even referred to him as God. Instead she called him the Fucker. "Don't you think it's odd that the Fucker didn't do anything to you?" she always asked me, and when one day I told her I thought the Fucker had done quite a lot to me, reminding her that I had sustained as many family losses as she had, she reached over to the wall and shut off her rotating bed, her breath sliding deep into her lungs, her mouth opening, her voice leaving her throat, hard and loud. "YOU STILL HAVE YOUR LEGS. NOTHING WENT THROUGH YOUR GUTS. YOU DON'T HAVE A HOLE IN THE MIDDLE OF YOU. YOU CAN STILL WEAR A BIKINI. YOU CAN STILL DIGEST YOUR FOOD. YOU CAN STILL GO OUT ON DATES. AND YOU CAN STILL HAVE BABIES. GODDAMN YOU!"

Immediately, I sank to my knees and laid my head on her belly.

"I'm sorry, Zellie. I'm so, so sorry." I grabbed hold of her hand and squeezed it, something slipping from my mind, a sheet, a curtain, some thin thing which had kept me from seeing that there was someone worse off than me, someone who has lost her whole family and her legs, someone who'd lost the function and beauty of a young body, someone who has lost a future.

After that I inquired about Zellie's chances for recovery, her long-range prognosis, and was told that for the rest of her life she would have trouble with her digestion, that her scar would fade and shrink, but not enough for her to feel comfortable wearing a bikini, that she would most likely be able to have sex, although she might experience some discomfort, and that she in fact would never be able to bear her own children. When I asked whether or not she would ever walk again, they said there was a possibility.

I took that as a good sign and devoted myself to Zellie's legs, traipsing up to the Morrisville College Library, taking out all the books they had on paralysis and healing, reading them between my classes, during my lunch hour, while Louise and Hillary chattered on either side of me, cracking them open during the long bus rides to and from the hospital, and then again up in my room at Mr. Antonovsky's late at night, before I fell asleep from exhaustion. I read scientific books, medical books, prayer books, books written by sixties gurus and health-food prophets, heal-yourself books, books on faith healing, books by anyone, I read them all. I found exercises to be regularly performed, nutritional regimes to be followed, poultices to be applied, herbs and vitamins to be tried, and if all of that failed, potions to mix to contact the higher spirits of healing.

I took all the poultices and herbs and vitamins I had gathered, all the vegetable juices and mung beans, and brought them to Zellie's room, where she received them with an air of suffering resignation. But she took them, she took my vitamins and allowed me to apply poultices to her spine and legs, she drank my vegetable juices and ate my mung beans, and she complained the entire time. "This will never work," she said, but it didn't matter what she said, I couldn't listen. There was no dissuading me from my path; what mattered was not to give up, not to stop, to keep going, to keep reading, to keep searching and finding, to keep mixing and applying and taking care. Stopping was the dreaded thing. Stopping meant standing still, meant lying up in my room at Mr. Antonovsky's on the bed thinking, ruminating, hating and raging against whatever unseen force had stripped me bare.

I don't know how much my poultices or vegetable juices or my mung beans did for Zellie's walking, but after a month's time, they let her get out of bed and into a wheelchair, and from that moment on, I pushed her everywhere I could think of—down the corridors, to the elevators, to the lounges on every floor, to the janitors' lunchroom, to the maternity section where all the babies were lined up in cribs, to Bo's room, where we sat in the clatter of her machines and stared at her. I couldn't wait to get up there after school, to get my hands on the plastic handlebars of Zellie's wheelchair, to push her anywhere her heart wanted to go, up this hallway or down that one, over to this lounge or back to that one, pushing her in the direction of progress, as if I could push us to the end of this, to that place where it would all be behind us.

When it came time for Zellie to take her first step, I brought her some bell bottoms and a pair of shoes I'd found in her half-burned closet, thinking that they might inspire her, but she cried, "They remind me of everything I lost," and I couldn't open her fifteenth-floor window fast enough to drop them.

She faced the parallel bars with courage and mustered the strength and really tried to take that first step, but her legs wouldn't work, nor would her feet, and then her spirit gave out, it was worn so thin, and she was sure that she could not walk and would never walk again. The physical therapist and his cheerful assistant tried to coax her, tried to encourage her, but she wouldn't allow it and said, "It's over. Can't you see that? It's goddamn fucking over."

I stepped in, as if I had some power over her, but before I even got her name out she screamed, "IT'S EASY FOR YOU TO SAY. YOU'VE GOT YOUR LEGS. YOU'VE GOT EVERYTHING. AND DON'T LOOK AT ME LIKE THAT—LIKE YOU'RE GLAD IT'S ME AND NOT YOU. FUCK YOU, HEMY. FUCK YOU!"

The physical therapist finally had to ask me to leave the room, because they needed Zellie to stop screaming. Her voice was re-sounding in the hallways, upsetting the sick people, who needed peace and quiet.

It went on for a few weeks, the physical therapist pushing Zellie up to the parallel bars, Zellie refusing at top volume, me sitting outside waiting, wishing that I could take part of her in-jury, one of her bad legs, part of that festering hole, a piece of her crooked spine, something so that I could shoulder some of it. It was too much for her, and I had everything. When it looked like there was no hope, the physical therapist cornered me in the hall and said, "Is there anyone who could reason with her?"

"Bo," I said.

"Let's call him up, and get him over here."

"She's already here," I said, "in room 201 J, in a coma."

I took out every book they had in the college library on comas and read them every chance I got. Louise started reading them alongside of me, during our lunch hour and late at night when she stayed with me up in my room at Mr. Antonovsky's. Her mother even read a few. I liked the ones that offered unscientific advice about how to break the spell of a coma, the ones that fu-eled a loping, desperate hope of communicating with the coma victim, of talking to their unconscious, of calling them back, giv-ing them reason to return. Though Zellie kept saying "It will never work," I wheeled her into Bo's room anyway and set her up on Bo's right side, while I took up the left and bent close to Bo's ear, and I whispered, "Bo, it's Hemy and Zellie. Don't leave us. Come back. Please come back." When I finished, Zellie said, "You think God would give us anything back? The Fucker took it away, you think he'd ever give it back?"

But after a few days she joined in, the two of us bending close to Bo, breathing in her gauzed-over ears, "Bo, it's Zellie and Hemy. Come back to us. You've been gone too long. We love you." These words, over and over, quiet, sibilant, whispered shushes, at first spoken for a few short minutes, until we built more steam, finally breathing them for an entire hour. There we were by her side, leaning on our elbows, whispering, mesmerizing, casting spells, all the while Zellie swearing it wouldn't work, me hoping it would. Hope was all I had. Hope that Zellie would walk again.

Hope that Bo would come around. Hope that Oscar was still alive. At night, when I lay awake in my bed at Mr. Antonovsky's, I closed my eyes and drifted in pools of hope, embracing gauzy, vaporous spirits, everything unseen, the supernatural, who knew what could help? I drank in the hope, breathed it in, called it home.

I had to wait for Zellie to get stronger before I could tell her about Oscar's remains and how I'd tried to kill Happy. I felt like I was keeping something important from her, like I was patronizing an old, religious woman whose heart was no good, but I couldn't tell her until after she had taken her first few steps and her spirit had returned, or at least some part of it. When I felt sure she was strong enough to hear it, I wheeled her down the corridor, to the big picture window on the fifth floor of Crouse Memorial where you could see the Syracuse cityscape against the sky, and told her about Happy. I sat down on the ledge and folded my hands in my lap. "I know you liked Happy a lot, but he bombed Bo's Place," I said. She listened intently as I told her how I had talked to the police and the firemen, to the people who had been injured in the bombing or had lost people, and how Spike Harris had taken me aside and told me to be careful talking the way I was about this Happy character, slowly working my way up to the worst part, which I uttered as quietly as possible: "I tried to kill Happy."

She stared at me, her eyes blinking like shutters in a windstorm.

"I found Lourde's gun in the ashes of our house, and Louise and I waited outside Happy's house, and when he came home with one of his women, I aimed the gun at him and pulled the trigger, but the bullet wasn't in the chamber. It was in the next one."

"I would do that to God if I could," Zellie said.

A few days later, I wheeled her down to the lounge and bought her a Coke and a bag of Fritos and told her about Oscar's remains. I said, "They told me Oscar was so close to the bomb that there were only remains." Zellie spit her mouthful of Fritos back into the bag, and I went on. "They wouldn't let me look inside the casket either, and I wanted to because I never really believed he was in there." She closed her eyes and spit one more time and then threw the Fritos away. A shaggy-haired boy not much older than me walked into the lounge and flashed us the peace sign, as if we were all members of a club that only required its members to wear bell bottoms and jean jackets and long hair. Zellie flipped him the bird and I waved awkwardly and apologetically for Zellie, for myself, for the whole embarrassing phenomenon of flashing peace signs, and he sat down near us, as if he had no idea that we weren't interested, and tapped his hand on his knee, tapped it to the time of the Led Zeppelin song that was playing over the radio, *Whole Lotta Love.* I wanted to tell him somehow what he had interrupted so that he would leave or at least move away to tap elsewhere, but Zellie said something that stopped my breath.

"I remember seeing Oscar go out the back door," she said. "I remember watching him go out the back door."

"When?"

"Before."

"Before what?"

"Before the explosion."

"Yeah, but when, Zellie? Right before or an hour before?"

"Right before," she said, but then she added, "I think."

"What do you mean, you think?"

"I *think*, Hemy!" she yelled. "How do you expect me to be one hundred percent sure? Jesus, a table leg went through me."

"What percent, then? Fifty percent? Eighty? What percent, then?"

Zellie thought about it for a minute. "Seventy percent," she finally said.

It didn't take me long to decide to dig up Oscar's casket, to see if he was really in there. I couldn't get the idea of it out of my mind, couldn't stop thinking about the seventy-percent chance that Zellie had seen Oscar go out the back door right before the explosion, couldn't get rid of the idea that there was nothing in his casket. I didn't feel comfortable asking Louise to help me, not after I had dragged her along when I wanted to kill Happy, but I asked her anyway.

Louise was very nervous, and during our short drive to the

cemetery in Louise's mother's car, she said, "It's not easy being your friend, Hemy, when you drag me into things like killing people and opening dead people's caskets, and that's a lot to ask of a person, and to tell you the truth, I think there is something wrong with you. I'm sorry to say that, I don't want to hurt your feelings, but I think there is something wrong with you, and you should see a psychiatrist."

I didn't mind her saying so, I told her, it was probably true, but even so, I was still going to do it. She sighed and pulled into the cemetery wrapped in her airs of martyrdom, me counting on her martyrdom fully, grateful it was there to be had. I was in no shape to do this alone. It was no easy task to dig up a grave, six feet under being a long way to dig in the dark if you were two skinny teenagers taking turns with a dull, rusty shovel from Mr. Antonovsky's garage. We guzzled a bottle of red wine I'd stolen from Mr. Antonovsky's pantry, and talked of lighter things, conscious all the while of this horrible weight, the weight of digging up the body of a brother and never saying a word about it, as if we were digging up something long ago lost, like a bottle, a ring, a photograph, nothing of consequence.

It was four hours of digging, our forced conversation giving way to silence, interrupted only by the sound of the shovel and our breath, an even rhythm of shovel, breath, shovel, breath, until we got down to the casket. Then it was two more hours of pulling to free it from the merciless dirt. Louise's mother would have fainted to see the rope tied to the bumper of her Ford Torino, the other end tied to the casket, the car heaving and digging in, pulling fiercely, tearing up the grass in a cemetery, of all places, while it dragged this casket out of the hard clutches of the earth. The casket kept getting stuck on the sides, so while Louise gunned her mother's car, I descended into the hole and guided it out, heaving and thrusting, breathing and sweating, all strain and grief. The whole time I pretended I was one of the prisoners in Stalin's work camps, like Mr. Antonovsky had been, digging and hauling rocks, shovels biting into the flesh of my palms.

Once the casket was out of the hole and sitting on the ground, the two of us fell back in the damp cold grass to catch our breath.

We stared up at the starless sky and then looked at each other and then at it and shivered. Who knew what unseen things might come flying out of it were we to open it? Who knew what wrath we'd invoke, how the dead would avenge this trespass?

"You do it," Louise said. She laid the shovel by my side, the cold steel point touching the tips of my filthy fingers.

I wanted her to do it, to open the lid, to tell me what was inside. I wanted a messenger between me and Oscar, just at first, and then I would do the rest. I would look myself, I would touch him if there was anything left to touch.

"I'm not going to do it, Hemy, so don't even ask," Louise said.

I pulled myself up from the ground, took hold of the shovel, and stumbled over to the casket, where I dropped to my knees and looked down at my thin, blackened arms, at my filthy hands, at my blue jeans which were matted with dirt. I thought, This is Oscar's dirt. In death, the dirt is like the blood is in life. I jabbed the pointed end of the shovel under the lid and gave it a few pushes with what was left of my strength, but it wasn't much, my muscles were now exhausted and lay like stuffing in my arms. But nothing. I tried it again and then again, but I couldn't break the lock.

"You're going to have to help me, Louise," I said.

She sighed and stared up at the faceless sky. "I can't believe I'm here digging up a casket, when just a year ago I was sitting on some porch steps waiting for you to kill Happy."

"I know," I said, "I'm sorry."

Louise pulled herself up from the ground and took hold of the end of the shovel. When I said "Go," the two of us pushed as hard as we could. Then, we breathed and I said "Go" again, and we went on like this: pushing, breathing, recovering, pushing, breathing, recovering, but nothing. It was as if the lid of the casket had been sewn shut with iron thread.

We heard the sound of a car on gravel and both wheeled around to face those red, whirling lights that seemed to show up at all my tragedies. "It's the police!" Louise said. "Let's run!"

"You run. I'm going to open it. I don't care."

She whimpered and started to run, then stopped, then started again, finally grabbing hold of the shovel, the two of us pushing with every last bit of gut we had left, glancing over our shoulders to see how close the car was getting, Louise worrying about getting caught, me worrying that we wouldn't get it open in time.

"Come on, Hemy. They're coming. You said we'd run."

I said we'd come all this way, we'd spent seven hours digging the thing up, we'd strained ourselves past endurance, I was going to see what was inside. With our adrenaline pumping, with all we had left in our weariness, we pushed one more time, and the lid to the casket popped open, making the sound of a vacuum-packed bottle.

The police skidded to a stop, not more than fifty feet away, and a beam of strong white light hit us. "It's that crazy Hemy Lourde and Louise Van Sant," the deputy said. Louise stood frozen in the lights, but I turned back to the casket and threw the lid back. When I moved to the side, the light from the deputy's flashlight fell into the casket and illuminated what was inside—a square red tin box, the kind of box people keep cookies in.

The sheriff clambered out of his car, huffing under his weight, puffed up with the power conferred by his badge, the deputy following. "Freeze," the sheriff said, but I didn't. I heard them racing towards us in the grass, the sound of their nylon coats brushing against their sides, their equipment knocking and clanging from their belts, and Louise's breath going ragged with fear. The sheriff yelled, "I said 'Freeze,' " but I didn't. I didn't even look over my shoulder to see if he had his gun pulled. I just tore off the lid and looked inside that red tin at a pile of pale white ashes.

They put Louise and me in the backseat of the police car and drove us through the dark hills to the Wampsville County Jail, where Bo and Lourde had done their time. They were at least good enough not to use handcuffs, and not for a moment did they suggest I give up the tin can, which stayed clenched between my fingers. Louise started crying into her dirty shirt-sleeve, and I knew it was all my fault. I should have left her out of it, it had nothing to do with her, so I put my arm around her and whispered, "Poor Louise," and wished for the words to tell her that it didn't matter, that there was a place outside of it all from which the world appeared different, the place where I now stood, a privileged place from where I could see the truth more clearly— how digging up a grave and being arrested was nothing.

When they took our mug shots and fingerprinted us, Louise broke down. "Now we'll have a record for as long as we live"— as if it would really make a dent in the rest of her whole long life. I knew enough not to care, and I did what I could to get her out of it, but there Louise stood with dirt covering her arms and face, ground deep into her clothes. When they put us into a holding cell, she started sobbing, and I felt worse about that than anything, because I'd promised her she wouldn't end up in jail.

"Louise, I'm sorry. I'll make it up to you," I whispered, and in the paltry light of the cell, I watched the tears spill down her face like small, silver rivers. When she said, "I've got a record now, and there's nothing you can do about that," I imagined myself stealing into the county offices at night, rifling through the county file cabinets, finding Louise's record and destroying it, Louise Van Sant meant that much to me.

When Mr. Antonovsky came to get me, he looked through the bars at me and Louise, both of us skinny and filthy, and hissed, "What are you doing, digging up a grave?"

I pulled off the lid to the ashes and showed them to him. "This is Oscar," I said.

"Eich," he wailed, "this is bad, very bad. You disturb dead this way, who knows what can happen." He turned nervously to one of the guards and said, "She is just girl, you know, girl who has lost whole family. This cannot be helped."

They arrested me anyway. The law was the law, they explained, and I had gone into a private cemetery and had dug up a casket, which was illegal whether it was your brother or not, the law being unable to take into account the emotional life of the criminal. At least they let Mr. Antonovsky take me home, and at least they didn't ask me to give up my tin can filled with Oscar's ashes.

I kept the tin can next to my bed, on the dark-stained wooden table that had come with the room, and sometimes at night I opened it and took the ashes in my hand and let them sift down through my fingers, imagining that I was touching Oscar, the essence of him, feeling oddly thrilled at moments, as if the parts that sifted through my fingers were the parts of him I'd touched that had so inflamed me. Sometimes I just opened the box and stared at the pale white ashes and tried to fathom if my brother, whose flesh had meant so much to me, had really come to this, but I didn't know if the ashes were his or not. Sometimes I imagined they were, sometimes I didn't, I wanted so much to believe he was still alive. When Mr. Antonovsky gave me a beautiful silk scarf his wife used to wear, I wrapped the tin box up in it, and quite a few times I walked up to the college floral shop and bought cut flowers which I put in the two slim white vases Gussy Keys had given me.

When I told Zellie that I had dug up Oscar's casket and found a box of ashes she said, "You're crazy, Hemy."

"I know," I said. "Everyone says so."

When we went in to see Bo, Zellie took up her position on Bo's right side and while I whispered the usual in Bo's ear, Zellie whispered, "Bo, you better come back. Hemy is losing her mind. She dug up Oscar's grave and found his ashes. She keeps them in a tin next to her bed, Bo. I think it's time you came back. You need to tell her to give the ashes back."

The lawyer Mr. Antonovsky called told me, by law, I was supposed to give the ashes back. "It's illegal to keep the contents of a coffin," he said.

"Arrest me, then," I told him, "because I'm not giving them back."

His name was Vic Ponti. Mr. Antonovsky had called him the day after I was released from jail. He was a twenty-eight-year-old lawyer who had settled in Morrisville to practice, and who fell two notches short of being handsome, his nose being too big and his jaw not chiseled enough, and although he had a full head of black hair, it wasn't long or stylish. There was nothing hip about Vic Ponti.

I wasn't the least bit interested in him, but I interested him. He didn't meet many sixteen-year-old girls who claimed their family had been killed by a bomb a dapper-looking man named Happy had planted in their bar when he felt he wasn't getting his percentage due for the protection he offered from the police for a still her mother ran. Part of him was amused by me, another part stricken. He knew the story of my loss (there was no one in town who didn't) and couldn't help but feel some compassion for my pending orphanhood.

He looked more than once at my legs, and when I asked him for a glass of water, he came back with water and three different types of soda in case I was thirstier than I had imagined; but when I told him my story, he stopped looking at my legs and listened attentively. I told it the way Mr. Antonovsky had told me to tell it, without passion, as if I had no interest in the outcome, as if I were a reporter merely relating cold facts, because he told me were I to put too much emotion in it, the lawyer would think I was a silly woman with big ideas. I spoke like a person who had just been lobotomized.

When I finished, Vic Ponti stared across his big oak desk at me, his eyes a mixture of teary sadness and hot interest, as if he wanted to come over and put my head on his shoulder while his hand snaked up my skirt.

Three days didn't go by before he called up at Mr. Antonovsky's and asked me out to dinner. I told him I would call him back later with an answer, if I could, and when I asked Mr. Antonovsky what he thought I should do, he said, "You must go, Hemy. Mr. Ponti take your case for nothing."

It was a long ride up to a restaurant in Syracuse, but it wasn't a silent drive like I had worried it might be. No, Vic Ponti was a good talker, and a decent listener, too. He asked questions and then listened to what I had to say, laughing half the time, he thought I was that funny. Over dinner he told me he had grown up in Queens in a poor Italian family of six daughters, and was lucky he'd gotten a scholarship to study law at Syracuse University, because there was no money to speak of in his family. I didn't have much to tell him that he didn't already know; my life was shorter by twelve years and quite public, but I told him about Bo's Place before the explosions, when Mr. Antonovsky and Coleman had tormented one another, when Oscar, Zellie, and I would do what we could to fuel it, when my life was simpler and I knew much less than I did now. Vic Ponti laughed at my stories, he had a wild, high-pitched, corny laugh that erupted too easily, and all night he would stop the flow of conversation to say, "Do Mr. Antonovsky again," or "Talk like Coleman," and because I felt compelled to, he'd taken my case for nothing, I found myself saying over and over again, "Eich, Mr. Lourde, I am paying customer," or "Here, Mastah, I play a song lif up yer spirits," while Vic Ponti laughed riotously, maniacally, like a small child.

Vic Ponti had a soft spot for mothers and sisters and insisted that we drive over to the hospital to see Bo and Zellie after dinner. He came in with me and met Zellie, and though I didn't invite him to see Bo, he followed me into her room and stood next to her bed alongside of me, squeezing my hand once or twice, as if to communicate his deep and lasting understanding or compassion or love, all of which started a cringing in my stomach.

And when later Vic Ponti tried to kiss me on Mr. Antonovsky's back porch, I closed my mouth and moved my head to the side and whispered, "Don't." Vic Ponti took my chin between his fingers and turned my head back to him, his lips falling on top of mine again. "Please," I said, pushing him away the way I might have pushed a dog from my crotch. "But I have feelings for you already," he whispered. "It's not my fault," I said, and Vic Ponti laughed wildly, slapping me on the back. "You're a pip, Hemy. A real pip."

DESERT

13

She turned over and picked up the German clock and read the time.

It's very late, she said. It's three A.M. She set the clock down and sat up and quietly undressed, pulling on her rose-colored night slip.

As he watched her he thought about how instead of enlisting Zellie to go off with her to extract their own justice, instead of this, she'd taken a turn towards hope. Why this turn and not some other? He thought it predictable, obvious . . . uninteresting, to use her word.

Did you become interested in goodness?

No, she said.

Then what?

Power, she answered.

Power? he said. It was nearly the last thing he expected her to say, but it interested him.

She turned then and their eyes caught, and he knew that she'd thought of it, that it all hadn't just happened to her without her questioning it.

He wanted to ask her what kind of power, but she turned away and pulled the covers over her shoulder. He sat back and lit a cigarette and it came to him then. Power to heal legs that were unhealable, he thought, to wake someone from a coma that was unwakeable.

Why did you dig up your brother's ashes and keep them by your bed like they were the ashes of—

A god? she said quietly.

Yes.

I could no more part with them than I could part with my own skin, she said.

He didn't understand this, and for a long time he heard only the steady syncopation of the train, the distant squall of a baby, short but piercing, and then the sound of his own breath. He thought of Zellie, of Bo, of Oscar, of their bodies. Had she wanted the power to free their bodies? He thought of her then, of how she had bound herself, of how she had tried to erase her own body, a woman's body, and he wanted to ask her, Was that what she was interested in—freeing her own body? But from what? he wondered. Then he thought of his own body, and panic swept through him, for where was his body now but in flight? It unnerved him to think of it, of his body in flight, as if it were imprisoned by something unseen by him.

When he woke it was very early in the morning, six A.M. by her German clock. She was still asleep on her side, her rose-colored slip edging halfway up her thigh. He reached over her delicately and pushed the curtain from the window. It startled him, the desert, gleaming white in the early morning sun, the waves of sand molded and hugging the land like curls pasted to a woman's forehead. It looked bleached and so picked clean that it frightened him. He tried not to see in that bleak landscape the metaphor for his inner life, for the passage he would next undergo, a journey into the desert, but he knew it was true. He didn't want to look inside, not really, nor did he want to see the land, but he knew he must or he would never find his way off the train, or anything else that took him away. Out of all the experiences he might have had, this was the one he'd been given, to go into the desert with a woman who had lived as a man. He told himself to clutch it to him, to say yes to it, but it was merely an idea. He didn't know if he could actually do it.

He turned to her and watched her sleep; he watched her chest rise with a long pull of breath and then fall slowly beneath the satin of her slip. He looked at her pale eyelids and at her mouth, which was full and pink, the small, sweet opening between her upper and lower lip attracting him greatly.

He put his arms around her and felt the satin of her slip against his bare chest and his long legs. He pressed his hardness against her hip and buried his nose into the softness of her neck where he could smell the faint scent of her perfume.

He couldn't imagine how she'd ever passed as a man. Her skin was too smooth, he thought, and he wondered again if she had made it all up. Hadn't she said it after all—I've always wanted to ride a train across the country and make up a whole story about myself?

He felt sick inside, sick at the thought that she might not be telling the truth. It sickened him too to realize that she was going to get off the train to spend the night in the desert, and that despite his aversion to the barren land, he was going to get off too.

They got off in Abilie, a minuscule town that was no more than three dusty blocks of two-story buildings, half of which were boarded up. The clerk at the drugstore/train station said there wasn't a motel in town, that if she wanted a motel there was one out of town, three, four miles or so, but there was no taxi. He said he would ask his cousin if he could swing by and give the two of them a lift out there. She agreed to that and was very grateful to him, she said.

It seemed odd, yet somehow interesting, when he found himself seated next to her in the back of a pickup truck, riding through nowhere Utah, sitting on top of their luggage, feed grain flying up around them. Neither of them looked particularly at home in the back of this truck, especially her with her gray skirt and black silk blouse and straw hat she had to hold down. He was wearing a sleeveless white T-shirt and khaki pants that stuck to him in the heat, and he had to fight to keep his hair from flying in his face.

She paid the clerk's cousin twenty dollars for the ride and arranged for him to pick them up the next day at noon.

After the man drove off, they both stood in the sand and the dust and looked around at the desert, at the old gas station, at the four-unit motel which stood just to the left of the station. It was whitewashed a shade brighter than the sand, and a mildew the color of brinish green had begun to work its way up from the bottom.

There was nothing else out there, not another house nor a building of any type, nothing but a road and the blue, unbroken sky. He could taste the dust in the back of his throat, could feel the grittiness of the sand on his sweaty skin, which felt overheated in the noon and blinding sun. It must have been one hundred degrees, he thought. She didn't say anything, but he could tell by the look on her face that she found it enchanting, though how he couldn't understand.

A heavyset Native American woman came to stand in the doorway. She wore turquoise leggings and a long pink T-shirt with the words LET'S BOOGIE stretched across her bulk. Her hair was long and flowed down her shoulders, beautiful and abundant, in contrast to her face, which was slack and pockmarked by time. There was nothing much in her expression save hardship and struggle. A boy of four or five wound himself around her leg and hid half of his face, looking out at them with one suspicious yet curious eye, filled not with struggle, but with tedium.

We'd like a room for the night, she said.

The Indian woman nodded.

The room they rented was whitewashed and barren, but large, and two-tiered, with a small kitchenette and a living room on one level and a bedroom and bathroom on the other.

As soon as they set their bags down, she went around the room and collected the plumes of plastic flowers in white glass vases and put them away in an empty drawer. She replaced them with her yellow-white candles, her ivory hand mirror and tortoiseshell hairbrush.

After that she went into the bathroom and pushed the sleeves of her black silk blouse over her shoulders. He sat down on the edge of the bed and watched as she washed her long, muscular arms with soap and then rinsed them off. It looked odd, and it made him think of how dirty her arms must have gotten after she had dug up Oscar's grave.

How long did it take you to get your arms clean after you dug up Oscar's grave? he asked her.

She turned and glanced at him strangely, as if she didn't know what he was talking about.

I don't know, she said, and then shrugged. She pulled a white towel from a metal rack and began to dry her arms.

I would think you would remember such a thing, he said. He took off his boots and socks and felt the cool floor under his feet.

What such a thing?

Washing the dirt off your arms.

Why? she asked. She finished drying her arms and pulled her sleeves back down.

Because you had the thought that the dirt on your arms was Oscar's dirt, like the blood of life.

She looked at him oddly, as if she didn't understand.

You said you looked down at your arms and had the thought that this was Oscar's dirt, dirt being like the blood of life.

Oh, yes, she said.

But it was too late, the suspicion had already taken root in his mind. She hadn't remembered it because she'd made it up, he thought. He was sure if it had been true she would have remembered it. It was an important detail. Maybe she had never dug up her brother's casket. It worried him, the idea that she might have brought him to this to awful place to toy with him.

When did you wash your arms? he asked her.

It was at Louise's house, up in her bathroom, she said. Why?

I was just curious.

She draped the white towel neatly over a small wooden chair. Then she walked into the bedroom and looked at him sitting on the edge of the bed regarding her as if she had done something wrong.

What's happened? she asked.

I thought you went back to Mr. Antonovsky's house after you got out of the jail.

She had to think about it for a moment.

I first went to Louise's to help her calm her mother down. Then, I went to Mr. Antonovsky's, she said.

Why didn't you say that when you told me the story?

If I told you everything, it would be too much, she said.

He knew that was true, but still he worried. She hadn't remembered washing her arms, and more importantly she hadn't remembered Oscar's dirt.

She took a white T-shirt from her suitcase and set it on the bed, and then walked over to the open door and stood, her weight on one hip, looking out at the long road, at the old gas station with its ancient Pennzoil sign, the old red pumps, the garage, whitewashed and pocked from years of sand blowing against it.

She turned and walked back to him, stopping when her bare toes touched his.

You are upset. What is it? she said. She bent her knees, knocking softly against his.

He just stared at her, unable to pronounce the accusation.

You think I am lying, she said, and she smiled.

I do wonder.

It upsets you—the thought that I could be lying to you?

Yes. I don't like the idea that I've been sleeping next to you, getting off trains with you, staying in strange hotels and motels with you, if you are not who you say you are.

First of all, I am who I say I am, and secondly, if I weren't, what difference would it make?

See, that's the sort of thing that makes me nervous, he said. That kind of what-difference-would-it-make stuff.

Well, would it make a difference?

He threw his arms up in exasperation. Yes, it would make a difference to me, he shouted. It would be the difference between having been told the truth as opposed to a lie. I would rather be told the truth than to be made a fool of.

Oh, so it's not so much the lie you care about, she said, smiling. It's the idea that you've been made a fool of that disturbs you?

Well, yes, if you want to put it that way.

She laughed, and after a few moments passed, she walked up to him.

I've told you the truth, she said.

She kissed his forehead lightly, and then found his eyes. She smiled, but when he looked into her eyes, he couldn't calculate what he saw—were these the eyes of a woman telling him the truth or were they the eyes of a woman toying with him? They swam before his eyes, flickering on and off, true, false, true, false, until he walked away.

Show me something, like your driver's license, he said. He shoved his fingers through his hair.

She stared at him a moment, and then said, Your doubts and fears have very little to do with me and my story. They are inside you. That's where you should be looking—not in my wallet.

She turned then and walked into the bathroom and closed the door quietly behind her.

He didn't know what to think, and for a moment he hated her. He wished she would beg him to believe her, but he knew it didn't make any difference to her if he believed her or not. He recognized it, her detachment, and he hated it.

She came out of the bathroom dressed completely in white— a long white skirt with a back slit and a white T-shirt. With the exception of a black ribbon, her hat was white, too.

Where are you going? he asked nervously.

I'm going to walk out on the land.

It's a desert, he said.

All right. I'm going to walk out into the desert. Do you want to come?

No, he said. I'm going to go over to the garage and get a soda.

The idea of walking across that land filled him with dread. It was without life and unpitying. Only vultures flew overhead.

All right, she said. Will you see if they have some bottled water?

He nodded and watched as she walked across the room, her hips swaying nicely beneath her white cotton skirt.

What do you think you'll find out there? he asked her.

Skulls and bones, she said, in a mock horror-film voice.

She laughed, but he didn't think it was very funny. He followed her out of the room and watched as she walked around to the back of the motel units and headed out to the godless desert that spread before him like some smothering blanket.

He watched her walk for a while, until it was too much for his eyes—her white clothes, moving across the blinding white sand, under a white sun. He walked in his bare feet over to the garage, where the Indian woman and her son were sitting. The woman was sewing what looked to be a traditional beaded head-dress, while the boy played a game on a Mac PowerBook. The little machine seemed so out of place inside this gas station. Time had stood still here. The glass counters were old and grimy, featuring a row of dusty cans of motor oil. There were yellowed papers everywhere, which seemed to have nothing remotely to do with present transactions and seemed instead to be props in a garage museum.

A television sat on top of a mound of these papers, the Indian woman quietly watching the O.J. Simpson trial. It seemed strange that O.J. and Nicole, a white woman who lay dead in the consciousness of America, beheaded, would be out here in the desert. And stranger still that this stoic Native American woman sewing a traditional costume would be interested. Still, it comforted him. He looked at the Mac PowerBook, at the fax machine in the corner, at the VCR, at Simpson's tired courtroom face, and it soothed him. It had not been vanquished. The desert had not vanquished civilization.

He crossed over the dusty drive and passed six depressed goats that were fenced in alongside the garage and pawing at the barren ground. He stopped near them and watched her standing out in the desert, her back to him. Was she looking, or were her eyes closed in prayer? he wondered. She had no fear of the desert, as he did. She could stand in its midst and not get lost, this thin, lone figure dressed in white. He felt it again in his heart, the breaking for her, for what she must have lived through. It was the consent he'd given to this breaking that made him fear—what if she was toying with him when he'd consented to feel?

He waited inside the room for her to return from her walk. At first he sat in the chair by the window with the door half-open, until he began to feel the dust and sand in his throat, to feel it on his hot, sweaty bare arms. Before he went to lie down on the bed, he stepped out of the room and glanced out at the desert again. She was still out there, now crouched on her haunches, as if she were bit by bit sinking into the sand. He couldn't imagine why she had to spend so long with it.

He went back into the room and stretched out on the bed to wait for her. His sleeveless white T-shirt and khaki pants stuck to him in the heat. It's Thursday and I'm in the desert, he thought. It's hot as hell and bleak and barren. He wondered where they were and what they were doing, *the ones he had left,* and sweat spilled from his hairline and dripped down his face. Guilt swept him, and he loathed it. He worried again that this quest of his was nothing grand, that it was nothing more than simple cowardice. He reminded himself of the rupture he'd tried to create, how he'd broken with his life to change himself completely, his thoughts, the way he saw the world. He'd climbed onto the train, he told himself, to become someone else. But a rude thought intervened—who and/or what had he ruptured?

He quickly lit a cigarette and went outside to see what had become of her, but she wasn't there. He looked around, but he didn't see her; it was as if the desert had reached up with its bony fingers and had taken her, reclaimed her, as if she belonged to it. He wheeled around out on the dirt drive and looked in every direction, but she was nowhere to be seen. Suddenly he felt himself to be a small piece of meat being cooked in this desert pan; while she'd been taken as the desert's own, he would be its burnt offering, sacrificed for what he had done.

He walked quickly to the gas station, to see if she'd gone there, but she wasn't there, and the Indian woman said she hadn't come in either. He hurried back to the room and found her inside, taking her hat off.

Where were you? he said, panting.

He knew the tone of his voice was too severe, as if she'd left him and had been gone for days.

I went out for a walk, like I said.

Her face was flushed and damp, her skin dusty with sand, but she looked content, fulfilled even.

He noticed she'd brought back a white skull—of what animal he didn't know, but whatever it was, it gave him pause.

Why did you pick that up? he asked her, pointing to the skull.

Someone asked me to bring one back.

I thought you said you didn't tell anyone you were leaving, he said, accusingly. You said you just got on the train without a phone call or a fax to anyone. Now you say someone asked you to bring something back. So you must have told someone you were going.

She laughed and said in a British accent, Elementary, my dear Watson. It proves she must have told someone she was going.

But he didn't think it was funny.

He walked into the bedroom, his bare feet lightly hitting the tiled floor. He stopped at the bed and sat down on the edge.

Did you tell someone you were going? he asked.

She looked at him and sighed.

Yes, she said. I did. Someone.

Who?

It's not important, she said.

A man?

She didn't say anything, and he waited another moment before he asked, A man on Death Row?

She gave him a look which told him he was pushing her.

I'm tired of this, she said. I don't want to play this game.

What game?

The prove-I'm-not-lying game.

She looked him straight in the eye again.

I don't lie, and if you're worried about it, look inside yourself.

She turned and disappeared into the bathroom, and he found himself following her to the door. He hated himself for it, but he wanted to be near her.

When he heard the water run, he slid his back down the wall, outside the bathroom, and sat on the floor with his legs drawn up to his chest. He closed his eyes and listened to the sound of the water. He was aware of everything—of his posture, of his breath, of the picture from the outside: a man sitting riveted outside a bathroom door, to a woman who took a bath inside, a woman who'd lived as a man. He tried to understand why he should be in this predicament. He didn't even trust her.

When she shut the tap off, he heard her movements in the water, lapping sounds, rich in the quiet of the desert. The thought of a naked woman sitting in bathwater aroused him. He longed to be in the water with her, their skin touching, their limbs entangling. He wanted to make up to her. He didn't want to feel alone now. If she was lying he'd discover it later, in a place that wasn't so awful.

He leaned close to the crack of the door and said, I'm sorry. I didn't mean to accuse you of lying. It wasn't a nice thing to do, and I'm sorry.

He heard her movements in the water and imagined her washing her face, her throat, her breasts.

All right, she said. I'll warn you, though—I tire of these sorts of things easily.

It annoyed him that she would say this, when it was she who had put the notions into his head. He would ask her nicely. He wouldn't accuse her again.

He moved closer to the door, until his lips were touching the crack.

In the beginning, he said carefully, when I asked you if the things you were telling me were true, why did you answer so provocatively? "Why would I tell you something I didn't want you to believe?" you said, instead of just saying, "Yes, it's the truth."

It was silly of me, she said. I was trying out my feminine wiles. It's been very confusing.

I'm sorry, she said. I can see now that it must have been. Forgive me.

He didn't know if she meant it or not, but he said, All right.

There was silence for a moment, and he took a deep breath and pushed his hair from his face. Then he said the thing that was uppermost in his mind.

Could I come into the bathroom and talk to you?

There was silence. Not even the sound of water.

Yes.

He stood up and opened the door and took a few steps inside. He sat down on the floor next to the tub, with his back against the wall and his knees pulled to his chest. They were facing one another, and he tried not to look at her, but he couldn't keep himself from it. That was why he was there, he reasoned. That was why she'd let him in, so he could see her body. He looked at her openly now and was surprised by how muscular she was. He'd seen her arms, how strong they were, her thighs too, but now that he could see her whole body at once, he was struck by how muscled she was. It wasn't that she wasn't womanly; it was just that her muscles were developed more than was usual for a woman. She had breasts, round, swollen breasts, and her waist, her hips, the delicate curves of her legs, her ankles, were all woman. And her face, so far from a man's, was beautiful, with a trace of red lipstick on her mouth.

He watched her pour handfuls of water over her shoulders.

It must have been strange for you during the years you lived as a man not to wear lipstick or any of the other things women wear, he said quietly.

No, it wasn't, she said. What was stranger was coming back to all these things after having not used them. Sometimes I feel like a man wearing red lipstick and fingernail polish.

How could that be? he asked.

She laughed. I don't know. Then she splashed him with water.

He pulled a towel from the rack and dried his face off. He laid the towel on the floor and watched as she washed her face, her fingers gently moving over her nose and cheekbones, her pale eyelids closed against the soap.

He asked very quietly, Am I the first man you've touched since you . . . ?

She rinsed her face with two handfuls of water. Yes, she said.

Do you ever wish you were a man? he asked.

She opened her eyes and looked at him. No.

But there was a time when you did?

I suppose, she said, but not like you think. However much women are disregarded, if you are a woman, you prefer it.

Do you still wish—

No. I am a woman, unfinished, but a woman nonetheless. There is no getting around it. Woman is stamped into me.

She rose after those words, as if to punctuate them, and he watched the muscles ripple under her smooth, pale skin, watched the two halves of her ass, so perfect, he thought.

He stretched himself out on the bed and watched as she put on a gray skirt and a thin white cotton blouse that he could see through. When she was done, she sat down next to him on the bed and threaded her fingers through his.

Could I see you? she said. She bit down on her lower lip softly.

What do you mean?

Could I see your body? She smiled shyly.

You want me to take my clothes off?

No, I'll take them off.

He agreed to it, though he felt awkward.

She looked into his eyes before she began to undress him, her look calming, as if she wanted to still him. She pulled his sleeveless white T-shirt over his head and looked down admiringly at his chest, at his stomach, his shoulders. He was in excellent shape, his muscles clearly defined beneath his taut skin.

She touched him gently with her fingers—his chest, his neck and throat, his belly. She said a few things very quietly. I love this part on a man, she said when she touched his side. This curve here, under the arm. It is beautiful. And later she said, I love this too. It was his throat, and the place where his jaw became neck.

She began to kiss him, then, his chest, his sides, his neck, his throat. The same places she'd just touched, she now kissed, kissed every spot delicately. He'd never been kissed this way, with such devotion, not even remotely. He wanted to ask her why she would kiss him this way, but he knew it would ruin things. Maybe it was because she hadn't touched a man in so long, he thought.

She carefully unzipped his khaki pants and slid them down his legs and over his feet, then his underwear and let them drop to the floor. She looked at him, at all of him, and said,

You are beautiful.

He thought he saw her eyes tear over, but he couldn't be sure. The light from the bathroom was very hazy and diffused. He wondered what might have been the reason. He would have asked, but she touched him with her fingers again, touched his legs, his inner thighs, that fragile flesh of his groin, kissing him in a way that felt devoted, sacred even. It was almost as if she were praying over him. He felt strange, as if she were making him too special.

When she finished, she lay down next to him.

Thank you, she said quietly, touching her lips to his bare chest.

He smiled and pushed his fingers up the back of her neck, into her hair. He put his arms around her then and held her. He didn't know exactly what had happened between them, but he felt himself on the verge of tears.

She was able to fall asleep in the heat, but he could not. He lay next to her, tossing and turning beneath the sheet, dust in his throat, as if the desert were trying to choke him. His mind was filled with stark white images, her hands and lips on his body. What she had done had felt sacred, and that disturbed him now. He didn't deserve to be touched that way.

He got up and pulled his pants on and walked into the little kitchenette, looking through the cabinets for something to eat. He found a small airline-sized bag of peanuts and ate them quickly. He heard her stir and then saw her sit up in the bed.

Are you all right? she asked. The thin strap of her satin night slip fell off her right shoulder.

Yes, he said.

But it wasn't true. He felt anxious, and wished he could have at least gone for a walk, to a bar or a diner, but there was nowhere to go. He was stranded out here with her, her story alive in his mind, this girl Hemy Lourde, stripped bare in his thoughts. He thought he loved her, the girl. But the thought stopped him— the girl didn't seem like her. He didn't know who she was, the woman in the bed.

He went to the door and opened it for some air, but the air was stifling and the goats depressed him. They shuffled anxiously in their pen, scratching at the sand for some nourishment when there was none, knocking and pawing at an empty can. Their bleats sounded starved. Suddenly he couldn't breathe anymore and closed the door.

She was sitting up in bed, squinting.

What's the matter?

Nothing.

You're pacing, she said.

It's the desert, I think.

Come here, she said. Lay your head in my lap.

He went to her and curled up next to her and laid his head in her lap. He felt like hanging on to her, but he didn't.

What's the matter? she asked.

I feel awful. Strange, and I don't know.

She slipped her fingers into his hair and began to smooth his scalp, to lightly massage it.

What could I do for you? she said.

He closed his eyes and concentrated on the pressure of her fingertips on his skull. He wished her fingers could somehow go under the bone and rearrange things. He thought of the rest, of the goats, of the things that drove him to pace, of her white fingers on his skin, her lips. What had their bodies done? he thought. He had no name for it other than tenderness. If only she'd been cruel, he thought, and he became aware then of how much he wanted to punish her for her tenderness. But why should this be? he wondered, and his mind reeled through violent punishments—striking her, throwing her down, beating her. He imagined ripping her apart with his teeth, sawing her in half, crushing her under his heel. His thoughts alarmed him, they were so brutal, so out of all proportion. She had only touched him.

He grasped desperately in his mind for something to guide him, until he remembered something he had read—whatever one so violently hates in another is nothing other than what he hates in himself. But what did he hate? he thought. The woman? Was he a woman inside?

He reached for her. Tell me what happened to Hemy, he said. There was a note of desperation in his voice he could not hide. What happened to Bo?

That would soothe you?

Yes. I could think of it instead.

She propped herself against the headboard, and he curled around her, his head in her lap.

All right, she said. Where did I leave off?

Vic Ponti was kissing you on Mr. Antonovsky's porch and you pushed his face away like a dog from your crotch.

I remember, she said.

She pulled the sheet over his legs and smoothed the hair from his face. Then she began, and he hung on to the thread of her voice as if it kept him attached to the living.

14

*B*o came out of her coma. I was in chemistry class pulling strands of plastic from a test tube when the main office called and told the teacher to excuse me because my mother had come out of her coma. The whole class broke into the most surprising, spontaneous applause. I watched their mouths smiling warmly, as if they were bearing witness to the justice in life, to the fairness, to the see-it-all-works-out. Something was missing from their faces, I noticed, a small flickering of spirit, generally centered in the eyes, the thin lines of slackness at the corners of the mouth I saw every morning in the mirror that bore witness to another way of thought which told me, Don't get your hopes up, she could be blind, she could be a vegetable, she could be both.

The whole way up to Syracuse, I tried to keep my heart down, to still it, to stop it from making plans, faltering inside my chest like it did, alternating between great loping hope and slashing fear. I carried it into Zellie's room, in cupped hands, ready at any moment to close my fingers over it, to leave it beating, evenly, without hope or fear. But Zellie was standing in front of her mirror, her weight twisted onto her good leg, sticking bobby pins into her hair as if she were pinning herself together. On one long breath she said, "Bo woke up at ten-thirty this morning and asked for eggs and pancakes, and then asked them to take the bandages off her eyes. She complained so much about them that they're going to take them off now, and we're going to be there with her. They told me that it is very likely that she will be blind, and they told her that too, although I don't know if she understood or not."

I tried to close my hand over my heart, to keep it from fear, but I saw Zellie's hands tremble as she stuck the last of the bobby pins into her hair, and I lost track of my faith, that small, flickering thing I sometimes held on to, sometimes not. "Is she still Bo?" I said, trembling myself, and when Zellie answered, "Am I still Zellie?," I lost my footing with hope too, as if it were a slippery cliff, because Zellie was and she wasn't herself, and which was which was now too hard to tell.

"Does she know?" I asked, the breath sliding out of me, knowing it would drive a nail into me were I to have to tell Bo that she'd lost her husband, her son, and her baby daughter.

"Yes," she said. "I told her."

I was faint with gratitude.

When we walked into Bo's room, she was sitting in a chair, connected to two machines which stirred and breathed next to her, her white, gauzed head held high, like a cotton bud holding its own against the wind.

"Hemy, is that you?" she said. When her thin, pale white fingers touched my hand, I said, "Yes, Bo," and my voice left me, and I thought how could this be Bo, this thin, trembling person, all gauze and white, this skinny little woman with a whispery, broken voice?

"Zellie tells me you're living with Mr. Antonovsky," she said. "Isn't that funny? You living with Mr. Antonovsky after what happened. Isn't life so strange sometimes?"

It had been so strange to all of us that none of us said anything.

"You must have had a time," Bo said, and though I didn't speak, a time line appeared in my mind, a time line that was jagged with deep, pitted valleys though I hadn't yet lived the days. They were all the same, furrowed and gouged. She grabbed my hands as if she were about to slip away and pulled me closer. "What have I done, Hemy?" she said, and though I couldn't find the words to tell her, I watched desperation twist her mouth, and in the silence that followed, I saw the gauze around her eyes become wet, then soaked, and like a helpless, inept bystander, I watched the water seep through the pulpy white mesh and slip down her face.

When the nurse came to get Bo, Zellie and I walked on either side of her wheelchair, like pallbearers at a funeral, not speaking, looking straight ahead, trying not to think of where it was we were going and what it was we were going to do, the word "blind" running through our thoughts, images of hands feeling everything, of feet walking uncertainly. Once inside the examining room, we held Bo up as she sat perched on the edge of the examining table. When the doctor's blunt-nosed steel scissors slipped through the white gauze, we watched carefully, mesmerized by his slow, steady cutting, by the clean, fruitful sound of the snipping, kept from the pointedness by the dimmed lights. When he cut through the last of it, the gauze fell away, dropped to the floor with barely a murmur, and our eyes were riveted to Bo's closed, pale eyelids, they had become our world.

"Take your time. Open them slowly, very slowly," the doctor said, reaching out to dim the lights even more.

Bo opened her eyes in one blink and stared straight ahead for a moment, then moved her eyes up, then to the right, then to the left. "I'm blind," she said, like someone else might say "I'm hungry." My eyes began to burn again, as if I'd left them out in the blinding sun, and immediately the doctor shined a small light in her right eye, then her left eye, peering into them curiously as if they were two smudged windows, after a few moments his hand dropping down to his side in defeat, as if that was it, there was no fixing them.

For days Bo drained her grief, her tears and breath like the rains and winds of a monsoon, coming quickly, violently, without ceasing. Zellie and I sat by her side, holding her hands, pressing Kleenexes to her blinded eyes, shushing her the way she had shushed us when we were children, knowing full well that the woman we'd spent so much time calling back to life was not the woman sitting before us. I wondered the whole time, where was that Bo, and where were Zellie and I, for that matter, life having twisted us past recognition. If you asked Bo a question, she would answer you, but there was no real way to talk to her, she just kept saying, "What have I done? *What . . . have . . . I . . . done?*" and though it was the most pointed and relevant question she could have asked, it was the one which was least possible to answer, for how could we have enumerated the ways, listed the things? It would have been cruel; it would have been pointless.

I stayed at the hospital for two weeks and slept on a cot next to Bo's bed, knocked awake at least six times a night when Bo reached out to make sure I was still there. Her arms didn't work very well, so I moved the cot right up against her bed. That way she didn't have to flounder.

I spent the days between Bo and Zellie, listening to Bo cry, helping Zellie walk down the hallways, feeling like I was the lead mush dog for a heavy sled, when I didn't have the slightest idea where we were going. I tried not to, but when I sat down in the lounge after they both went to bed, I felt my future lurking outside the smudged hospital windows, a long, skinny, frayed thing, like a ragged garden hose stuck in the mud, winding through gutters and alleys, through oily garages and fetid cellars so pocked with holes that by the time you came to the end of it there was nothing left but a dirty silver lip, dry as a bone.

When Bo stopped crying a few weeks later, she asked for a telephone, and in the first hour after it was installed, she called a lawyer, a stockbroker, a bank, and a home-repair place called Levitt's. When she put the phone down, she said we were moving back into our house as soon as it was ready. We wanted to so much, Zellie and I believed her, until the doctor pulled us out of Bo's room and whispered in deep, sure tones that Bo couldn't be left alone, that she had what they called an aneurysm and that any kind of trauma, even a relatively minor one, could kill her. She needed to go and live in a place called Cedar Valley Rehabilitation Center to recover, her physical problems being such that she needed constant supervision and extensive medical and physical therapies that couldn't be gotten in the home, certainly not the home we could provide. It was the aneurysm, it was quite serious, he said, and he admitted that it was doubtful that Bo would ever be able to come home, at least not in the foreseeable future. I started thinking of Bo like an egg perched on the edge of a counter, and let Zellie tell her that she wasn't coming home, she was so much better at giving people bad news than I was.

One of the hospital officials took me into her office the day before Bo left and told me that Bo didn't have any more money.

Our house insurance denied the claim due to the illegality of the stills, she said, and the money Bo had had was now depleted, due to the hospital fees, and even though Bo and Zellie were now on Medicaid, anything personal they might need would have to come from another source. From me, she was trying to say.

So I went over to the college the next day and got a job working on the dinner shift at the Seneca dining hall, chopping vegetables for the salad, serving hot food from behind the glass counters, afterwards slipping into the dish room along with two heavyset women with hulking pink arms and no teeth, intercepting dirty trays coming in, one after another.

When the hospital told me Zellie had to go and live in another kind of rehab place, one that was less intensive than Bo's, but a rehab place nonetheless, I got another job, helping Louise clean Mrs. Taintor's student house on the weekends. I almost lost the job two weeks later for chasing Louise down the hallways with a sponge filled with Uncle's pubic hairs, Uncle being Mrs. Taintor's drooling old uncle. When she caught me running down the hall with his pubic hairs on a sponge, she fired me. Louise's mother marched down there after dinner and interceded on my behalf. "You can't fire this girl," she said. "She has a family to support. Shame on you." Then she turned to me and she said, "Leave Uncle's pubic hairs alone, Hemy. Do you hear me?"

Once both Bo and Zellie were settled in and had everything they needed, I thought it was time I asked Bo about the bombing. I'd waited long enough, I thought, through Zellie's flipping bed and Bo's squall-less breathing, and now I wanted to know what she thought about Happy and his part in the bombing of our house, but Zellie said, "Don't you dare," and grabbed my arm and shook me. "Look at her."

It was true, you just had to look at Bo, and you could tell she was doing all she could to hang on. There she was in a wheelchair, wearing black sunglasses, red lipstick, and her old moviestar dresses; her hair was still black and curly, but it was now thin and wispy. Half the time either her arms or her hands didn't work, and when they did she had so little control over them that she banged into walls and beds and tipped over everything from waste baskets to trays of scalding hot food, but you couldn't tell

Bo anything. We had to sit quietly by and watch her, she wanted so desperately to learn the place, and if we tried to give her so much as a hint, like "Bo, the wall's in front of you," she'd say, "Don't tell me," as if it were a test she were trying to score well on. The staff wanted to take her wheelchair away, but Zellie and I persuaded them not to. "It will kill her," I told them. "You don't know Bo," I said.

"She has to make her own way. She has to be the best cripple," Zellie said.

It took about a month before my life began to lose all connection to the life I had led before the bombing, as if someone had come along and erased it from the blackboard and started drawing something else, something more difficult, more tortured, something much more twisted. I went to school, and after school I worked in the dining hall, and when I finished there I caught a bus to either Utica or Syracuse to visit Bo or Zellie, depending on whose turn it was, and when I got home I went up to my room at Mr. Antonovsky's and Louise and I read books on spinal-column injuries. When they seemed hopelessly bleak, Louise brought over her mother's book of saints, and we spent our nights figuring out which ones Zellie and Bo needed, making various combinations, like Saint Osmund, the patron saint of spinal injuries, and St. Raphael, the patron saint of blindness. The next time I was in Syracuse, I went to the Catholic store and bought over ten different saint medals for Zellie and Bo, and in a small ceremony Louise and I devised we hung them around their necks.

Sometimes after Louise went home, Vic Ponti came to visit me, and because Mr. Antonovsky thought him the catch of all catches, it didn't bother him when he knocked on the door and found Vic Ponti lounging around on my bed. Mostly Vic Ponti talked to me, told me about things I'd never heard of and then burned to know about, he talked about them so appealingly— things like paintings in a Parisian museum called the Louvre, and movements in art like dada and surrealism, and writers like Beckett and Brecht, and books like *Malone Dies* and *Death in Venice*, which he lent me one after the other.

I sometimes looked at him in the soft light of my lamp and thought how intelligent and refined he was, how lovely really, but then I would remember something he had done when he took me up to visit Bo one night, and the idea of his goodness would vanish from my thoughts. We were sitting next to Bo in her small room at Cedar Valley and he pretended to grab one of my breasts and stick one of his fingers up what he called my "monkey," because Bo was blind and couldn't see. Even though it happened only once, I couldn't help but think it was an indication of some deeper darkness, like a small blemish can be evidence of a cancer raging within.

I rolled around on the bed up in Mr. Antonovsky's room with him, and we kissed enough, but I wasn't very interested in letting Vic Ponti grab my breasts or stick his finger up my so-called monkey, although he was, and it was no lie that we argued about it constantly, him insisting that there was something wrong with me, me insisting that I was getting over someone who had left me. When we were alone in my room, I often felt as if we were sitting on the branch of a tree, me a sparrow, Vic Ponti a mountain lion, him pretending he was nothing more than a sparrow, while I looked into his eyes and saw something dark and seething, something primitive, a black, flesh-devouring instinct, crouched deep down inside him.

"What are you going to do?" Vic Ponti was always asking me. I think he secretly wanted me to fall into his arms crying, "Oh, Vic, I don't know what I'm going to do!" I was so afraid of my future that sometimes late at night, after Louise or Vic Ponti left, I went and stood along the highway like I used to when I had stayed with Gussy Keys. I didn't want to get hit by Mack trucks this time. No, I wanted the trucks to stop and pick me up and take me the hell out of there, and when they hauled themselves up the hill, driving past me, I was filled with the deepest, strangest regret, as if they had invited me to come along and I had refused.

One night Vic Ponti found me standing on the highway and slammed to a stop in his white Corvette. I climbed into his car, and after a few moments of silence he turned and said, "Why don't you marry me?"

When I didn't say anything, Vic Ponti glanced at me across the darkness. "You think you're too good for me?"

"Of course not," I said, though on some level I did. I only had to remember him pretending to grab my breast in front of Bo because she was blind and couldn't see him.

"You think you could get someone better?"

I thought I could, but I didn't say so. "I thought maybe I would go to college," I said.

"I'll put you through college," Vic Ponti said. "Where would you like to go? Syracuse University? Cornell?"

"What about Harvard?"

"We don't live in Cambridge. We live in Morrisville."

When he came up to my room, I let Vic Ponti touch me, the idea of being put through college so tempting, and all in all it wasn't so bad, letting Vic Ponti touch me, not as bad as I had imagined. It wasn't great either, certainly nothing compared to being in my bed with Oscar, although I didn't let myself think of it much anymore, it was too painful. It was pleasant enough, being touched by Vic Ponti, but it let loose nothing wild inside my body. My heart just sat there, nothing turned over in my stomach, my hands were quite content lying in my lap, and not for a moment did I feel like we were two cars speeding down a hill with no brakes. Maybe it was foolish of me, but I wanted that feeling. It was that or nothing.

When Coleman found me standing on the highway a few weeks later, he gave me some hope. "Look at you," he said when I climbed into his car. "You're all grown-up looking now." When I told him I felt like I was pushing sixty, he looked at me again and said, "You've had a string of bad luck, girl. It's time something good happens for you." I told him, "Amen, brother," and when he let me off at Mr. Antonovsky's house, I went upstairs and fell to my knees in front of Oscar's ashes and prayed to God that something good would happen.

Zellie had a hard time at the rehab place in Syracuse. She complained all the time that everyone was crippled and said she couldn't eat, it made her so sick to see them. The woman in the room next to her was a paraplegic and had a constant strand of drool coming from the corner of her mouth, like a waterfall in slow motion, Zellie said, and the woman across the hall had big steel leg braces that clomped day and night. "I'm not crippled enough to be here," she kept telling everyone, as if that would cut the strings that connected her to the drooling woman, to the woman who clomped night and day. I would have gladly taken her back to Mr. Antonovsky's with me, but the counselors said, "She needs more help than she lets on."

Out of the blue Vic Ponti sent her a book on Frida Kahlo. He thought it might be of interest to her, considering Frida Kahlo had been impaled by a railing in a train wreck around the same age Zellie had been impaled by a table leg. He had no idea that it would change Zellie's life, that she would read it and send me out to buy all the books and prints I could find on Frida Kahlo, to buy everything that had anything to do with Frida Kahlo. The books she read voraciously, treasured, fingered carefully. The prints she hung on the walls of her room, stared at, conjured dreams in, prints of Frida's paintings of her own ruined spine and body. She wore her hair like Frida's, and took up the habit of smoking short, fat cigarettes because Frida smoked them. She even started to consider the possibility of having a boyfriend, because maimed and all, Frida Kahlo had had a great love with the painter Diego Rivera. I asked her once, kiddingly, if she wanted me to buy her some black paint so she could draw her eyebrows together like Frida's were, and she revealed to me her secret desire, the one that had been born and had grown up in the past weeks, walking the late-night hours in her mind when she couldn't sleep. To paint like Frida Kahlo, that was what she desired now, and afterwards, after this shy confession that filled her with such marvelous hope, she nervously handed me an art-supply catalog with all the things anyone would need to paint. I took it back to my room and totaled it up, shocked that it should come to five hundred dollars, but it was her twentieth birthday, and she didn't get to go to college like normal girls. She didn't even have a boyfriend. What she had was an indentation in her stomach the size of a baseball, a digestive tract so knotted she had to eat pudding for breakfast, lunch, and dinner, and a spinal column that was collapsing.

"Ask Vic Ponti if you can borrow the money," Louise told me. "He's got it."

I wasn't worried that he didn't have the money. I was worried that I'd have to roll around on the bed with him more than I cared to, but I wanted so much to cart those art supplies into Zellie's room on her birthday that I walked over to Vic Ponti's office and said, "I need five hundred dollars to buy art supplies for Zellie's birthday. She wants to paint like Frida Kahlo."

"Are you asking me for five hundred dollars?"

"No, I'm not asking for it. Just loan it to me, and I'll pay you back."

"How are you going to pay me back?"

"I'll get another job," I said.

"You already have two."

"So I'll have three."

He pushed his chair back and walked around to the front of the desk where I was sitting and perched himself on the edge. "Hemy, why don't you just marry me. You can quit your jobs and go to college to study whatever you want, and you won't have to worry about Bo and Zellie being taken care of."

It sounded like the best thing I had ever heard of—the quitting-the-job part, the Bo-and-Zellie-being-taken-care-of part. The part I didn't like was the marrying-Vic-Ponti part.

I looked down at my hands, up at the ceiling, anywhere but his eyes, they were so pleading, and asked him if I could think about it. He told me to take as long as I liked, and when I left his office I had a check for five hundred dollars.

When I told Bo that Vic Ponti had asked me to marry him, she asked, "Do you love him?"

"No," I said immediately.

"Good."

"Why 'good'?"

She took my hands into her own and squeezed them. "If you want to be a woman, love a man," she said. "If you want to be a great woman, you must build a fortress around your heart." She paused here and then said the worst thing she would ever say to me. "You can never love a man, Hemy." Suddenly I saw workmen erecting huge concrete walls around my heart, and my eyes began to burn again, as if I were being exiled from my own self, severed from my sentience, never to know the secrets of my heart, to live, in essence, the life of the lobotomized.

Bo touched her fingertips to my eyelids and whispered, "You have a great fate ahead of you. Don't ever forget that. Never," she said. "Do you hear me, Hemy Lourde? You have a great fate ahead of you."

I was shocked to hear her speak this way, about my fate. She hadn't so much as mentioned it since the bombing, and I couldn't bear to bring it up either, especially the part about me changing the course of history, it embarrassed me so much.

"It doesn't feel like it," I told her. If I had let myself I could have gone on for hours, for days, telling her exactly why it didn't feel like it, giving her the detailed history of my heart and all it had passed through, like a soldier would tell of wars he'd fought and wounds he'd gathered. I didn't, because I knew she would blame herself, there was no one else to blame.

The whole question of whether I should marry Vic Ponti started her praying three hours a day, like she had before the bombing, and all that praying gave her so much strength, they couldn't keep track of where she went in her wheelchair. They started calling her "the Wind." "One minute she's there, the next minute she's gone," was what they said. She learned her way around the whole building and got to know everyone in the place by the sound of their voice, some by the sound of their walk, and she talked to everyone—the staff, the patients, the janitors, knew them all by name. She helped in the kitchen baking cookies, making stews, mopping the floors. She answered the phones for the secretaries when they wanted to take breaks. She planted marigolds and petunias in their flower boxes, and organized staff picnics outside. She learned how to read Braille and helped wash the clothes and fold the laundry.

Then, at night, when it was quiet, the visions came, lots of them, more even than before the bombing. Her prayers had activated them, she said, but they weren't about Vic Ponti and me, like I thought they might be. No, they were about other people, people outside our family, sometimes people Bo just barely knew, like Clementine Burcott, an old farm woman who lived a mile down the road from our old house. Bo had a vision about this woman, and called her and told her not to sell her farm to the man dressed in a business suit. When Clementine asked her how she knew a man in a business suit had offered to buy her farm, Bo said she didn't know how she knew, she just knew, and not to sell the farm to him. "Someone else will come along who is better for you and your farm. You just have to wait." And someone did, a younger man and his wife, who knew farming the way Clementine Burcott did, who loved it with the same passion, a couple who'd lost their own farm in a fire.

She had a whole rash of visions about these people, and though I advised her against it, Bo didn't care, she called every last one of them. And these poor people, struggling with their pained lives, were touched by her concern, amazed that anyone would have a vision about them, they felt they meant so little. They called her back, thanked her, some of them weeping, some of them driving over to Utica to take her hands into theirs, to thank her in person, to weep in her presence, they were so grateful. Her visions had changed their lives. By the end of the summer Bo's former larceny, her godlessness, her greed, her foolishness, became pure and simple wisdom. "It takes something like horrible misfortune to bring a person closer to God," became the official line on Bo.

I figured if all these people could talk to Bo about their lives, I could ask Bo about Happy and Oscar, because the questions hadn't gone away.

I leaned my elbows on the cool stainless-steel counter in the kitchen where Bo was making cookies and I said, "Do you think Happy planted a bomb in our house?" Bo's hands stopped, and as if the word "Happy" were directly attached to a nerve, I saw blue, touchable veins pulse at her temples.

She straightened her sunglasses with her left hand and said, "I don't know," and when I asked her, "Were you in a fight with him?" she answered, "I was always in a fight with him." She lost her breath and the color in her face vanished, and though I knew I was walking on her raw, flayed flesh I asked anyway. "Don't you think he did it, Bo?"

Bo stopped cutting in the shortening and clutched the knife to her chest. When her voice came it was deep and angry, hoarse as if underused, strangled even. "It was the biggest, most fatal mistake I ever made, getting involved with that man. The enormity of the mistake I can't even begin to utter. If I let it, it would swallow me whole. It is unspeakable, and it will follow me through the rest of my life, to my grave and through my next twenty lives."

"Yes, but if he did it, Bo—"

She turned quickly and shook the knife at me. "You hear me, Hemy Lourde. That man is not the sort of man you accuse of bombing your house and killing your family, not if you want what's left of that family to live. Do you hear me?" When I said, "Yes," she said, "Good, then," and I decided against telling her that I had tried to kill him.

I waited a few days before I asked her what she thought had happened to Oscar, when she was outside on the patio, turning over the soil in these long planters. She looked like the old Bo, the long, dark dress, the red lipstick, and sunglasses. She was even wearing a silk scarf tied loosely at her neck.

"Where is he, Bo?" I asked.

She straightened her back and tipped her head up toward the sky. Then, she went back to her planting. "Oscar isn't quite among the living, nor is he quite among the dead," she said wistfully. When I asked, Did it mean he was dead and his spirit had lingered, refusing to go over to the dead, or did it mean he was living and his spirit was consigned to some living hell?, all she would say was, "I don't know." I pressed her, I told her I wanted her to have a vision about Oscar so we could know, but she said the visions were gifts, she never went looking for them. They came to her, not she to them. If she had a vision about Oscar, she would have one. Otherwise, she wouldn't, and it would remain unknown to both of us.

I thought it best not to tell her that I had dug up his grave and stolen his ashes.

By the time I went to bed that night, I half believed that Oscar was still alive and living in some sort of horrid half-life state. Perhaps he had been wounded in the explosion, I thought, and had run out of the house. In his fear and confusion he had stumbled into the woods, just beyond the field, where he had gotten lost, and no longer had the strength to carry himself out. Wounded and forgotten, he was now just barely alive, foraging for food in the woods, his mind lost to madness, his body ravaged by cold and starvation.

Whereas before I had floated in hope, blinking in the darkness of my room at Mr. Antonovsky's at a universe both obscure and enormous, I now knelt down before the ashes. I longed for Oscar, I craved his flesh, I wanted him back. I folded my hands and stared transfixed at the box of Oscar's ashes which I had wrapped in Mrs. Antonovsky's silk scarf. I became aware of the importance of asking for the right thing. I understood I couldn't ask for his life if he was in fact dead, and I understood too that it would be worthless to ask for something good to happen, that good was relative, that it did not come because you suffered, that it had another rhythm, another principle, that I did not understand. So what I finally asked for was the truth. I was interested in the truth, so very carefully I asked for a sign, any sign regarding the truth of Oscar's state, and then, though I told myself not to, I asked for something good to happen.

I prayed first thing in the morning, and instead of standing on the highway late at night, I stayed in my room and prayed for contact. I prayed in front of the ashes, I prayed on the buses that took me to Syracuse and Utica, I prayed out in the woods. I prayed so much and so often, Louise started calling me Little Bo. She prayed with me sometimes up in my room or out in the woods, smoking cigarettes between prayers, and if she didn't pray with me, she would call or come over and ask, "Any word yet?"

I searched for signs in everything. If the toast came out black, I thought it meant that Oscar was among the dead; if a dark-haired college student cut ahead of me in line, I thought it meant that Oscar was among the living. Louise finally told me that when the sign came, it would be big and obvious. I was wasting my time on these little things, she said, and if I didn't stop I would eventually drive myself nuts.

So I waited for a bigger sign to appear, waited for something good to happen, and then something happened, though it seemed neither a sign nor something good. Late one night Cedar Valley called Mr. Antonovsky's house, and after he woke me and steered me down the stairs, I stood in his living room, the cold receiver against my ear, and heard through my sleep that Bo had died. They said she was folding the sheets when the Lord came for her. It was the aneurysm, they said. It had been a ticking bomb from the start.

When I hung up the phone and told Mr. Antonovsky that Bo was dead, my legs buckled and I sank to his living-room floor, to my knees. He tried to pull me up, but I thought I might never get up again. I thought I might sit there on Mr. Antonovsky's floor, forever, like a fallen church bell.

"Hemy," Mr. Antonovsky whispered. "I'm so sorry." With great difficulty he lowered himself to the floor and put his arms around me, drawing me to his chest, where I first felt a vibration emanating from deep inside, then heard him humming a tune, a simple string of notes from a Russian lullaby. When I saw his hand on my arm, his finger keeping time, the deep gully in his palm where Stalin's shovel had bitten into his flesh, I pressed my eyes shut. What did I know about suffering? I listened to his tune, to the husky wheeze of his breath, to the note of sorrow, the mournful goodbye he sang to his whole life and now to mine, Mr. Antonovsky who broke rocks in Siberia for Stalin, and who after all that had it in him to give shelter to the girl who had shot his dick off. Mr. Antonovsky's tune stopped and was followed by his tears, the sound of which summoned my own, and as his body shook with loss, my tears streaked down my face, slowly, like a liquid procession of ants, carrying grief back to their anthills.

15

*T*he man turned over on his other side, laying his head down in her lap again. He was crying, and he didn't want her to see his face. He thought how men bore their own tears worse even than they bore a woman's.

What's wrong? she said quietly.

I don't know. And it was true, he didn't.

She pushed her fingers through his damp hair, and he squeezed his eyes shut, the tears slipping down his cheeks. He felt himself losing to her, as if he had fallen into her world, when suddenly he saw himself hiding in the midst of a rack of dresses in a shop his mother had dragged him to, his heart pounding. He was no more than eight years old, he remembered, and rather than go inside the dressing room to zip or button up her dresses, he had hidden himself in the racks. It frightened him to have to help her decide which dress she looked most beautiful in, as if it were him she wanted to look beautiful for. He hated her breathiness, the sickening smell of her perfume when he had to be too near her, the way she hugged him in a clutch that seemed to go on forever.

Do you want me to go on? she asked him.

He sensed her control, the way she was parceling her story out, and it terrified him.

Would you like me to stop? she said again. She slipped her hand into his. The idea of her stopping terrified him as well.

No, don't stop, he said. Tell me the rest, what you did next, how Zellie felt when she found out.

He tried to cover the sound of tears in his voice, but it was impossible.

Are you sure? she asked. She leaned over to look at his face.

Yes, I'm sure. He wiped his eyes with the sheet.

But you're upset. It might upset you more, she said quietly.

No, it won't upset me more. If you stop talking, it will upset me.

All right, she said. She leaned back against the headboard, and he drew his knees up underneath the thin sheet.

Thank you, he said.

16

$\mathcal{I}$slept some that night, maybe a few hours, three at the most. When I woke up, I found Mr. Antonovsky sitting by my bed on one of his dining-room chairs, a mottled pink wool blanket draped over his shoulders, his huge hand wrapped so tightly around mine, mine was now warm and sweaty, red from the pressure.

He asked me how I felt, but I had sunk past language and had no desire to communicate anything, no desire to hear the sound of my own voice. The world felt black and speechless to me now, as if someone had gone inside me and switched off all the vital electrical currents, all the lights, all the valves. With hands the size of mitts, he brushed the hair from my eyes as tenderly as if he were a ballerina and whispered, "I understand. Life take something away after it take so much, the soul shuts down from horror. But your sister, she needs you now. You must go to her, Hemy."

While Mr. Antonovsky drove, I sat in the front seat of his car and stared down at my hands, so thin now, lying in my lap like a pile of bones. He reached over and patted them. "Say something, Hemy," he said, and I looked over at him, my eyes burning as if I'd put them in the dryer. "I just want to hear your voice. It is sweetest voice." I reached up with my skinny hand and gestured towards him. "Would you like this dance?" His eyes softened and something bubbled up from his throat, a laugh, a sob, I couldn't tell which. "Oh, yes," he said, "by all means," and he pressed his hand against mine and began to hum a waltz, the two of us driving down the icy roads, my hand pressed inside his palm, our hands suspended above the stick shift where they drifted back and forth in time to Mr. Antonovsky's hummed waltz.

You should have seen his eyes, two bright flint sparks surrounded by dark, sad waters, and you should have heard his voice when he said, "This Zellie, she's all we have left, we must treat her like God."

When I walked into her room, I found Zellie crying in her bed. "You didn't come," she cried. "Bo died and you never came." I looked into her eyes, past the flood of her tears, past the bloodshot whites, and saw Zellie, a small, skinny thing, heartbreaking in her need. I was all she had. I didn't even take my shoes off, I just crawled into her bed and held on to her, her body shuddering against mine, my fingers pressed against her crooked spine, my thoughts vaulting backwards to the time when this would not have been possible, me holding on to Zellie with all my might. A still, I thought, a metal thing, spitting and wheezing, no brain, no heart, a metal spitting thing blew up and did all this.

For a week I stayed with Zellie and listened to her remembering Bo as all breath and breezy dresses flowing, while I remembered Bo in a wheelchair, her eyes bandaged, asking, "What have I done?" I felt a sense of relief for her. It must have been pure hell to have gone on living after the still you made to feed your family had exploded and killed half of them.

I followed Zellie around the hospital, then the rehab center, gazing over her shoulder as she painted the stitches and scars of her wounds, and when she got tired, I bundled her up and we walked the streets of Syracuse like a couple of sailors on leave, talking about a future, though I didn't speak honestly. In the deep quiet of my mind I was packing my bags and leaving on a night plane to some great and faraway place, like India or New Zealand, Germany even, where I could study the things Vic Ponti had told me about and change my name to something else, forget everything that had happened and begin again. Zellie wanted something easier, to study painting at Syracuse University, to have a sunny apartment and a boyfriend as captivating as Diego Rivera, along with enough clothes to fill a big walk-in closet.

The whole town of Morrisville turned up at Bo's funeral, at least twenty people standing up at the memorial service giving testimony to the fact that Bo had changed their lives, Birdy Washington dedicating a memorial fund in her name, holding herself back from calling Bo a saint, but that's what she wanted to say. The whole time I was thinking, You have a few visions and everything is forgotten: Bo's corruption, her flagrant disobedience of the law, her bad influence dropped from their minds, as if they had never happened, and in the wake of Bo's visions, she had reappeared to them as a saint.

After the funeral, the women crowded around me and Zellie and touched the sleeves of our dresses, our shoulders, the backs of our hands as if we possessed some residual visionary powers of our own, and later a few of them cornered me in the kitchen, Louise's mother included, and told me they had a feeling Bo's powers had been transferred to me. It was rude of me, but I laughed. "I prayed to God for something good to happen, and my mother died," I said. By the time it was over, all I wanted to do was sit in a corner and drop inside myself, like a pen slips into an inkwell.

Vic Ponti and I dropped Zellie off at the rehab center and left her painting a cow's brain she'd ordered from a specialty laboratory, brains now instead of scars, in honor of Bo. Vic Ponti wanted to know where she was going when she got out in a month, and when I told him she would live with me in my room at Mr. Antonovsky's, where else, he turned and said, "I told you I would take care of Zellie if we got married."

"Would you pay for her to go to Syracuse University to study art?"

"Yes."

"Could she live in a good apartment?"

"I don't see why not."

"Would you buy her good clothes?"

"Of course," Vic Ponti said.

I was sorry Bo had died before she got to tell me whether I was supposed to marry Vic Ponti or not, because I knew I couldn't marry someone like him without Bo's permission, especially not when she had told me I could never love a man, that I had a great fate ahead of me, that I would change the course of history. I didn't know if I believed her words, but they were impossible to dismiss, full of allure and finally unforgettable, and they sat now in my mind like some sort of precious, inscrutable gift it wasn't yet time to open. No, I couldn't do it without Bo's permission.

"You have to find out what Bo would say," Louise said. "You can't say yes or no until you know."

When I asked her how I was going to know, Bo was dead, she pulled me over to Oscar's box of ashes and said, "Kneel down," so I dropped to my knees again and prayed to know Bo's answer about whether or not I should marry Vic Ponti. I prayed every chance I got, every free moment, in any place I could find a semblance of solitude, I prayed until I was exhausted. If I prayed less than three hours a day, I would have been very surprised.

I looked for the signs in everything and rolled around on the bed with Vic Ponti, one night slipping into the next night, a whole chain of rollings, trying to imagine if it was good enough for a lifetime, fighting off his tongue, his lips, his hands, which were always digging too deep, dipping too far, looking into his eyes, hoping not to see that black flesh-devouring instinct crouched deep inside him, but seeing it anyway.

When nothing much happened, Louise decided we should see a medium, a person who had more experience than we did contacting the dead, a woman with great psychic powers, strong enough to summon someone as tremendous as Bo. So we looked through the Syracuse yellow pages and found her, found Zynia, a spiritual advisor who claimed to have great psychic powers and to have read the cards of past mayors and governors, and who lived on Grant Street, not more than ten blocks from Zellie's rehab center. Louise figured if she'd read the cards of mayors and governors, she could cope with Bo, but Zynia was not what either Louise or I had hoped for. She was tremendously thin, not like the plump European mediums I'd seen in the movies, and dressed, not in big, flowing, flowery dresses, but in a pants suit—a pair of tan double-knit pants with a matching coat. "She could have at least worn a scarf or something over her head," Louise whispered when Zynia left the room for a moment, but it was true, there was no trace of affectation, nothing put-on or mysterious about Zynia Drumbolt. She could have been the Avon lady.

When she led us into her kitchen, I was disappointed. It was just a kitchen, a shabby little kitchen with teakettle wallpaper and

a steel-legged table with four steel-legged padded chairs, uphol-
stered in a blue-green plastic. I wanted it to feel mysterious and
otherworldly, shrouded with intrigue. I wanted that kind of experience, otherwise I doubted I would believe what was told to
me. There should have been some candles burning around the
room, or some beads or curtains hanging, if not around the table, then in the doorway, or at least some incense smoking from
a metal burner. I would have taken a crystal ball, something to
give me the feeling that this woman was in touch with the other
side. "Let's get the hell out of here," I said to Louise when Zynia
left the room for a moment. I meant it, I would have walked out,
what did I care about Zynia Drumbolt, but such blatant rude-
ness bothered Louise. She still had a sense of propriety. "We
have to stay and hear what she has to say."

So I played along, I gave over my money and told Zynia I
needed to know whether my dead mother wanted me to marry
Vic Ponti or not. She considered it for a moment and then dispensed with her tarot cards and asked us to hold hands, reaching up and turning off the overhead light, this swinging bulb
with a cheap metal cover, as if to create the right atmosphere.
She asked us to close our eyes, and after she closed hers she began taking in great big deep breaths of air, never saying whether
or not we were supposed to do the same, though we didn't;
Louise and I couldn't even look at each other for fear that we'd
burst out laughing, and when she began swaying from side to
side, her head rolling on her shoulders, I could no longer even
watch her, she looked so ridiculous.

But there she was, Zynia, swaying back and forth, me and
Louise attached to her through her hands, trying not to rock from
side to side, Zynia swaying, taking in deep breaths of air again,
swaying, breathing deep, swaying, breathing deep, Louise and I
moving with her, straight-backed and rigid, and then all of a sudden she went stock still, as if the spirit of Bo or someone had
possessed her, and her forehead wrinkled in deep concentration.
I was waiting for her to speak, to say something. I thought the
dead person's voice was supposed to come through the medium,
but there was no voice coming through Zynia. She just opened
her eyes and it was over.

"You can marry him," she said.

"That's it?" I said.

"Your mother says you can marry him."

The first thing I said to Louise after we got out of there was, "Bo would never have said that."

"You don't know," Louise said. "Bo's words probably had to travel a long way. Who knows, maybe it was like that game Telephone. You know, where one person says something and by the time it goes through a bunch of people, it all changes. Maybe that's what it was like." I told her that was bullshit, that the woman was a fraud, Granny Clampett with a deck of tarot cards, no advisor to the spirit. "I know," Louise said, "but while she was doing it, I swore I felt Bo in the room." It went straight to the pit of me, the core, the idea of feeling Bo in a room, any room, the wanting, the desperation to feel her, it didn't matter where, to know she'd come out on the other side and was still there. At the thought that I couldn't feel her, the weave of me was threatened, her death like moth bites, small, delicate holes, tiny at first, eating at what strung me together.

We almost didn't go up to the rehab center to visit Zellie, I felt so sick about it. It was bitter cold too, and since neither Louise nor I wanted to walk the ten blocks, Louise said, "Let's just take the bus back, and we'll call her from my house." When the wind bit into my cheeks, I agreed, but as we headed towards the bus station, I knew I couldn't go home. I had to see Zellie, there was nothing else I needed to do. "You can go home, Louise, but I have to go see her."

Louise came with me anyway, and it was a good thing, because no sooner were we in the doors than two nurses were offering us chairs, telling us that Zellie had attempted suicide. One hundred butabarbs stolen from the pharmacy, after she'd cut her arms up with a razor blade. She was sedated now and under twenty-four-hour surveillance, they said, and one of the nurses led me and Louise in a deathly, hushed procession down to Zellie's room, where the shades were drawn and Zellie slept. My heart beat uneasily to the rhythm of suicide, the word "su-i-cide," not so far from "seaside" in sound, but so far in meaning, so distant they were from each other, so at odds, and so much death already, how could she think of such a thing? When the nurse left, I pulled the sheets back and looked at Zellie's arms, two limp flower stalks wilting by her sides, all gauzed and bandaged, through which I could see hard red lines beneath the cotton weave, twenty-five cuts, twenty-five slices on each arm. I know because I counted.

Another nurse asked me to step outside the room and gave me a telephone number written on a small scrap of paper. "Dr. Redding is a psychiatrist who is very good, especially with cases like Zellie's." When I asked what was a case like Zellie's, not knowing, never having heard of such a thing, the nurse answered me with the words "She's a self-mutilator," and then the list followed, the row of cigarette burns down her right leg, the knife cuts on her rear end, the punctures on her left thigh, the cutting open of her old wounds. There were more mutilations, but the nurse was good enough not to go on.

I was appalled, and when I asked with hot indignation why I hadn't been informed of so much as one of the cuts or punctures or burns, I was told that Zellie had specifically asked them not to tell me. I argued that I should have been told, I was all she had left, who else was there to tell, and when the nurse spoke up loudly that Zellie was not a minor and I was not her guardian, my temper rose up from below. "Who the hell do you think her guardian is?" I yelled, my voice filling the hallway, because what was I but Zellie's guardian, her only flesh and blood, her mother, her father, her sister, her friend, her only anything? "There is no one else!" I yelled. "I am it, this is it, I am who she has left, do you understand?" and I hit myself with a fist, hit my chest, so it made a loud, dull sound, so that the nurse wouldn't mistake me for anyone else. "Of course you are," she said. "I'm sorry, so sorry." I nodded and slipped the piece of paper into my pants pocket, knowing that before the day was out I was going to have to call this man, I was going to have to get this man to help her.

I went back into the room and sat down next to Louise and watched Zellie again, like I had so many other times, watched her breathing, watched her taking up space, wondering what she'd be like when she opened her eyes again. This is my life, I thought, sitting by bedsides, watching people breathe, waiting, would they live, get better, looking under gauze at their wounds and cuts, attached to them through their bandages, released only by death, by the long, shiny, sleek caskets slipping past. My temper rose up again, monstrous this time, urgent with the need to pick up the chairs and heave them through the windows, to tear the curtains down, rip them to shreds, to take an ax and break into the walls, tear into them like a ravenous claw. I could hardly keep myself from doing it, I was so filled with fury at life for having taken my family, for having left me with a sister who attempted suicide and carved herself up with knives, for having done so with such rabid indifference, for not having given one damn. I pressed it down, for Louise's sake, for Zellie's sake, kept it just beyond my throat, which was pinched off and tasted of vomit.

"What did the nurse say?" Louise asked.

"She said Zellie needs to see a psychiatrist."

"I could have told you that."

"Don't say that, Louise. Look at her."

The two of us sat there for an hour, looking at Zellie, at her soft, beautiful face, at her arms that were marked up with fifty razor cuts, at her life, which seemed somehow to be waiting over in the corner, not certain as to whether it was needed or not. I would have stayed all night, but the rehab center wouldn't allow it, so Louise and I put our coats on and walked down the bleak, frozen streets of Syracuse to the bus station, the whole time something horrible happening inside of me, as if a demon were gathering itself in the pit of my stomach. The gorge was so thick in the back of my throat I could barely swallow. I could have killed someone, with my own two hands I could have killed someone, strangled them to death. I held it in, thrust it back, and kept walking down this desolate street, the rain like a cold mist, a clammy veil I wanted to throw off, Louise trailing after me like a dark, anxious sloth, saying "What's wrong?" every other minute, because she could feel the evil leaking from me.

When we got to the bus station, I took a few staggering steps past a couple of black men watching a coin-operated TV and

told Louise I was going to puke, she'd better get me to the bathroom fast. She grabbed me by the elbow and pulled me, staggering, through the grimy station, across the filthy floors, and into
the bathroom, where she announced, "She's going to puke, you
better get out of the way," everyone moving away, quickly, gladly, abandoning their ablutions altogether.

She kicked a stall door open, and I dropped to my knees just
in time to vomit into a toilet bowl stopped up with toilet paper
and so many floating turds that it made me puke more just to
see them. Poor Louise, standing over me, her hand on my shoulder, the people in the bathroom staring at her. "She got food poi-
soning from McDonald's," she said; she felt she had to offer them
something. Crouching down, she rubbed the back of my neck
with great pumping motions, and I threw up until there was nothing left in me and fell against her, a moan leaving me, long and
unbroken, low and howling, like the cry of some deranged wolf.
I'd heard it before, in the front of Gussy Keys's car when my house
was burning, and I didn't want to hear it again.

It was unbearable, the sound of it, so I grabbed the toilet-
paper holder and tried to rip it off the wall, and when it wouldn't
give way, I tore at the paper, pulling and ripping and heaving
it everywhere, Louise dodging my flailing arms, calling out my
name, "Hemy, Hemy," as if that would bring back the sense.
I ripped the metal Kotex box off the wall and threw it against
the back of the toilet, then picked it up a few more times and
heaved it against the metal walls, the sound was so good, thwack
after metal thwack, until it ended up in the toilet bowl. I dropped
to my knees and threw my head back, tipped it up to the filthy
ceiling, and pounded the sides of the metal stall, right side, left
side, right side, left side, like an ape in a small zoo cage. "Ahhh-
hhhhhhhhhhhhhhhhhhhhh."

Then I blacked out for a moment, and Louise grabbed hold of
me, rocking me back and forth, saying my name, as if the sound
of it would summon my sanity. And when the time came, she
picked me up, opened the stall door, and helped me limp across
the tiles, a spectacle for the eight people who were still in the
bathroom. They all stopped and stared at us, horrified, as if I
were possessed by the devil, and at the last moment Louise, big

brave Louise, turned to them and said, "Take a picture, why don't you. It lasts longer."

Once we were on the bus, Louise put my head in her lap, and her hand began the constant motion of soothing me, and in this way we rode back to Morrisville, the wind sucking and howling outside the iced-over windows, Louise's hand just kept going, and I wondered how you got through something like this, when you didn't have any reserve, when the savings account of your strength had long been withdrawn. It seemed your heart should just stop and that would be the end of it, but mine hadn't. No, it lay inside my chest, beating strongly, evenly, without pause.

Louise took me back to my room at Mr. Antonovsky's and fell asleep on my bed, her arm wrapped around my shoulder. I lay next to her for a few hours, thinking crookedly about Zellie and her cuts, about Vic Ponti and the medium, about my howling in the Greyhound bus station, and how dear Louise was to me. Then, somewhere after one in the morning, I put my coat and boots on and I walked outside in the freezing cold and through the silent streets of Morrisville over to Vic Ponti's house, where I knocked on his door. It was strange, I almost never came to his house. I suppose it was because I knew we would have ended up in his bedroom, and that "no" would carry far less weight in his bed than in mine.

He opened the door, clutching a black robe. "Hemy," he said. "What happened?"

"Zellie tried to commit suicide," I said, "and she cut her arms fifty times with a razor blade."

Vic Ponti stepped outside in his bare feet and put his arm around me. "Come in," he said.

I didn't want to go in, though. "I just wanted to tell you something."

"What?"

I looked down at my boots and then up at Vic Ponti. "I'll marry you," I said.

"You will?"

I nodded and Vic Ponti threw his arms around me.

17

She stopped speaking when he began to cry. It started softly at first, but then it burst from him noisily. His head was in her lap, and hurriedly she kissed his ear, his neck, sweetly, as if to calm him.

What's wrong? she said softly.

Couldn't she see it—he was up to his neck in her emotion. He was drowning in it.

You know what's wrong, he said.

He was barely understandable, his voice was so choked by tears.

No, I don't, she said.

He disentangled himself from her arms and looked at her. She appeared so calm, he feared that she was enjoying his tears. He quickly wiped his face with the palms of his hands. He could scarcely believe that he was weeping, he had rarely wept in his life, and never in front of a woman. And that's what she was, a woman, cunning, teasing, always wanting to come out on top.

You're toying with me, he said. In fact he feared it greatly.

She moved to put her hand on his shoulder, but he shrugged her off. Make him cry, then soothe him, that's what women did. That's what they lived for. To break a man.

How am I toying with you? she said quietly. She moved to her knees.

He took his hands from his face and looked at her—at her smooth, unlined face, aroused only slightly, he detected, by his tears.

You're toying with me, and don't say that you're not, he said. You want to see me break.

What do you mean?

She reached out to touch him, but he moved away from her, to the edge of the bed, where he dropped his feet to the floor and lowered his face to his palms, taking in deep breaths to stop the sobbing. His neck was bent and beaded with sweat.

I'm not trying to break you, she said.

Very carefully she moved closer to him, the satin of her slip swishing against the sheet.

Why would I want to do that? she asked.

He looked up at her and a host of reasons ran through his mind: she saw through him, she knew what he'd done, she wanted to break a man because she couldn't be one, she wanted to bring a man to his knees.

You're lying to me, he said. You're making it up to play some kind of mind game on me. He grabbed his T-shirt from the bottom of the mattress and pulled it over his head.

That is nonsense, she said. What reason on this earth would I have to make up a whole story to play a mind game on you?

For the same reason you left your life in ruins, he said.

It was in ruins because I'd lived as a man and now I've started to live as myself.

He turned on her now.

You couldn't have lived as a man. You don't have the slightest idea what a man is. You aren't a man and you never will be.

Exactly, she said, dropping her hands heavily into her lap.

He stared at her and felt the pain of a mind confused by time and circumstances. He didn't know what to think now, he'd made such a scene, but it broke his heart, this girl Hemy Lourde, and he didn't want to be made a fool.

Let me see your driver's license, he said.

Without even waiting for her answer, he grabbed for her purse, which was next to the bed, but she sprang up and snatched it away first. He was astonished at how fast she was, how cagey.

So you don't want me looking at your driver's license? he said, sure he had struck a nerve now. He tossed the hair from his eyes.

No, it isn't my driver's license I'm worried about.

Oh, no? Then why did you grab for it so fast?

There's something in it I would prefer you not see, she said. She held the purse against her chest.

Yes, the driver's license.

Think what you want, she said, and sat down on the bed. When the straps of her rose-colored slip fell off her shoulders, she pushed them up with her thumbs.

He hung there for a moment. It was so awkward between them now. They were two strangers in a motel room in the middle of a desert with no hope of getting out until the morning.

Her face softened and she said, I am not lying to you. You need some sleep. You're not thinking right. She held her hand out to him.

Show me the driver's license, he said.

She looked so deeply into his eyes, he felt it scorch him.

I am not obliged to show you anything, she said. You asked me to tell you my story—I never suggested it—

Yes, he yelled, you turned to me on the train and told me you've been living as a man for five years. You were the one who started the whole thing, you were the one who said the first word that ever went between us. You had something on your mind, lady, and something up your sleeve.

I don't know why I told you, she said. As soon as I said it I was sorry I had. I apologized. It just slipped out. I wanted to tell someone. I'm sorry, but even so it was you who pursued this story. I did not ask to tell it to you.

At the thought of her story, of the girl Hemy Lourde, he began to cry again. It angered him that the girl had such power over him just now, when he was out in the middle of a desert with a woman he didn't trust.

She cocked her head to the side and looked at him. Who are you? she asked.

She looked at him strangely, as if she were trying to recognize him.

Do I know you?

He pushed the hair from his eyes. Why do you want to know now? he said.

Because we're not just a man and a woman on a train anymore, she said.

No? What are we?

We've become entangled, for some reason, though I don't know why. I'm trying to understand. It is something, that I am sure of. I've told you who I am, and I'm asking now who you are.

He wrestled with himself over the answer, and then finally he said it.

Oscar Lourde, he said.

The air inside the room dried up.

Her eyes blinked rapidly, as if the words, "Oscar Lourde," were attached to the nerves that made them open and close.

He swallowed and watched her carefully.

She pinched her eyes shut for a few moments. He wasn't sure if she was praying or summoning patience.

He heard his voice.

It was my fault the still blew, he said.

She opened her eyes and stared at him.

I tampered with it so that I could give Happy the extra percentage he wanted without Bo finding out—that way everyone would get what they wanted. But the still blew up.

She looked at the wall behind him, as if to rest her eyes while her mind went ahead in thought. Then her eyes shifted back to his face.

Where did you go after the explosion? she asked. She spoke so matter-of-factly.

I went into the woods for a few days, he said. Maybe it was two days later, maybe three, I don't remember. I came out because I was starving. I didn't know what to do, so I hitchhiked to Syracuse and found Happy.

She nodded her head and considered that for a moment.

Why didn't you come back? she said quietly.

He looked down at his hands and spoke softly.

I knew it was all my fault. How could I come back?

She pushed the sheet from her legs and rose up. Barefoot, she walked to the door and opened it. She took in some air while he watched her, the way the satin slip clung to her hips, the way it plunged down her back. He could hear the goats scratching at the hard, caked dirt. The sound of it made him nauseous.

Without turning around she spoke again.

Why are you so worried that I am not telling you the truth?

I thought you knew, he said. He sat on the edge of the bed, his feet on the floor, his hands on his knees.

Knew what?

Knew that I was Oscar Lourde and were punishing me for having left you. I thought you were making up the story to torment me.

She stepped outside and stood there, motionless, her back yet to him.

How did you find me now? she said.

I looked your name up in the telephone book, and I followed you.

How did you even know I was in New York?

I didn't, he said. It's just that I ended up there. No matter where I went I always looked your name up in the phone book. For the last twenty years I've been looking up your name in phone books. This time you were there.

How did it work out so nicely—me sitting next to you on the train? Me just getting on the train, and out of all the seats I could have taken, I sit next to you?

She turned and glanced over her shoulder. Her eyes were sharp, her mouth straight, no tension, no mirth.

I followed you to the train, he said. I'd been following you for weeks. I don't know how it happened that you sat down next to me, but it doesn't matter—I would have found you no matter where you sat. He shoved his fingers through his hair.

She hung there for a while, standing motionless, her spine straight, her neck long, not speaking, just breathing. He sensed that was what she was doing—just breathing.

He was waiting for a flood of questions: when is your birthday, when is mine, what are the names of our grandparents, our cousins, how was our house laid out?

But she didn't. Instead she walked back into the room.

Before she could sit down on the bed, he rose up and moved towards her and threw a haymaker. She blocked him with a bolo punch. He blocked her bolo, but just barely. He wasn't expecting it.

You've been practicing, he said.

She sat down on the bed, her eyes never leaving his face.

I haven't thrown a bolo since I was fifteen, she said.

He eased himself down next to her, his movements small and careful, as if the moments were made of filament.

He spoke very softly, his words just barely breath.

Where were we when we threw our last punch? he said.

Their eyes caught and held. It was as if they were now in some elevated state, a theater of some sort, where every word was important, every gesture counted.

In the hallway, she said softly.

Just before I read you my play?

Yes, it was. She smiled.

What'd I throw. A haymaker? An uppercut? He spoke quietly, carefully.

A haymaker, she said.

I remember the last time I saw you before the explosion, he said.

Something new appeared in her eyes. A darker heat.

I saw you from my window, he said. I watched you ride your bike down the driveway. You were wearing a pair of wide bell-bottoms and a peasant blouse, and your purse was on sideways and hanging down your back. Your hair was blowing in the wind so I couldn't see your face.

Was that the last time you saw me? she said quietly.

I saw you again later that night, he said, barely speaking the words. They were all breath.

I saw the fireman throw you over his shoulder and put you in Gussy Keys's car, though I didn't know her name then.

Where were you? she said.

I was in the backyard in the sunflowers. I heard you scream my name.

A few tears fell from his eyes and he brushed them away. She was startled by them, he could tell, and her lips parted.

Why didn't you come and help me? she asked softly.

Because it was all my fault, he said. You have no idea . . .

More tears fell from his eyes, and she reached out and brushed them away. Her touch was so tender, he thought, it was almost unbearable. He felt so undeserving.

I saw you many times after that, he said, speaking even softer.

Where? she said, her voice like breath now too.

I came back to Morrisville many times to see you. I saw you at the cemetery standing between Louise Van Sant and Mr. Antonovsky. I saw you watch the caskets going into the ground. I had no idea that you were thinking you would have to come and dig mine up because you didn't believe I was in there. You knew I wasn't. I was behind a tree.

Her eyes never left his face.

I used to come and stand outside your door at Mr. Antonovsky's, he said. Sometimes Louise would be there and I'd hear you laugh, but there were times when I heard you cry.

And you felt so little compassion for me that you never knocked on the door? she said.

I wanted to. You have no idea the magnitude of my crime—I was no good anymore. He cried again, deep into the palms of his hands, a long, plaintive cry.

You have no idea the life I've lived, he said.

He felt her hand tender on his shoulder, and it only made him cry harder.

Happy changed my name to Vinnie Dupre, he said. He was part owner of Rosie's supper club, and I started off there in the kitchen, busing tables and washing pots. I lived in Happy's apartment, in the back room off the kitchen. It was a small room, but it was the only place I had. I lived to see you, even if it was the smallest glimpse. Just seeing you walk down the street gave me hope.

Then, Happy opened another restaurant, a swankier place named Artemus, and I became a cook and worked even longer hours. I was there for years. It wasn't so bad, but then Happy brought me into the business. You don't say no to guys like Happy, so there I was, twenty-two years old, running drugs and numbers for Happy, everybody slapping me on the back calling me Vinnie Dupre, good ol' Vinnie Dupre.

The tears began again and he stopped speaking.

She touched his tears with her fingers, and they rolled down the back of her hand.

What happened? she said.

I got out, he said. I hurt too many people. I saw too many things.

Like what did you see and who did you hurt? she said gently. She crossed one leg over the other, the satin of her slip swishing.

Like this Jewish guy who ran a small newspaper store just off of Onondaga Avenue. Happy wanted to run numbers out of there, use the guy's place for a front. Rausha was the guy's name, and he didn't want to do it. He was old and he had an old, gnarled-up wife, and he didn't want to have anything to do with it, so Happy asked me to stay on top of him. Every day I had to go over to his shop and hammer the guy a little, let him know that if he didn't do it there could be some consequences, an unfortunate fall, a nasty accident, he liked his grandchildren, didn't he? I hated doing it, the little guy shaking, his wife twisting a handkerchief in her hands. It went on for about two weeks, and then the old guy shot himself. When I went into the shop the next time, the old woman was weeping all over the newspapers.

He stopped speaking, and the tears streamed down his face. She brushed them away again with a gentleness he had not even known existed, and he was no longer certain of anything—whether she believed him, or whether she didn't believe him at all and was toying with him, or whether she didn't believe him and was compassionate anyway. He wasn't even certain why he had told her this. He only knew he felt himself drowning in emotion—his, hers, he couldn't distinguish between them anymore. He had gone too far now, to a place he'd never been before, as if he had swum so far out into the ocean that he could no longer see the land. He saw no truth anywhere. He was merely stranded, his reason lost utterly, his guilt gnawing at him like teeth.

Can you forgive me? he said.

Forgive you for what? she said.

He paused and then said, For leaving you.

He saw her eyes change. It was as if she took them back. Then she rose up and walked to the door.

Who are you and who did you leave? she said quietly, without turning to him.

He understood then that she hadn't believed him, that she'd been playing along. She'd indulged him and it hurt him. It served only to make him trust her less, to confirm his fear that she had been lying all this time. It made him sick to his stomach, the idea that he was in the middle of a desert, cracking up inside a decrepit motel room with a deceiving woman.

He rose from the bed.

See that, he said. You're not straight with me. You're toying with me.

She turned and walked back to him.

I'm toying with you? she said, raising an eyebrow.

You don't believe me, yet still you ask me questions as if I am Oscar Lourde.

Are you? she said.

He looked at her, sick that he'd lost her eyes. They were empty of him, of their heat. He didn't know what to do, so he jammed his feet into his boots and walked out of the room, into the muggy night.

He stood on the porch for a minute, feeling his heart race inside his chest. When she didn't come after him, he left the porch and hurried past the goats and the gas pumps. He crossed the gas station drive and hastened to the road, where he walked quickly in the direction of the moon. It was so quiet the slap of his boots on the pavement was loud. He wiped the tears from his eyes. He was crying like a girl, for Christ's sake, and his heart was pounding. What the hell was wrong with him? Get ahold of yourself, man, he told himself.

He was amazed to find himself hurrying down this empty road, out in the middle of the desert, crying, after he had just left a woman in a motel room, a woman whom he had told he was Oscar Lourde.

He suddenly felt choked with guilt, more guilt than he'd felt before he'd climbed onto the train, guilt for all of it—for what he'd done, for getting on the train, for telling her he was Oscar Lourde. He hadn't broken past anything, he realized. His guilt was the proof. He stared up at the sky and thought, The great fucking triumph of Western civilization: it had evolved to nothing more than a ravenous watchdog. Yes, he thought, take all the cruel, dark, bastard impulses and deny them, and then watch them all turn inside, driving themselves like spikes into the souls of every poor fucking bastard who ever believed for a minute they could be vanquished.

He opened his mouth and howled FUCK, as loud as he could, feeling the pleasure of the anger in his throat, and after he fell silent a wave of relief swept him. Suddenly he felt elated about what he'd done, all of it—climbing on a train, telling the woman in the motel that he was Oscar Lourde, leaving his life in ruins. He now relished the idea of the broken dishes, the heaved chairs, the overturned table, their terrified screams. There was a certain gratifying pleasure in having inflicted the suffering, rather than turning it against himself. He stopped in the road to savor it.

A surge of immense joy pumped through him. Was it freedom? he wondered. Had he made it happen? Had he broken beyond all that had so bound him? His heart began to pound, and he thought perhaps he'd done it. What was here, he wondered, in the crack he'd made, in this small break? What lay beyond the narrow lines of thought he'd always had? What other ideas were there? What other thoughts? He wanted to have them, to think them. What were the things he'd never before imagined? What other words could be written? He wanted to imagine them, to write them. He wanted to discover something truer than what he now knew, to become someone else.

But nothing came into his mind. There was only the desert and his heart, which had begun to pound in dread.

Then a thought came to him. What if he kept going? What if he followed his darkest impulses, all of them? What would he have then? He saw it unfold before his eyes: destruction, nothing but destruction, and he felt sick at the thought. Was there nothing else? Was there only guilt or destruction?

His mind fell into confusion, and his heart pounded in his throat.

Many men had lost their reason only to find another, he told himself. There was a long list of men who had gone before him, both literally and figuratively, to the desert. One had to be willing to suffer a terrible unraveling in order to come out the other side. Perhaps he was merely in the passage.

Unexpectedly he heard his own voice in his throat. It was a sob, as agonizing a sound as the goats pawing the barren earth. He couldn't stand it, and in the intolerable silence that followed he discerned his own unbearable smallness, the limits of his own mind, of own his reason, and he understood how utterly imprisoned he was by them.

He felt his chest tighten, the asthma attack coming on swiftly. It felt serious, the constriction, so severe he feared he might pass out. He gasped for air and pulled the inhaler from his pocket and breathed in as deeply as his lungs allowed. He closed his eyes and struggled to wait for it to work, struggled not to panic and make it worse. The panic he had had as a boy had been unbearable. He wondered if it was the desert, if it was the air out there that somehow reminded him of the sickening, closed–up air inside the oxygen tent, of the suffocating presence of his mother, always there, always touching him.

He gasped for air and took another blast from the inhaler and tried to keep himself from the panic that always made it worse. But it filled him, and he crouched down on the pavement and pulled his knees against his chest. The sound of his wheezing breath was so loud in the quiet, he couldn't keep himself from imagining his death. They would find him curled up on the road, he thought, blue in the face. Part of him was relieved at the thought of it. He would be let out of it then—the struggle, the endless, tedious struggle, of this thing and then another.

But slowly, he began to breathe again. As his bronchial tubes dilated, he gulped in the air. How greedy his body was to live, he thought. What an unshakable, unrelenting instinct, life. He stood up and looked around him, as if the desert might hand him something, an insight, an awakening, but there was nothing. And with nowhere else to go, he turned and headed back. To her, he thought.

When he saw the lights on in their room, he wondered what he would say to her. He wouldn't say anything, he decided.

When he found her asleep, he stood over her. He felt hurt. He would have liked her to be waiting, worried that something had happened to him. He wanted to call her a bitch, but he remembered her touch, so gentle it had been nearly unbearable.

His eyes fell on her purse, and he picked it up and carried it quietly out of the room, out to the porch, where he heard the goats shuffling. It was a horrible accompaniment to the unbuckling of it—the sound of their dried-out hooves on the cracked ground—

so he walked over to the gas pumps, away from them, and in the light from the lamp overhead, he opened her purse and slipped his hand inside. He pulled out one thing after another: a black wallet, three tubes of red lipstick, a roll of stamps, a small 35 mm camera, a black hard-covered notebook, a small two-sided mirror, two Kotex napkins, and a couple of Bic pens. He laid them side by side in a neat row on the concrete island where he was sitting.

He tried to imagine what the Indian woman might think were she to glance out the window and find him sitting on the concrete island, in a white sleeveless T-shirt and khaki pants, the contents of a woman's purse placed next to him, neatly in a row. He couldn't help but see himself in this way—sitting on this concrete island, staring at a row of woman's things, out in the middle of an unending desert.

It was the black portfolio with the delicate string that he finally separated from the other items, but it was the wallet he first opened. It was empty of photographs, of name cards, of credit cards, of a driver's license. The only thing inside was one-hundred-dollar bills. That and a price tag stuffed between two crisp bills. Everything was new, he realized—the wallet, the purse, the camera. She'd just gotten them. He didn't know what to think.

He put everything back into the purse except the black portfolio. It felt so secret to him, this hard black folder, like it contained her beating heart. He wasn't sure why, but he liked the idea of taking it out into the desert, of opening it in the sand, of looking at it in the small, round beam of a flashlight he'd found sitting next to one of the red gas pumps. He walked out into the desert until the sounds, both alien and hostile, made him stop. He dropped to his knees and gently laid down the portfolio. He then untied the strings, and it fell open in the sand. There was a stack of about twenty typewritten pages, which he thumbed through and then read in stealth in the round yellow beam of the flashlight.

Dear Dr. Mattair,

I apologize it's taken me so long to compose this, but my vision has not cleared completely, and my balance, though it has improved

*greatly, is no more than rudimentary. It has been hard to type for
long periods of time, not to mention the hesitancy of the mind to
relinquish the story of the body's greatest suffering.*

*I offer this story in way of an interpretation. In truth, it is only
half of the story, one wing of the butterfly, the other wing, its echo,
known to me as well, is more difficult to tell. I will write of it later. I
trust you understand.*

Bellevue, April 7, 1995

I married him in the heat and bloom of summer, a
beautiful blazing June day. A June bride, of all things, a
white dress frothing about me, little white satin slippers
on my feet, thick and lasting, white everywhere, in my
hair as baby's breath, on my hands as gloves, even my
underwear was white, but it was all just dress-up, a
masquerade, more like cross-dressing, a man passing
as woman, and my heart, hardly white, was deeply
empurpled and black, like the heart of a cow pulled from
the deep freeze.

I walked down the aisle, and the people stood disguised
like an array of orchids in their shades of pastel and
white, their hats and gloves like petals, a whole assembly
of executioners, smiling sickly at me, their smiles all
fakery, their eyes saying sorry for your pain, I'm glad
it's yours and not mine, how awful. Yet they consented to
pretend that this wedding was like any other, and the
priest, knowing full well that it was otherwise, waited
for me at the end of the long, red rug.

On June 5th, 1976, I, Hemy Lourde, passed away.

June and July passed without a consummation. I
wouldn't do it. The thought of it was withering. I slipped
from his fingers, a thing more spirit than flesh, and
moved through the half darkness of his room. I invented
small games to play, like, "Do you know what I'd do if I
ended up in the Sahara Desert without a camel?" and
proceeded to tell him, while he sat on his bed, amazed that
he should find me in his room at all, a flame in a white

night dress, a fierce imagination, nothing more. When his fingers fell on my shoulders I'd slip away again and think of something else.

By August, his fingers began to fall on me all the time, and it became more difficult to slip from them gracefully, he dug in so deeply. After a while, I had to fight my way out from under them, and when I stood apart from him in my white night dress, I no longer amused him. I was now a thing that wouldn't. I should be grateful for his affections, he said, no one else would ever want me, a cursed family, a madwoman for a mother, a sister who cut herself with razors. I was no prize, a country rube, no culture to speak of beyond what he'd taught me, it was a lucky thing he'd come along. Who else would have married me?

There was a hole in me I hadn't known of, where the words slipped through.

It was in late August, on his queen-sized bed, that Vic Ponti finally took what was his, the room dark except for a light burning in the closet which stretched out across the beige wall-to-wall carpeting in a long, thin finger.

"Don't be nervous," he whispered as he pulled my white night dress from me, like wings from a fly. I whispered, "Maybe we could rent a drawer at the morgue for an hour, the mortician could drug me, and when you're done, you could just knock on the drawer and holler."

Vic Ponti smiled, and I felt his lips on mine, like two pieces of warm rubber moving haphazardly, his hands running wildly over my flesh, his fingers pressed deeply into my most hidden parts. It drove my head into the cradle of his neck where I hid. "I don't want to do this," I breathed. "It has to be done," he said, and he jabbed himself inside me. I went rigid, and the world shrunk to a radius of two feet, I was aware only of Vic Ponti's legs pumping between mine and of his hand wildly navigating his member down my frozen aisle. "It hurts," I said, but he couldn't hear me over the suckish sound of his own breath. He was laboring above me, gaining momentum; the unclean smell of his hair flooded my nose, the retching sound of his breath filled my ear, I had never witnessed

such a ragged loss of self-control. I was a greaseless
socket, dry and sleeved in metal, and a grave,
uncomfortable feeling crawled into my conscience, as
if I had been asked to run a marathon without legs.

It was never any other way, and I screamed at night to
save myself from it. I even broke his nose once and put a
bruise the size of a fifty-cent piece on his left ribcage. I
was his wife, he wanted me to be quiet like a child holds
still for a night diapering, and when I wouldn't, he just
took me.

Once a month I slid a check across the kitchen table
with my fingertips and watched Zellie's fingertips take
over. A $1,000.00 check written out to Zellie Lourde,
signed by Vic Ponti. He paid for Zellie's apartment with
the walk-in closet, her food, her clothes, her art supplies
that were exactly like Frida Kahlo's. Then separately,
Vic Ponti paid for her tuition at the beginning of each
semester and for her medical insurance which came due
in quarterly payments. Zellie cost $20,000.00 a year.

The thing about it—he never complained.

I coordinated my schedule at Syracuse University with
Zellie's so that I could walk her to her classes and walk
her home to help her out of her braces to rub her skin
where the metal bones had chafed. They had to be taken
off her at night and put back on her in the morning,
which I did every day of the week, save Saturdays and
Sundays. An older woman named Doris Briggs, who lived
down the hall, helped Zellie on Saturday and Sundays for
$400.00 a month, $25.00 for each changing.

While Zellie studied painting, I studied photography. I
took pictures of everything, to prove they existed, but the
photographs were like small thoughts on the edge of an
unending storm. All that happened in the evening cast a
long shadow across them.

I tried to tell Louise Van Sant when the two of us
climbed out onto her roof and sat under the eaves. I spoke
in a voice that was half aching, half bold, the backbone
almost lost, and told Louise Van Sant everything I could

bear to utter about being married to Vic Ponti. Louise listened, her eyes wide, and heard my hushed voice speak the mean words Vic Ponti had uttered, but about the taking, I never said a word. Louise Van Sant looked up to me, I wasn't the sort of person you pushed around.

I told Mr. Antonovsky though. We were sitting in his living room, across from each other in the sister chairs, the chairs we had sat in when I had tried to apologize for shooting his dick off. It was no easier now, this three years later, trying to tell him about my marriage, but I told him as best as I could, saying in a voice crushed by shame, "He hits me, Mr. Antonovksy, and forces himself on me."

Mr. Antonovsky said, "You must give him what he wants. This is way of men. This is how men are. It cannot be helped."

"You hit Mrs. Antonovsky?" I breathed quietly.

"I didn't have to. Mrs. Antonovsky, she never say no to me."

"She said no to those men in the camps," I said.

"I know, and look where it got her. Bludgeoned to death."

"But, still," I said. But still.

He reached over and patted my hand. "You are so young, this is problem. You will get used to it. All women do. It is not so bad when you accept that this is way."

It rang in my mind at nights. This is how men are.

———————

When Vic Ponti decided I was frigid, I tried to defend myself by telling him that I had once had true sexual feelings for a boy. He wanted to know who the boy was, accusing me of lying, pushing me to give up a name, laughing at me when I wouldn't divulge the name, saying of course there was no name, because there was no boy, pressing me so hard against the wall of my own mind that I finally admitted that the boy had been my brother, that I had had sexual relations with Oscar.

Vic Ponti feasted on this. He ushered it in, warmed his hands over it, gloated. It became his prized possession—I had had sexual relations with my brother. I was perverted, that was what was wrong with me, he said. I could only be excited under circumstances that were perverse, not under normal circumstances, such as he offered me. It was not normal for a woman to want her brother, and that it came out so early in my life was just proof of the depth of my perversity.

So Vic Ponti took me down to St. Mary's Catholic Church when no one else was there and held my hand in the ethereal light and air that permeated the stained glass windows. He patted me and tried to comfort me, because he understood that having a sexual problem such as I had was a trying thing.

I sat next to him in the quiet of the church and squirmed inside, feeling caught and pressed down below something so dark it was suffocating. When he spoke to God on my behalf, something with hard wings beat in my heart. "Help her, God," he said aloud. "Please God, take this woman and make her whole." I whispered, "Take this man, God, and make him impotent." And Vic Ponti laughed, but I didn't.

How could I be frightened, I asked myself, when the light in the church was so soft and diffused, when the altar lay pallid under a garment of silence, stilled for the time being, but breathing nonetheless, as if it lived on in the absence of the Fathers who tended it, like a baby asleep in a crib?

But the praying had no effect. It seemed it made me flinch more; it got so whenever he so much as touched me, whenever he even mentioned sex, I started to shake, like I was freezing cold, and when red rashes broke out on both my wrists, ringing them like raw bracelets, I had no idea why. I tried to feel naturally, like he told me to, but I lay underneath him and stiffened. The worst violence hacked through my brain, brutal acts, one after the other, heinous, grotesque, sick—his body riddled with bullets, thrown onto a busy highway, ending up under countless wheels, pulp crammed into the tire treads, bit by bit worn away, ground into the concrete until he no longer existed, not a single particle. No ashes, no bones, nothing left behind, perhaps a stain, which the rain would wash away. That's what I thought when his fingers touched my breasts and dipped inside of me.

Oh to slit his fat throat, I thought, with piano wire.

Louise Van Sant noticed there was something wrong with me. "You're not the same," she said when we sat shivering on her roof, under the eaves. "I know," I said.

When Vic Ponti decided I was a lesbian, he stopped taking me to the church. All the while I drove back and forth to Syracuse, tending to Zellie, sitting in my classes, the thought arrested me, it stopped my heart, the thought that I was a lesbian.

Then in the spring of that first year of marriage, it happened. I was in the Art History Library looking through a book of color plates when I saw one of a voluptuous, naked woman wound coyly around a red divan. An unmistakable thrill rose from my groin and raced through me with drunken glee, wanton even, thick with juices, and I knew then that it was true. In the warped logic of a mind lost I decided that there was no place for me but a convent. A nun, that's what I'd become. A nun in a convent. A lesbian nun in a convent. That must be why Bo had told me that I could never love a man, that must be my destiny. To be a great nun, a great lesbian nun. Yes it made perfect sense, chilling sense. I'd take Zellie with me, get special dispensation for her, a room with good light so she could paint.

At the dinner table I told him my idea. I even had a convent picked out. There was one in Goshen, New York. I wanted to go, I said, and though I didn't say it aloud, he heard my words—TO GET AWAY FROM YOU. He picked up his steak knife and cut me.

I lay in bed for a few days, amazed. I'd seen all sorts of things done to flesh—burns, cuts, mutilations—but never to my own. Mine was cut to the bone, they said. I wondered, did the knife touch the bone? Was there a twin line on my bone now, echoing the one on my skin. When my bones lay in the ground, would someone be able to dig them up and after looking at them say, "Someone cut this woman deep"?

They gave me Demerol for the pain, and my eyes rolled back and forth while he brought me trays of tea and cake and apologized in the most meager of voices.

When Vic Ponti told me, among other things, that women were inferior to men, I was shocked. I'd honestly never heard of such a thing. Bo had never said anything about it, nor had Lourde, nor had Oscar, nor had any of my teachers or friends. No one had even suggested anything of the sort. But then I remembered something long forgotten—how Lourde's last written words had been: BETTER TO FALL INTO THE HANDS OF A MURDERER THAN INTO THE DREAMS OF A WOMAN IN HEAT.

When Vic Ponti screamed, "History is filled with the great deeds of men, not women. Who in the hell do you think built this world?" I didn't know how to answer him.

But between lunch and dinner on a cold, blustery February afternoon, I went to the Syracuse Library and looked up women, searched for women in history, in art, in politics, in reference books, in the book of Who's Who, ran my fingers through the card catalogue, looking for women. For weeks I collected their names in a notebook, gathering over a hundred names, and I would have gone on had Vic Ponti not said, "So what, I could sit here and in two minutes name you two hundred men right off the top of my head." And he did. He sat there in the kitchen, eating a piece of steak, and rolled out a few hundred names even as I cried out for him to stop, screamed for him to stop. "BENJAMIN FRANKLIN, NAPOLEON BONAPARTE, GEORGE WASHINGTON, ALBERT EINSTEIN, ABRAHAM LINCOLN, FRANK LLOYD WRIGHT, VINCENT VAN GOGH, DEGAS, RENOIR, REMBRANDT, YEATS, SHELLEY, D. H. LAWRENCE, HENRY MILLER, THOMAS WOLFE, GANDHI, J. D. SALINGER, SHAKESPEARE, CHARLIE CHAPLIN, ROCK HUDSON, CARY GRANT,

HUMPHREY BOGART, ALEXANDER GRAHAM BELL,
JACK KENNEDY, GENERAL PATTON. . . ."

When Mr. Antonovsky lost his toes to diabetes, they put
him in a nursing home. He didn't last more than three
weeks there, it was too much like Stalin's camps, he told
me, and even though I told him I would get him out, he
died. One night he just died, and I never stopped thinking
about Stalin, of the concentration camps Mr. Antonovsky
had made it through, my mind returning every day to the
question: How had he survived? How had any of them
survived?

Then I lost Louise Van Sant when she got married
to a young man named Ryan Mourn and moved to
Pennsylvania, where he had a job working on a road
construction crew. Louise Mourn made him lunch and
sat at home, getting fat in her pregnancy, knitting baby
bonnets, and collecting little clothes.

After that I did many things, a series of things, a line,
a string, a whole list of things.

> I took care of Zellie,
> took classes,
> took the bus,
> worked at Dan-dee Donuts,
> Ethel's Ice Cream,
> then the Blue Bird Restaurant,
> at nights,
> to earn money to pay for a car,
> which Vic Ponti was opposed to.

Lots of sugar and sticky hands and tedium and male
customers hanging around trying to make conversation
with a girl so edgy, so uncomfortable in her own skin,
hiding behind her hair, behind the counter, feeling terrible,
and these male customers, they had no idea.

I became friends with a man named Alan Ryce, a nice
blue-eyed blond-haired man with puffy lips and Popeye

arms who burned with equal passion to write novels like
John Steinbeck and to make love to me. I tried a few times
up in his apartment in Syracuse, but I couldn't, and not
because I was married either. Being an adulteress would
have pleased me, but it was the strangest thing, what
happened to me. I felt like Pavlov's dog. Trained,
conditioned in behavior, conditioned to feel violent hatred,
hot-pounding, killing instinct when someone, anyone now,
so much as touched one of my female parts.

This became the secret, the thing I closed inside, walled
in, surrounded with barbed wire. Everything I could spare,
all the extra blood, the antibodies of my emotions—all that
could be commandeered was rushed to this . . . thing, this
wound with no scar, with no mark, to protect me, to pad
me, to keep me from being provoked or seen or known.
The rest of me operated on what was left.

And all this while Zellie got better. She improved so
much that she could go without the braces for longer and
longer periods of time. She even got herself a job selling
tickets at the Salt City Playhouse, where she met the man
who built the stages for the plays. She slipped right into
bed with Frank Pinter and moved through love freely,
normally, the way I had that night with Oscar.

It was hard for me to come in the early evening to help
Zellie with her braces or to give her a check and have to
wait out on the sofa while Zellie and Frank Pinter finished
making love in the bedroom, not because the sofa was
hard or because I felt inconvenienced, but because I'd lived
with Vic Ponti all this time so that Zellie could have this
apartment, this living room, the bed on which she was
making love to Frank Pinter.

It seemed now that Zellie was the one who had
everything, and I was the one who had the hole punched
in me, the one with the knotted digestion, the twisted
spine.

A year slipped by accompanied by terrible thoughts,
the worst of thoughts, maggoty sorts of thoughts, of

decapitations, of terrible axings, of drawings and quarterings, all my own.

One day you're all right and the next day, it seems, you've been bundled up and flushed down the toilet into the deep black of a territory never encountered before, endless, vast in its dreariness, finally suffocating. No one ever said so, but life was suffering, constant and unmitigated, from the moment one first rose to the moment one dropped off, gratefully, to sleep.

The days passed by me, nudging me out of the way.
Every morning it was this:
Okay, get out of bed.
All right, now walk to the bathroom.
Just brush your teeth now. That's all you've got to do. Brush your teeth.
All right, now undress yourself. Just do that.
Okay, now take a shower.
Good, now dry yourself off.
All right, get dressed, wear anything. It doesn't matter.
Drink some milk. Only half a glass if that's all you can do.
Good, now put your coat on.
Walk down the stairs.
Two blocks, just two blocks to the bus stop.
The rest of the day was a series of moment by moment commands. Now walk up the hill. Open the door. Walk down the hallway to the classroom. All right, now sit down. Get out your notebook, and a pen. Take notes if you can.

What happened to me? I would ask, and then my mind would reel through the possibilities.
Losing my family.
Losing Louise Van Sant.
Losing Mr. Antonovsky.
Being married to Vic Ponti.
Losing.

* * *

I cried some nights when I felt my body jailed, my spirit withering in the hell of depression.

When a paralyzing anxiety began to accompany the depression, as if they were companions unable to travel alone, it was as if a cover from a terrible hell had been opened and I had been thrown inside, the cover tightly sealing over me. I sank slowly into speechlessness, into a deathly silence, like a sun falling under the horizon, never to rise again.

Certain things became unendurable, like riding in a car or on the bus, though I had no idea why. I understood only that they were two situations in which I felt I could not easily escape, but why I wanted to escape, I did not know. It became so difficult, I would often think how it would be preferable to cut a finger off rather than ride in a car.

The anxiety went on unmitigated, the minutes, the hours, the days grew exaggeratedly long; I felt every second go by in the worst sort of self-consciousness—self-consciousness of each breath, each heartbeat, they were its measure, of every moment as if the next one would be the fatal one, the one in which I fell to the ground and began to foam at the mouth in a dramatic and unalterable loss of mind.

Two years passed in this way, and the rashes on my wrists grew more inflamed, as if they were the voice of some silent consuming disease which raged beneath my skin.

One night I pulled out Lourde's green trunk and Oscar's ashes. Then, in the corner of the living room I set up a little table. I wrapped Mrs. Antonovsky's scarf around the tin box, and brought out the vases Gussy Keys had given me. I even trudged through the snow, down to the A&P, to buy some carnations. When I dropped down to my knees, I wanted the whole assembly to be perfect, to be just the way it was when I'd first devised it up in Mr. Antonovsky's room.

But I couldn't stop the flood of thoughts, ambitious in their darkness, oppressive in their bleakness, relentless in their pursuit, thoughts of death, of suicide, of images of axes at my neck, pills sliding down my throat. There was no room for prayer with all these thoughts, and after a few tries, the silk scarf and the tin and the vase and table fell under dust.

It was in June, the third summer I was married to Vic Ponti, that I ran into the field behind his house, to get away from him. He'd called me a whore and spit on me because I didn't want to sleep with him, and before he could throw me against the wall, I ran into the field. It was waist-high in wheat and my only hope was to get lost in it. Vic Ponti's voice, screaming my name, drove me into its deepest midst. When I couldn't hear him anymore, I stopped to catch my breath. I became aware then of a house nearby, but it looked abandoned and was so skinned of paint, so broken-kneed and collapsed, so quiet it seemed it was holding its breath. It never occurred to me that anyone lived there, until I heard, "Is that you, Hemy Lourde?"

All gravel and throat, the voice sounded full of cigarettes, the way Bo had sounded near the end. I looked up and saw Birdy Washington, her old baggy face flush with the window, her still body on the bed, a small pea in a ragged pod, her jaw practically on the windowsill. She'd been watching me. Birdy Washington was the woman who had stood up after Bo's funeral and had dedicated the Bo Memorial Fund—the woman who had had to hold herself back from calling Bo a saint. Bo had saved my life, she had once been fond of saying.

She was living in the back room of her son's house now. It was a shed, to tell the truth. There was a room between it and the main house where the washer and dryer were. It was in perilous condition. A hole yawned in the floor, and since nothing went on in Birdy Washington's room, it stayed still for so long a bee's nest had grown in the corner. And there was Birdy, like an old toenail, lying in the yellowed sheets, the bees flying around her head.

"Oh, they don't mind me," she said when I mentioned them. She swore they never stung her.

Her daughter-in-law, Gwenivere Bing, left Birdy back there to rot. Once a day she came, usually in the morning, and she changed Birdy, emptied her piss pot, and left her some food. Then, the door closed, and the bees came out.

I crawled through the window the next day with a few things in a suitcase and cleaned Birdy Washington up. I put on fresh sheets and changed her gown, and when I found bed sores on Birdy's backside, I took care of them the way I'd taken care of Zellie's and Bo's. Then, I nailed a board over the hole so that Birdy Washington wouldn't lose a limb down it.

I came and went through Birdy's window all summer long, bringing Birdy whatever she wanted, Brazil nuts, chocolate chip cookies, cotton blankets, Gauloise cigarettes. When Birdy complained that it was too much, I said, "I am the wife of a well-off man. Someone should benefit from it."

That's when Birdy realized how much I didn't. Benefit. And while Birdy urged me to leave, I brought her pack after pack of Gauloise cigarettes, the type she craved ever since Gwenivere Bing had told Birdy she wasn't getting any more cigarettes. And the two of us smoked the cigarettes down to the nubs while the bees flew around our head. The whole time, between and after puffs, Birdy Washington told me that I didn't have to stay with a man I didn't love.

I didn't say anything for a while, but I was glad that the truth was out in the open, that Birdy knew it, even if Birdy was just this yellowed old thing hanging on by her fingertips.

"I hate his guts," I said one day, and for a moment we both paused and sucked in our breath. When our eyes caught, Birdy put it together.

"Zellie," she whispered, and I sat straight, my eyes stuck on Birdy's, I didn't move so much as a part of myself.

"You're not your sister's keeper," she said.

"Who is then?"

"If your sister knew how much you hated that man, do you think she would want you to stay?"

In exchange for these words, I brought Birdy Washington whatever Birdy Washington wanted—creamed herring, speckled trout, German pretzels, chocolates, silk pajamas. If Birdy Washington wanted me to carry her halfway across the field, I did. I dressed her in a sun bonnet and carried her bones across the field where we sat in the wheat and smoked cigarettes and lunched on boxes of Godiva chocolates. All on his tab, I would think. If Gwenivere Bing ever saw us she never said anything.

"What does she say?" I asked because it wasn't like you couldn't notice any difference in Birdy's room—a white chintz comforter, striped peach curtains, and a wicker rocking chair for Birdy Washington to rock in.

"She knows who you are," Birdy said.

Who am I? I wondered.

When Birdy Washington figured out how I got the long scar on my arm, she grabbed my hands and shook them, her big hollow eyes gathering themselves for a storm. "You steal as much of that man's money as you can get your hands on," she said, "and you get the hell out of there."

A few days later Birdy told me something else. We were sitting in her room, the curtains fluttering at the rotted windows, the bees flying around our heads, when she said, "Bo told me to tell you to leave that man. You were never supposed to marry him."

I lost my breath at the mention of Bo.

"How?" I said.

"How what? How do you leave that man?"

"No, how did you talk to Bo?"

"She came into my mind this morning is all."

I believed Birdy Washington. I believed Bo had come into Birdy Washington's mind during the morning. I bent over in my lap and hung there, my breath stopping and starting.

Birdy Washington's hand came out of nowhere and sat on the back of my head. "Honey, you might as well have some fun while you're young," she said. "Because when you get old, they pitch you out in a shed and throw your food at you."

That's what Birdy Washington said.

I stole money from Vic Ponti, three thousand five hundred dollars, and shoved it into the lining of Lourde's old green trunk. On November 15, 1977, I walked out of Vic Ponti's house and into the first snow. I put the trunk into a grocery cart and wheeled it downtown where I caught the 6:00 bus, but not before he knocked me down and spit on me again. "You're crazy. No one is going to want you, you crazy, fucking woman." When I climbed on the bus, stone cold and shaking, the last thing in this world I wanted to be was a woman.

When Zellie opened the door and found me standing there with Lourde's green trunk, she didn't quite understand.

"I left him," I said and dragged the trunk, leaking and snowy, into Zellie's living room.

"Why?" Zellie asked.

"Because I hate him."

Zellie hadn't known, hadn't known any of it, but when I started to tell her, it seemed there had been an idea in her head all along, a shadow in her mind, a stalking shadow at the bottom of a well, only now just risen.

Over a cup of coffee, I slid the money across the kitchen table, the money Zellie was going to need for her last semester of tuition, one quarterly payment on her medical bills, and three months rent and food money. I gave it to her in cash, in $100 bills.

Zellie immediately pushed it back. "This is your money. I can do something for money."

"You're going to have to," I said. "This will only keep you going for four months. I'm sorry, Zellie, but—"

Zellie pressed her finger to my lips. It was too much to hear, the reason why, she knew it anyway, there was no need to speak, not now. When Zellie saw the scar on my arm, she sank to her knees in the living room.

Late that night I crawled into bed next to Zellie and lay

in the darkness listening to her breath as I had when her
bed had flipped, when she'd taken too many Demerols,
when she'd sliced up her arms. Zellie's breath and my
own heartbeat, and with that I began to remember myself.
The girl who put saint medals around Bo and Zellie's
necks, with Louise Van Sant officiating, the girl who dug
up Oscar's grave and stole his ashes, the girl who'd lived
up in Mr. Antonovsky's reading books on spinal cord
injuries and comas, the girl who rolled around the bed
with Vic Ponti, trying to imagine a lifetime of it, the girl
who went to see a medium and asked if she should marry
Vic Ponti or not.

The girl who married Vic Ponti.

18

There were a few loose sheets of paper in the back of the portfolio. The first one was blank, but the second one was written on. *"August 10th, 1995,"* it read. *"I am on a train to Los Angeles. Just after I was released from Bellevue, I left. I've met a man on this train, but I don't want to know his name. Names open hearts."*

Bellevue, he thought. Had she been in the mental hospital? His heart started to pound. He thumbed ahead through the rest of the pages, but there was nothing but blankness, white sheets against the desert sand. She had not yet written the other half of the story, he realized. He closed the portfolio and turned the flashlight off, and for a few minutes he just sat on the desert's floor. What had he just read? he wondered. Was it a story, with characters named Hemy and Zellie, Oscar and Bo? Had this woman just climbed onto a train and decided just for the hell of it to tell the man who sat next to her a story she'd written? He remembered again what she'd said: *I've always wanted to take a train and make up a whole story about myself.*

He shook off the sand from the black cover and shuddered. He had felt the girl Hemy lose herself, lose the thing that had made her Hemy Lourde, and it made him sick.

He stood up and ran towards the light and came to rest against the light pole, grateful for the low hum, for the presence of the moths and mosquitoes that swooned above him in the yellow light.

He remembered the portfolio, how it was clasped under his arm. It felt like it was beating under his arm, like her closeted heart. He worried then that she had felt his trespass, but when he went back to the room he found her sound asleep.

He slipped it into her purse, which he still carried, then sat down on the edge of the bed and pulled the sheet up over her bare shoulder. He looked at her long, thin neck, at her closed, pale eyelids, and wondered who the hell she was. She flickered on and off before his eyes—a bored writer taking a train, toying with him. Over and over again, Hemy Lourde, mental patient; Hemy Lourde, writer, then mental patient. Only briefly did she appear as just Hemy Lourde.

He smoked a cigarette and paced the floor in the living room trying to decide where he could lie down if he wanted to go to sleep. How could he climb into bed with her after he'd told her he was Oscar Lourde? But the sofa wouldn't comfortably accommodate a midget, and the floor was dirty tile, sandy and pocked.

He sat down on the sofa, and when he heard the goats, he winced. It was the way they shuffled in the caked dirt, the lone bleat, like an expired breath of some deep, bone-tired anguish, that made him sick. Then it was quiet, and he couldn't stand the silence, either.

The sheet had fallen off her shoulder and her bare back hung there blazing. He could feel her presence as if it were breath on his neck. His impulse was to slide up next to her, to reclaim her. Whoever she was, he was drawn to her.

He could no longer stand the stillness, the loss of momentum, and stretched out on the sofa. He threw his legs over the arm, they were so long, and closed his eyes and tried to steady his breath. He felt his heart hammering in his chest. He closed his eyes tighter and imagined himself swimming in water, in lakes, in springs, in still pools, in turgid waters, finally in the ocean, where he washed up on shore, the only person left on the earth. He felt utterly lost and clung to this idea. It was large and had the power to hold his thoughts.

He imagined the cessation of human life, the end of man and woman on this earth—no more cars, no more jets, no more nuclear bombs or cellular phones or information highways. Nothing. Just a relieved place. He sensed the earth's relief anyway to be rid of its most difficult and ungrateful guests. He envisioned the scarred yet quiet body of the earth, recuperating for a few million years, healing from the vast assault of human life, unchecked, rebalancing its ecosystems, replenishing its plundered resources.

He got up from the sofa, and for reasons he didn't quite understand, he took a sheet of paper from the desk drawer and sat down at the small desk and wrote rapidly:

It's August 19, 1995. It's 6:08 A.M. I am the last human being on the face of the earth, and feel bound to record the following:

There is a Catholic mission in Rwanda where the Hutus systematically hacked the Tutsis to death while they hid behind the pews in the church or under the desks in the classroom or in the swamp in the valley or up in the trees. It was said that when the Hutus tired of killing, they incapacitated the Tutsis by cutting the tendons in their arms and legs, whereupon they went off to have lunch and returned later to finish the killing. When a man named Boutros-Ghali, Secretary-General to the United Nations, went to speak with the Hutus and the Tutsis, the Hutus claimed that the Tutsis were waging a campaign of extermination. The Tutsis claimed the night attacks by the Hutu extremists rendered peace negotiations impossible. The air in the room grew very thick with welled-up anger. When they finally stopped speaking, Boutros-Ghali spoke. "You are mature adults," he said. "God helps those who help themselves. Your enemy is not each other but fear and cowardice. You must have the courage to accept compromises. That is what a political class is for. You must assume your responsibility." He then took up his papers and left the room.

He threw down the pen and pushed the chair back. He tried to breathe, to still his heart, but he couldn't. He was afraid, he realized.

Sweat poured from his hairline as he rolled the note up and took the pale skull she'd found out in the desert and then thrust the note through the hole where the nose had once been. He didn't know why, but he took it outside and walked around back, out into the desert about one hundred feet or so. When he dropped to his knees in the sand again, he felt himself coming unglued. She's winning, he thought. She's winning. He threw the flashlight down and began digging a hole with his bare hands. Once he'd dug a hole two feet deep, he lowered the skull with the letter thrust through its nose. Then, he buried it.

When he returned to the motel room he felt crazy. He tried to sit on the sofa, but he couldn't. He paced loudly back and forth, hoping he would wake her, but she was sound asleep. When he could no longer pace or sit, when it was unbearable to be alone a minute longer, he walked over to the bed and shook her awake.

What? she said, opening her eyes.

He waited a moment before he said,

I'm not Oscar Lourde.

She stared at him, her green eyes blinking rapidly at first, then slowing down, finally settling into his. Her face was flushed from sleep, her satin slip damp against her warm body. His white T-shirt stuck to him in the heat.

They stared at one another, he vowing not to speak, straining to hold quiet. He wanted her to speak next, to hear what thing had passed through her thoughts. It took a while, but she finally spoke.

Okay then, she said. She pushed her long fingers through her hair.

He didn't know what to make of that—"Okay then." What could it mean? But he held still and waited for her to say the next thing.

Come to bed, she said. She threw the sheet back. Her legs were bare, her night slip wound around her thighs.

He pulled his T-shirt over his head and slipped out of his khaki pants and crawled into bed next to her. He wrapped his arms around her, but kept himself utterly quiet to see what she would say.

Then he heard her voice. It was a whisper, warm breath on his throat, low and straight.

Who are you?

I have no idea, he said. His throat welled up and his eyes burned suddenly. He pulled her to his chest and heaved for breath. Then he held himself back from any further sound. When she tried to look at him, he held her tighter.

Then she said, Just sleep, as if she understood everything.

He had no idea who was in his arms, and he knew she had no

idea who held her. Then it was fair, he thought, at least for now it was fair.

When he opened his eyes the next morning, it was late. He could tell by the light in the room that much of the morning had already passed. When he realized she wasn't in the bed with him, his eyes darted around the room for fear she'd left, but she was sitting cross-legged on the sofa with her eyes closed. She was wearing a long navy-blue skirt with a side slit, and a pale yellow blouse. When he threw off the covers, she opened her eyes.

You've got about a half-hour before the clerk's cousin picks us up, she said.

He stood up and grabbed a couple of towels from the rack.

Come and talk to me while I'm in the shower, he said.

But she didn't.

When he came out, he asked her, What's wrong?

She was kneeling on the floor packing her suitcase. Where is my skull? she said.

His heart pounded hard. He even heard it in his ears. How could he tell her that he'd buried it out back with a note to a future civilization thrust through its nose?

It gave me the creeps, he lied, and I pitched it out.

Go get it, then, she said. It wasn't yours to pitch. She closed her suitcase and zipped it shut.

He rolled up the sleeves of his white shirt and went out to the back and stood in the hot noon sun staring at the spot in the sand where he'd had his pathetic moment last night. The sand was flung every which way, as if someone had wrestled with something there.

When she turned up behind him, it startled him.

Where is it? she said.

I don't know. I guess I threw it pretty far. He stared out at the desert, as if he were looking for it.

I promised someone that skull, she said matter-of-factly.

A man on Death Row? he said.

Their eyes caught, and he watched her carefully.

Yes, she said.

She turned then and went back into the motel room, and he

wandered around in the desert, under the glaring sun, until he found another skull. It wasn't quite as big, but she didn't care.

It's fine, she said.

It sat in the palms of his hands, warm and sandy.

When he handed it to her, he asked, Why would a man on Death Row want a skull?

She pulled her suitcase across the tile floor. Who knows these things? she said. When I was in a hospital I wanted nothing but red rosary beads.

You're not Catholic? he said.

No.

Why were you in a hospital?

I'd rather not say, she said, and she walked out the door.

When they were riding back to town in the back of the pickup truck, she laid the skull in her lap. It was eerie the way it sat there, its teeth shivering in its mouth. He was sitting on one of the tire humps, she on the other. The wind was blowing hard, and the grain was flying up every which way.

I'm sorry I told you I was Oscar Lourde, he called out to her. His hair blew across his face.

He wasn't sure why he chose this moment out of all the moments to tell her. Most likely because it was hard to talk with the wind blowing.

She was sitting with one leg crossed over the other, her hand holding the slit in her skirt closed, her red lipstick bright against her pale skin. The wind blew her dark, short hair straight back, and she just stared through her sunglasses.

You don't have anything to say? he said.

He felt vastly uncomfortable, as if he were a lumpy mountain perched delicately on a smooth pond.

She looked away for a moment and then looked back.

I don't know what to say, she said.

She looked away.

I'm sorry I said it, he said again.

It was ungainly, this second apology.

She nodded nonetheless.

They rode in silence, the teeth in that skull chattering, the grain flying up all around them.

You never believed me anyway, did you? he finally asked her.

No, she said. I would know Oscar Lourde anywhere. And—

But she stopped herself.

And what?

I know where he is, she said.

Where?

But she wouldn't say, and he asked her if he was in that box of ashes.

Please, she said. She straightened her sunglasses and looked away.

He nodded, and they rode through more desert and past billboards offering springs and Kool cigarettes, streams and Newports.

He moved closer to her, to a cardboard box that stood between them, and put his hand on her knee.

I'll tell you my name, he said. It was all he felt he honestly knew about himself.

She reached out and pressed her fingers to his lips.

No, don't tell me. I don't want to know now, she said.

He remembered what she'd written, *"I've met a man on this train, but I don't want to know his name. Names open hearts,"* so he kept his name to himself.

While they waited awkwardly on the Abilie station platform for the train to pull up, she turned to him and said, I think it would be best if we got back on the train and didn't see one another anymore.

His heart pounded hard.

Why?

Something is wrong, she said. The scene last night . . .

I was worried you were making up your story, he said. I mean, come on, it isn't an ordinary story. We were out in the middle of the desert, for Christ's sake, and you're picking up skulls for men on Death Row. What am I supposed to think? he said.

I know, she said. It must be hard. But you must consider what it is like for me. I tell you my story, because you ask me to, and then you don't believe me. You tell me you're my dead brother, Oscar Lourde.

It sounded awful put that way, but he couldn't think of it. The train was heading down the tracks. It was coming on fast. The urgent sound made him feel desperate. He didn't want to lose her. He wished they could go back to the place where she was kissing his body so that he could redo his part, not say the words—Oscar Lourde, that is. But it wasn't this way anymore. He had ruined it.

I promise I won't do it again, he said. He felt a few drops of sweat roll down his backbone.

I don't have any more brothers, she said coolly.

That's not what I mean, he rushed to say.

When she picked up her suitcase, he reached out and touched her arm.

Please, Hemy.

The sound of her name stopped her. She turned to him.

What?

Please don't do this, he said.

He had never said those words in his life.

You said we weren't just a man and a woman on a train anymore, he said. You said we'd become more than that, that we'd become entangled.

Yes, she said, but we should go back to being a man and a woman on a train. A man and woman who don't talk.

She smiled, and he stood powerless as the train roared up to the platform.

Over the sound of the engine, he shouted, Then why did you let me sleep with you?

He spoke so loudly, another passenger—an older man—heard him and he felt embarrassed.

I am kind, she said politely.

This is not kind.

I am not always kind.

Can't we at least have dinner?

No, she said.

He turned and saw the older man watching him.

The doors to the train opened, and she picked up her bag and climbed the stairs. He climbed up after her and watched her disappear down the aisle. His heart hammered so fast, he sank down in the first available seat. He feared he would never see her again. He imagined looking for her from that moment on, searching cities for her, wasting years of his life trying to find her.

He rose from his seat and hurried to the deluxe bedroom car and knocked on the doors, one by one. He got an answer to all but three, and no one claimed to have seen her.

He searched the entire train, checking all the smoking lounges, and didn't find her anywhere. He worried that she'd gotten off, that she'd gone back to the desert. He rushed back and knocked on the three doors that hadn't been answered before and found an elderly man in one of them. No one answered the other two. He made another frenzied sweep of the train, and not finding her, he went to his own room and lay down.

He was hot and sweating and out of breath. He kicked off his boots and unbuttoned his white cotton shirt. He wasn't supposed to smoke, but he did anyway, four cigarettes in a row. You don't even know who she is, he kept telling himself, she could be a mental patient. But still it didn't matter.

He went back to the two doors where he had knocked before, but once again there was no answer. He traversed the train another time, shortly before dark, and found her sitting in the cafe car talking to some man. It stabbed him to see her at the table with this other man. The guy was nothing, he thought. He was balding and had the air of a bore. He slipped into the booth next to him.

Hi, he said to her.

She said, Hi. She said it softly, sweetly even.

The other man nodded his head, but he didn't pay any attention to him. He poured his attention across the table to her.

I've been looking all over for you, he said.

I'm sorry.

He was being terribly earnest, and he could see it was making the other man uncomfortable.

I should be getting back, the other man said.

He obliged the man's exit, making it easy for him to get out of the booth. As soon as he was gone, he found her eyes.

He could see that she'd been crying.

What's wrong? he asked.

He reached across the table and delicately touched one of her pale eyelids.

She didn't say anything.

Is it because I told you I was Oscar Lourde?

She just stared.

Because I saw you naked in the bathtub and then you—?

Tears fell from her eyes and rolled down her cheeks. She didn't speak, or move, and he understood that he'd stirred her. He felt her too. He felt in those tremulous moments the woman Oscar Lourde must have possessed and then run from.

It thrilled him.

She rose to leave, and he let her go. He found her a couple of hours later in one of the smoking lounges. She was sitting in a red vinyl chair, her arms on the ledge, watching out the window. They were now in the desert of Nevada. The sand didn't shine as brightly in the moonlight nor was it as smooth as it had been in Utah. There was more scrub brush here and there. He sat down next to her in a companion chair, and for a long time they didn't speak. He watched out the window too, as the desert raced past.

After a long time, she turned and looked at him.

You are not going to leave me alone, are you? she said.

No, he said. I cannot.

Why?

His impulse was to say Because I love you, but it frightened him to say it. How many times he'd said it to others, only to have to pull it back.

He wanted her to look away first, but she didn't. She'd regained herself, he could see. Her eyes were straight again, precise even, like lighted hallways.

I don't want to lose you until I have to, he finally said.

He reached out and touched the back of her hand with his fingertip. When she held still, he said carefully, I want to know the rest of your story.

He spoke quietly, lowly, the way he'd spoken last night.

But you don't believe what I say, she said. She lay her head on her arm and watched him.

It is hard to forget what you told me when we first met, he said quietly. How you've always wanted to get on a train and make up a whole story about yourself. And the story you've told is very strange, if not unlikely.

She picked up her head. Believe me or not, she said. Just make up your mind.

It was a confusing idea—that he could just decide to believe her or not, independent of what the truth really was.

But what is the truth?

I'm telling you the truth, but still you question it.

Why not get off the train? he said. Why not call Zellie up so I could talk to her? She could validate your story.

He thought it a perfect idea, but she shook her head. She sat back in the red vinyl chair.

I don't have to prove anything to you.

You wouldn't let me look inside your purse, he said, and that made me suspicious.

I am under no contract with you which says that it is my duty to show you what is in my purse, she said coolly.

You're right, he said, but we're not just a man and a woman on a train anymore, goddamnit. It isn't that clean anymore. I don't care what you say. I want to know who you are.

I am Hemy Lourde, she said loudly.

What was inside your purse that you didn't want me to see?

An envelope, she said.

But he didn't remember an envelope. Could there have been an envelope that he'd missed? he thought rapidly. Perhaps there were compartments inside of her purse that he hadn't checked. But he couldn't ask that.

You read my journal, she said. She stared into his eyes, until he had to look away, but he didn't speak. His heart just pounded hard in his chest.

I took it out this morning to write in it, and I found sand between the pages, she said.

He couldn't say anything. He felt ridiculous, small, and when he saw himself crouched in the desert, reading her pages with great stealth in the beam of a flashlight, he was deeply ashamed.

Why had he done it, he wondered. What had taken possession of him?

Please forgive me, he said. I don't know what came over me. It was unconscionable.

Did you read the entire thing? she asked.

Yes, he said. I'm sorry to say I did.

Her face reddened and she stood up. She started for the door, as if she might walk out of his life forever, but he rose from the chair and quickly touched her arm.

I'm sorry, he said. Please don't go.

Their eyes caught.

I want to know you, he said. I want to know the rest of your story.

Why? she said. Why do you want so much to know?

Because I care to know. Can't a person care to know? he said. He knew this wasn't true, that there was more to it, but he couldn't find the words to tell her that he was searching for something, that she'd gotten mixed up with it, and he couldn't do without her now.

Yes, she said answered. A person can.

When he saw himself sitting in the chair, holding on to her wrist, telling her he cared to know, he felt foolish. He wanted to get up and walk out of that smoking lounge. He wanted her to follow him down the aisle, begging him not to leave, but he heard his voice.

Please sit down and tell me what happened after you left Vic Ponti, he said.

She held still a moment, searching his eyes, as if to penetrate his question, to discover his need. He struggled not to look away.

I will tell you, if you tell me, not your name, but who you left and why.

He tossed his hair from his eye. Okay, he said, though he didn't know if he would tell her the truth or not. If he had to, he would lie, he decided.

She resettled herself in the red vinyl chair. He looked away then, out the window, and images raced through his mind—his hands overturning tables, plates and glasses falling to the floor and shattering, food spilling everywhere. He saw his arms sweeping across dresser tops, framed photographs falling, jars of creams, of perfumes breaking, the air suddenly saturated with feminine scents. He saw their faces, their eyes red and swollen with tears, wide open in fear, but even so their hands outstretched, as if to ask him back.

Her voice interrupted him. Who is going to go first? she said.

He turned to her then. You, he said.

All right, she said. Where do I start?

After you left Vic Ponti.

She hunched down in the red vinyl chair and put her feet up on the window ledge. The slit in her navy blue skirt fell open and revealed her long, pale legs. He couldn't take his eyes from them. She cleared her throat and pushed her fingers through her short hair. He lit a cigarette, and this time he didn't just sit back and listen. This time he watched her carefully—her every movement, her every gesture.

19

$\mathcal{T}$he rashes on my wrists disappeared. They vanished almost immediately after I left Vic Ponti, but even so, I couldn't forgive myself for having married him at all, images of myself lurking around his house, a skinny, broken thing, haunting my thoughts. Something had to be done, some sort of severing had to be accomplished, a bloody line drawn between the girl who'd married Vic Ponti and the person who lay in the dark of Zellie's bedroom. I feared so much that if I didn't do something, whatever had driven me to Vic Ponti would gather itself in the dark, unexamined recesses of my character and follow me again. Trembling, I sat on the edge of the bathtub holding a knife, and near the long, deep cut Vic Ponti had made on my arm, I now cut another mark, a curved line, an arc, as if to turn the direction of my life forever.

I dropped out of college and enrolled in a couple of night classes, working at Equitable Life Assurance Society during the day, paying group medical claims for the Meat Cutters Union, while Zellie took a few painting classes and worked part-time at Salt City Playhouse selling tickets. When her boyfriend, Frank, left her for another woman with fewer scars and more sanity, she had no choice but to quit, she couldn't stand to see him every day, the way he just brushed past her booth and said hello, as if it were nothing that they'd stopped sleeping together, stopped the constant exchange of I-love-yous. He wanted to be friends, that was all.

So Zellie got another job selling tickets, downtown at Loews movie theater, but it was all she could do to sit in that booth and ask, "What show? How many tickets? Ten dollars, please," forget about asking her to figure out a plan. Her health, a delicate thing to begin with, slipped, and like it or not it was up to me to haul it back, to keep her from love's sacrificial altar, where twice she sliced into her wrists over this man Frank, who now said hello to her as if they were casual acquaintances and nothing more.

When I realized we weren't going to be able to pay the rent, the tuition, and the bills, I moved us to a poorer neighborhood, one that was falling down around itself. We could barely make it there either, and more than once I had to let the electric bill slide or the phone bill go unpaid for a few weeks, because it was more important to get this or that for Zellie, she was in such constant need. I didn't know what to do, this man Frank broke her so much, so I finally went and talked to him one night, Zellie waiting up in her room, chewing on her fingernails, but there was nothing to tell her when I came home except "He doesn't love you anymore. He's got another girlfriend, Zellie. Her picture is up on his wall."

But she couldn't realize it somehow, and I finally had to drag her out of her bed and force her to kneel in front of Oscar's ashes, like I had done so many times myself and now did again. It was just like before, though, like when she was in the hospital and wouldn't get out of her wheelchair to walk. "WHAT IN THE HELL AM I SUPPOSED TO PRAY FOR?" she yelled. "SHOULD I PRAY TO GET MY LEGS BACK? OR SHOULD I PRAY THAT MY SPINE STOPS CAVING IN? WHAT, HEMY, WHAT THE FUCK SHOULD I PRAY FOR? YOU THINK THE FUCKER WOULD GIVE ME ANYTHING WITHOUT TAKING IT BACK?" I told her I didn't know what she should pray for, it was up to her, but I know when I finally got her to kneel down in front of those ashes, she prayed to get Frank back. I bore her flowers at the altar, flowers piled in heaps, carnations, irises, occasionally roses when she had a few extra dollars, and listened to her feelings about this man with the shabby heart, while I had different feelings, not of a broken heart, but rather of a wounded animal that crept around inside me, slowly and at different hours.

We tried to burn the memory of Frank Pinter and Vic Ponti one night in the middle of our living room in the dead of January, when I'd been unable to pay the heat bill. We felt desperate, sitting up in that apartment, the windows iced over, knocking in their panes, the two of us wearing almost everything we owned, huddled together on the sofa. I finally dragged a metal waste can into the middle of the living room and set fire to our old newspapers, that giving us the idea to burn the rest—Zellie's old love letters, the photographs she'd fingered to death, the notebooks inked up with her regrets and blurred with her tears, then Vic Ponti's bad poems, his letters, his pictures, his books, in the end everything that he'd ever touched.

The fire grew dangerously large, then claimed us, there was something riveting about it rising up untamed in the middle of our living room. Something wild came over us then and we began to move around the waste can in loping strides, a few cries coming from some deep-down place that had been closed off until now, our arms jerking up and down, as if we were pumping ourselves of something.

Our clothes ended up in the fire, and as the sweat slid down our backs, we were swept up into a feverish ecstasy, our cries growing longer and fiercer, our arms moving wildly. Had there been war paint, we would have painted our faces, had there been spears we might have plunged them into hearts, but all we had was a belt buckle with the letter O for Oscar de la Renta. Delirious, we heated it in the fire, and after Zellie branded her forearm, I branded the heel of my right foot. When I asked her "What does the O stand for?" she said "Other," but for me O stood for Oscar Lourde, and I relished the throbbing in my heel and only wished I had put the O someplace closer to my pulse, like at my wrist, or near my ear, or over the top of my heart.

When we woke up the next morning freezing, I quit my night classes and went out and got a second job—the night shift, mopping the floors of Crouse Memorial's charity ward. I pushed a mop up and down the hallways, swabbed the rooms, quietly working my way around the beds where most of the time the patients slept, all the while kept company by the hum of respirators, by the nurses' soft rubber-soled shoes, by the labored breath of the ill. I felt strangely at home among them, as if I were one of them, and had just risen from my sickbed to wash the floors.

Sometimes I woke them, mopping around their beds, but it was usually their pain or fear that woke them, and there I was in their room while they cried out for someone, anyone, a nurse, and the nurses were overburdened, there were so many poor people in need of their attention, all crying out in the night. So I put the broom up against the wall and sat down on a chair and held their hand until a nurse could come. I listened to the words they used to tell of their pain, and I said, "I know, I know," at least a thousand times, and somehow I did know. I knew everything they spoke of, I'm not sure how.

When I started to help the nurses turn and wash the sick, I had to know them, the ones I touched, and I talked to them when they were able to talk and found out something about them, sometimes more than I meant to, they needed so much to tell someone everything. The stories, they were of such sad strength, stories of broken homes, of violence, of no love, not a shred, and now on top of that there was a gangrened toe or a bad heart or a failed kidney or a gunshot wound to the head, to the chest.

I did them favors sometimes, wheeling them out to the telephone booth when they couldn't sleep, stealing into the kitchen for a biscuit or some corn bread when they were hungry, telling stories when they couldn't stop the flood of their own tortured thoughts.

One night I showed a woman whose mother was in a coma how I had helped Bo to come out of hers, sitting the woman on one side of the bed, while I sat on the other. I told her what to whisper and how long to whisper it, and asked if she had a sister or a brother, an aunt, or someone who could whisper it with her, it would help. The next day she brought her brother, and they asked me to stand near them while they whispered, to make sure they were doing it right. "Whisper with more intention," I told them, "whisper what you mean, not just 'Come back, Mother,' but *'Come back, Mother.'* In here," I said, hitting my chest with my fist, "it comes from in here. You have to intend it, it doesn't work if you don't intend it." They thought I did it so well, they wanted me to do it with them, so I sat next to the brother and whispered in this old woman's ear, *"Come back, Clara, your children want you to come back, they love you."*

Another woman found me in the hallways and asked me to teach her the whisper, the name Clara's daughter had given my method of calling back those lost to coma, her husband was in a coma, she said. She wanted to call him back too, so I went to her husband's bed and took one side, while she took the other, and I taught her how to whisper to a person in a coma. Other people found me in the hallways then, they'd heard about me, and asked could I whisper to their mother or father, husband or wife, and I did, what else could I do? Sometimes I got home very late, it took so much time sitting by their bedsides, in knots of families not my own, and there was still the mopping to do. I sensed I had some kind of power, though I didn't know what.

A few years passed like this, and then I met a man a couple of years older than me, a man who came at night to sit with his mentally retarded uncle named Irwin, who was terrified of nights in the hospital, memories from another hospital crowding out what little reason he had in his mind. He came in around ten o'clock and sat next to Irwin until the poor man fell asleep. To keep him from his own treacherous thoughts, he got Irwin remembering Bible passages, because in health Irwin preached. While I mopped, I heard Irwin preach, amazed that a man with a mental age of seven could remember such long biblical passages and had such ability to mimic the preachers he had listened to all his life. "Brethren," he'd say, "repent your sins. The day of judgment is at hand. Repent now, Jesus forgives you. He died on the cross so that you would be forgiven. . . ." It was amusing, of course it was, Irwin was no preacher, and sometimes he got things mixed up, and whenever he did he would say, "Wolfe, I got that mixed up. Now what am I going to tell the people? I muffed it." And in the softest of voices the man would say, "It's okay, Reverend Irwin, you're only human. They will forgive you, as Jesus forgives them. Just go on." And Irwin would say "Amen" and be off again.

When one night the man didn't come, Irwin became so agitated that the nurses didn't know what to do with him, so I put my broom against the wall and sat down next to him. "Reverend Irwin," I said, "I am in need of one of your sermons, the poor sinner that I am." And Irwin forgot about the nurses, straightened his gown, and began to preach.

The next time I looked up, the man was standing there. I had never really looked at him before, never noticed his singular, particular features, I saw so many patients, so many visitors in the course of a night, but now I looked at him, found myself stranded for a moment in his wanting brown eyes. He had dark hair, nearly black, stringy and slightly greasy, which fell into his right eye and gave him a defiant, hoodish sort of look. He wore an old black sweater whose polyester weave was strained to threadbare at the elbows, holes whorled from around the neckline, where small pats of his white flesh flashed indecently, and a pair of army boots, weary with lines, whose toes curled up slightly, as if they were much too big. He was short, I noticed, shorter at least than I was, and when he smiled, I saw that his teeth were stained brown from nicotine. He seemed tainted to me then, as if the brown, the stain, were indicative of a deeper rot, a more intransigent ruin, and it so effectively compromised his image that I was repelled by him.

When he sat down next to me as if the two of us might go on all evening listening to his retarded uncle preach, I rose quickly and grabbed hold of my mop, but not before he had a chance to reach out and touch the back of my hand.

"Thank you," he said. "That was very kind of you." He had a low, slightly effeminate voice.

I would have forgotten about him had he not been waiting outside the hospital when I got off work the next night. He was hunched down inside his leather coat, ravenously inhaling a Camel cigarette. The coat was beat up and marked with lines that gave it a mauled look, as if an alley cat had used it to sharpen its nails.

"I never got to find out your name," he said. "I wanted to find out your name." He was nervous, I noticed, his head motions quick and jerky, his hand motions almost stabbing.

"Petunia," I said, and kept walking.

"My first girlfriend's name was Rose," he said. He tossed his hair from his right eye and hurried to keep up with me.

He shagged after me, up to the movie theater, walking two

quick wigglish steps for my every one, talking excitedly, animat-
edly about some right-wing conspiracy he'd read about in the
newspaper. He said his name was Luke or something, and for a
long time I thought of him as "that Luke guy," though I never
called him anything, nor did he ever call me anything.

He managed to see me at least once or twice a week, to meet
me outside the hospital after he visited his uncle, when I was on
my way home from work. He always walked with me up to the
movie theater to meet Zellie, and when I went across the street
to a Greek diner to wait for her to get off work, he came with me.
We sat in a booth and had a cup of coffee; it was no more than
ten or fifteen minutes that we sat there.

I slowly discovered he was intelligent and articulate, the brown
teeth, the dark hair, the clothes having thrown me off, but now I
understood that it was a guise, that he was quite learned, having
read almost every book I could think of and more that I had never
heard of. It was his revenge, I understood, dressing that way, reading Proust and Joyce in seclusion, only to mention it when you
least expected so as to watch your image of him shatter. It pleased
him greatly, but still I didn't care.

When his uncle was released from the hospital, he didn't wait
outside the hospital for me anymore. Weeks passed, and I thought
that was the end of him, that I'd never see him again, and I missed
him, but one night I found him waiting for me outside with five
red roses.

"I would have gotten you petunias, but it's winter," he said.

"My name isn't Petunia," I said. "I'm sorry I told you it was."

"I know. It's Hemy Lourde."

Our eyes caught then.

He took me to one of his favorite Italian restaurants, a place
called Angelina's, and bought me a big plate of spaghetti and
meatballs, which I ate while he read me an essay he'd written
against Richard Nixon, even though we were long past the days
of Nixon. I paid more attention to the sound of passion in his voice
than I did to his words, it was so strong, it gathered in his eyes
until it was a storm raging in the middle of all that great brown.
When he was done, I told him it had moved me, for it had, not

the words so much as his passion. He smiled and thanked me, and a moment later he said, "I think about you all the time."

I didn't know what to say, I rarely thought of him except when I was with him, and found myself instead talking about Vic Ponti, as if Vic Ponti were the reason I couldn't admit the same, confessing my terrible marriage, and though I never intended to, telling him Vic Ponti had raped me countless times. Countless times, I said. My confession came quickly after his disclosure of having been an alcoholic, but even so, I was shocked at how easily it sprang from me, as if it had been poised beneath the waters of my calm like a geyser. He reached across the table and pulled a hair from the corner of my mouth, as if to tell me he was sorry; his hand was small, but his touch was sweet and some part of me relished it, until he smiled and those stained brown teeth erased any moment we might have had, they seemed to exist to ward off everything.

I let him help me walk Zellie home that night because he'd taken me to dinner, it seemed only right. And when the three of us walked up the hill, bent against the wind, Zellie struggling in her braces, me holding her up, while he shuffled after me like some sort of Ratso Rizzo character in those beat-up army boots and leather jacket, his stringy hair falling into his eyes, I wondered when I would be let out of it, escorting the crippled, the maimed, the unwhole.

When we got to the apartment, Zellie and I excused ourselves and went into the bedroom so I could help her out of her braces. I would have rubbed her back where the braces had cut into her skin all day, but he was out in the living room, waiting, I could feel his presence like it was something heavy and breathing.

I found him sitting on the edge of the sofa, and when I sat down next to him, I could tell by the way his brown eyes had softened that he'd seen or heard at least some part of my nightly ritual with Zellie.

"What happened to her?" he asked quietly.

"She was badly injured in an accident," I told him. I knew he wanted to know the details, but I didn't tell people about my family, it was too much, you needed hours to tell it.

"You take care of her like that every day?" he asked quietly.

I nodded, and though it hardly seemed possible, he burst into tears, and it so embarrassed him that he hid his face in the palms of his small, fluttery hands and apologized, "I'm sorry, Hemy, please forgive me, I'm sorry, God, who would believe this."

"It's okay, Luke," I said. I didn't know what else to do, so I patted his knee. He took his hands from his face and looked at me out of his frozen-brown eyes and said, "It's Luther, not Luke."

"I'm sorry, Luther. Please forgive me."

He nodded, and we sat on the sofa, awkwardly, stiffly, and just when I was about to suggest that he should be going, that I had to help Zellie do something more, he asked me, "Could I kiss you?" The idea repelled me, it was out of the question, and yet I couldn't tell him that, saying instead how he shouldn't ask a woman a question like that, it was too awkward a thing, as if he should have just leaned across the darkness and kissed me.

When I lay awake in the dark of Zellie's room that night, I couldn't get him out of my mind, the way he cried, the way he asked if he could kiss me, the way I'd talked to him so easily. It didn't seem quite possible.

After that, whenever he met me at the hospital, he came home with me and Zellie, pretending that he was interested in fixing the things that were broken in our apartment, like the toilet and the loose tiles, although he wasn't very handy. Sometimes in the midst of it, our eyes would catch, and I saw how inflamed his were, how hot and brown and desiring, and I felt bad I didn't feel the same way. When he brought up the subject, which he couldn't help himself from doing, I told him about Vic Ponti and the bad marriage, until it was so threadbare that it wasn't worth mentioning.

At Christmastime, when we were in the diner, he handed me a small box he had carefully wrapped in red foil paper, which I opened slowly. Inside was a small note card, carefully lettered in his hand, which read, "Hemy, so that brute physical strength will never win out over a spirit as fine as yours," and underneath was a gift certificate for lessons at the Karate Institute. I almost cried at his thoughtfulness, he had touched the wound so carefully. And then I felt sick, I had gotten him nothing.

When he asked me to come to his apartment for dinner, I felt I had to, he had given me a gift when I had given him nothing. I was afraid to go, I imagined he lived in squalor, that cockroaches scuttled across his floors, along the walls, but I was wrong, his apartment, though run-down, was elegant, the drawing room of an old Victorian house, with tall ceilings and well-kept hardwood floors, long French windows, on either side of which were walls lined with overstuffed bookshelves. It was sparsely but nicely furnished—a small dark sofa, a leather armchair, and a black marble coffee table.

He wore a pair of crisp black slacks, neatly creased, and a white shirt, black wool vest, and a pair of black shoes he had polished to a shine. His nervousness was so huge, it had taken on a presence of its own, so much so I felt I could have reached out and touched it. I wanted to tell him not to be nervous, that it was only me, a woman who'd seen people in their worst moments and had never turned away, but there was no way to tell him, so I left him to shimmy back and forth from his kitchen to his living room, bringing in the food, the dishes and the silverware.

While I sat on his sofa, he sat across from me in a black leather armchair, our plates in our laps, and though I had often thought how easy it was for the two of us to talk, as we sat there I couldn't imagine what we had ever talked about, what he had ever listened to so carefully. I knew almost nothing personal about him, I realized, like where he'd come from, or who his family was, even what he did for a living, nor did he really know much about me beyond my marriage and Zellie. I had avoided any other mention of my family.

I didn't know what to say so I told him about the karate class I'd taken, and he told me he took karate too, that he'd taken it for years. He said he'd been teased as a boy because of his family, and that he had had to learn to protect himself. Then he reached out playfully and threw a punch to see if I knew how to block it yet, and I froze, it felt so much like the ease that had gone between me and Oscar, like the punches Oscar had thrown me across the dinner table, and impulsively I reached across the table and brushed his hair back, out of his eyes. He closed his mouth, and for the first time I looked at him.

It shocked me, the sight of his face, he looked so much like

Oscar, the straight black hair, the black eyes, the white skin, and for a moment I thought I might sink to my knees, but I didn't. I had never really seen him before. With the hair out of his face, he was suddenly attractive, his mouth full and sensuous, his eyes black, his nose straight, his skin white, pale even.

His full name was Luther Wolfe, and later, I climbed up the ladder after him to his bedroom—a small room above his living room, with a mattress and a bookshelf and a small light. We swapped stories sitting on the mattress, his heartbreaking in its loneliness, its isolation; poor Luther had it hard, raised by his grandparents on a dirt farm near Buffalo, his mother having left him there, no father to speak of. His grandparents were first cousins, and only one of their four children turned out normal, Luther's mother. The rest were retarded, two aunts and an uncle, adults when he was a child. Irwin came first. Then Sally, a woman in her thirties, who was no more developed than an infant and wore diapers and wailed often. Then there was Dorothy, who was the best off—she could do the dishes and help with cooking, run small errands, dial the phone, and look after Sally to make sure that Sally didn't put the carpet ravel in her mouth. Whenever Sally did, Luther said, Dorothy's voice came, strong and clear, "Ma, Sally's eating the carpet ravel again!"

Luther Wolfe had to sleep with Irwin in a tiny room and keep him out of trouble, and between the preaching and the touching, Luther said, it was sometimes more than he could bear—Irwin's fingers touching him in the dark, wandering over his face, dipping into the holes of his nose, his eyes, his ears, digging into the hollow of his shoulder blades. He called out, "Gramma, Irwin's touching me again!" And his grandmother's voice would blast from the darkness: "Irwin, stop touching Luther or I'll come in there and whoop you with the stick!" The stick was sufficiently frightening to Irwin that he stopped touching Luther for a while, five, ten minutes, then the memory of the stick would fade, and the feel of Luther's flesh under his fingertips would get to be too much, and he would have to reach out and touch Luther's child skin.

It was Luther's job to look after Irwin, who was nearly thirty years older than him, to bring him back to the farm when he wandered away, to keep him from preaching too loudly, to help him eat his meals, to dress him in the morning, to undress him at night, to clean him up, to tell him when he had to go to church, to keep him quiet in the pews, to tell him what was right and wrong. "He was my child," Luther finally said.

It was a transistor radio which saved him, he said, a small transistor radio that connected him to a Buffalo radio station, where he listened to opera and learned to speak Spanish, where he first heard radio plays and political debates. If his grandfather hadn't given him that transistor radio he thought he might have perished. That's what he said, "perished."

I put my arm around him, and in that way I told him about my life, about Bo and her stills, about Happy and the explosion and all the rest, amazed at the power the story held, the power disaster holds. And when I was done telling him, he leaned over and kissed me.

It seemed as if there was no time between the moment Oscar had kissed me and now, my heart picked up the fast, unhalting beat, as if where it had left off. It was as though I were back in my bedroom during that rainy August night, with Oscar, with what felt like a horse kicking against my ribs again, writhing and teeming with temper sharpened by the passing of years. Now, after so many years tethered to some horrid outback of a post, I called it to action, and it leapt into my stomach, slammed against my heart, broke loose of its tethers, crashed against my ribs, shimmying awkwardly to break loose of my bones, my tendons, my ligaments, all that webbed me together, and I contained it, though just barely, and used it like fuel. He's not my brother, I thought, and it was in large letters, HE'S NOT MY BROTHER, breaking across a sky white with morning, in the high, lavish voice that announces wars are over. I forgot everything and became all lips and tongue and slamming heart, hungry for a taste of male flesh, for the scent, the touch, the breath of a man. And that horse inside me broke loose of my internal body, independent of what I feared, what I wanted, and raced forward on its own.

"Something is happening, I don't know what it is," I said. Luther Wolfe smiled and within moments the world we lived in, the world of Syracuse, of Crouse Memorial, of absent mothers and fathers, of concrete and asphalt, was lost and we became something else—two bodies, longing, eyes riveted, big and open, staring, curious and amazed, hands loping, unsure but driven. Voices in my mind called out, "Hey, hey, you hardly know this man," in a variety of grave tones, none of which dissuaded me, because when he took my hand and placed my fingers on the elastic waistband of his underwear, I slipped my hand past it, holding my breath, not knowing what I would find this time, afraid that it would remind me of Vic Ponti, excited that it would be too great. Hard, the skin silken velvet, unbearably soft, it was again the most thrilling thing I'd ever touched. My fingertips moved over the heartbreaking skin, my hand tightening around it, holding it, pushing it against my belly, which hurt with a longing that had so long ago unfolded inside, forgotten by me until now.

Tears dropped from my eyes, it was too much, the way it had come back to me, Oscar on its breath, Vic Ponti lurking around the edges, black as death. I took my hand back, and Luther Wolfe's voice came, deep and somehow perfect, as if it matched some hidden tone inside of me. "Are you all right?" he said.

"This is so strange," I said, and Luther Wolfe brushed the hair from my face and said, "I know," and fell softly back on the pillow. We searched one another's eyes for something, for a clue, a reason for the swift, abrupt change. "I care for you a great deal," he whispered. I nodded, as if it were true, and we lay there for a long time, not saying anything, just breathing, waiting for what would come next.

Then he took my hand and whispered in the deepest, faintest voice, "Will you see me again?" and I said in a voice stripped of everything save breath, "Yes." We lay there quietly, still possessed of one another, still longing, wondering how everything had changed in a moment's time, how had we found one another, could it be true?

His voice came again, barely a voice, less than a whisper, a sound between a voice and silence, and fell into my ear: *I want to be a good man to you.* That voice fell headlong into my ear, the perfect pitch, and touched that which had never been touched—

needs, deep-down needs I didn't know I owned. That voice awoke them, and I fell utterly.

I went to see him every night after that. As soon as I got Zellie home and out of her braces, I changed my clothes and hurried over to Luther Wolfe's apartment, where he was often waiting on the street, he was so excited to see me. Sometimes he ran to me, he couldn't wait, the smile on his mouth seductive, the light in his eyes hot and precious. He was boyishly sweet and threw his arms around me, his exuberance intoxicating. We climbed the ladder to his bedroom and dropped to the mattress, where we stayed until three or four in the morning, finally parting on the street, I had to take care of Zellie in the morning.

I lived and breathed Luther Wolfe, and he lived and breathed me.

There was something about his bedroom, warm and tucked away, that gave us license to speak, and we told each other everything. I turned myself upside down, emptied myself out for Luther Wolfe, gave him everything there was, and he listened like no one had ever listened, watched my hands, my mouth, my eyes, with his dark, lit-up eyes. I was Luther Wolfe's offering and he took me gratefully.

Up in his room, he showed me scrapbooks that documented his life, photos of when he was a boy on his grandfather's farm, thin as a stick, big-eyed, sorrowful and burdened, his uncle Irwin always lurking nearby, his transistor always in hand or hung from his neck with twine. Then his student days at Syracuse University, dressed absurdly, in hippie pants and atrocious boots, one pair red with heels three inches tall, where he was a political activist, first a Marxist, then a Leninist, pictures of him parading through the riots, bricks in hand. Then all the girlfriends standing under Luther Wolfe's arm, there were many, dark-haired, most of them, except for a tiny woman named Winona, who had blond hair and nearly ended her life over him after she had stalked him for six months.

He'd been bad when he drank, he said, he'd hurt a lot of people, broken a lot of hearts, a whole string of them, had had to make a lot of amends. I said I couldn't imagine him as a drunk and closed my eyes to it, hung on to the fact that he hadn't had a drink in twelve years. "He's still a drunk," Zellie told me. "Once a drunk, always a drunk," but I never thought of Luther Wolfe as a drunk. He prayed every night on his knees with his hands folded, like a sweet boy. He played the violin beautifully, expertly, you should have heard him, the songs he wrote, the voice he sang with, playing the violin the way some people played the guitar. He sat on the toilet cover and played while I took a bath, and at nights he sang in my ear. He taught history at an all-boys Catholic school, and knew eighteenth-century Russia like I knew hospitals, knew more about opera than I could imagine, could sing whole parts of *Turandot* on request.

Some nights I just touched Luther Wolfe. He lay still for me, watching, while I touched his body, I had never really touched a man. With the backs of my fingers I touched his arms, his sides, his chest, his back, then I opened his legs and touched inside. I kissed every inch of him, Luther Wolfe lying there, watching with his dark, lit-up eyes. It was perfect, my fingers and lips on his skin, the light from the kitchen falling on us, illuminating us just barely, but enough. For a while he didn't ask to touch me, he knew about Vic Ponti, and let me have my fear that I couldn't be touched, that Vic Ponti had ruined me. He let me wrestle with it in the faint light of his bedroom, this squeamish, sickening thing, deep in my guts, this animal that had crept around inside of me, heavy-footed, since the day Vic Ponti first pressed himself on me.

When we finally made love, it happened slowly, Luther taking our clothes off, pushing inside of me, moving delicately, hips of silk, his eyes catching fire. His hands touched me then, I was a pale wafer, worried I might crumble, but something in me breathed, then fanned to life. Then I wanted him, wanted his touch, his scent, his sweat, his breath, his nerve, his gut, and whenever I got scared, I returned to his eyes, his dark, lit-up eyes, I knew them already. "I love you," he whispered to me. "I love you hopelessly." And I whispered back the same. "I love you hopelessly too." "You are my life, you are my blood," he said. "I love you utterly."

No one had ever told me about the power of taking a man inside of you. Certainly Bo had never said. It was only when Luther Wolfe was inside of me, my legs wrapped around his back, his mouth on mine, my hands like fevers on his skin, that I real-ized it was a serious thing, taking a man inside, it could change a life, alter the look of you. Someone should have warned me, given me something to read, pointed my way, it was too fraught with power to have gone unmentioned. Still, I didn't know, and when he was inside I realized I loved him and how much, and the emotion robbed me of breath. It was almost too much, the sense that came over me, of splitting myself open, taking him in-side, as if in doing it I'd done something else, something more permanent that I couldn't take back. I found his eyes then, and he looked down at me and whispered, "You are who God gave me," and I cried.

When he fell asleep later, I sat up and pored over him, my eyes passing over his naked, sleeping body, the light so soft and dusty on his white skin, it was heartbreaking in its faintness. It was so clear, as pure as anything, his beauty, my desire, my love, there wasn't a single blemish.

I had never known such happiness.

When I knew Luther Wolfe well enough, I put him in the bath-tub and scrubbed him, washed his hair and cut it so that it no longer fell in his eyes. And though it took some doing, I got him to go to a dentist who cleaned the nicotine stains off his teeth and polished them until they were white again. I manicured his fingernails and his toenails, and bought him a pair of boots with two-inch heels, I was self-conscious that I was taller than him. We danced in his living room then to songs he hummed in my ear, but even with the boots I was still taller. I'd catch sight of us in his mirrors, and it stabbed me to see myself bigger than Luther Wolfe, but up in his bedroom where he made love to me, Luther Wolfe was bigger than me.

Sometimes late at night before I left, we sat side by side on the only chair in his kitchen and ate big, thick slices of bread with raspberry jam slathered on top. When we were done, I'd some-times ask Luther Wolfe to sit on my lap and I'd hold on to him and breathe in the scent of his skin, burying my nose in his neck, while he did the same. "I love the way you smell," he'd say. Then we'd bite each other's cheeks like a pair of dogs.

He wasn't perfect, he was shorter than me, his walk was wig-glish, his hands fluttered and stabbed, he smoked so much his teeth were always stained, and he was so nervous he couldn't sit still half the time. I never knew about what, but there was a rest-lessness that worked on Luther Wolfe, you could see it in his feet, in the way he shoved his chair back, hurried heavy-heeled to the kitchen for a cracker or a fig. You could see it pursue him, push him from one room to the other, light up his cigarettes, turn his head back and forth quickly, make his hands stab the air. I didn't know what it was and wondered if he was running from his uncle Irwin's fingers, trying to get away from that man, or maybe he wanted a drink, but he said no, that held no appeal. He ranted about politics, and some nights he fell asleep when I wanted to talk, yet I treasured Luther Wolfe, I adored him, I lis-tened to everything he said. I cleaned him up and made him mine. I thought Luther Wolfe and I had found each other, two orphans, the same almost, meant for each other. I was sure for all the things I'd lost, I'd been given Luther Wolfe.

When Luther Wolfe said I was his wife, that we would get married and have a few children, it scared me that I loved him. As if to signify that it was wrong, I got a bladder infection that wouldn't go away, no matter how many rounds of antibiotics I took. Finally after seeing three doctors, I was told it was hyper-active, who knew why, and I had to take a drug from that mo-ment which numbed it and turned my urine orange. Bo's words came back to me in a lather, a heat, *You can never love a man,* in my ear now, pressed up against my thoughts: *If you want to be a woman, love a man. If you want to be a great woman, build a fortress around your heart.* It weighed on me that I loved Luther Wolfe and went home to him every night to lose myself in his flesh. It bothered me that I could have stayed in bed all night with him, Luther's breath close to mine, that I could possibly have passed a lifetime in this way. I was relieved I had to go to the hospital every day, that people needed me, I could have stayed all day and washed and ironed Luther Wolfe's shirts, could have fetched his coffee, bathed him, waited by his side, listened to his voice, watched him all day. It was awful, the feeling, where did it come from? It shamed me, I had never once thought of myself in this way, Bo would have been appalled, I knew. There was no one to ask, Where did this feeling come from?, it was so powerful it drove me so I had to run from it.

I finally went to the library and looked up women, this time rifling through the card catalog wanting to know if it was just in me, this obsession, or was it in women. I went back in history as far as the written word went and shuddered in the silence, thousands of years of silence, not a word from a woman, only Sappho somewhere in 600 B.C., and what did she write but love poetry? There were women before Christ, women written by men, filled in by men, but they were there: Penelope, who spent a whole epic poem waiting for her husband, Odysseus, to return, and Queen Dido, who fell hopelessly in love with Aeneas, who, once having seduced her, realized he had lands to conquer and men to kill, and left her brokenhearted, whereupon she killed herself with a sword. And Antigone, who defied her uncle by performing funeral rites for her brother, and after being walled in, killed herself. My heart stopped when I saw myself digging up my brother's casket, stealing his ashes, and placing them on an altar.

I went on, through the centuries, hundreds of years, no word from women, the voices lost to earthen walls, to vaulted ceilings, to cloistered halls, not a trace, the pages they wrote eaten away by the moths and worms, thrown out, most of them, with rotted food and ragged clothes. I feared what they might have said, what they had written from worlds shrunken, from sights shortened, from bodies confined by rooms, by the needy fingers of children, their thoughts contained in a circle that began and ended with the imposed knowledge of their secondness. I was almost relieved not to hear them, they might have been an embarrassment.

Eventually they slowly began to speak, to write, to be heard. I collected their books on a cart and sat down at a long, wide table, unoccupied except for me. I opened them randomly, reading whatever stood in front of me, doing so rapidly, as if I were starving and could not eat fast enough. I read about women, about men and women, about romance and children, about women in literature, women in cinema, women writers, women poets, women scientists, women's bodies, women's minds, women's women, until a hand came out of the blankness and touched my shoulder and a voice said, "The library is closed." I shut whatever book I was reading, slipped into my coat, and walked out of the library, down the stone steps, walked the ten blocks back to work, and what I remembered, what stood out in my mind from all the rest, was a sentence that Victor Hugo's mistress Juliette Drouet wrote him, one of the countless sentences Juliette Drouet wrote in the seventeen thousand letters she sent Victor Hugo: *I want you to tear your clothes as much as possible, and I want to mend and clean them all myself.*

Almost a century separated me and Juliette Drouet. I had lived through the women's movement, I'd heard about the oppression of women, had seen it mapped out, had felt it on my own skin when I was married to Vic Ponti. As a girl I had not been kept in the house, taught to sew and cook, to look forward to marriage and children, was never once pushed in this direction, never thought of these things, didn't cook, didn't sew, thought little of children, almost nothing of marriage, yet I understood Juliette Drouet perfectly, could have written Luther Wolfe a sentence like that, could have written him seventeen thousand letters. The difference was, I dared not.

I hated this feeling, loathed it, that I could have written Luther Wolfe seventeen thousand letters, that I could have written, *I want you to tear your clothes as much as possible, and I want to mend and clean them all myself.* I wanted to run, I wanted not to feel so much, I wanted not to know that my heart and mind pulled towards him, like a tree bent under an implacable wind. It was terrible, I hated the intrusion, the possession, but there was Luther Wolfe, warm and loving, with those dark, lit-up eyes. Perhaps Bo knew this of me, perhaps that is why she had told me, "If you want to be a woman, love a man. If you want to be a great woman, build a fortress around your heart."

In the dark of Zellie's bedroom, I worried for the first time that greatness would never come now, that either it was gone from me forever because I had loved a man, or because I had loved a man there was no room for it to appear. What if I renounced my love, just gave it up, left Luther Wolfe, forgot him, and bit by bit built a fortress around my heart? I wondered.

I hadn't known it until now, but I wanted to be great.

What will I do? I had once asked Bo, pale and warm, shaky in my fifteen years, my knees buckling in the living room, Bo's hand on my arm, her breath on my face. You'll change the course of history, she had said.

Change the course of history.

The idea, so slippery, hung on the edges of my consciousness, a bastard thought, I could barely claim as my own. Only a madwoman would tell her daughter that, I thought, yet I felt pulled in the other direction, pulled to a back room in my consciousness, where I allowed myself to imagine changing the course of history. I thought then of great people, of greatness, of attaining it, rising to it, and suddenly I felt the sacrifice, much had to be sacrificed, loving a man was but one thing. It seemed it would be endless, the sacrifice. The path appeared in my mind, not as an image, but as a feeling, claustrophobic, it was so narrow, so difficult to navigate. But even so, great like what? Great like Napoleon? What great deeds? Great like conquering nations? I felt angry at Bo for not having left me with the slightest clue. Great like what, Bo? *Great like what?*

I had never felt the present so surely, heard its breath now, its heartbeat, as if greatness were sitting next to me, waiting, a sense that it wasn't in the future anymore, but was now, it had waited long enough. But there was Luther Wolfe, having fallen asleep at my side before I went home to Zellie. He was a beautiful sleeper, on his back, his hands near his face, his fingers curled faintly, his head turned slightly.

If Zellie was envious she never said, but she got worse, as if to punish me for having Luther Wolfe, and one day in the middle of winter, she collapsed on the street, and I had to put her in a cab and take her back to the rehab center. While the doctor examined her, I discovered that she had stopped doing the exercises, she was so lost now without Frank, without me, now that I had two jobs and Luther Wolfe, she'd stopped doing everything that was necessary, eating even, and there were marks again on her body, knife marks on the undersides of her arms, which the doctor cleaned and bandaged.

While the nurses settled Zellie in her room, the doctor pulled me aside and told me that he thought she'd need to stay for at least six months, maybe a year, her spine needed that much attention. She needed psychiatric care also, he said, an expense barely covered by Medicaid, which meant I would have to come up with a great deal of money. It wasn't enough to help her home from work every night, to help her out of her braces, to make sure I was there in the morning to help her into her braces. It wasn't enough, she needed more.

I walked down to her room and sat in the chair next to her bed and watched her sleep, knowing as I sat watching her that I was losing money, money I was going to need to pay for the psychiatrist. I touched her face with the tips of my fingers. She was a beautiful woman, her skin radiant, like Bo's, I thought, it was a shame. I envisioned Bo making that still, marveling over her own cleverness, building it piece by piece until there it stood in all of its gray metal splendor, spitting and breathing, gathering itself for the moment it would explode and be replaced by two more that would blow up and ruin one girl's life and chances, to say nothing of mine.

I stayed most of the night with her, rubbing her back and her legs until my hands were worn out, knowing that I would never be released from this duty, that my hands would always know the feel of her flesh, the shape of her bones, until one of us finally gave up and died.

When I went to Luther's, I paced back and forth in his living room, threw my hands up and down. How could this be fair, I said, her life on top of mine, her breath, my breath, was it fair, hadn't I lost enough? When would it stop, the loss, all the loss, how was it fair to take so much from a person? I loved her, but it had been years, back and forth, back and forth, my whole life seen on a worn carpet, a path worn from my room to hers. Was it wrong to want to live, to want my own life, to be free of her collapsing spine, her self-mutilations, her endless heartbreak, hadn't I lost enough, hadn't I been through enough hell, what was this?

I stopped then and sought Luther Wolfe's arms. It didn't seem possible, but he opened them reluctantly and then held me sparingly, his embrace stingy, and when I pulled back to look in his eyes, I was shocked—I found nothing. I had fallen from them entirely, had become nothing in a moment's time. What had I done, what had he seen? What had happened? He saw through me? saw past me? the light fell badly on me? my face contorted in ugliness? It was maddening to know the course of one's life could be altered by a fact so illusive. I looked fat? weak? I was too naked in telling him my story? What displeased him? But he wouldn't say, he wouldn't agree that anything had displeased him, but I knew it had.

20

She stopped speaking and rose up. She went to the small metal sink next to the vinyl chair in the smoking lounge and splashed water on her face.

So what happened? he said.

She dried her face with a few paper towels and then threw them in the trash.

It was over, she said.

What do you mean, "over"?

She turned to him.

It was over.

How could it be over?

It was, she said.

He took his feet down from the window ledge.

It couldn't have just been over, he said. You must have said something. You must have talked about it. You must have done something.

She leaned her hip against the metal sink and pushed her fingers through her hair.

Yes, she said, but even so it was over.

What happened?

The life drained from her face.

Please, he said, you must tell me.

He understood then why he wanted to know—he wanted to know how other men severed their women from them.

But isn't it your turn? she said. She forced herself to smile.

No, you must tell me the rest of the Luther Wolfe story, he said. Then I will tell you.

He pulled gently on her wrist, and she sat back down in the red vinyl chair.

Why did you hate the feeling of being possessed by Luther Wolfe? he asked her quietly. He was curious about this fact. He had always assumed that women were this way, that they *were* possessions, as if they had no choice in the matter. He had thought they enjoyed it as much as they enjoyed breathing, but she'd said she hated it. He was glad she'd said it. It was something he understood completely.

Why did you hate it? he said again. He watched her carefully, aware almost for the first time that she had a world all of her own.

It was too much, she said.

Too much what? he wanted to know.

Feminine, she said.

She smiled, and he suddenly felt himself allied with her, as if deep down they were the same. His own guilt lifted for a moment, and the images that passed through his mind ceased to disturb him—the broken dishes, the overturned table, the creams and photographs smashing on the floor. There could be too much feminine, he thought. She had even said so.

Tell me what happened next, he said.

All right, she said, but I will not tell the details. The corners of her mouth turned down, and he saw it again, the sadness, as if she'd laid husbands to rest, watched whole crops fail, buried stillborn babies in small pine coffins.

What will you tell, then?

The sense of it. That is all.

He touched his fingers to the back of her hand.

All right, he said.

21

The nights passed awkwardly between us, Luther Wolfe wasn't the same. Every time I asked him what had happened, he said he didn't want to talk about it, he said it nicely at first, but I picked away at it, I was desperate for his liquid brown eyes, for his breath in my ear. But he was absent from his eyes, his breath never touched my ear, his voice turned harsh, lacerating, hoarse with anger, this man who had once talked to me about everything. I didn't understand and longed to, I coveted understanding like I had never coveted anything, I pressed him over and over, what was it? But the more deeply I pressed, the meaner he got, until I sensed that whatever worked on Luther Wolfe, whatever pushed him from room to room, was behind his silence, a beehive he didn't want touched. If I poked too hard, I sensed something would come flying out, but somehow, with no words, he convinced me to tiptoe around it, to leave it alone altogether.

When I looked into his eyes, I found nothing but cold distance. The future was gone, no mention of it, the talks of a trip here or there, glaringly absent now, as if such pleasures had never been mentioned. I had no hold anymore, he had slipped away, my hands ached from reaching, from trying to grasp, my mind froze in a panic, uncertain as to how to be, calculating every word, every move, self-consciousness stiffening me like arthritis. My stories no longer meant anything to him, what I'd said to make him laugh brought out only the stringiest of laughs, as if manufactured to keep me from embarrassment.

I got mixed up with whatever drove Luther Wolfe from room to room. I spoke and he lit cigarettes, raced away. My flesh lost all appeal, his, he took away. I was in pain I would have traded for physical pain, for severed limbs, gashed eyes. I went around all day, gored, my thoughts confined to this, stuck, there is no way to reproduce the agony of it, the length of it, the hours and hours and hours of it. I struggled in the hospital to put it aside, to concentrate on the patients, but I could barely manage it. I posed instead and came to loathe who I was, this servile, huddled thing, disfigured inside.

I learned to quiet myself in Luther Wolfe's presence, it was the only way to keep him in the room with me. It became a game, to quiet myself until I was so silenced and stilled that whatever drove Luther Wolfe from room to room was momentarily lulled and he was able to stop for a few minutes. It was as if a hummingbird had come to rest next to me, and I could barely breathe lest I would scare him off, this man who used to spend whole evenings in bed with his arms around me.

I took photographs of Luther Wolfe in the morning when he was asleep, with a box camera he had showed me how to use. He was always naked, always beautiful, his strong body tangled in the white sheets. I took hundreds of photographs of him, he had no idea, and kept them in my locker at the hospital.

The weeks turned into months, and one night Luther Wolfe met me at my apartment and told me he couldn't go on any longer. I was picking him apart, he said. His nerves were in shreds. It was late, after midnight, and whatever drove him from room to room was upon him fully, he could hardly sit still, he was strangled for air, his eyes jerked from my face to the door, this short little man with the nervous, stabbing hands. He wasn't ready to make a commitment, he'd never once made one, he couldn't, he didn't know how. It ruined me, these words, but still I tried to keep him there, I reminded him of what we had, but it was too late, he said. He was gone from me, and though I tried to press him to me, his will won out, and finally when it was unbearable for him, he ran out of my apartment.

I pursued him through the streets, desperate to know what had taken him away, and ended up outside his locked door, banging my fist against the cold, chipped wood, crying, "It's me, Luther. Why are you doing this?" And he stood on the other side crying, "You have to go away. Go away, Hemy. You have to go away." "You said I was who God gave you," I said. "I know," he said. "I'm sorry." "I love you, Luther. I miss you," I said. "I love you too, and I miss you too, but it can't be," he said. This went on for fifteen minutes and might have gone on longer had he not opened the door a crack and said through bared teeth, "If you don't go away, Hemy, I'm going to call the police."

I felt something rise out of me, a thin plume of smoke, vital it seemed, like the smoke of a burning soul, and suddenly I saw myself beating my fists against the door of the man I'd first met— the short man with the stained brown teeth and the dark, greasy hair, who had so repulsed me that the possibility of ever kissing him, much less making love to him, had been so completely, utterly out of the question—and I was so horrified, I vanished from his doorstep.

M O U N T A I N S

22

She stopped speaking and rested her head against the back of the red vinyl chair. The air was getting cooler, more fragrant. The desert of Nevada was giving way to the mountains of northern California. The land sped by, half brown, half green, the trees sturdy, the hills promising mountains.

That was very sad, he said.

He watched her pale white throat as she swallowed.

The idea of it made him uncomfortable. He hated to admit it, but he understood Luther Wolfe. He lit a cigarette and watched the way the blue-gray smoke made for the open window—wildly, almost ecstatically.

What do you think changed Luther Wolfe's feelings? he asked.

He saw that I was not perfect, she said.

But it was nothing, he said. You were upset.

He was afraid, she answered.

Of what? he asked. Of women?

She looked at him. Perhaps, she said. But I was not whole, either.

She paused, then sighed.

I was not a great woman, she said.

He wouldn't have feared you had you been a great woman?

How could I know? she said.

It impressed him that she did not lay the blame entirely at Luther Wolfe's feet, that she shouldered some of it herself.

Could you ever love like that again?

No, never, she said. One cannot and remain whole.

He didn't know why, but this relieved him.

He sensed again that she was not the girl Hemy Lourde, the

one who'd loved Luther Wolfe, that she was in fact quite different now. He now imagined that her living as a man was a complete obliteration, that all the breaks she'd had before were small ones, combining to make this great, momentous one. The one which had truly obliterated her.

His mind confused again when he saw himself straining to understand her. What had she to do with him, goddamnit?

He reached over and took her hand. When she held still, he felt better. He'd almost lost her, telling her he was Oscar Lourde.

It's your turn now, she said, without opening her eyes.

Let's go back to your room, he said. He wanted to be back in her room, to assure himself that she was not lost to him.

She turned to him and opened her eyes.

Tell me first, she said.

He found that he could not tell her the truth, not then. What he ended up telling her was not exactly a lie, but it wasn't the truth, either: he told her that his mother was dying of lung cancer. She was always calling him, five, ten times a day, telling him this was wrong, that was wrong, could he bring her this, could he bring her that. It got to be too much, and he finally asked his sister to come from Ohio to watch her for a while.

When he finished, she said, You're lying. But then she smiled, as if she found it amusing.

Why wouldn't I tell you the truth? he said, in imitation of her.

I don't mind, she said. Someone's lie is as revealing as their truth.

Like living as a man? he said.

Yes, she said. She smiled, then turned and looked out the window, the smile fading slowly from her mouth.

When they were back in her room, she went into the small bathroom to wash her face, and he stretched out on her bed, as if to reclaim his territory. In the quiet, he thought of the similarities between her story and the story he'd told her when he was pretending to be Oscar Lourde: he'd thrown a punch to prove he was Oscar Lourde, and the decisive moment between her and Luther Wolfe came when Luther Wolfe threw a karate punch across his coffee table. And then there was the matter of the way she had first touched Luther Wolfe—exactly the same way she had touched him the night before. What was he supposed to think?

When she came out of the small bathroom, she kicked off her sandals and sat down on the bed, her back against the wall. He watched as she opened her compact mirror and applied red lipstick to her mouth. Then she wiped it off, and with a lighter touch applied it again. When she put the lipstick away and turned to him, there was something in her eyes he hadn't seen before, something fierce, almost wolfish.

Am I a woman? she asked him.

Of course, he said.

I wonder sometimes. It's ridiculous, being a woman. The things you want men to say, the things you care about, some of the things you want. I swear to you they are ridiculous.

Like what? he asked.

She smiled and shook her head no. She was not going to say.

Instead she took his hand and began to kiss it, then kissed his wrist, his forearm, the hollow of his elbow, kissed all the way up his arm, to his shoulder. At first he didn't understand what she was doing, until he saw all the lipstick traces. There was a trail of them, and he thought of wiping them off, but he liked them there.

He leaned close to her then and kissed her deeply on the mouth. When he pulled back to look at her, she smiled, her lips faintly red from the lipstick. He pushed his thumb into her mouth to see what she would do, and she sucked on it, her eyes never leaving his. The image of her lips around his thumb, the back of his hand stained with her red lip marks, made him hard. When she reached down and touched between his legs, he found her mouth again. She opened hers as far as she could, and after a moment he surrendered to her and opened his too. He had never kissed in this way, with fully opened mouths. Her passion had the pull of something unseen and savage, and he pushed her backwards, crawling on top of her, as if to gain control.

What are we now? he whispered. A man and a woman on a train?

A mixed-up man and a ridiculous woman on a train, she said, smiling.

He laughed.

I'm the mixed-up man?

Aren't you? she said.

Yes, I suppose I am, he said.

But he hated to think of it.

Why are you the ridiculous woman?

Because I am in this room kissing you, and you are a mixed-up man, she said.

He laughed again and pressed his nose into the smooth whiteness of her neck and kissed her with an open mouth. He felt her melt, like Luther Wolfe must have. When he kissed her neck again, she folded into him.

Then something went cold inside of him—the idea that he was holding on to some bored housewife from New Jersey who had thought through the telling of her story so well, she had even left her identity back in the dresser drawer of her suburban bedroom. The idea repelled him. He would have preferred her to be a recently released mental patient.

He pulled away and lay quietly next to her.

What's wrong? she said. She turned on her side, her green eyes suddenly penetrating.

Nothing, he said.

He put his hands behind his head and imagined going to Morrisville to ask the townspeople if there had ever been a Hemy Lourde who lived there, a Lourde family. Then the hospital in Syracuse to find out if a woman named Hemy Lourde had ever worked there. It wasn't a completely elusive truth. There were things he could check if it ever came to that.

He looked at her, at her pale forehead, her faintly red lips. He was barely touching her, but it seemed he could feel her heart beating as if it were his own. He didn't want to break the silence, but the longer he lay there the more the questions burned. He had a lot of them, he realized, and he could feel the time falling away, bringing them closer to the end. And he had not begun to understand.

He pulled a cigarette from his shirt pocket and lit it. What happened after you left Luther Wolfe? he asked.

She looked at him, then lay back down and closed her eyes. Her voice came again and he was grateful.

23

I went to Zellie and told her Luther Wolfe had broken up with me. She opened her arms, and I fell into her lap. I cried into the folds of her dress, my forehead pressed against the cold, hard metal of her leg brace, Zellie patting the back of my head, glad she wasn't alone any longer. She knew every inch of the path, every step of the way—Luther, Frank, Frank, Luther, they were indivisible now. She had seen it coming, she said, it was no surprise, Luther Wolfe wasn't who he said he was. Who was he? I said, and as quietly as she could she said, "He was air."

I lay up in my apartment, holding on to the mattress, hands like knobs, words running through my mind, "Luther Wolfe left you, he left you, he didn't love you, it's over, he's never coming back," followed shortly by a harried refrain of "Maybe he'll come back, you never know these things, he could come back," yet in all that time Luther Wolfe never called, not even once. That weighed heavy on me.

For two weeks I sat in the emptiness. I sat with my back up against the headboard of Zellie's bed, my knees pulled to my chest, wondering how I had come up so empty-handed. I hardly ate. I wouldn't have noticed the day turning to night had I not needed to visit Zellie. And when I came home I sat on the bed with my back against the headboard, and when sleep came, if it did, I just lay down on my side and pulled a coat over me. I thought often of those pills Gussy Keys had given me in the hospital, wished I'd had some, but there was nothing. But even so, the trouble with my bladder vanished as if Luther Wolfe or something about him had triggered it, as if it had been a sign or a warning, and now that he was gone from me, I no longer had to take the pills that turned my urine orange.

My mind traveled slowly and laboriously through swollen, elephantine thoughts, down a path worn bare with memories of Luther Wolfe, as if there had been no greater, where I asked questions over and over, what had happened, why did he leave, answering them variously, he was afraid, something was wrong that I didn't know, it was me, I shouldn't have gotten upset about Zellie, the answers changing over the hours, sometimes combining, sometimes mutating, stuffed for a short time into the question's raw wound, a brief anodyne, until it began again. There seemed to be no stopping it, the grief came up in gusts, nothing to keep me upright but the headboard behind my back, I was grateful it was there. There were no answers, just like there was no comfort, you had to know that and press on. To what, there was no saying. I'd opened my chest to Luther Wolfe, just opened it the way I would open a door and let someone in. It was trained to Luther Wolfe now, all that red, pink skin, delicate as paper, trained to Luther Wolfe, all of it bloated now out of all shape, heart, lungs, guts, running together.

I should have listened to Bo. I should have built a fortress around my heart. There hadn't been a wall, not a fence, not so much as a stone.

The worst was at night when there was no place to go, no one to talk to, when I sat up in my apartment and remembered Luther Wolfe, remembered how he smelled, how he sounded, how he tasted. And when the phone rang, it was never Luther Wolfe, it was someone calling about the phone bill, the electric bill, the rent. They were all due, but the money sat on the dresser, I couldn't bring myself to give it away.

Weeks went by in this way, with me lying in Zellie's bed, the phone ringing all the time. I had to answer it, it could have been Luther Wolfe, but it was never Luther Wolfe, it was AT&T or LIL Electric or the landlord, they wanted their money. But the money never moved, I never touched it, it sat on top of the dresser, perfectly still.

Then an image came into my mind that plagued me at nights

when I tried to sleep. Ushered in by the silence, it hung in my mind, strong, offending, finally riveting, I couldn't stop searching it, marveling over its strangeness, amazed that it had appeared at all. It was an image of me superimposed on Luther Wolfe, although I could not see through myself. I was in front of him, my back pressed against his chest, both of us upright, our arms out straight, slightly apart from our bodies, where we were joined at the wrists. We shared the same veins, our arms merged at the wrists, the veins which joined us popped in such throbbing, pulsing relief that every vein, every capillary was visible, thick and swollen, grotesque even. It was unsettling, but what was worse was the night my neck turned in the image and I sank my teeth into Luther's Wolfe's neck and began to suck his blood. I felt an implacable hunger, a devouring need for his life, for his blood; his absence had carved a hole in my guts which hungered, which starved, which needed and wanted. I was a vampire, sucking at Luther Wolfe's blood. For days, the image burned in my mind; while I sat still and alone on Zellie's bed, the table next to me strewn with desiccating plates of food, I pored over this image, strangely attracted to it, repulsed at the same time by my own horrible, devouring need, by my teeth sunk deep into Luther Wolfe's neck.

No wonder he left me.

Then one night I saw something that I had not seen before— through the cuts in my wrists where we were joined, it was I who poured my blood out to Luther Wolfe. I had given Luther Wolfe all my blood, he had it all, and I was lifeless without it—that's why I had none. I was struck by this, by the fact that I had so easily, without thought, opened my veins to Luther Wolfe.

When the phone and electricity were shut off, a man from a collection agency turned up and started banging on my door. When I couldn't stand it anymore, the banging on the door, the dark nights, the knowledge that I had given Luther Wolfe my life's blood, I threw Zellie's clothes and mine into Lourde's old green trunk and dragged it nearly fifteen blocks to the rehab place, over grass and sidewalk, across streets, the scrape irritating, my breathing loud and uncontrolled, like an ape's, I thought, the night above me in a black, cold starless sky.

When I got to the rehab center, I was sweating and crying, my hands frozen from the March cold. "I've come to see my sister," I said, expecting at least some consideration, I'd dragged the trunk a long way, but the old security guard didn't care, he told me it was past visiting hours, I couldn't see her. He turned back to the small black-and-white television he was watching, as if I hardly mattered, just a crying, sweating woman, no more, and I shoved past him, dragging the trunk after me, oblivious of his hoarse voice as he yelled for me to stop, I had no right, threatening me with a pack of security guards.

I went straight to Zellie's room and shook her awake.

"Get up," I said. "We're leaving."

"What do you mean, we're leaving?"

"We're getting the hell out of here," I said. "There's nothing here for us. We should have left a long time ago."

"What are you talking about?"

"We're going to New York," I said. "There's better luck there."

"How can you say that? Bo's mother died in prison there."

"Bo was born there," I said.

I went over to her dresser and started pulling her clothes out of the drawers and putting them into the trunk.

"What about my rehab?" she said.

"New York has a lot of rehab places."

"This is too soon," she said. "It's midnight, what about our apartment, you can't just leave it, and all the stuff, and—"

"We have to leave now," I said loudly. "The rent's due, they shut off the phone and the electric, and a man bangs on the door every day. I've got the money in my pocket, Zellie. If I pay them, we'll never get out of here."

"Is it because of Luther Wolfe?" she said.

I closed my eyes briefly against the pain, it flared up like a flame and scorched my heart, and when I opened them I said, "I don't want to breathe another breath in the same town as Luther Wolfe."

There was such fears in her eyes, but she said, "All right," she knew I meant it. She pulled her braces out from under the bed, and in the silence I helped her put them on, neither of us speaking, the two of us knowing without having to say a word that our lives, for reasons we didn't understand, were made up of violent beginnings and endings. While she packed the rest of her clothes, I went out into the hallway and found her wheelchair. I couldn't wait to push it, to push Zellie and me out of this town forever, it held nothing but hell.

I pushed her down the hallway, the trunk balanced on the arms of the wheelchair, my breath ragged in my own ear, my heart beating hard, like a slamming fist. When a trio of security guards caught up to us and told me that I could not take this patient out, I had no right, I did not stop, I did not speak, I just pushed the wheelchair, it had never been so clear to me what had to be done. And when they physically barred our exit at the front doors, I looked at them and opened my mouth and my voice slid out: "This is my sister. I am the only person she has. We lost our family in a bombing. A table leg impaled her, and you see she is crippled. I am leaving this town, and I will not leave her behind."

Patients and nurses had gathered in the hallway and now gaped at us. The security guards stood frozen, looking from one another to me, to the gathering of nurses and patients, waiting for someone to say something, to decide what should be done about me. One of them finally turned to Zellie and asked her, "Do you want to leave?" and when she said, "Yes, I must," he sighed, as if this were simply beyond his reserves, and then finally, who knew why, he opened one of the glass doors and stepped aside, and I wheeled Zellie out. I pushed her down the sidewalk in silence, and when she finally spoke it was to say, "You're crazy," and I said, "I know. I had forgotten until now."

I wheeled her to the Amtrak train station, all breath and bone, pumping down the street like a machine, I had a purpose, something I could focus on, I could have pushed her to New York. When we got on the train it was past two o'clock in the morning, and while Zellie slept with her head in my lap, I counted the money I had in my pocket, trying to imagine if it was enough. I didn't know, I hoped it was, and put it away and sat in the darkness of the train, feeling the thrill of running away. I relished the idea of Luther Wolfe calling on the phone only to discover it had been disconnected, or stopping by the apartment to find I had been evicted, my furniture strewn all over the lawn. I imagined his shock over and over again, it gave me such pleasure.

I pressed my forehead against the window and slid down in my seat, my eyes fierce as they hooked on the dark waters of the Hudson River. A spitting, clawing anger thundered up from my gut and blazed in my throat now, the old voice coming back, the voice of a pit-bulled prick, Fuck you, I've had enough, get the hell out of my way.

It was morning when we emerged from Penn Station, a bright, sunny morning, the sky filled with buildings that offered an abundance, an almost ridiculous abundance, a sense of endlessness that was exhilarating. There were no memories here other than Bo's, no real history, Luther Wolfe had not breathed here, it was perfect. The past lay behind us, I thought, a ruin.

While Zellie sat at a booth in a diner finishing her breakfast, I went to the pay phone near the door and looked up rehab centers in a thick phone book that hung from a wire. There were six that I thought might be good, and with Lourde's trunk balanced on the arms of Zellie's wheelchair, I pushed her from one to the other until she settled on a small beautiful place called Our Lady of the Immaculate Heart Rehabilitation Center, located on a quiet side street in Little Italy. She liked the look of the nuns in their black habits, their faces stark and pale inside their hoods, their hands thin and gentle, on the verge of prayer. She loved her room especially, the walls were white, the blanket on her bed navy blue with white trim; the window faced a courtyard with a small fountain, the sky was unobscured, the light beautiful for painting.

The nuns let me stay with her in her room that first night, the two of us huddling in the clean and quiet, watching with amazement as the habited nuns passed our door, their feet barely making a sound. I was especially struck by the piety in their posture, always inclined towards God, as if every movement were a prayer, I had no piety inside.

We fell asleep to the sound of their rosary and then awoke in the morning in a pool of sunlight.

*   *   *

I left Zellie after breakfast, when they took her for physical therapy, and went to look for an apartment nearby. I couldn't afford much, but I found a studio two blocks away from Our Lady of the Immaculate Heart, a studio with wooden floors and a tin ceiling that went up over fourteen feet. The windows were tall and French and faced Elizabeth Street; the room had once been a drawing room, the elegance still there, only faded, but I could feel it as if it had veins that still coursed beneath the layers and layers of paint. At the back was a small, old-fashioned bathroom and kitchen with old, stained, round-edged porcelain and fat, rounded knobs. Below me was an Italian restaurant named Filomena's, and next door lived a drag queen named Baby Faith, who wore wigs and red high heels and makeup, I had never seen anything like him. On the other side was a stoop-shouldered old woman named Fatima who listened incessantly to opera, Puccini mainly, and above us, two families lived, one of them Puerto Rican, the other Italian.

For two weeks I sat in the emptiness, I had no furniture, and read books I'd taken from the library, books on women—*Women's Writing, The Second Sex, The Vindication of the Rights of Women, The Female Eunuch*—I wanted to know what kind of thing I was, of what type, of what order. I read them near the windows where I could see the sky and no one could see me. When I was done, I lay there for days, the books standing around me like walls, while a conception of woman formed in my mind; she rose from the mud of my imagination, a most unfortunate being, a being called the weaker sex, second, the other, given the lower attributes, the corporeal, sensible, natural, while attributed to men were the spiritual, the intelligible, the transcendental. She was a mirror held up for men so that they might see themselves, she was a hole, the unsymbolizable residue, excluded from the social contract, cast out, used as an object of exchange, the dark continent, the defective man, castrated, castrating, a being with no subjectivity of her own. A creature finally silenced and ground into the dust.

I could just see women working in their kitchens, children ringing them like skirts, bent over sickbeds, wiping and washing, serving, while men sat in the kitchens, stood in doorframes, watched and thought, She was born woman, poor thing, she's not quite human.

An image formed in my mind of woman as a swampy vessel, unthinkingly attached to a biology, which forced her to look for a man, insert a man, and finally give birth to a man's child, as if there was only this purpose, to become a mother.

It was a history of slavery I read, I had never realized the extent of it. I felt it suddenly, the words I read echoed my existence, I had never known it quite before, but the words now intervened to give voice to that which had gone unspoken. It was true, I felt second, I felt every bit of it, the lesser, the lower, the left out.

When one woman wrote, "We lack our subject, our verb, our predicates: our elementary sentence, our basic rhythm, our morphological identity, our generic incarnation, our genealogy," I understood her exactly.

I looked around my apartment, at the barren white walls, at the emptiness, at myself lying alone on the mattress, books piled up around me, and I thought: I am a woman who loved a man, my sacrifice so predictable, it was nothing, I have no lover, no money, no job, no education. Even so, I didn't want to be second, underneath, without a voice. I wanted out, I wanted something else, something more, and then I had a thought that stopped my breath: I wanted the fate Bo had told me was mine, the one that would be great, the one that would change the course of history.

But suddenly I was afraid that I had ruined my fate, I imagined that fate had a particular time, a particular rhythm. I feared that it had hovered above my life, waiting for the perfect moment, and when that moment had come, I was in Luther Wolfe's arms, and it had no choice but to go elsewhere.

I lay blinking in the darkness. I hadn't listened to Bo, she had told me: "If you want to be a woman, love a man. If you want to be a great woman, build a fortress around your heart." I was filled with remorse to imagine that I had given up greatness for Luther Wolfe, that I wouldn't change the course of anything, much less history, because I'd loved Luther Wolfe. I lost my breath and lay there panting. Luther Wolfe was nothing. I had given my life for nothing.

There was barely light in the room when I sat up and arranged myself cross-legged on the mattress Baby Faith lent me, the way Bo had, and closed my eyes. For an hour I sat like that and breathed in and out, asking to know if there was still a fate for me or not, prayed to know what I could do to get it back if it had left, pledged myself to it as if it were a groom. I wanted to go forward wrapped in a great fate. I wanted to be a great woman.

I wanted to change the course of history.

When it didn't seem enough to sit cross-legged on the bed, I stretched myself out on the cool wooden floor, face down, my arms extended out crosslike, the way Bo had done long ago, and swore on a whispered breath that I would do nothing but seek my fate. I offered up my heart then, cut by Luther Wolfe, and vowed to build a fortress around it.

I rose from the floor, something more needed to be done, a rite performed, a sacrifice made, and in the early morning light I stood in front of the bathroom mirror and cut my hair to an inch of my scalp. I threw away all my dresses, and from that moment on, I wore nothing but dark pants and jackets, black boots, as if I were in mourning, and when I finally took a job, I made one last sacrifice. I gave up my name. I said it was Oscar Lourde.

No one at the job asked me specifically about my name, this was not a place that cared about names. It was a place I could walk in, could move through easily, it didn't require much of me, Bellevue was its name. I didn't need to say much, sometimes nothing at all, all I had to do was wash people, wash old men and old women. They put them in a line outside the showers, in wheelchairs, dressed in robes, their special soaps in small plastic buckets on their armrests. I worked in a large marbled shower, with a wooden seat where the old people sat, one after the other. I washed them, their arms, their legs, their backs and faces, their hair, if they had any. I rinsed them carefully with a hose, and then slowly dried them off, starting at their feet and working my way up their baggy skin. I washed twenty of them a day, sometimes twenty-five. I knew them by their hammer toes, by their gnarled hands, by the fleshy hang of their buttocks, the curve of their legs, but mostly by their eyes, sunken and fierce like two spits of fire.

At night I visited Zellie at the rehab center, in her room, that's where she was happiest. I brought her paints and canvases, brushes and posters of Frida Kahlo's work, which she hung on her walls. All day long she painted, not her own wounds anymore, but the others' wounds, they sat for hours, the patients baring their maimed flesh for Zellie to paint. Once, she painted me standing against her wall, my hair dark and short, dressed in a black suit, the faint outline of a white dress beneath it, the bare suggestion of white shoes beneath the black boots.

When I went home at night, I tried not to imagine Luther Wolfe next to me, but often I felt his skin on mine, heard his voice in my ear, saw his dark eyes, his full, wanting mouth, smelled the skin on his neck, heard us laughing. I saw our life through a window I could neither break nor touch. And every night I gave him up, every night I lay face down on the cool wooden floor, like Bo had, and gave him up. Again and again, I gave him up, Here, take him, he's yours, and I asked for my fate instead. Please, I said.

I looked for it every day, looked for signs, something, any change, small or otherwise, but two years passed without the slightest movement. I walked through the streets of New York, through SoHo and the West Village, sometimes to the Upper East Side, where Bo and her mother, Georgia, had lived in a Park Avenue apartment. There were bookstores I frequented, cafes where I sat and drank hot cocoa and read books. I went out to restaurants and to the movies late at night, I picked up my camera and took photographs of the old people in the showers, of Zellie's friends at Our Lady of the Immaculate Heart, and developed them in a rented darkroom.

Even so, the two years passed in the deepest, most profound silence. I hardly said a word, except to Zellie and to Baby Faith, occasionally to Fatima, the woman who listened to opera, I kept myself so quiet. It seemed nothing much happened, until I gradually began to notice how I could see that things were not often as they appeared, like the Korean man who ran the market down the block. He always screamed at his small, harried wife, and she hopped on his every word, her shoulders hunched forward in defeat, her lips tightened. He was cruel, but what was less obvious was that she had helped him to it.

*   *   *

Then, one hot August night, Baby Faith knocked on my door, he wanted to introduce me to a man named Jack Tortorre, a young man who came by on the weekends to visit the Italian family upstairs. I'd seen Jack Tortorre before, we'd passed on the stairs, but I had thought nothing of him, I still thought of Luther Wolfe. He had dark, tightly curled hair and liquid black eyes. He was medium height and was lean and agile, with muscled arms beautifully marked with blue, touchable veins. He wore a pair of loose-fitting black corduroy pants and a blousy white shirt, and black boots. He was an actor, Baby Faith said, he'd just finished a Hollywood movie, not the lead part, but a good part, a part that put him next to Robert De Niro or Al Pacino, I couldn't remember which. It was awkward, Baby Faith didn't know I'd made a vow, that the last thing I was looking for was a man, but it was the two of them who invited me to walk down to the Feast of San Gennaro, so I agreed.

Jack Tortorre had a presence, I felt it almost immediately, an electricity ran through him that didn't run through everybody. It made his gestures precise, his movements fluid, it lit his eyes and kept his mouth wet. You sensed he'd been chosen; for what, you didn't know, but you felt inclined to follow him, as if he would end up in thrilling places. I was surprised he showed me as much interest as he did, I had such short hair and wore such dark clothes, I told him my name was Oscar. I imagined he needed an Italian woman with dark hair and dark eyes, who wore dresses that flowed to her ankles, and high-heeled sandals, red perhaps.

The three of us, Baby Faith, Jack Tortorre, and I, walked through the crowds and ate sausages and drank red wine, we even rode the Ferris wheel. I was grateful for their company, I was tired of sitting alone in my apartment, but when Baby Faith met someone he knew and the two of them disappeared, there I was with Jack Tortorre, alone.

We kept walking through the Feast of San Gennaro, as if we hadn't really seen it all. I watched him the whole time, watched how he walked and used his hands, it appealed to me greatly, he lived so much in his own skin. I tried to imagine his nature, wondering what it felt like inside his chest, imagining it was so much less complicated than mine, and I wanted it instead. I watched him when people came up to him and slapped him on the back and said, "Jackie, how are you, how are you?" And I watched him nod his head, saying he was good, he was good, and I watched him when he introduced me to people and lied and said, "This is my friend Maria."

"Maria?" I said after they'd left.

"Oscar's a man's name," he said. "You don't want a man's name."

"Yes, I do," I said.

"You don't want to be a woman?"

I didn't know what to say. How could you tell someone you'd just met that you thought you had a great fate, that you were waiting for it and couldn't let your nature get in your way, you'd already done that.

"You want to be a man, then?" he said.

"No."

"What do you want to be, then?"

"Is there anything in between?" I said.

Jack Tortorre laughed, and I saw in his eyes the hot, wanting look I'd once seen in Luther Wolfe's. A thrill rose in me, unexpected and unwanted, but a thrill nonetheless, and I realized how much I was attracted to him, in a way I had never experienced before—so suddenly, it struck with such power. I felt I could have taken him right then and there, in some dark corner, behind a vendor's stand, down a side street. I had never known such immediate desire, I didn't understand, I knew this man not at all.

I forgot myself and invited him into my apartment, offering him a cup of tea, the two of us sitting on my mattress, sharing the cup, I had only one. He teased me quietly, Was I Francis-Francine? he said and then laughed, and when I asked who Francis-Francine was, he said, "A half-and-half." He ran his finger slowly and dramatically from his left ankle up to his neck. "On one side he was a man," he whispered. "His leg was hairy, and he wore a wing-tip shoe and a black sock. His chest on this side was bare, and he wore a man's watch." Then he ran his finger up his right side, even slower this time, and did so so suggestively, I wished he were touching me instead. "On the other side, she was a woman," he whispered. "She had a hairless leg and wore a high-heeled slipper, one breast in a cup of a bra, and bracelets on her wrist." He outlined my lips with his finger and said, "This side of her mouth was lipsticked, and her hair was long and curly." He pushed his fingers through my hair and cupped the side of my face. "Francis-Francine, the amazing man-woman," he said.

Then he wiped a drop of tea from my lip, and I swooned. I wanted to take his finger inside my mouth, I wanted his lips to touch mine, I wanted him, all of him, his bone and sweat, his nerve. He wanted me too, and there we were on a mattress, alone, sharing a cup of tea, our fingers brushing, our eyes meeting. It was nothing when he leaned close to me and kissed my mouth, and it was nothing when I kissed him back; it was pure and perfect, our desire, there was promise in it, his mouth so wet and warm, his hands strong, his body taut and eager, and there we were pressed up against one another, in agreement about this devouring. I remembered something I'd read, though I'd never remembered it before, it just came into my mind whole and unbroken: *The single word love in fact signifies two different things for man and woman. What woman understands by love is clear enough: it is not only devotion, it is a total gift of body and soul, without reservation, without regard for anything whatever. This unconditional nature of her love is what makes it a* faith, *the only one she has. As for man, if he loves a woman, what he* wants *is that love from her; he is in consequence far from postulating the same sentiment for himself as for woman; if there should be men who also felt that desire for complete abandonment, upon my word, they would not be men.*

I was this kind of woman, with this kind of nature, and when I saw myself banging on his door, crying, "Jack, it's me, let me in," it drained from me, all of it, and I sat up.

"What's the matter?" he said.

"I would like to, you can't imagine, but I can't," I said.

"Why?" he said. I stared into his eyes, they were beautiful, so dark and hot and full of want, and I wanted to lose myself in them, it was in me, but what was in me was not in him, I thought, though it appeared so now, and I didn't want to lose my life to it again. I told Jack Tortorre he had to go, I was sorry, but I couldn't sleep with him. He used all of his powers, his lisp, his crooked smile, desire in a man was no weak thing, but for that moment my will surpassed his, and I showed him to the door. He didn't understand, but he left, and I lay awake half the night reckoning with it.

I was stunned, I had lived almost cloistered, in such deep silence, for two years, and in a matter of a few hours a man had ripped through the calm. I wanted the silence back, the turbulence was foreign, but it seemed so far away, as if I'd never had it, and yet how could that be, I'd awoken to it only this morning? I thought of his eyes, his mouth, the pressure of his body against mine, the smell of his warm flesh. They stuck in my mind like the phrase of a song, and I tried to keep myself from looking at that small teacup we had shared, but it fascinated me and I stared at it as if in its fragility it held what had happened between us.

I put the teacup in the sink, and when a small light welled up in my room, I rose from my bed and stretched out on the floor, face down, my arms stretched out, and gave Jack Tortorre up. Here, take him, he's yours. I felt long, all bone and sinew and heart, and I asked for my fate again, I was ready for it, please.

Two days later, just after midnight on a rainy, cold night, Jack Tortorre knocked on my door. I stood frozen near the sink, trying to decide whether I would answer or not. "Oscar," he said, "I know you're in there. I saw you come up, and I didn't see you go down."

I moved towards the door, attracted by his voice, it was so deep and low and exciting, and I pressed my forehead against the cold wood of the door.

"I can't let you in," I whispered.

"Why not?"

"My grandmother is here, and she is sick," I said.

"You're lying."

How could I tell him I wanted a great fate, that I wanted to change the course of history?

"I want you, Hemy," he said.

The sound of my name on his voice went through me, I was made of so little.

"How do you know my name?"

"I had to know it."

I said nothing.

"I can't get you from my mind. I just want to see your face. I won't do anything but look, I think of you constantly," he said.

I said no, and he told me how he loved the shape of my mouth, how my lips drove him mad, how my eyes burned in his mind, he begged to see my face, just for a moment, my eyes, he would do nothing but look, he promised. The way his voice importuned was so thrilling, I forgot and unbolted the door, even as my mind told me not to. I opened it a crack and instantly fell into his eyes, they were so full of desire. Suddenly his lips were on top of mine, I tried to pull away, I must, I told myself, but his arms were around my waist, and I was in the hallway, pressed against the wall, the weight of his body warm and heavy against me, his mouth on mine. I wanted to pull him into my apartment and lay him down on my mattress and take him, I had never been so attracted to anyone, but I remembered how Luther Wolfe had once told me, "You are who God gave me," and I was wounded all over again. Then, I thought of a line I'd read, *To love like a man is a first step away from social and biologic destiny,* and I thought, Yes, of course, to love like a man, that was how, but then I understood I didn't know how to love like a man, that I only knew how to love like a woman, and that if I let Jack Tortorre in, it would be he who loved like a man and me who loved like a woman.

I pulled away, but he cupped his hands to the side of my face and sought my eyes. "I have never known a woman like you," he breathed. He kissed my forehead as if to anoint me, and I thought, I could love him, but I didn't want to, I didn't want to lose my life again. He could ruin me, I knew, and I remembered then how Bo had told me she had felt it pass her, but that I would do it. "Do what?" I had said.

Change the course of history.

I said, "You must go now." I pulled away from him abruptly and slipped into my apartment, and before I closed the door I looked back at him and saw the loss in his eyes. Better his than mine, I thought, and I sat down on my mattress, barely breathing, and heard nothing but his knuckles on my door and his voice calling my name, knowing how much it hurt to want and not to get, to lose the flesh most precious to you.

He left my door, and I lay back on my mattress, completely stilled, and heard only his footsteps as he descended the stairs. When he was gone and there was nothing, I wondered how I could have opened the door. He could ruin me, I knew, he could never be let in again. But how could I trust myself, I'd given him up before, and still I'd opened the door. I had to do more than give him up, fate was no small thing, it asked of us all we had, there was no halfway.

I looked around the room, as if there were something, I felt so desperate. There was nothing but Lourde's green trunk. Even so I was drawn to it, I don't know why, and in a moment of abandon I wildly pulled out everything I'd been carrying around in the bottom of that trunk since the explosion, all the burned objects, Lourde's gun, Bo's cracked bowl, a few pots and pans, Oscar's boxing gloves, Oscar's typewriter, the tin of Oscar's ashes, which I had carefully wrapped in a wide strip of elastic Zellie had once used to give her back support. I unwound the elastic from the tin and set it in the center of all of the objects, and looked at them all, they were my crosses, my statues, my idols, these blackened, ruined things.

I knelt in front of them. "I want the fate, Bo," I said, "more than I want Jack Tortorre." I felt something come over me then, as I had felt once before when I was in Lourde's room after the explosion and had looked down and found the darkened remains of a family photograph on the floor by my feet. I had felt something not quite made of bone and blood pass through me, as I now felt. I was aware of being in my empty apartment, of kneeling in front of those burned objects; I was aware of looking down and seeing the wide strip of elastic in my hands. I stood up then and walked to my bed and laid it on my pillow. I took off my blouse and flung it at the end of the mattress, then I unhooked my bra and dropped it in the wastebasket. I took the elastic and began to wrap it around and around my bare chest, until I was completely bound.

I knew it was strange, but even so I didn't stop, and when I was done, I pulled on a white T-shirt and stood in front of the mirror, where I saw a boy, a teenage boy, no, older, I saw Oscar Lourde. I hung there, mesmerized by my reflection, by this man-boy I had become. Do you want to be a man? I asked myself, even as I feared the answer, trembled inside, for I didn't *want* to want to be a man. There was nothing but hysteria in that, cutting breasts off, shaping genital flesh into a bizarre little part, pinkie-finger sized, a sad appendix, nothing more, then growing hair and muscles where there were none, and looking around for women to sleep with. No, that was not it, I did not want to be a man.

What was it, then? I asked myself, my mind straining to understand the unconscious reason. Did I hate so much being a woman? Was it so difficult to be a woman it had driven me to this act, desperate, it seemed to me, to erase my womanhood? Or was I covering my body to prevent myself from attracting men, so I wouldn't lose myself to another? Perhaps I was bandaging the nature that lay inside my chest, I thought, or perhaps I was wrapping it as if it had something to undergo, a metamorphosis, an evolution. I didn't know. All that I understood was that my devotion to the fate Bo had breathed to me seventeen years ago was now absolute.

I wanted to change the course of history. It was that or nothing.

I began to pray differently after that. I sat cross-legged, my back against the wall, my eyes closed, there were no words now, no vows, I watched my breath, the in-and-out pull of my breath, that was the prayer. And between my breaths, there was a place when the air was blown out, before the net breath was taken in, a space, silent and empty, where I asked to know. I sank deeply, losing myself to it, craving the sense it gave that there was something to know, something extraordinary, and I huddled in the stillness for hours and listened.

When an old woman started talking to me as I washed her in the shower, I heard her. She was going blind and was terrified, the thought that she would be lost to darkness horrified her. She couldn't sleep at night, she was afraid to shut her eyes, afraid that when she opened them again she wouldn't be able to see at all, so she kept them open all night, rested them on the frame of the doorway, where she could see the faint yellow light from the hallway, to make sure they didn't quit. You couldn't possibly know what eyes were until you were losing them, she told me. Her name was Lausy Hayes, and I started to think of her at night, imagining her struggling to stay awake, her eyes pinned on the fading yellow light, proving to herself, moment to moment, how she could still see. Then one night it came to me that Lausy Hayes was right, that she was going to go blind. It was strange, this knowing, it was a sense, yet I heard it, I heard the words, and I knew she would be blind.

When I washed her next, and my hands moved carefully over her large-boned body, across her chest, which rose and fell harshly, finally to her withered face. I washed her cheekbones and looked into her cloudy blue eyes and watched them move incessantly, they were searching for their sight. When I saw myself looking for Oscar in the ashes of my house, searching through them for a piece of his shirt, his shoe, anything, I knelt down and took her hands. "Lausy," I said quietly, "I want you to try something for me." I was as surprised as she was to hear myself speak, I'd been bent over in silence for so long, but now she nodded, as if it were only logical that I should, and in that damp, steamy shower, where the water dripped and echoed in the marble stall, I asked Lausy Hayes to close her eyes for five minutes, to watch her breath instead of her thoughts, and in that space between her breaths, I told her to ask for her sight. In the stillness that followed, I told her to listen for the answer. It may take a while, it wasn't magic, I said, but it was all we had, and she nodded as if she understood.

Then, while I held her hand, Lausy Hayes sat naked on my wooden bench and closed her eyes. She breathed deeply in and out, the air in her chest rasping, the veins straining at her temples, her fear was so great, but she did it, and when she was done, I thanked her and told her she must try it twice a day, as an experiment, nothing more. "You've nothing to lose, Lausy Hayes," I said, and she nodded, she knew it was true.

Lausy Hayes came for a wash more often, she preferred doing the breathing in my presence, she said. There was an air about me, she said, so I washed her, then sat next to her on the wooden bench and held her hand while she breathed. I sat in the steamy air and breathed along with her. We rarely said anything to one another, but one morning she squeezed my hand and said, "I think I understand something. Thank you, sir."

It shocked me, the use of "sir," it was the first time anyone had openly referred to me as a man. Lausy Hayes was nearly blind, but even so I saw myself as Lausy Hayes must have, a tall, thin figure, flat-chested, dressed in black slacks, black boots, and a white T-shirt, short hair, no jewelry of any sort, just a mannish wristwatch. It had happened so slowly, the transformation, first the hair, then the clothes, then later the binding. There had been no conscious intention on my part to look like a man, it seemed almost accidental, but now I understood the effect—I had taken on the look of a man. Yet it confused me, I felt so little like a man.

The next time Jack Tortorre came and knocked on my door, I opened it. It was late, Thanksgiving night. I'd eaten Thanksgiving dinner with Zellie, a whole table of crippled people, and the nuns in a large room with long tables draped with white crepe paper, behind which hung dark red religious paintings. When Jack Tortorre knocked, I opened the door a small crack, I wanted to see his face, he was alive, and within moments I was in his arms, the two of us inside my apartment, the mattress beneath us, a devouring begun like I had never experienced, all the waiting had only heightened it. Our mouths, the pleasure, his hands on my body, his mouth, open, greedy, his eyes hot and wanting in a way I had never seen, to match mine, I kept thinking, Luther Wolfe had only been a boy. "I think of you constantly," Jack Tortorre said. "I cannot get you from my mind. I walk the nights desolate for you. The days are empty. I think only of you." I listened, drunk from the sound of his voice, my vow wiped out in a matter of seconds by his voice in my ear, his hands on my face, I was made of nothing. It would have progressed, I seemed not to possess the will to stop it, until he came to the elastic which bound my chest—a gate, a wall, it came between us now. "What is this?" he wanted to know, appalled that I should be bound. He thought at first that I was wounded, that I'd been punctured or pierced, that an infection raged inside my chest, but I told him no, it was nothing like that, but when I tried to explain it, I found I could not, how could you tell someone you couldn't love them, you had a fate? He wanted to unwrap me, but I wouldn't allow him, I couldn't, there was will in that. I forbid him and he begged, he could bear no part of me taken from him, but I would not be unbound, I could not be, it was not time. I should never have let him in, I realized. I made him leave, I pushed him to the door even as he cried, and then I sat with my back against the wall, confused, as if it were beyond me, any fate at all. I heard him walk down the stairs, I heard the front door slam hard, I heard the click of his heels on the cold concrete sidewalk, then there was silence.

I breathed in the quiet of my apartment, aware of the moments, aware of myself, of my body, how heavy and bound to this earth it was, all spirit had left me. I was at least relieved that Jack Tortorre was no longer outside my door. He could kill me, I knew.

When Zellie was let out of Our Lady of the Immaculate Heart, we moved to a bigger apartment a few blocks away, a one-bedroom with a large kitchen you could actually have a table in, and Jack Tortorre never found us. When Zellie discovered I bound my chest, it did not seem so strange to her, she'd grown accustomed to my dark, masculine clothing, to calling me Oscar. "A bomb blows up a family, leaving two sisters behind, there's no telling what they'll do," she said. I thought of all the cuts and burns she'd made on her body, and I wondered if I was driven by a similar impulse, but I didn't begin to know.

We slept together at night, Zellie with her curved spine, me with my bound chest, the Lourde sisters, we were all that was left. We weren't Italian, but Zellie decided she loved everything Italian, Frida Kahlo herself had resembled Italians, and little by little, our apartment became Italian—candles burned on our windowsills, on small altars next to pictures of the bleeding Sacred Heart, crosses hung here and there, big pots of tomato sauce bubbled on the stove, and Zellie moved about in long, elegant dresses, red mostly, copying paintings of Fra Angelico and Tintoretto, Verdi playing on the radio.

She worked a few hours a day in an Italian grocery, sitting behind the counter, taking people's money, learning Italian so she could speak to all the old people who came in. Then she came home and painted and cooked our dinner.

While we ate, she liked me to tell her about the old people I washed, to do imitations of them, it reminded her of the old days in Bo's Place. It wasn't kind, but I liked to make Zellie laugh, so I brought her stories from the hospital, like the sight of Harold Rubin, the old vaudevillian, sitting on the wooden bench in the shower, his pale skin bunched up underneath him, his feet barely touching the floor, saying in his Yiddish–Brooklyn accent, "You ever heard of Danny Doyle, eh, Oscar? No? He was one of the greats, you never heard of him, Danny Doyle, you must have heard of him, no, all right, so you can't know everything. How about Vinnie Doyle, you gotta know Vinnie Doyle, you don't know Vinnie Doyle, God bless you, Vinnie Doyle, no one remembers you but me, and look at me, Vinnie Doyle, you're a poor slob, I'm the only one remembers you." I mocked them all, even Lausy Hayes, I mimicked her blindness, her trembling voice; I courted irreverence, welcomed impiety, I was no saint.

When Lausy Hayes began sleeping at nights, an old black man named Leopold Harry sat in my shower and started talking to me. He was a large man, big-boned and raw-handed, and his eyes were deeply sunken and clouded with cataracts. He'd lost most of his toes to diabetes, but most noticeable was his chest, puckered and scarred from burns he'd gotten in a race riot when someone threw gasoline on him and lit a match.

He wanted to know what I'd done. " 'Cause you done something," he said. "Lausy Hayes crying every night about her eyes long as I been here, and now all of a sudden, the night quiet. What you did?" I asked him, "Why do you want to know?" and he said he thought often of suicide, of taking the pills he'd saved, there seemed no sense in going on. When I saw myself sitting up in Gussy Keys's upstairs bedroom late at night, holding pills in one hand and glasses of water in the other, I asked Leopold Harry to bring me the pills the next time he came to my shower. I said I'd hold on to them, I'd give them back as soon as he wanted them. Then I asked him if he would try something, an experiment, I said it was, but he said he was too old for experiments. I told him he only needed to close his eyes for five minutes and watch his breath instead of his thoughts, and between his in breath and his out breath he was to ask where his spirit had gone. "Then, in the stillness, listen for the answer," I said, but he said he couldn't do that, he wasn't that sort, so I nodded and washed him, and weeks passed in silence.

When Leopold Harry spoke to me again, it was to say, "Lausy Hayes blind as a bat now, she not crying, neither. What you done?" he said. I told him that it was Lausy Hayes, she was a good listener, it had very little to do with me, but he said he was sure I had something to do with it, Lausy Hayes was a blind bitch, and now he wanted to try whatever it was Lausy Hayes was doing. So I sat down next to Leopold Harry on the wooden seat in the marble shower, and he closed his eyes and watched his breath and listened. It began to fascinate me, the power of grace, the core that lay deep down inside someone, that when touched, sent things up, answers, strengths, occurrences, as if power dwelled down there. There seemed to be nothing else in the face of a life that could take your family, your legs, your spine, your lover, strip you of everything, make loss the only thing you knew.

Leopold Harry came every day after that so he could do what he called the breathing. It was better when I was there, he said, he was sure there was something special about me.

I became more careful with my words then, and spoke even more sparingly to the old people in the showers. It was strange, the effect my silence had; it seemed the less I said, the more they wanted to hear my words, until a few more of them began asking me to teach them what I'd taught Lausy Hayes: a woman who heard ringing in her ears night and day, she was losing her mind, another woman who could hardly breathe, she'd smoked herself into emphysema, and a man who had two inoperable tumors at the base of his spine that caused him such pain, he wished death would take him. When they asked me to teach them what I'd taught Lausy Hayes, I was careful with my words, speaking only what was important, all other words fell away.

Somewhere in the midst of it I began to wonder if the old people would have listened so carefully to me had they known I was a woman. In many ways I did not hide that I was a woman, that had never been the point. I did not move my hands as a man did (if I'd thought of it, I would have been incapable of thinking about anything else), and though my voice was naturally low, I did nothing out of the ordinary to lower it. When I spoke on the phone, people often called me "miss" or "ma'am," it was only when they saw me that they were persuaded I was otherwise.

I had really only made three concessions to maleness, other than the short hair, the bound chest, and the wearing of men's clothes: I continued to take karate lessons, knowing the physical advantage it gave me, and as a result my muscles, particularly my thighs, were greatly enhanced. I had, as well, ceased shaving my legs and armpits, and though I was not terribly hairy, I was certainly hairier than the average woman, given that she is not supposed to have much hair at all except on her head. And I kept none of the standard personal effects of a woman, such as lipstick or nail polish or sweet-smelling bath soaps. All else, such as wearing phony mustaches and/or socks pinned into my underwear, seemed ridiculous to me, and I never bothered, although Zellie once made me a mustache from her own hair, which I kept in a drawer in my bedroom.

I didn't easily understand myself, either. I often felt confused about living as a man. The contradiction was not lost on me, bound and living as a man when I wanted to become a great woman. Whenever I thought of it, which I couldn't help doing, I pushed it away, there was something terrifying about it. I didn't understand what drove me, I only understood I was driven.

When a man named Francis Mumford asked me about the hocus-pocus I was conducting in the shower, I asked him why he wanted to know, and he held his hands out to me. They were almost unrecognizable, twisted backwards, his fingers swollen to the size of sausages. He was a thin board of a man, wiry yet bent, his gray hair thin and wispy, his half-steel, half-black glasses held together with safety pins.

"What about your hands?" I said, and he answered, "They hurt, what the hell do you think?" So before I washed him, I taught him how to watch his breath and told him in the space between his breaths to ask how the pain could go away. Then I told him that in the stillness that followed he should listen. "Will it make the pain go away?" he said, and I answered, "I have no idea."

"What do you mean, you have no idea?" he said.

I said, "You have nothing to lose."

Francis Mumford tried it, and though the pain in his hands never faded, he found if he listened to a certain kind of opera, Wagner mainly, he forgot the pain, his mind simply left it.

His friend Edward Christy came to me after that with a tumor on the right side of his head the size and color of a football. It was taking one thing after another, he said: his left eye, his balance, his ability to speak. He thought he should talk to me about it me before his tongue thickened beyond recognition. When he asked, "What can you do about this tumor?" I said, "Nothing."

"That's what I thought," he said, and a few tears slipped down his wrinkled, drawn face and dripped off his chin. A few of them dropped to the floor of that marbled shower, and before I washed him, I taught him how to watch his breath and told him in the space between his breaths to ask how he could accept the tumor. Then I told him that in the stillness that followed he should listen.

I started to stay longer at the hospital at night, washing the old people and watching them breathe—a job I couldn't name. I told them they could do this in their room, in the hallway, that was the beauty of it, it could be done anywhere, but they believed it was best in my shower, when I was present. So I sat with the men, I held the women's hands, I didn't want to disturb the momentum of grace.

Then, late in the spring of 1992, a man named Reverend Beacon turned up in my shower. He was a tall black man in his forties, highly educated, Yale or Harvard, full of an energy you could see working in his eyes. He came to Bellevue a few days a week to visit patients. I had seen him in the hallways, in the rooms, we'd nodded to one another, but I had never really spoken to him. But now he stood in the warm, moist air of the shower and said he'd heard about me and wanted to meet me. I nodded and watched in silence as he walked quietly to the shower stall and sat down on the wooden bench where the old people always sat. He folded his hands and looked at me a few moments before he finally spoke.

"I have work for you, Mr. Lourde," he said.

"What?"

"It's difficult work, but I think you're the kind of man who could do this sort of work."

"What sort of work?" I asked.

"Work on Death Row," he said, "with men on Death Row."

"Why would you think of me?"

"You have conviction," he said.

"What is the work?" I asked.

He told me over breakfast in a small diner across the street from Bellevue. He said the work he wanted to do was not sanctioned by the legal community, but that it ought to be. He called it an experiment, and then very quietly, he told me exactly what he had in mind—a strange, unorthodox idea, an idea that seized my imagination and made my heart beat fast. He had no idea how much I relished the illegality of it, the lack of authorization, the law had once authorized a man to bomb my house and family, leaving me cold. When he was done speaking, he sat across from me in silence, his large black hands lying still on the table. "What do you think?" he finally said. I told him I would consider it, but even so I felt strange, I was not who I said I was, and I couldn't help but wonder if he would have asked me had he known I was a woman.

24

She stopped talking and looked out the window. She was lying on her back, he on his side, his arm draped across her waist. The train sped through a valley, green with pine trees and patches of grass. It was completely dark now, but the sky was brilliantly clear and illuminated the snow-capped peaks of the Sierra Nevada Mountains rising up in the distance.

He looked at her and then reached out and touched her mouth with the tip of his finger.

What was the experiment? he said.

Her eyes never left the window.

It was very strange, she said. Almost embarrassing.

Why? he asked.

She smiled, but the smile faded, and a distant, sad look settled into her eyes, as if she'd seen more than she'd ever cared to see.

He wanted her to tell him about the men on Death Row, but she said she was too tired and was going to take a small nap. She shut the lamp off and closed her eyes then, and he watched the light pass across her face as the train sped by the night lamps. He was going to lose her, he thought. In another day, she'd be gone.

The thought bothered him, and he began to feel as if he could not breathe, as if he might smother in the small space behind the red velvet curtains. He rose quickly and swept the curtains back. He sat down in the chair beyond them and took a few deep breaths of air. He thought of the word "fate," she'd used it so much, but he'd never really believed in fate. He believed in chance. He wondered now if chance possibly functioned within the confines of fate, as if fate were the larger vessel. Or was it the other way around, did fate float in the hands of chance? Perhaps something that appeared as chance was not, he thought: for example, his sitting next to her on the train. Why her, of all people, a woman who had lived as a man, especially in light of his own predicament? He was tempted to believe it had been fate, but he could not say for sure.

He lit a match and held it out and watched her in the small flickering light. Her face was so white, so delicate. He could just see her lying stretched out on a wooden floor, her pale, determined body, yearning for her fate. He loved this image, he didn't know why. When the match went out, he looked at her in the dimmer light and wondered again, what if he were not looking at Hemy Lourde? What if she had never sustained those moments with Jack Tortorre in a hallway? What if she had never bound her chest? What if she'd never stretched out on any floor, anywhere, had never asked for her fate even once? What if this woman had lived an uneventful life and had made this all up? He felt it would break some small but vital part of him if she had lied. A woman would have made a fool of him. But beyond that, he sensed he would lose himself in a way that would be intolerable. He hated to admit it, but he was counting on her.

He remembered the envelope, and his eyes fell immediately on her purse. The impulse took him, and he knelt down and quietly opened it. It was as if he'd opened her heart.

What are you looking for? he heard her say.

He quickly closed her purse and returned to the chair. He felt ridiculous, like a petty thief.

The envelope, he said quietly. There was nothing else to say.

If you found the envelope, you would feel you could believe me then? she said. Her hair was softly mussed and her face flushed from sleep.

Her voice wasn't harsh, or sharp. It was soft, just a question, as if she were trying to understand, but he couldn't bear it. It made him feel more ridiculous, like a small boy who'd been caught going through his mother's bras.

Yes, he said. It would help.

He waited a moment.

Will you show it to me?

She drew her long legs up. No, she said.

Why not?

Because I am not obliged to prove to you my identity.

You're not obliged to do a damn thing, he said loudly. I'm asking you to, as a favor. Do it for me, goddamnit, so that I can rest easier.

No, she said.

Why not? What difference does it make? You could easily put my mind at rest—

No, she said.

Why not?

She pushed up on her elbow. I will not play this game, she said sharply.

What game? What goddamn game? he yelled.

The prove-I'm-not-lying game. I will not play. Believe me or don't.

I'm asking to see one white envelope. That's all I'm asking. Just as a favor, to put my goddamned mind at rest.

Take a stand, man, she said forcefully. For once in your life take a stand.

Fuck you, he said.

He rose up and walked out of her room. He didn't know what else to do. He listened for her voice as he walked down the aisle, but she had no name to call him. She wouldn't have called him anyway, he knew.

He had nowhere to go, so he retreated to his room, where he lay in the darkness. He felt humiliated, being caught with his hands in her purse. She'd pushed him to it, he thought, telling this bizarre story that no one would easily believe, and then when she had a chance to prove it was the truth, she wouldn't. Instead, she twisted it around and made it seem like he was the sort of man who could not take a stand. No, no, it was her, there was something devious about her. She was toying with him. Why else wouldn't she show him the goddamned white envelope? Anyone else would have. He told himself that it didn't matter, that this little train trip and this little man-and-woman-on-the-train interlude would fade quickly from his memory. He wouldn't return to her room. He would give her up, forgo her story. Forget her.

He thought this would release him, but he began to writhe uncomfortably on the cot, turning from one side to another. His feelings drove this unbearable motion. It seemed they'd gathered and risen *en masse* from the depths of his psyche and swarmed inside him now. He'd courted this, he had ushered it in, but now that it was upon him he wished it away.

He should never have gotten involved with her. The idea that she had anything to do with him seemed absurd to him now, a mad thought. She who was all breath and emotion. He could just hear her saying, *Suddenly his lips were on top of mine, I tried to pull away, I must, I told myself, but his arms were around my waist, and I was in the hallway, pressed against the wall, the weight of his body warm and heavy against me, his mouth on mine. . . .* It sickened him, he felt so sunken in all her emotion, as if he had been a stone which had fallen into its vast pond and had descended to the bottom.

He watched his mind work to supply him with proof that she was wrong—her folly to live as a man, taking her own body hostage, her ridiculous efforts to give those poor old sick people some kind of hope where there was none. But she was aware that she had taken her own body hostage, he thought, and she was aware that there was nothing she could truly do for the old people. She'd even told them so.

He lunged about in his mind trying to find something, some way in which to reject her once and for all. Was she some sort of Christian ecstatic? A moralizing humanist? A cloddish Western convert to Buddhism? He wanted to label her something he could sneer at, something he could loathe, but she never spoke of Christ, she didn't deny the rabid drives, nor did she denounce suffering. She invited it in as if it were a welcome, if not necessary, guest.

Fuck her, he thought.

It was the violence of her living as a man that his mind finally turned to. It appealed to him greatly, the way she had bound and concealed, snuffed out all that was woman. He relished this idea, and wondered if it was this that had excited him from the start.

When he imagined himself becoming his sister (it was something he could not keep himself from doing), growing his hair down his back, shaving his legs, binding his own genitals, and wearing white dresses, calling himself Nina, some part of him trembled. Somewhere inside it held some appeal, and when he couldn't deny it, it horrified him.

When he wondered if he was a woman trapped in a man's body, he saw his mother cast deep inside of himself, and suddenly, he could not breathe. He thought he might smother in the small space he now lay in, and tried to take a few deep breaths of air, but he couldn't. He reached for the inhaler, pressed it into his mouth and took the adrenaline into his lungs. There was no running anymore, he told himself. He held his breath and asked himself, did he want to be a woman? It would destroy his life, he thought, rearrange it so profoundly he would be unrecognizable to himself.

But no, he did not want to be a woman.

Did he hate women then? he asked himself. Did he really want a final divorce from them? The thought of it drove his heart. He tried to still himself by watching his breath, the way she would have said, but he felt like Lausy Hayes, terrified to even close his eyes. He hated the turn inward, he realized. It frightened him more than anything else, and suddenly he wanted to see her again. But why? he asked. He thought he'd gone over that, that he'd decided to forget her, to forgo her story. Yet he wanted to return to her now. Why, goddamnit? But he didn't know why.

He let two hours pass, hoping she would come looking for him, but she didn't. He got up then and returned to her door. He knocked, but there was no answer, and when he knocked again, he heard her stir inside, but she didn't come to the door. He felt how tenuous his position with her really was, and that made him knock harder, until he felt the sting of tears in his eyes. He left abruptly.

He coursed through the train, going from one car to another rapidly, and finally settled down in the smoking lounge, where he smoked three cigarettes, one after the other. When he remembered her touch, how delicate it had been, how gentle, he wondered, Could a cruel person touch that way? but he had no idea.

He stood up and went to the sink. He threw water on his face, and when he glanced in the mirror, he saw fear in his blue eyes again. They must have seen it in his eyes, he thought, the ones he'd left. It bothered him to think that that was their last image of him—the man with fear in his eyes. But he realized it was his back they'd seen last. His back going out the door.

It took a while, but he returned to her door and knocked again. She didn't open it, but he heard the lock click. He turned the knob and pushed the door open slowly.

He quietly closed the door and sat down in the chair. She was sitting on the bed, her long legs stretched out in front of her, dressed in crisp black pants, a white T-shirt, and black boots. It shocked him. Oscar Lourde, he thought, and his pulse raced.

Why did you change your clothes? he said.

I was tired of wearing skirts, she said.

Why?

Imagine being a mermaid, she said, smiling. She uncrossed her legs and recrossed them. He noticed her boots, black and pointed, and missed her sandals, the thin straps crisscrossing over her delicate ankles.

I am sorry that I opened your purse, he said.

All right, she said.

The room went silent. It wasn't that there was nothing to say. There were so many things to say, all of them delicate, all of them requiring such care that it was hard to know where to begin, how gingerly to step.

I want to know the rest of your story, he said quietly.

He realized he'd come for that. He needed to hear the rest of her story. The sound of her voice, the thread of her story were a sort of lifeline to him now. He felt he could not do without it now. There was thought of violence in obtaining it. If need be, he would rob it from her.

I wouldn't blame you if you didn't want to tell me, but still I want to know, he said.

He smiled then and fumbled for his cigarettes. He couldn't

forget the fear he'd seen in his eyes when he looked in the mirror. He knew she was seeing it now, and it disturbed him.

All right, she said. Come and lie next to me. I can't tell the story without you next to me now.

He was grateful she spoke in this way. He recognized the words—they were a woman's. He moved to her bed then and stretched out next to her. When she threaded her warm fingers through his, he forgot his anxiety.

For a long time they lay in the silence and watched out the window. The mountains were very close now. He was relieved that all that wounded desert land was behind them. He could feel the air growing even cooler, and he became aware of the train's climb, of its ascension.

She turned to him and spoke quietly.

It's strange, she said, the rest. She bit down softly on her lower lip.

I know it must be, but I want to know.

He reached out and pushed the hair from her forehead.

She closed her eyes then, and her voice came.

25

*I*t was a hot July day when we finally began the experiment. By the time I arrived in the morning at the New Jersey prison, most of the details had been worked out by Reverend Beacon, Dr. William Henry Mattair, and I. We'd spent months figuring out exactly what was to be done and when and how, it was no easy matter. We had gone over every detail, considered the ideas over and over, checked them for any flaws, but even so it was difficult from the start, the crimes the men committed, the feeling of being in some underground hell came to me often.

I spent nearly two hours getting there the first morning, on trains that roared through close, dark tunnels, switching three times, shuffling from train to platform where mobs of people moved heavily in the heat. Men played violins sometimes, stopping for the racket of the train, then resuming, the strain of notes almost holy down there.

Then the prison, with barbed and razored wire, rose up against the gray sky, the heat unbearable during the walk down the sidewalk to the side entrance. I was aware how little this place had to do with women, how little it had to do with the kind of people I'd always known, how little I belonged there. The towers, the barbed wire, told me that, but it was the air around the place, like harsh male breath, scented with rage and sweat, that I inhaled and smelled more deeply the further I followed a guard named Bristol through the maze of concrete hallways and locked doors, the click of our heels on the floors, the sound of our breath, the rustle of our clothes as loud as if a thunderstorm were underway. My eyes caught on Bristol's thighs, two moving tree trunks as we walked down one corridor, then another. He was an enormous man, tall and heavyset, with one deformed, cauliflower ear, which he tried to hide by wearing his hair over it, but it was so misshapen and protruding that the hair could not cover it completely. As doors opened and closed behind us, the feeling of being in a submarine came to me—rivets, metal, concrete, no air, nothing but clanging heels.

I was taken to Karl Gerhardt, who was waiting for me in a closed-up room. He was the assistant Reverend Beacon had chosen, and though I'd spent a great deal of time with him, I knew him barely at all. He didn't talk much, not at least at first, and had given me the impression that he was a closed-mouthed worker, uninterested in personal affairs. He was a slight, small-handed man with tiny round glasses and a nervous face, eager and terrified looking at the same time. He had a bad left arm, maimed in some way by a childhood accident, though I was never told what, nor did I ever see the arm—he always wore a sleeve over it and kept it close to his side, and never once did he mention it. I didn't like him, not even from the start, and he was acting so serious now, as if we were two priests on the verge of administering communion to the Pope, that I had the strongest urge to do something impious, like grabbing hold of his maimed hand and shaking it, but I didn't.

Karl cleared his throat slowly, as if to remind me of the gravity of the situation, and handed me the folders of the three men we were to work with on Death Row. I laid their photographs side by side and looked at them again while he and I sat in this airless, windowless room at the end of a long conference table that was scarred with cigarette burns. I had met the men a number of times, I had talked to them extensively, but even so it was still strange to look at their photographs now. There were nine of them on Death Row, nine condemned men, and no executions in fourteen years, but only three were part of the experiment: John Guyer, William Heathens, and Harold St. Hilaire.

I laid their photographs side by side and looked at them: John Guyer, rail-thin, with large, indented temples and slicked-back black hair, which had receded deeply, leaving him with a prominent, jutting forehead which overshadowed dark, heavily lidded eyes; devoid of light or wit, they were the slow, dull eyes of a lizard. Next to him, William Heathens, with his abundant brown hair and large blue eyes, looked angelic: his face sculpted, the planes of his cheekbones angular, the light falling on them pleasingly, his eyes frozen in the stare of a child. And Harold St. Hilaire, whose eyes were neither blue nor slow, but rather arresting, and framed by large, black glasses, they were the most penetrating, intelligent eyes I thought I had ever seen.

I put their photographs away and read about their crimes again, though I knew them by heart. John Guyer, Caucasian, thirty-two years old, met up with three women on the night of July 9, 1985, walking up the stairs to the exit of the New Jersey PATH train on Bay Street in Bloomfield: Sharon Cousins, fifty-five, Beverly Talth, fifty-seven, and Joanna Hayword, twenty-four. John Guyer was heading down the stairs when the women were walking up. Their fear was obvious. Sharon Cousins was scrambling up the stairs when John Guyer shot her in the back. When Beverly Talth started screaming, he forced her to her knees and shot her in the back of the head. At gunpoint, he first forced Joanna Hayword to perform oral sex on him and then raped her on the embankment just outside the train exit. He then shot her in the head.

William Heathens, thirty-five, Caucasian, walked up to a parked car on Dundee Avenue in Paterson, New Jersey, on April 1, 1984, and opened fire with machine gun on a young couple having sex in the backseat of a Ford Torino—Jackie Slater, nineteen, and Keith Williams, twenty.

On the twenty-fourth day of May 1989, Harold St. Hilaire, Caucasian, thirty-eight, robbed the 7-Eleven on Pompton and Bradford in Cedar Grove, New Jersey, whereupon he fled to a nearby neighborhood and entered the family home of Ellen and James Cotton, on Ridge Road, where they lived with their children, Emily, twelve, Sarah, ten, Paul, seven, and Godfrey, four. Harold St. Hilaire herded the Cotton family into the cellar, where he held them hostage for over twenty-four hours, after which time he hanged them by the neck from the rafters.

I closed the last file and looked up at Karl, his mouth open, his eyes small and tight as he gauged me. I imagined he tried to see inside me as if he longed to find my weakness, any weakness, but I pulled myself in, stared back, careful to keep my eyes quiet. I didn't say a word. I pushed the files away and Karl got up to get a glass of water, which he slid across the table to me. I thanked him, took a few sips, then put it down.

I'd spoken to him many times before, of course, but just to make certain, perhaps for myself as well, I asked him if he understood that it was an experiment, what Reverend Beacon, Dr. Mattair, and I were going to do with the men on Death Row, an unauthorized experiment, and he told me of course he knew this, Reverend Beacon and I had told him. I wanted to know again if he was bothered by this fact, by the illegality of it, and he said that he was not. I asked him what he thought of the experiment, and he told me that it interested him enormously, that's why he had agreed to be a part of it. I did not pursue this point, I assumed that his reasons for getting involved were, on a certain level, as unknown to him as mine were to me; I was not unaware that I was beginning an experiment with three men on Death Row as a man named Mr. Lourde, with only the vaguest understanding of my personal motives.

When Karl said everything had been prepared for me, as I had requested, I told him I was ready then to go upstairs to the cellblock so we could begin, though in truth I had never felt less ready for anything in my life. I followed behind him, down one corridor after another, watching the back of his head, the stiffness of his neck, as he guided me down a few darkened hallways to the older section of the prison, which wasn't in use anymore.

We took an elevator up a few flights, and while we stood in the silence, I found Karl's presence irritating. I sensed he regarded me skeptically, or at least my abilities, as if underneath it all he was hoping I would fail. I didn't know why I felt this way, he had said nothing of the sort, but somehow I sensed it.

The elevator opened into the old part of the prison and we stepped quietly into the corridor. It was an eerie place, unheated, with walls that sweated water. Every step we took echoed, and whole blocks of cells stood empty, a decrepit ceiling hanging over them all, crumbling even at the slight breeze we caused passing underneath. There were four cellblocks on the floor, ten cells per block. They were very small, the cells, no more than ten feet by eight feet, and the walls inside were cold to the touch and scabbed with peeling yellow paint. Outside each cellblock was a small walkway, no more than six feet wide, where the prisoners had once walked to and from their cells, and beyond this inner area was the catwalk, where the guards had once paced. Just beyond the catwalk were large windows, heavily barred and mottled so that the outside was not perfectly clear. The sky was visible, but mainly you could see the razored wire which rose up outside the prison. Some light came in through the windows, so that the cellblock wasn't completely dark.

I followed Karl into a small room just beyond the bank of black-handled levers which opened and closed the cell doors, where his personal belongings were—a coat, a black satchel with papers, a bottle of Evian water, some cookies, a Tupperware container filled with spinach salad. He'd been working up there for weeks, preparing it for this morning. He put something away and then turned to me.

"Are you ready?" he asked me. His eyes probed mine, looking for doubt, for indecision.

"Yes," I said.

He opened the door to the inner area just outside the block of cells, and we walked quietly to the place where an altar had been set up—some five feet outside in the walkway. The altar was low to the ground and was already set with the things I'd asked for: four blue tapered candles, a flat black incense burner, four small yellow bells, a bronze gong, and a red satin prayer book. Karl asked if the items weren't religious, and I said only in the context of the religion itself, I brought no religion into this.

A large chair equipped with chains was bolted and chained to the floor in the cell we had chosen—one of the middle cells in a row of ten. The men were to be chained to the chair as well as being shackled and chained themselves. I would have preferred this not be the case, but the warden would not allow it any other way.

There was a large black pillow for me to sit on, the altar being that low to the ground. There was an extra pillow for Karl, and when I finally settled myself on mine, I noticed that the morning

light spread through the block of cells evenly, that despite the cool-
ness of the floors, of the cells themselves, it was already growing
hot and humid.

Karl told me to ring the bells, that Bristol, the guard, would
hear them and bring the men, one at a time. When I rang the small
yellow bells, we heard movement outside the cellblock, the shuffling of feet, the jangle of chains, and I felt sick right down to the
pit of my being.

Karl turned to me then and said, "John Guyer is first this
morning."

John Guyer, I thought to myself, the one who had shot three
women in the exit of the PATH train, raping the youngest one
before shooting her in the head.

The jangle of chains grew louder, the shuffling of feet too,
heels and soles against gritty concrete. Then I heard the lever being pulled from outside the cellblock, and the cell door clanged
open. Bristol appeared outside the cellblock with John Guyer, and
after he opened the outer door with his key, Karl and I watched
as he escorted John Guyer down the walkway, towards the cell.
He shuffled slowly, his legs shackled at the ankles, his hands in
wrist cuffs, his orange jumpsuit colorful amid the gray, his temples even more sunken looking in the dull light. Bristol guided
him into the cell, and after John Guyer sat down in the chair,
Bristol fixed the chains that were attached to the chair across John
Guyer's chest, and when he made his last, final adjustment, one
greased lock of John Guyer's hair fell and lay like a dark gash
against his forehead. There he was, the condemned man, sitting
chained across the chest to a chair which was chained and bolted
to the floor, his ankles in leg irons, his wrists handcuffed to a belt
around his waist. He looked like a man sitting in the electric
chair. I had known it would be this way, but upon actually seeing it, I felt sick.

Bristol left the cell, and moments later I heard the thrust of
the lever being pulled outside the cellblock, and the door to the
cell slammed closed, the sound harsh and final, particularly in
the silence.

"Good morning, Mr. Lourde and Mr. Gerhardt," John Guyer
said. His voice was high and hoarse.

"Good morning," I said.

John Guyer squinted in the half-light, trying to discern my features as I tried to discern his. His eyes were hooded and dark and slid away. He wasn't a big man, but it was obvious he had tried to make up for it, building up his biceps, which I could see plainly enough, under the rolled-up sleeves of his orange jumpsuit. His right arm was completely tattooed, from his wrist up to his shoulder and around his neck, though I couldn't see what the tattoo was, and he wore soft black shoes without laces.

He nodded to me and I nodded back, chilled already by his reptilian stare, and when he smiled, I noticed his mouth was thin, slotlike.

I lit the blue tapered candles and Karl picked up some incense and lit it with the flame of one of the candles. He laid the sticks down in a bed of ashes in the incense burner, and I then picked up the yellow bells one by one and rang them. I felt self-conscious about ringing them, I was not a religious person, and suddenly I wished I hadn't asked for them. Nonetheless, I never forgot the way those bells sounded up there in the morning light, reverberating in a place so hostile, a moment where beauty and horror embraced.

"Mr. Guyer," I said. "We're going to chant the Goza Buddhist prayer first this morning." Over the past few months Karl had taught the men the prayers.

John Guyer nodded, and I watched him fold his hands as best he could within the confines of the handcuffs and the waist belt. Then he closed his eyes and Karl handed me the prayer book and then for close to ten minutes Karl, John Guyer, and I chanted this prayer, over and over, a Buddhist prayer Reverend Beacon had taught us all. "*Soregashi senzo daidai narabi ni toshu shinko no menmen; naitoku shinko no menmen; onoono senzo daidai no sho shoryo, tsuizen kuyo sho dai bodai no tame ni. Soregashi senzo daidai narabi ni toshu shinko no menmen; naitoku shinko no menmen; onoono senzo daidai no sho shoryo, tsuizen kuyo sho dai bodai no tame ni. . . .*"

I watched John Guyer sing the chant just as I had once watched the old people breathe, and I tried to imagine how I was actually going to tell if John Guyer was praying right. That was my job—to make sure he prayed right.

I took him through another prayer, a prayer from the Bhagavad Gita, which we repeated over and over again, this time the words in English: *Even the worst sinner becomes a saint when he loves me with all his heart. This love will soon transform his personality and fill his heart with peace profound. This is my promise, O son of Kunti: Those who love me, they will not perish.*

Our voices were harmonious and syncopated yet I couldn't help but wonder where the words went inside John Guyer's mind. What did he make of them, words like *Even the worst sinner becomes a saint when he loves me with all his heart*? Where did the words travel, what paths did they take? How was his mind constructed that he could walk down subway stairs, take a look at three woman who feared him, and kill them all, point-blank, in cold blood, boom, in a matter of seven minutes, and then saunter down the stairs and catch a train to Manhattan? How could these words float amongst the words that had led John Guyer to this? What would it look like, these words drifting about in the same mind that had conjured such an unspeakable scene? Could it possibly do anything to say these prayers? Could it ever untwist that which was twisted?

When I thought of John Guyer's mind, I saw a dark cave, where steams and vapors, where full winds blew. I watched John Guyer again, and I tried to imagine what Sharon Cousins's husband would see if he were here. What would he think of John Guyer praying for his food and air? For the water he washed himself with, he had to perform three good acts a day; for the pallet he slept on, he was to speak honestly for one hour a day with Dr. Mattair; at night, for a blanket and pillow, he was required to write five pages of his thoughts.

What would Joanna Hayword's mother think of this experiment? I wondered. For that matter, what would any of the relatives of the dead think of it? Would they be interested to know if spiritual transformation was possible in men such as these—not necessarily for moral reasons either, there was no moral imperative; it was more a matter of inquiry than anything else. It was an experiment that was entirely voluntary, not one of the condemned men had been forced into it, they had agreed to it on their own and were free at any moment to be let out of it. Nothing had been promised to them either, no extra time, no money, no reprieve, no stay of execution, nothing. They were only told they might find some peace. Even so, I couldn't imagine what Beverly Talth's mother or her husband or her children, or for that matter what any of the relatives of the dead, would have thought of this experiment.

I hit the gong three times and we all fell silent.

"Mr. Guyer, we're going to finish up the hour with meditation," I said, and I told him how he was to watch his breath instead of his thoughts, just as I had told the old people, and John Guyer nodded, closing his eyes again, repositioning his folded hands, as if to fold them better or deeper. Karl sat as I sat, and the two of us watched John Guyer carefully, watched to see if his meditation was sincere or not. It seemed of the utmost importance that we know, as if the truth of it mattered up here, as if something larger were at stake than this man's breakfast and morning air, although I couldn't say what.

It didn't take too long before the silence brought me to the crimes John Guyer had committed against Sharon Cousins, fifty-five, Beverly Talth, fifty-seven, and Joanna Hayword, twenty-four. I tried to imagine this slight man, sitting now in meditation, after having chanted several sacred Buddhist chants, after having repeated a prayer from the Bhagavad Gita, shooting Sharon Cousins in the back and Beverly Talth in the back of the head, then raping Joanna Hayword before he shot her in the head as well. I tried not to see him forcing Joanna Hayword to her knees, but I saw it. I saw him raping her on the embankment, tearing her clothes off, her girlish voice screaming, his hands slapping at her mouth, at her neck. Suddenly it was too much for me, this sort of holiness in this most unholy of places, the sight of this chained man in a chained chair, behind bars, a man who'd killed and raped, and myself, a woman disguised as a man. A small noise came up from my throat, tiny, but John Guyer and Karl heard it and opened their eyes and looked at me. I averted my eyes, dropped them to my lap, and they looked away finally. I was almost sure I wouldn't last out the day, that I wouldn't get through Harold St. Hilaire and William Heathens.

When the meditation finally ended, Karl retrieved from a small cart a tray of food Bristol had brought—scrambled eggs, two slices of buttered toast, and hash browns on a plastic plate, a plastic cup of orange juice, another of coffee, and a plastic spoon wrapped inside a paper napkin. Bristol went inside the cell and unlocked the cuffs from John Guyer's wrists, took the tray Karl had pushed through a small opening, and handed it to the man. While he sat bent over it, I watched, spellbound, as this man devoured his food, knowing two strange things about this meal—that he had prayed for it, and that I had the power to decide if his praying had been good enough or not.

Karl leaned close to me and whispered, "How do you know he prayed right?"

"It is intuitive," I said. "There is nothing scientific in it, Karl. What do you think?"

His eyes blinked a few times behind those small, round glasses.

"How do you take their air away?" he said.

"If I sense they are going through the motions, rather than giving their energy to the prayer, they get neither the food nor the chance to go outside in the garden for their air," I said. There was a finality in the tone of my voice, and without meaning to, my eyes fell on Karl's lifeless arm, and he nodded, then looked away.

The next two came, one after the other—Harold St. Hilaire and William Heathens—both of whom shuffled in, shackles clanging, and who were chained to the chair which was chained to the floor, both of whom said hello to me, scrutinized me with different eyes, William Heathens's blue and frightened, and in the case of Harold St. Hilaire, deep and black as loam. I conducted more chants, more prayers, a half hour or so of meditation, while I imagined all their crimes and was repelled past all understanding, wondering what I was doing here, sensing the prayer words were pure raindrops falling into a fathomless cesspool. It threatened to swallow me, the hopelessness of it, prayer in the face of such monstrousness. I counted eleven people dead, two men, five women, four children, one woman raped. That's what lay between me and them.

When Bristol took William Heathens away, Karl walked me

to a bathroom, where I nearly threw up my small breakfast of fruit into a filthy, pockmarked toilet.

After lunch Reverend Beacon came with me to the prayer cell and sat through the lunch prayers, where we heard the same shuffling, the same sound of chains, where we watched the condemned men walk to the cell, only to see the same strange sight of them (burned now into the back of my eyes) handcuffed, chained to a chair, which was chained to the floor, all of whom were behind bars. I shall never forget the sound of their voices joined with mine and Reverend Beacon's in prayer, then their voices alone, when they told us the three good acts they had performed that had gotten them their water for the day.

At dinner prayers, I listened with fascination to the personal prayers the men spoke out loud to me: William Heathens spoke of his victims, of their relatives, whom he knew by name, saying he prayed their pain be lessened every day, apologizing three times to the men and women he had wronged. I didn't know what to make of it, it was so strange, their names on his lips, his crimes given voice. It didn't come easy for John Guyer, this public apology, words were not easy for him. He said, "I ask forgiveness from Sharon Cousins, Beverly Talth and Joanna Hayword, from Mr. Talth and Mr. Hayword, from the Cousins family, who I've hurt past words. I am sorry," this last whispered so quietly I could barely hear. Then, when they had finished and began to say the prayers and the chants with me, something happened down in that dark cellar, something I can't really explain.

Something small gave way inside me, and I felt a sorriness for the men, however paltry. How could I feel nothing at all, them chained to that chair, barely able to move, their lives condemned, a living hell, while they prayed for their victims, for their families? How could I not realize that it was the best they could do now, the only thing left to them? Even still, the bodies lay there before them, they would never go away. That was the thing about it, from the start, but there they were, these men, their voices joined with mine in prayer, the sound of it extraordinary, really, you must remember the place, and I found myself believing, what I'm not sure, but believing, perhaps it might work—that a transformation might be possible, that they might master themselves, that they might gain the inner freedom to make another choice.

John Guyer's mother was Puerto Rican, his father German. He had two older sisters. At the time of his childhood his father was an alcoholic, his mother a certified schizophrenic who was in and out of mental hospitals most of John's young life. His father and mother argued constantly, his father often beating her. There was much difficulty in the family, desertions, chaos, more beatings. Then when John was eight years old, his mother shot his father in the heart with a neighbor's gun and left him dead on the bedroom floor, whereupon she tied John underneath the bed and took her daughters to visit her sister in Trenton, New Jersey. John remained tied beneath the bed for nearly a week, his dead father decomposing not more than two feet from his eyes.

John Guyer was the easiest to learn, he liked to talk, and so it didn't take me long to discover his love of guns, of weapons of every kind, he had a collection on the outside and was very knowledgeable about most firearms. He loved every war film ever made and knew nearly all of them, particularly World War II films. He hinted at an interest in Hitler and at a loathing of Jews and blacks, but under the circumstances of our prayer together and his interest in his meals, he kept it to himself. He had a girlfriend, a small, dark-haired Puerto Rican girl who would have married him, he said, if he'd wanted to get married, although he didn't and never would. It wasn't for him, marriage, and he confessed to having hit her quite a few times. "Where is she now?" I asked him, and he said, "Gotten herself knocked up quite a few times, that being the only thing she was ever good for."

Harold St. Hilaire's mother and father had given him to his grandparents to be raised when he was a year old. It was never quite understood why this was done, as Harold's other brothers and sisters, one younger and two older, remained with his parents. He lived with his grandparents until he was sixteen years old. It was a household wherein Harold's grandfather routinely beat his grandmother, and enlisted Harold to take part. Although Harold did, he did so with great hesitancy. He began reading at a young age, to escape. His grandfather ended up accidentally killing his grandmother, beating her so hard one day that she bled to death. Afterwards, his grandfather hung himself, and Harold returned to his parents.

Harold St. Hilaire was thirty-eight years old, his hair dark and partly grayed, he wore it straight back, though it never stayed that way—it fell towards his face in curls. There was something irrepressible inside of him, which he wore in his eyes, not one quality but a mixture of qualities, like mockery, evil, and amusement. He had the most sensuous, confusing mouth I had ever seen, the way he held it, the way he used it, the way it worked together with his eyes—a full mouth, it was almost womanly, and the way he drew his lips up was bowlike.

He was a medium-sized man, and though he moved as a man, some of his gestures defied masculinity and would not have been out of character for a woman. Small parts of him flared up, as if acts of defiance, like a woman: his hands moved too quickly sometimes, yet it was just a momentary impression, fading almost instantly, and when he walked his hips swayed a little, it was barely noticeable, but it was there and it worked on you, leaving a vague, diffuse impression of woman.

He spoke quietly, it seemed he almost whispered, yet there was great drama in his voice, as if he were filled with secrets and was going to let you in on one. He was a quiet man, more interested in his food, and hence more reluctant to talk, but he admitted to liking pool and having been quite good at it, good enough that he made a living hustling from time to time. He was a big reader and had read every book in the prison's library and had to order books, three, four a week, he went through them like water. He liked thought, he said, liked reading about thought, about what men thought, it fascinated him. As for women, he didn't care much for them, he said. Had no real use for them, they never cared for him either.

William Heathens was continually stalked and raped by his father from the age of four until he was sixteen, after which time he ran away from home, never to return. Though his mother knew, she did little to stop his father. His grandmother tried to intervene, but she was frail and nearly blind. When William finally ran away from home, he began robbing small stores for money. He lived on the streets for as many as five years.

William Heathens talked some days and was silent other days, there was no anticipating his mood. What he liked more than anything were his Dobermans, he had three of them on the outside, a photograph he carried in his back pocket at all times, worn and fingered, commemorating their attachment to him, as he stood tall and golden-like amongst them, like a Viking who had conquered lands. He loved his grandmother, William Heathens said, a small German woman he'd carried in his arms at the end, carried her from the porch chair to the bed and back again in the morning, read her the newspaper, and brought her tea. She died when he was fifteen, he said, and it was never the same after that.

It wasn't like working with the old people, working with men on Death Row. The men on Death Row did not follow me easily. They were more reckless, more daring, they'd committed acts that would forever separate them from the rest of society—they had murdered. There was always danger there, and I had to fight to stay in control. It was in our minds where the struggle took place, their eyes against mine. It took all I had, but I never flinched, and yet I always felt unbalanced in their presence, always on the edge, never truly equal to it.

I struggled with the prayer and meditation, it hollowed me out sometimes, calmed me at others, illusion became much easier to see, but just when it seemed most at hand, some sort of awakening, it all left you, the remotest sense of the spiritual world, and there you were sitting with yourself, no one miraculous, just yourself, with your breath and your beating heart and your hunger, the walls rising up around you. I often opened my eyes and saw the men, John or William or Harold, murderers every one of them, and I thought how I could barely move myself sometimes, how could they, their dead holding on to them?

When I told Dr. Mattair this, he said, "Aren't you a murderer?" and I had to agree with him. I'd shot a man, I would have shot another had the bullet been in the chamber, yes, I was a murderer too.

* * *

I found the weekly analysis session with Dr. Mattair perhaps even more difficult than working with the men. Everyone who was involved in the project—Reverend Beacon, Karl, and Bristol—had to undergo this one-hour session once a week, and in turn Dr. Mattair underwent an hour a week with a Dr. Moore in New York. I liked Dr. Mattair, he was an elegant, tall, unconventional man with a flamboyant air about him. He was as different from Reverend Beacon as two men could be, Reverend Beacon being quiet and obscure, a man of few words who spent much of his time in a small office outside the cellblock where the guards had once eaten their meals. Dr. Mattair, on the other hand, spent more time on the floor, quietly observing the men, moving languidly through the cellblock, picking his spot from which to observe, a red scarf often around his neck. He wore the most impeccable suits and sat on a chair, one long leg swung over the other, staring out of thick glasses, he was nearly blind.

The room we met in was indescribably close—a small cinder-block room, there was just enough space for a long leather sofa and for the chair he sat in. We were so close, I could hear the rhythm of his breath behind me. The walls were barren and so without inspiration that I closed my eyes rather than look at them, and for an hour I was to tell Dr. Mattair my thoughts.

Ordinarily it was not difficult to talk to him, he had an easy, disarming way about him, but in this room I found it hard to speak; I was now required to speak as if I were a man, with male thoughts when I could only guess what they might be. Everything I thought to say had to be passed through a filter, my true experience completely veiled, if not obliterated.

The first day, I could barely talk, I spent most of the session realizing the implications: I could not simply tell of my life, my family, my feelings—they were a woman's. No, I had to consciously rearrange the stories, substitute Oscar for Hemy, male for female, man for woman. It was quite difficult, and to explain the large gaps of silence I fell into, I told Dr. Mattair that the process was quite foreign to me—speaking out loud on a sofa, while he sat behind me. He said he understood, that everyone found it difficult.

The first thing I told him was about my family, it took me weeks, I had to so carefully restructure the story. Instead of Oscar being killed, I was killed; "My sister Hemy died in the explosion," I said, and then I went on to explain how her death had devastated me, telling him that I had in fact dug up her grave, confiscated her ashes, which I still had in a tin can. I mentioned too that I had had incestuous relations with her; it slipped out amid the details of the bombing and all the loss, this fact, small it seemed, in the midst of all the rest, it was becoming more difficult to control what I said. When I added that it had never progressed to actual lovemaking, although I had wanted it to, the room went silent, and I understood that inadvertently I had said something that held a certain weight in this small room, suddenly more weight than the bombing of my family, which I could not imagine ever being overshadowed by anything, but now inside of this room, the mere mention of incest caused it to fall into shadow.

"I never understood why I was incestuous," I said, as if that would erase the word, lighten its weight, but the repetition of it only called more attention to it.

When Dr. Mattair asked, "Was there any other incest in the family?" the question surprised me, I hadn't expected it. But then something surfaced in my mind that I had not remembered until now—the night Lourde had asked me and Zellie at the dinner table if we were playing Hide the Wienie with any of the boys.

So I told Dr. Mattair this and added, "He told them that if they were, he didn't want them sitting at his dinner table. I think it made my sisters cringe."

"A father asking his teenage daughters if they are playing Hide the Wienie with any of the boys is vulgar and would make any daughter cringe," Dr. Mattair said.

The room went silent for quite some time while I thought about this, the understanding that I had cast Lourde in a bad light coming to me immediately.

"He was drunk and having a hard time. They'd rejected his plays," I said, as if this would help excuse Lourde. But then Dr. Mattair said nothing, and the silence weighed on me. I warned myself to be more careful, but when I next spoke it was to say,

"The night I first kissed my sister, was the night she shot Mr. Antonovsky. She shot his dick off, you know."

"Why would she do that?" Dr. Mattair asked.

"It was an accident," I said.

Silence followed again, and I became aware of the significance that shooting Mr. Antonovsky's dick off took on inside of this room, isolated as it was now from the rest of the story, from the furor in Bo's Place at the time, from the necessity of shooting him, from Zellie's loud voice commanding me to shoot him.

I tried to cover it up by saying, "I felt sorry for her," but when Dr. Mattair asked me, "Was that why you kissed her?" I struggled to remember what it was about Oscar that had made me kiss him. I thought of him holding me in his arms at night during the rainstorms, and I wondered if I should say I held my sister during rainstorms because she was afraid of them, and that had led to other things, or if I should say that I, as Oscar, was afraid of rainstorms and that my sister would sometimes come to my bed and comfort me. I imagined that I shouldn't be afraid of rainstorms if I were Oscar, so I said, "I used to hold her during rainstorms. I was trying to comfort her that night, and somehow I ended up kissing her."

When Dr. Mattair asked me, "What made you decide to kiss her?" I had no idea why Oscar had decided to kiss me. It had come as quite a surprise to me, and I wondered now if I should say I didn't know, or if I should make something up—say how attractive my sister's lips were, her breasts heaving under her nightdress, but it was laughable, and in the end I couldn't bring myself to say the words.

"I don't really know," I said.

It went on this way for a whole hour, time during which I was never so conscious of being a woman. I could not forget for one moment that I was a woman, that I was an impostor, and oddly, it was not so much that I was living a lie that disturbed me as it was that I did not understand why I was living one. I was aware too that these sessions were not like anything else I had ever experienced. I did not understand the rules, the ritual, all I understood was that it disoriented me, brought things to mind, associations that I didn't normally have.

* * *

When I was with the men now I began to feel like a cat out-side a birdcage, perched on the edge, breathing quietly, riveted to the men as if through instinct, eyes toiling to miss nothing, as if something inside that cage stirred me to a flush, pushed my heart, drove my blood through constricted veins. I did not fail to notice this, nor did I fail to acknowledge how safe I felt disguised behind the short hair, the flat chest, the lowered voice, the ratio-nal way in which I conducted myself, the man I had fashioned. I often wondered if I was spying on them, trying in some uncon-scious way to fathom them, as if the only way I could ever under-stand them was to pretend I was one of their kind, as if this was the true experiment that was being conducted, this one where I was a woman dressed as a man, listening to their souls speak as men, listening with the ears of a woman. But I didn't know.

I often remembered what I'd thought when I'd first visited Bo and Lourde in jail—how strange it was that you could just go along as part of a family having a fine time, and then a still your mother shouldn't have made but did make blows up, and be-cause a black piano player and a fat white man hate each other, you end up standing in your living-room-turned-bar with your father's gun in your hand, shooting the white man in the groin, and then there you were in jail talking to your mother and father behind reinforced glass.

Now when I stared through the bars at the three men in their orange jumpsuits and leg shackles, I thought how strange it was that you could shoot a man in the groin and have it be the decid-ing event which prompts your mother to tell you that because of it she realizes you have a great destiny ahead of you, that you will change the course of history, and that because of this great fate you can never love a man, and then when you lose your family in a bombing and your sister survives as a cripple, you marry a man you don't love to help take care of her, and after he hits you and forces himself on you enough times, you leave and strike out on your own, working long and hard, and out of the blue comes a man, and you think because your life has been so hard, life has given you this man to love, and you forget what

your mother has told you about your destiny and about not loving a man, you love him anyway, and then one night you fly into
a rage because the burden of your crippled sister gets to be too
much, and he leaves you, and there you are, alone, worrying that
you gave up your fate for this man who left you, and you want it
back, the man wasn't worth it, so you vow you'll build a fortress
around your heart, like your mother told you to, you'll search
for your fate, and you cut your hair, you change your name, you
refuse the passions of a passionate man again and again and
again, you bind your chest, you watch your breath and listen in
the silence, and you wash the old people and teach them to do
the same, and then you end up working with men on Death Row,
and now here you are, in another prison, bound and dressed like
a man, and you don't know what or who you are, and through
the bars sit men, like the man Happy who bombed your family.

When Dr. Mattair got the warden to loosen up on the restrictions in the cellblock, the atmosphere up there began to change.
The restrictions had been quite severe—a grim silence hung in
the emptiness, a metallic echo accompanied each movement, each
voice, the men themselves chained and then chained again inside the cell, nothing could enter into the cellblock other than the
bells, the candles, the pillows, and the prayer book. Not even so
much as a sheet of paper was allowed in, the warden was so para-
noid about this unauthorized experiment. But somehow, Dr. Mattair managed to quiet his fears, and very slowly we were allowed
to introduce new elements into the quiet emptiness, one thing at
a time, each striking in its newness.

Music came to us first, piped in at scheduled times through
an old public announcement speaker. We listened to country-
western, which John Guyer liked, and classical, which Harold
St. Hilaire requested, and Bruce Springsteen, who was William
Heathens's favorite. Karl liked show tunes, Bristol preferred jazz,
Dr. Mattair favored opera, and even Juan, the janitor, had his
preference—Elvis Presley. After a while, Juan became our unoffi-
cial disc jockey, playing old records from a room on the other
side of the cellblock, often announcing them in a faux announcer's
voice: "And now, we have a selection from Bruce Springsteen's

fabulous double album, a request from William the Heathen." It was often funny, especially when he played one of Bristol's favorites, calling him Lurch LaMotta, because Bristol walked like Lurch and had a cauliflower ear like Jake LaMotta. He didn't like Bristol, and Bristol didn't like him either. Even so, the sound of music up there was so singular, it seemed rare, extraordinary even.

Then Dr. Mattair began a mural on the wall just outside the cellblock, and before the men entered the prayer cell in the morning they were allowed to draw or paint or paste something on this wall, whatever they wanted, wherever they wanted—images or words clipped from magazines, photographs, drawings. It wasn't too long before it became a fascinating collage of their darkest impulses: images of guns, of violent explosions, of blood and death, of mangled bodies and war. It took months before around its edges began to appear other images, of beautiful girls, of shimmering beaches, of sunsets and mountaintops.

These things, small in and of themselves, began to alter my relationship to the men, somehow bridging the gulf between us, until one cold afternoon I found myself laughing hard when William Heathens told me a story about his father, speaking in his father's accent, the accent of Mr. Antonovksy. While he sat chained in the chair in that orange jumpsuit, shackled and handcuffed, his brown hair soft around his angular face, his eyes blue and childlike, he told me about the time when he was a boy and had wanted to change his name to Clark, because Superman's name was Clark. When he told his father his desire, his father had laughed and said, "No, no, no, you don't vant this name. Just listen." And then he sang in his Polish accent, "Hoppy berthday to you, hoppy berthday to you, hoppy berthday, dear Claaaaaaaaaaaaaaaaaark," with such a short, flat, awful *a* that I laughed, laughed much louder and brighter than I should have, we were in a prison, on Death Row, and when I looked up at William Heathens and our eyes met, I realized he was sexy. It was terrible, but William Heathens was sexy, and for a few moments I was overcome with the wildest urge to lay him down in the corner of the cell, tear his clothes off, and make love to him. The urge was almost intolerable, and it shocked me that it should

rise up in so dark and decrepit a place, with a convicted murderer, a man on Death Row. I tried not to look at his mouth, at
his lips, at the way his tongue touched his lower lip, the way he
sometimes bit softly down on it, it wreaked such havoc inside
me, but it seemed the harder I tried not to look, the more I looked.

When he spoke one particular prayer, a prayer from the Bhagavad Gita, his eyes fluttered shut during the last stanza, and I
watched him as he spoke:

> Give not your love to this transient world
> Of suffering, but give all your love to me.
> Give me your mind, your heart, all your worship.
> Long for me always, live for me always,
> And you shall be united with me.

I watched him, admired his face, he was handsome in a rugged
way, his mouth full and boyish, his arms strong and sculpted
from lifting weights. For a split second, I saw past the bars that
separated us, the chains that bound him to the chair, the shackles that tied him to the floor, and though the prayer he spoke
was to God, I imagined he spoke it to me. When he opened his
eyes, I averted mine quickly and pretended to look at the small,
orange flames of the candles, but he had seen me looking at him.

I thought of him that night, in the faint light of my room, in
the warmth of my bed, the idea of taking William Heathens in
the corner of the cell, taking him with all my breath and sweat,
with all my pent-up, thwarted passion, taking him in a blaze, and
all the while I wondered where it came from, this fierce, strong,
overpowering urge, wishing that it would go away, that it would
let me out of its grip, this was a man on Death Row, and I was
living as a man.

If anyone sensed I was not a man, it was William Heathens. I
sensed he had an attraction to me, although I didn't understand
how, me sitting there with brutishly short hair, bound breasts, as
male as I could be, but there we were, truly, a man and a woman,
inflamed, two beasts in this hard world, our instincts rising up
from down in some dark communal well. I did not fail to notice
this, and I prayed to forget.

* * *

It wasn't long afterward that I made my first mistake with John Guyer. It drifted out of my mouth in the form of a question. "What were you thinking when you forced Joanna to her knees?" I asked him one chilly morning when he we had finished our third prayer. He looked up through the bars that separated us, his darkly hooded eyes sliding away within moments, it was impossible to capture his gaze.

"Thinking?" he said. His eyes moved sideways back to mine for a moment, then slid away again.

"Yes, what went through your mind?"

"I don't know," he said. He now stared at a spot on the floor, his eyes cast down, his forehead appearing larger and more prominent, and white as paste.

"You must have thought something," I said.

John Guyer laughed nervously, shuffling his feet on the floor, his laceless black shoes small, almost girlish, the shackles on his ankles clanging.

I looked around to make certain that Karl wasn't lurking somewhere before I asked him, "Did you think she was there for your pleasure?"

"No, I did not," he said.

"What did you think when Joanna was screaming?"

"I wished she wouldn't," he said.

"You wished she would be quiet and do what you wanted?"

"Yes," he said again.

"Why do you think she was screaming?"

"She didn't like it."

"Then what did you think?"

"I wasn't thinking," he said.

"Surely you had thoughts," I said loudly. "Surely you must have thought something, something about these women. You saw them on the stairs. Did you believe they weren't quite human?"

"No," he said.

"Then what?" I demanded to know. "Then what were you thinking about them? That they were lesser, there for your taking?"

"No," he said again.

"THEN WHAT WERE YOU THINKING?"

"NOTHING, I DIDN'T THINK NOTHING."

I stopped myself from going on, the shame drilled through me, the nakedness of my questions apparent to me even as I asked them. Vic Ponti was everywhere, his voice, his breath, his cold touch.

"I'm sorry, Mr. Guyer," I said. "Sometimes it's hard to understand. Please forgive me."

I looked at him, his hair carefully slicked back, his temples sunken as if the doctor had pulled him from his mother's womb with steel tongs, his eyes big, the sleeves of his orange jumpsuit rolled up, his tattoos, a collection of snakes inching up his arm and wrapping around his neck. He was sitting in the chair, his small black shoes side by side on the floor, his hands folded in his lap. We'd just finished the St. Francis of Assisi Prayer: *Lord, make me an instrument of thy peace. Where there is hatred, let me sow love.* . . .

He nodded his head as if to tell me this time he would forget it, he'd forgiven worse in his life, which I didn't doubt, and I was grateful he was big enough to overlook it, it was unfair of me, undignified.

It was after this that the memories of Vic Ponti returned to me, fetid and diseased, the days I had lived with him coming back to me now, I could feel the pull of that horrible box I had once descended into. My mind seized on a day when Vic Ponti and I were riding in the car, I had no idea why; it wasn't a special day, there was nothing remarkable about the day, except that I remembered feeling an utterly hopeless despair, an oppressive anxiety at being caught in this car with him. It stood out among my other feelings, not because it was so dissimilar from the others I always had, but because it was more profoundly stark, the despair deeper, more weighted, as if during that uneventful car ride I had descended farther or had edged closer to oblivion, as if something unseen was drawing me quietly towards a final parting with the world, not bodily, but emotionally, as if I were being lured, courted even into vanishing.

I couldn't remember anything but that and couldn't imagine why the memory kept returning to me, it seemed to hold nothing other than this, no great happening, no indelible image, only this depth of despair. I began to wonder if something terrible had happened before I had gotten into the car, if Vic Ponti had beaten me savagely or drugged me, but I could remember nothing. When strange red rashes appeared around my wrists again, when bracelets of raw, chapped skin ringed them both, I was convinced that something must have happened, for I couldn't help but remember how the rashes had mysteriously broken out after I had married Vic Ponti, and had disappeared without a trace not long after I left him. I wanted to tell Dr. Mattair about Vic Ponti, to push up the sleeves of my coat and show him the rashes, so as to make the connection between John Guyer and Vic Ponti, telling him how much John Guyer reminded me of Vic Ponti, not so much physically, but rather in judgment, the blackness I felt lay in their souls remarkably identical, but there was no way in which to tell him, unless I was willing to say that Oscar had been sexually abused by Vic Ponti countless times, or that I was not Oscar Lourde to begin with.

As it was, I had to say something about this conversation with John Guyer—everyone knew about it, it was a small, intimate group, you couldn't yell like that and not have everyone know, if not hear. Bristol was often nearby, a man who in his silence heard everything, Karl kept a constant vigil on me, and Juan could have been anywhere pushing his broom.

I lay there for a long time on Dr. Mattair's sofa, listening to his even breathing, before I said, "I wish I hadn't asked John Guyer the questions. It wasn't right of me." And when Dr. Mattair asked me, "Why wasn't it right?" I answered, "It is not my job to question John Guyer's behavior."

He asked me then why was I so interested in John Guyer's behavior, and I thought to myself it was because I wanted to understand how John perceived women, I didn't understand what a man thought when he raped a woman. I was interested in the idea that they might not perceive women as human. But I couldn't say this because I wasn't sure if a man would ever wonder such things. So very carefully I answered, "I'm curious how a man could rape a woman. My sister was raped by a man once, and she was upset by it."

When Dr. Mattair then asked me, "Would you like to rape a woman?" I immediately answered, "No."

"But you're interested in why John Guyer wanted to?" he said.

"Yes."

"Why is John Guyer's sex life so interesting to you?" he asked next, and I wondered in silence if John Guyer's sex life was interesting to me. I couldn't imagine wanting to sleep with him, the thought repulsed me actually, but I didn't think I should answer that. I wondered then if Dr. Mattair imagined that I, as Oscar, wanted to sleep with John Guyer or be raped by him, but this I truly could not imagine. So I asked myself, why would John Guyer's sex life be interesting to Oscar? But again I had no idea.

I finally said, "I don't know that John Guyer's sex life is interesting to me. I was merely letting my emotions get the better of me. I was horrified by the thoughts of what he did to those women."

"Do the sex lives of the women interest you?" Dr. Mattair asked me.

They didn't particularly, but I thought they might interest Oscar, since he was supposed to be sexually interested in women. But it might be perverse to say yes, I thought, under the circumstances, but then again to say I was not interested might not be normal either. I finally answered, "I don't know."

There followed a long silence which weighed greatly on me, while Dr. Mattair was not made the least bit uncomfortable by it. He in fact made use of it, settling into it, until it finally forced me to speak.

"I'm just curious about what men—other men, that is—think about women. That's all," I said.

"What's so interesting about what other men think of women?" Dr. Mattair asked me.

I tried to imagine what it would have sounded like if I had spoken as a woman and had said, "I'm just curious about what other women think about men." I imagined this didn't sound too preposterous, that certainly a woman could honestly wonder what other women thought of men, and that it then followed that a man could wonder what other men thought of women

without it being strange or out of the ordinary. But then it occurred to me that my comment was revealing, that it implied that
I was actually interested in what I as a man thought of women,
that it didn't really matter at all what other men thought of wom-
en, what mattered was what I thought of women. When Dr. Mattair left the silence alone, I felt myself stranded, for I couldn't
answer that question—what I as a man thought about women,
because I couldn't really know. What I was truly interested in
was what I thought of men as a woman.

I felt strangely speechless then, as if I were being silenced, as
if some hand were being held over my mouth, although Dr. Mattair had neither touched me nor silenced me, not in the true
sense, and I desperately wanted to leave. I checked my watch
and saw that I had ten more minutes to fill, and I didn't think I
could do it.

My head began to pound, and when Dr. Mattair broke the silence and asked me, "What man's thoughts are you interested in
knowing?" an image came into my mind, an image of John Guyer
sitting inside a cell, on a bunk, his legs hanging down listlessly,
but there was something wrong, I had never seen John Guyer
sitting on a bunk, I had only seen him chained in the prayer cell.
When I looked more closely I was shocked to realize it was Lourde
I saw in my mind and not John Guyer—it was Lourde I had seen
sitting inside a cell in Wampsville Jail, his legs hanging down
listlessly. I remembered how this image of Lourde had thrilled
me as a girl, how I had wondered in the dark of my room if the
still and the bombing weren't all his fault, as if through some silent, unseen means he had compelled it all.

Then, for some reason the sheet of paper with Lourde's last
written words came into my mind, and though it made no logical sense, I said, "Do you know that my father's last words were:
'It is better to fall into the hands of a murderer than into the
dreams of a woman in heat'?"

The words, uttered in that small cinderblock room, were so
stark, so final.

"Did he fall into the dreams of a woman in heat or into the
hands of a murderer?" Dr. Mattair asked.

"A woman in heat," I said. But then I saw Bo, struggling to keep Lourde happy, making a still so that he wouldn't have to get a job, a still that blew up his family.

"Maybe she was a murderer too," I said.

"Why would your mother want to murder him?"

I could not imagine that Bo had wanted to murder Lourde, or what reason she would have had for wanting to, yet the more I thought about it, the faster my heart beat.

"My heart is pounding," I said.

"Why is that?" Dr. Mattair asked me, but I didn't know.

When I went home that night I felt strange, mad even, and I didn't know what to think, all the things I'd said, and me with bound breasts, dressed like a man, calling myself Oscar Lourde, directing men on Death Row in prayer.

I watched Zellie cooking dinner in our kitchen and wondered where it had gone, the urge to be like her, cooking or bent over someone's baby, I had become some strange thing, I didn't quite know what, and when I thought if the men knew that I was not Oscar Lourde, if Dr. Mattair knew, it froze me.

In the dark after Zellie went to sleep I sat down on the wooden floor in our living room and pressed my back against the wall. With closed eyes, I watched my breath and asked what was wrong with me, why was I bound and living as a man. Instead of listening in the silence, I slowly descended into the minefield of memory, searching for a piece in the vastness of my memory, the piece that would cause me to understand my existence. It felt so vast, like looking for a small chest sunken deep below the floor of an ocean.

I was transported back to the time I was with Vic Ponti, the idea of riding in the car with him returning to me again. I approached it as if it were a tightly sealed box I wanted to open, but had neither the hands nor the teeth to open it with. I tried to remember what had preceded it, what had followed it, but I could remember nothing, only that the day was hot, that when I looked out the window, I felt myself so far away, I feared I might never return. I tried to capture the memory in my imagination, to hold it down, stealing up on it from every direction I could think of, to discover it and rob it of its essence, but it yielded nothing.

When Harold St. Hilaire began to talk to me, I was surprised, he had always been so reserved. It was always about what he'd read, he declined most times to talk about himself, so we talked about philosophy, he'd read many of the great works and could quote long sections from heart, eloquently. It disturbed me at times that he could speak so beautifully that the Cotton family drifted from my thoughts, the six of them coming back into stark focus later, I would see them hanging from the rafters, when I was on the train or back in my apartment. But Harold had a voice that could mesmerize, that could cast spells, and he was not unaware of his power.

I felt compelled to read the books he talked about, lest I appear uninformed in his presence, and I went so far as to memorize certain passages, and marked many others I felt were interesting, bringing them up nonchalantly, as if I had read them ages ago. What I couldn't help but notice was that they had little to do with women, in some cases the word or concept of woman not appearing for pages, sometimes chapters, whole treatises, they figured in so little. I mentioned this to Harold St. Hilaire one day, a casual remark, and he said, "Women are the niggers of gender, that's why. Their set purpose is to make men, something from which a man never fully recovers, but it makes them inferior, contrary to popular opinion." He looked out through the bars which separated us, his black eyes flashing both evil and amusement, magnified just slightly by the thick lenses of his glasses, his gaze so penetrating, I felt naked in front of him, as if he had reached under my coat and torn my binding off.

When he pursed his lips and smiled, I realized that this was a subject that interested Harold St. Hilaire greatly, and he was hoping it was an interest of mine as well, that we could talk man to man. "I know there is the argument that women were kept from genius due to their socialization," he said, "which I don't underestimate, but there is now a hundred years behind us where women have not been in chains, and as a group, such as men are a group, they have not emerged with a truly brilliant body of work, in any field." He paused a moment, then added, "I can say these things. I am a man on Death Row." Unable to move his hands freely (they were handcuffed), his long, tapered fingers rose gently in a delicate, fluid motion, offering me a slight hint, a trace of the feminine, which vanished as soon as he stilled them.

I swallowed, and very carefully I mentioned to Harold St. Hilaire that I believed there was at least one field in which women had an enormous body of superior, brilliant work—literature. I said I thought women had made a considerable contribution to literature, but he strongly disagreed, saying there were a few isolated incidences of brilliant women writers, such as Virginia Woolf and Simone de Beauvoir, but for the most part he did not see women as contributing much in the way of literature, saying that they did not write about enduring themes, they wrote about being women in relation to men, generally in a sentimental way. I asked was it not an enduring theme, the subject of women under male dominion? It has certainly endured, I pointed out, to which he replied, "Good try, Mr. Lourde."

When he said, "It is in woman's nature to be subdued," I asked him was it in a Jew's nature to be led to the gas chambers, was it in a black's nature to be led into slavery, some of these Jews and blacks were men. No, I said, let us look to the ones who did the leading and let us ask what was in their nature to want to lead others down such a lousy road. To which Harold St. Hilaire replied, "Superiority."

When I went home at night, Harold's words often stayed with me, and I would wonder if it was a fact, a fact of nature like the color of one's eyes or hair, a fact of nature, the secondness. What if it were true, what if women were second, the lesser, inferior, not as brilliant, as reasonable, as fierce, as godlike, and never would be? What if they were actually swampy vessels with a specific biological function? What if, frankly, this was the worst thing a woman ever had to know?

Inside, I took it on, wore it, pressed it to me, my secondness. Underneath the clothes, I was secondness, a subcreature, walking the master's land, knowing more about the master than the

master knew of me, reveling in it, rubbing up against it, this secondness, pushing after a while, until I was heaving myself against
the wall of it.

I began to watch Harold carefully, especially when he tended
his altar or his section of a garden, both of which Reverend Beacon had added out in the catwalk. The men were now let out of
their handcuffs and chains long enough to take care of small gar-
dens that thrived in the diffused light, and small altars which
they had made out of thick cardboard and had glued to the wall.

Harold was the most attached to the altar, bringing to it all
the items he'd managed to replicate of an obscure Indian religion
named Jainism. He'd come across a book in the prison's library
and had created his section of the altar based on the pictures he
had found in this book. He built a cardboard incense-stick holder,
a small lamp, and a tiny dish into which he put red powder. He
framed two pictures he cut from the book, one of the Hindu saint
Satya Sai Baba, the other of Mahavira, a Jain saint who was almost God, he told me. There was also an idol of Ganesh, a man
with an elephant's head, who was the Hindu god of prosperity,
which he had made from clay.

It wasn't so much the altar as the way Harold St. Hilaire tended
the altar that was fascinating. The movement of his hands, freed
of the handcuffs, riveted me, they behaved so gracefully, as if they
had a life of their own, separate from him. While his sleeves hung
over the backs of his hands, he put his thumb in the dish of red
powder called kanku and touched it to the foreheads of Satya
Sai Baba, Mahavira, Ganesh, and then himself. "Chandan" was
the name of the mark, he said. He touched the things so delicately it almost made me weep.

One day while he was tending his altar, his hands lightly touching the photographs of Mahavira, of Satya Sai Baba, he said that
he did not think women should be beaten or mistreated in any
way. He thought they should have equal political rights, which
he believed they now had. "Biologically they need to be emotional," he said, "and hence sentimental, and capable of long, enduring love, otherwise they would abandon their children, the most

important being the male children, us." He included me again, another man. "The same thing which makes them good caretakers," he went on, "their emotions, makes them poorly equipped to be rational thinkers and hence build the world, such as men are and do. It's all dictated by nature, and nature is nothing you can argue with," he said. "It is no one's fault." He glanced at me, his eyes filled more with mockery than evil, and I noticed the masking tape holding his thick black glasses together.

I moved closer to the bars. I could have reached through them and touched Harold St. Hilaire, I could have touched his dark, curly hair, his slender, effeminate hands that moved like swans.

"Was it rational to hang six people from the rafters of their home?" I asked him quietly, he loved the rational so much.

"No," he said. "It was not rational."

"Wasn't it emotional?"

He did not answer.

"Wasn't it the most extreme of emotions—anger, hate, revulsion—the most complex, and hence emotional?" I asked, my voice a little loud.

"Yes, it was emotional, in this way," he agreed.

"Then it follows that your act was in some way womanly."

"No, it was not womanly, for no woman, or very few, would ever commit such a crime. Women are incapable, for the most part, of such extremes. Their range is quite narrow."

"But what about it being emotional, such as you say women are?"

He turned slowly to me, his eyes dark and piercing. "You are toiling upon barren ground, Mr. Lourde," he said.

I shoved my chair back and stood up. "I think not," I said.

When I turned, Karl was standing there, his maimed arm hanging lifeless by his side, his eyes flashing behind those tiny round glasses, he was thrilled to have witnessed a small piece of my unraveling.

The next time Harold was tending his altar and turned to me and said, "Women are no more than slaves," a violent rage rose up in me suddenly and unexpectedly.

"Yes, perhaps, but even the slave can master the master's dialect and use it against him," I said.

"She is not interested in the truth," Harold said.

I moved my chair closer to the bars. "How should you know what she is interested in?" I asked. "Do you think you can speak for women?"

He was surprised by the tone of my voice, it caught him off guard, and for a moment he froze. Then he turned back to his altar and touched the red powder delicately to the picture of Satya Sai Baba and said matter-of-factly, "She has no voice."

Harold put down the picture of Satya Sai Baba and stared at me.

"I read a woman philosopher who said that when she reads a man's work, whenever she comes across the word 'woman' in the text, she substitutes the words 'my mother,' and then she understands completely."

Harold threw his head back and laughed hysterically.

"What makes you think you can speak like a woman or for a woman?" I yelled. "Are you a woman?"

He stopped laughing immediately, and his eyes plunged deep into mine. "No," he said. *"Are you?"*

It was as if his eyes, given a sudden power of focus like no other I had ever seen, bored through my dark clothes, past the elastic binding, straight into my heart, his gaze not merely unmasking me, but rather going further, emasculating me so suddenly and fiercely I felt castrated.

When I went home that night, I stole into the bathroom and in the silence and stark white light placed myself in front of the mirror, where I slowly began to unbutton my shirt. My hands started to shake, I hadn't looked at myself in years. It horrified me to think how I never took the binding off anymore, leaving it on while I showered, drying it afterwards with Zellie's blow-dryer. But I took my shirt off now and hung it on the doorknob, my eyes chancing to fall on the rash that bordered my wrists, straying then to the image of my chest in the mirror, which was bound with elastic the color of flesh. I stared at my collarbone, fascinated at the way it lay beneath my skin, the curve so delicate and feminine, so different from a man's, and my neck, so stemlike and pale it embarrassed me. I pressed my fingers underneath the elastic, near the right side of my ribs, and found the small silver pin, which I unclasped and held in my left hand while I unwound the elastic, one wrap at a time, daring myself to look, as if the sight of myself would put an end to all of it—working in a prison with men on Death Row, bound and living as a man— but I didn't get very far. It felt dire, what might happen were I to finish the unbinding, as if it might result in a fatal stroke. My heart beat so fast, I quickly rewound the elastic, and swiftly, with fingers long ago trained, I pinned it underneath and pulled my shirt back on. I sat down on the edge of the porcelain bathtub then and hunched over in my lap, crossing my arms tightly against my chest, as if the elastic weren't enough, and it was there, pulled deeply into myself, that I listened to my short, shallow breath and knew that there was something wrong with me, something more than I had ever imagined. It wasn't a matter of being bound and living as a man, as if it had been my choice; no, I had no choice—I couldn't be unbound.

I asked myself again why I had bound myself, *why*, it was finally too strange, too bizarre, and an answer came up so cleanly, the words were startling, as if my mind's voice had spoken: *You should have been a boy.* I had never heard anything so clearly, but where had this voice come from, I had never heard it before, and the words, they were so precise, wrapped perfectly in silence. But why, why should I have been a boy? I asked, but there was no answer, only the pounding of my heart.

After this, when I sat down on the floor in the living room at night with my back pressed against the wall, I closed my eyes and watched my breath and asked in a voice that grew louder what was wrong, what had happened to me. I found myself lost again and again in the vastness of my memory, searching for that piece that would cause me to understand what had happened that I was working with men on Death Row, bound and living as a man. Every night, I took hold of, fingered, brushed over and over the memories which had always stood out, the ones I had always looked to, as familiar to me now as my own hands, the ones which I had nurtured, paused in front of, recalled, passed by

time and time; the ones that are the markers, the signposts you
have seen so often you almost cease to see them, but even so
they have always supported the idea of your life, they were its
main pillars, its stays, and when added together offered up a tale,
a story of your life, which you lived by, swore by. I am this way
because . . .

My mother made a still and opened up a bar, she was trying
to outdo her own mother, she loved her husband so much, she
wanted him to write plays, then it blew up and I shot a man in
the groin to save Coleman, and this fact changed my life, it was
the deciding event which prompted my mother to tell me that
because of it she realized I had a great destiny ahead of me, that
I would change the course of history, and that because of this
great fate I could never love a man, and then when I lost my family in a bombing and my sister survived as a cripple, I had to
work so hard that I finally gave up and married Vic Ponti to save
my sister, but he ruined me, he put inside of me a wounded animal which crept through me at strange hours, and then I met another man, I thought life had offered him to me, and I loved him,
lost myself to him, until he left me, and there I was alone, worrying that I had given up my great fate for this man, and I wanted
it back, so I vowed to do as Bo had told me, to build a fortress
around my heart, and I cut my hair and changed my name, I refused the passions of a passionate man again and again and again,
I bound my chest to keep my vow, I watched my breath and listened in the silence, and washed the old people and taught them
to do the same, which aroused the attention of Reverend Beacon
who had convinced me to work with men on Death Row . . .

But I could discover nothing.

When Dr. Mattair asked me why I was so interested in argu-
ing with Harold St. Hilaire about women, I said, "Because he
says ignorant things about them, as if he is an authority."

"Are you an authority on women?" he asked me.

Of course I was an authority on women, but I couldn't say
this, Oscar was not an authority on women, and I suddenly felt
entrapped by my own words. Silence engulfed me, and I longed

to be gone from this small room, to escape Dr. Mattair's questions, to be let out of this arrangement.

"No," I said. "I don't think I'm an authority on women. It's not that. It's just that he's a man, and it's presumptuous of him to assume he can speak for women."

"Can you speak for women?" he asked me, and I thought, Yes, of course I can, but even so I didn't know what I would say were I to speak for women. I wanted to, though, I wanted to speak for women, I wanted to scream for them, to scream at the top of my voice, and then perhaps the words would come, but I felt so hopelessly silent, as if I had no words, no language.

Would Oscar want to speak for women? I thought, I must speak like Oscar, and I was fairly certain that Oscar would not be interested in speaking for women, just as I was not particularly interested in speaking for men, they spoke very well for themselves. "No," I finally said, "I can't either."

"What is so interesting about speaking for women?" Dr. Mattair said.

"Have you ever heard them speak?" I asked. "Have you ever listened to them?"

"Why does it interest you so much?" he asked again.

"We are amid destruction, amid men who personify destruction," I said, but I stopped myself from going on.

As the silence hung like gloom in this small space of cinderblock and concrete, I was never so aware of being a woman. This was a place, I suddenly realized, farthest from women, a place where woman did not exist, where the idea of woman had been erased. There were no women. They never walked inside this place, they never spoke here, never laughed here, their voice was utterly lost, barred forever from this place. Woman did not exist here. She had been walled out entirely. In fact, there was no place where woman's absence was more complete, and here I was, dressed as a man, calling myself Oscar Lourde.

Then Dr. Mattair broke the silence to ask me, "Who wanted to destroy you?" and immediately I had the sensation of being held down, deep in some airless, dark hole, where I was utterly speechless. My heart pounded, and I felt myself being drawn closer to insanity, as if the line which cordoned sanity from insanity was thin, diaphanous, a membrane through which the fluids of one passed easily into the fluids of the other, and suddenly, without any provocation, I wept violently into my hands, and Dr. Mattair never said a word.

I felt then as if at the center of me a vital pin had broken.

When I was with William Heathens I tried not to watch him moving about in the catwalk when he tended his part of the garden or his altar, but I was drawn to his movements, to his long strides, to the slow swing of his muscled arms, to his childlike blue eyes, as if there were some comfort there. I was especially curious about what he brought to this altar, feeling ridiculously pleased when he brought certain things—a faded photograph of his grandmother, a piece of fabric that reminded him of a dress she had once worn, a necklace he made out of aluminum foil.

It amazed me how the attraction had no respect for the fact of our positions, and that no matter how silent we were about it, never breathing a word of it, it remained between us, insistent, obstinate, and unrelenting. He watched me also, and often stayed near me, and when our eyes chanced to meet, I sensed in his look, his confusion, sometimes desperate, he did not know I was a woman.

Whenever he was in the catwalk, I was never unaware of the fact that I could have reached out and touched the muscled flesh of his upper arm, his cheek, his boyish mouth. He was not unaware of it either, the nearness of our flesh became a torment, and one late afternoon he edged so close to me, our hands almost touched through the bars. I saw the pain, the confusion in his eyes, he was worried that he was attracted to a man. His mouth began to form a word, but he did not speak. He finally whispered, "What are—," but then he stopped abruptly and turned and walked back to his section of the garden.

My heart began to pound hard in my chest; I felt utterly silenced, incapable of speaking so much as one word—what could I have said, a woman dressed as a man, yet I wanted to know what he would have asked, even as I knew I could not have answered his question.

It remained between us, though, these two words—"what"

and "are." They burned there. Whether he was in the catwalk or chained inside the prayer cell, whether we were silent or praying, I could hear them, and if not them exactly, then the question, which over the weeks became clear to me: *What are you doing?* This question never left me. I took it everywhere with me, I asked it of myself every free moment I had, and though I never knew why, something about this question caused my bladder to ache in the same way it had ached when I was with Luther Wolfe—it began anew, the pain, and I was forced again to take the drug that turned my urine orange.

I heard the question most when I was with John Guyer, the silence between us having deepened, becoming so profound he began to feel like a dark, impenetrable weight on the other side of those bars. Sometimes while we meditated I had the illusion of floating up into the air, as if I was made of something entirely different, opposite, perhaps from him. It seemed to be a measure of our complete misunderstanding of one another, we were two creatures nearly unfathomable to one another. I sensed in him a dark mystery, as if he were a terrifying wall I could not scale, and at nights I began to dream John Guyer was trying to kill me.

When I told Dr. Mattair this, he asked me why John Guyer would want to kill me, and before I had a chance to think, the words "Lourde did" came out of my mouth, and neither Dr. Mattair nor I said anything for a long time, the words, *Lourde did,* hanging in the air of that small cinderblock room, trying to escape. I had never once had that thought, and where it had come from, I could not imagine, but later, in the dark of my bedroom, when I asked myself why I had said it, I became aware that there was something to it, that the words were attached to something terrifying at the bottom, at the brink of my mind, but I did not know what.

How many times my mind went over the story of my life, sifting through it for another piece in the vastness of memory, for a piece I had perhaps missed or neglected which once discovered would radically alter my perspective, would throw light on it all. As each night passed, I grew more and more desperate to know, pressing the memories, pushing them, finally shoving them up against a wall, to force out of them some answer. I began to focus my concentration more and more finely, as if it were the ground glass of a microscope, all the while straining to see, prying, digging into the memories, turning my mind into a probing instrument capable of boring through the cement of fixed memory, of moving relentlessly downward. It was as if I were seeking the hidden, as if something unseen lay beneath the markers of my life, something that had directed the sequence of events which had always formed the story of my life, as if the sequence itself had been put in place to lull me, to keep me on the same worn path forever so that I might be saved or kept from seeing the truer order, the hand beneath it all—a dark, sprawling hand, I imagined, with countless fingers, like fine filaments, an invisible circulatory system of the mind, a huge network of veins and arteries, which carried the blood of thought back and forth, as if in fact there were a living thing breathing deeply at the base of me, a frightening contagion of roots that crawled up from the seething black soil of my mind, like an ancient tree that had touched everything I had ever said or thought or done.

But it was elusive, and I couldn't discover it.

It made little sense to me when I touched William Heathens's hand, I was not at liberty to forget myself. Juan was sweeping the prayer cell not more than ten feet from me, Karl was in and out of the cellblock, bringing candles to the altar, adding new pages to the prayer book, Bristol was standing guard in the catwalk, reading a comic book. But when William came over to the bars and looked into my eyes, I forgot them, I forgot my anxiety, something about him made me forget. We were not more than twelve inches apart, it was a clandestine moment, an important moment, I sensed, a moment in which he had decided to say something to me. Even though there were no words for us, no way we could truly speak, I wanted to hear him, as if his words would soothe me. He stood there, his eyes filled with desire and confusion, his fingers clutching the cold metal bars that separated us. He whispered, "Why am—," and then stopped speaking, and I imagined he was trying to ask me why he was attracted to me. I desperately wanted to let him know that it was not what he thought, I did not want him to suffer. "It's okay," I said, as if that could possibly explain something.

"What's okay, Mr. Lourde?" he asked quietly. His eyes burned as he stared through the bars at me.

I couldn't imagine what I should say, I tried to think of something, but there was nothing. *Your attraction to me is all right, I am a woman. You're attracted to me because I'm a woman. I am a woman dressed as a man.* There was simply nothing I could say, not one word, not so much as a sound that I could make, so I reached out and touched the back of his fingers, that was all that was left to me. He froze, and then, though I couldn't quite believe it, he grabbed my hand and squeezed it. "I think about you all the time," he whispered fiercely. Horror then filled his blue eyes.

I heard someone behind me and turned to find Karl standing there, his mouth hanging open, as if to underline his shock. He had heard us, he saw our hands touching now. I dropped my hand immediately and moved away, William Heathens turning abruptly back to the altar, an anguished sound coming from him.

"What were you just doing?" Karl hissed. Underneath his obvious shock, I sensed how deeply he relished this moment, as if all along he had been waiting for this.

"What did it look like I was doing?" I whispered. I knew of nothing else to say.

"It looked like you were touching William Heathens's hand, that's what it looked like, like the two of you were having a moment," Karl hissed.

When I next went to Dr. Mattair's office, I said right away, "I touched William Heathens's hand." I couldn't stop myself from saying it.

"Why would you do that?" Dr. Mattair asked.

My eyes wandered over the cinderblock wall, up to the ceiling, while I considered what I would say. "It was a gesture of compassion," I finally said.

When Dr. Mattair asked me why I was feeling compassionate for William Heathens, I thought how I hadn't felt the least bit compassionate, I wanted to sleep with William Heathens, but Oscar could not say this, he would appear homosexual. I thought of William's history again, how his father had raped him from the age of four to sixteen, and I said, "I was feeling compassion-ate for him because his father raped him."

I hated the way that sentence hung in the silence, how a sen-tence like that, so carefully considered by me, could be uttered with an innocence and yet hang there so nakedly.

"Sometimes fathers don't always control their impulses," Dr. Mattair said, and I thought of that, of fathers being unable to control their impulses. "Children are very sexy," he went on, "and all fathers are attracted to their children, but they cannot allow themselves to act on these impulses."

My heart started to bang again.

"A child's nervous system cannot tolerate the stimulation," Dr. Mattair said, and he kept speaking in this vein, but I was so suddenly and inexplicably seized with panic that I no longer heard his words.

"I think I might faint," I said.

"Why?" Dr. Mattair asked me.

"I don't know," I said, and within moments my arms began to go numb. "My arms are going numb," I said. I wrung my hands like someone possessed.

"Why?" he asked, but I didn't have the slightest idea.

I bolted upright. I felt if I lay on the sofa another minute, I would lose my mind, that it would disassemble right then and there and I would be left insane.

"I can't lie here," I said.

"Why?" Dr. Mattair asked.

"I'm afraid if I do, I'll go insane."

"Why would you want to go insane?" Dr. Mattair said.

"What are you talking about?" I said. "I don't want to go in-sane. I fear it tremendously." It struck me as such an odd thing to say, and it annoyed me immensely, but I couldn't think of it and spoke now of anything else, of the men, of the model of a sailing ship Dr. Mattair had in his office, of the headache that had begun to bloom inside my head, describing it thoroughly, down to the timing of its pulse, discussing its possible origins, telling him of other headaches I had had, trying to find some safe, neutral ground on which to stand, but there was none.

* * *

Anxiety began to accompany me wherever I went, it came to inhabit me like some pitiless demon. When I was at the prison, I was able to quell it enough to sit with the men, to conduct the prayers, but when I left it consumed me, its appetite was ravenous, a furnace which burned my flesh.

I became plagued with thoughts of explosions then, of stabbings; whenever I walked on the street now I imagined being shot in the back, every time I rode in a cab I envisioned crashing. I found myself thinking more about Mr. Antonovsky and Stalin's work camps, the question which returned to my mind over and over again: How had he survived? How had any of them survived? At night I was unable to sleep and writhed in the dark, and every time I approached the anxiety, asked it what it was, the closer I drew to it, the more I was filled with it.

Night after night I pressed my back against the wall, and with my eyes closed, descended into the minefield of my memory, searching for that piece that would cause me to finally understand. I brushed over and over the memories again which had always stood out, the ones I had always looked to, the ones that had always supported the idea of my life, which when added together offered up the tale, the story of my life, which I had lived by, sworn by.

Innumerable times I recounted the story, focusing my attention more and more finely, boring again through the cement of fixed memory, moving relentlessly downward, straining now to see the hidden, that unseen something which lay beneath the markers, that dark, sprawling hand which I knew was there, until one night with blood pounding at my temples, I veered off the path of worn memories, rushing deep into the woods of my thoughts, plunging into an abyss, dark and tangled, where I again found myself sitting in the front seat of Vic Ponti's car, cut off from everything, from the air, from the wheat fields that sped by, as if I were encased completely in glass. It shocked me that I should return to this, yet even so, something was different about it now, I sensed it stood alone, naked, detached from its usual associations, as if I had before seen only the shadow it had cast, and I sunk myself deeply into the thought of it, feeling again the deep, weighted despair, descending farther into oblivion, allow-ing whatever unseen hand was there to draw me quietly towards it, to lure me, seduce me into going, guided only by my senses, waiting to be seized by the bite of truth.

My heart beat so fast, I felt myself in peril, yet I kept going, I kept track of myself, watching my breath, never losing awareness of where I was or what I was doing, my mind pulling downward, falling beneath the surface I had always known, finally descending into the deepest sadness, the deepest silence, a freezing cold, as if I had been delivered to the bottom of an ocean in the icy, dead black of night. Then a sense came to me, a terrible, chilling recognition that Vic Ponti had been only one wing of the butterfly, that there was another one, unseen by me as yet, an echo of it, as if the experience of Vic Ponti had happened before, at someone else's hand.

I pressed closer, and then, though it didn't seem possible, something even deeper, a hole, a depression, opened up, and I suddenly possessed the strangest knowledge, as if all this time it had been perfectly preserved beneath the surface, like a carefully excised heart sealed off completely in a glass jar.

The front seat of a car came to me first, the image of a dashboard, barely visible in the darkness. The recognition that I was in the car, the dashboard my vantage point, I could see nothing above it, I was only two years old. The sense that it was late at night, I had been pulled from my bed, ripped from countless sleeps, driven somewhere, it was always Lourde who drove. His window cracked an inch or two, the wind causing a persistent, high-pitched whistling. That sound, plus the sound of the car, the sense of motion, the feeling of being helpless and terrified, of knowing I was being driven to a place where there was no one, the sense that it was growing more and more unsafe by the moment, there was no one to save me, no mother, no hope, I was profoundly trapped.

The idea of a game came to me, a game I was forced to play in the front seat of his car, a game called Hide the Pickle, a secret game. Always at the beginning, his voice, low and sweet, gentle even as he tried to entice me into playing the game, vague bits of words, *going to play again, see how many ways.* There was something wrong with the game, I didn't want to play, I never wanted to play, and it scared me to be asked to play. I sought his arms, arms that at other times had held me, but there was no comfort, my need annoyed him. There were no other arms, I knew of nothing to do but seek him again and again, the tone of his voice changing in a matter of moments, his patience evaporating so quickly it was jarring, his voice turning harsh and lacerating, this man who had only moments ago been so kind. The touch of his hand, at first so gentle, became hard, grasping, then forceful, his hand clapping over my mouth again and again, extinguishing my voice, my struggle growing, the power in his arms, multiplying until it felt infinite. Shivering, my small legs were spread, my arms strung up above my head, his hands on me, choking me, my small nipples rubbed raw, hard things thrust into me. The scramble of my small legs, its utter and hopeless futility. How swiftly I was overcome, how easily I was beaten, thrown from one end of the car to the other, an awful sense of how many ways there were to play this secret game, Hide the Pickle, how I had been forced to play them all.

Night after night, until I could speak.

No images now, only a language of the body, my bladder aching, my windpipe cut off, my jaw unhinging, weight crushing my chest—the traces left, my body a page, his evil inscribed forever in my flesh. How utterly helpless, unfathomably powerless, a sand castle against a wrecking ball, a paper doll beneath a golem.

Then, much vaguer, much more difficult to grasp, the idea of torture, senseless, less comprehensible, strung up with rope, tied at the wrists, my arms pulled over my head, the rope tied to a door handle, to a tree in a pitch-black woods, to a boat winch, while horrible dark water spread out before me. The sense of a woman appearing, yet only a trace, a feminine laugh, the hem of a dress, sometimes in the woods, in a boat, the two of them retreating, then gone completely, leaving me for what felt like hours. Then, the sickest silence descending, a speechlessness like no other.

The thought again, I should have been a boy.

A two-year-old and a full-grown man. Then Bo standing in the kitchen of Cedar Valley making cookies. "Don't you think he did it?" I had asked her, meaning Happy and the bombing. "It was the biggest, most fatal mistake I ever made, getting involved with that man," she had said. "The enormity of the mistake I can't even begin to utter. . . ." I had said, "Yes, but if he did it, Bo—" and she had turned quickly. "That man is not the sort of man you accuse of bombing your house and killing your family, not if you want what's left of that family to live. Do you hear me?"

Bo sitting in her wheelchair, blind. "If you want to be a woman, love a man. If you want to be a great woman, build a fortress around your heart." How she'd really said: "I've loved that man, that's why I'm not a great woman." Her husband, writing his plays up in the attic, sitting there with his terrible knowledge, this man who relished evil secrets, the sort of secrets where he inflicted evil, of which the person was completely ignorant, where he went not only undiscovered, but unsuspected as well. Lourde without conscience, taking Bo's child from her bed, playing this secret game, then handing her back to Bo, knowing he had gotten one over on Bo, the child could not speak, the child could tell no one, Bo had had the dreams of a woman in heat. "And I wouldn't feel the least bit of guilt," I remembered him saying when he talked of killing Happy and leaving his dead body in a field to be eaten by vultures.

Being like Pavlov's dog, trained, conditioned in behavior, conditioned to feel violent hatred, hot-pounding, killing instinct, when someone so much as touched one of my female parts. I had always thought Vic Ponti had trained me. Vic Ponti was nothing.

How I'd shot Mr. Antonovksy, how I'd nearly shot Happy, how I'd gotten into bed with Vic Ponti seeking comfort in the arms of a tormentor. How I'd dug up Oscar's ashes and knelt before them. How my thoughts had returned every day to the concentration camps, to Stalin, to Mr. Antonovsky, asking, How had he survived? How had any of them survived?

Lourde, the father, the maker.

The rashes around my wrists,

the bladder infections,

the binding.

The body spoken.

The idea of a fate, of any kind of fate, vanished, and I found myself reinterpreting Bo's words: "You have a great fate ahead of you. You will change the course of history." Now: "I know what happened to you, your fate will be strange. I wish I could change the course of your history."

And I understood my life completely.

26

She stopped talking. She was lying on her back, her eyes pressed closed as if to shut out the horror. He was on his side and now rose up on his elbow to look at her. When she opened her eyes and looked straight into his, he was surprised how clear they were. He could not imagine what was in her mind.

What? she said softly.

But he didn't know what to say. All she had told him foundered in his mind, trying to assume some sort of shape. There were so many things to consider, he didn't know where to begin.

You must have hated them, he said softly. Bo and Lourde. Especially Lourde.

Yes, she answered. I cannot lie.

But not anymore?

She smiled and reached up and traced the outline of his lips with her finger.

What did Zellie say when you told her?

She believed me, she said.

Do you think it happened to her as well?

Yes, she said.

But she doesn't remember?

She doesn't want to.

He could understand that. It was forbidden knowledge, he thought, the route to it perilous, the break she had fallen into disturbing. But when she had said the words *And I understand my life completely*, he longed for such an understanding, for a moment when his life would make such sudden and terrible sense to him. But even so, he feared the break he would have to fall into. There was no getting there without that, and what if he could not climb out?

Come here, he said, and he wrapped his arms around her. She fell into them so easily, he thought, and without meaning to, he imagined her as a two-year-old, naked in the front seat of Lourde's car. It was this more than anything else which had disturbed him. Its association with the words *Better to fall into the hands of a murderer than into the dreams of a woman in heat* deeply unsettled him. Hadn't he admitted to himself his own understanding of these words? Then, it came to him again, Lourde's violence against his small daughter.

She turned onto her side, and he lay down on his back and studied her as she watched the Sierra Nevada Mountains speed past. He thought then of the men on Death Row. Of all of the men, it was Harold St. Hilaire he best understood, but then he had the sudden and horrible thought that she had made up this whole story so that he could discover Harold St. Hilaire in himself. Was it possible that she could have been so clever?

He looked at her, at the softness in her face as she watched out the window, and he thought, what if all she had told him were true? What if it had nothing to do with him? And felt himself close to tears.

Did you go back to the prison? he said.

Yes.

For a moment he could see the strain, as if it stretched out taut beneath her pale skin.

What happened?

She glanced at him.

I will tell you, but then it is over—the telling.

All right, he said.

But he dreaded the end of her voice, for what would there be then but his own thoughts, his own life, the break into which he was falling. He knew now that it would not be simple, that taking a train across the country was only the beginning, and he feared what lay ahead. He took hold of her hand then, and just after he touched his lips to the back of it, her voice came, one last time.

27

$\mathcal{I}$ asked Dr. Mattair many questions about the men on Death Row, as if I were interested in the clinical answers. William Heathens raped by his father, John Guyer tied beneath a bed, his father decomposing, Harold St. Hilaire present during the violence against his grandmother: how did a person survive such ordeals?, I wanted to know, and Dr. Mattair answered me, without asking why I asked (yet I sensed he knew), his voice a guide in the most visionless fog.

In this way, I lived again as if I were two years old, with emotions that felt too great for me, as if I still possessed a small body, a nervous system that didn't have the capacity to make sense of the strong tides of violence, as if I still possessed a mind with no language. I edged through the city, speaking to no one, I ate almost nothing, I didn't sleep easily. I wept sometimes and lay often with my ear pressed against the small black speaker of a tape player, listening to the ocean. Twice, I nearly chose insanity. The path was suddenly so clear—to cease speaking, to lapse into profound silence. The sight of me stilled and silenced would have been proof, that was the appeal. This went on for a long time, longer even than I dare mention; I was not truth's equal, not for some time.

It was Lourde's death inside of me that took so long. If only I had guns or bombs, but there was no such advantage in the mind, in the end nothing more than will. For weeks, the worst violence hacked through my mind, brutal acts, one after the other, heinous, grotesque, sick, but the power he had over me felt infinite, as if he lived somewhere deep in the pit of me, a seething golem, breathing my breath, warming his hands over the heat of my blood, using my life.

At last I succeeded in gunning him down, riddling his body with bullets, throwing him into a field my mind offered where he was picked apart by vultures, heaving what remained of him onto a busy highway where he ended up under countless wheels, pulp crammed into the tire treads, bit by bit worn away, ground into the concrete until he no longer existed, not a single particle. No ashes, no bones, nothing left behind, perhaps a stain, which the rain would wash away.

I watched the men pray and close their eyes in meditation, watched them bend over their earned breakfasts and lunches, their dinners, watched them breathe in their earned air. I sometimes looked up and saw in William Heathens's eyes that hot, wanting look, but instead of returning it, I glanced down, hoping that by giving him nothing, it would die instead of him. Certainly, we never spoke of it again.

When Dr. Mattair managed to arrange it so the men didn't have to sit chained in the chair that was chained to the floor or wear handcuffs while they were in the cell, it frightened me. They were attached only to the chair now, at their ankle, on a chain that allowed them some movement within the cell, and somehow their release and my fear caused something to drop away, a sheet, a curtain of the mind. In a moment's time I saw how a life could fold back on itself, as if it had been reaching to the beginning, as if in making a dark return to the start in the form of a prison and convicted men, a mind's need would be fulfilled, its need to comprehend evil, to touch it and alter it, as if in altering it it might possibly mitigate the original circumstances.

It is incomparable, such a moment, the moment when the mind drops a shackle it has been caught by for so long. Like the struggle of a hill, the tedious and long crawl, the moment the top is reached, the view so clear, how rapidly you descend the hill, the ascent over, with what unimaginable ease you depart.

The mystique of the men, of the prayer fell away, and in a moment's time it vanished, my need to be with them, and I knew then that I would leave the prison behind.

*   *   *

On my last day, one of the tapered blue candles I used rolled near the prayer cell. It was a cold day in December, we could see our breath in the air, and when I moved to retrieve it, William Heathens lunged forward, falling to the bars just as I reached to pick up the candle, his body at a slant, his right ankle chained to the foot-long chain that was chained to the floor. He quickly reached through the bars and grabbed my neck, pulling me up to my knees. I felt the bars against my chest, pressed across my face, I could see William Heathens's eyes closer than I cared to, like a mad dog's, I thought, I could feel his breath, smell it, foul with cigarettes. "Mr. Heathens," I said, but he squeezed my neck tighter and I began to choke.

"What are you, one of them big-armed women?" he hissed.

"What is that, Mr. Heathens?" I managed to ask.

"One of them women trapped in a man's body."

"No," I said. "I am not."

"I think you're some kind of a fag," he said. "There's something weird about you."

"There is," I said. "You are right."

I realized then how deeply I had deceived him, that it was no good, this lie, and I wanted to tell him immediately, I wanted to come clean in front of him, in front of all of them—nothing had ever been so clear to me. I was hoping he would allow me to talk to him, to tell him the truth, but he cracked my skull against the bars, then once again, and I tried to speak, but my throat was crushed off, not a sound made it out. I could barely breathe.

I tried to tell him the truth, but he said, "You faggot, you lousy little faggot, with your prayers." And I heard no more, he slammed my head against the bars another time, and I lost consciousness.

Then, he stripped me from my clothes, and when Karl Gerhardt found me I was lying unconscious on the concrete floor, bleeding from the head, skinny and naked, a woman.

28

She stopped talking, and neither of them said anything for a long time. He lay on his side, holding her, her head in the cradle of his arm. The image of her lying naked and unconscious on the prison floor, bleeding from the head, remained fixed in his mind. Once in the silence he squeezed her hand, and she squeezed back.

He glanced out the window and noticed that the train had begun its descent from the mountains. The forest was thinning, the grasses disappearing.

Were you badly hurt? he whispered. His lips were touching her ear.

Their eyes caught when she took his fingers and slowly guided them through her hair, over a long, thick scar that ran from her right ear to the crown of her head. Another wound inscribed in her flesh, he thought. He thought then of her body, of his body. Did it imprison the soul, or was it, like she said, imprisoned by the soul? He didn't know, but he wondered what, if anything, had been inscribed in his flesh. He was certain something had, but he didn't want to think of it. He pulled her tighter to him and touched his lips to the scar on the crown of her head.

You were recently released from Bellevue? he asked.

Yes, she said.

How long were you there?

Eight months, she said.

What did Zellie do while you were there? he asked.

She came to the hospital every day and sat by my bedside, as I had done for her so many times. She brought me food and pushed me around in the wheelchair. I think it was one of her greatest joys to take care of me. You should see the painting she did of me—me with white bandages on my head, wearing sunglasses.

He searched her eyes.

It didn't break you? he said. He imagined it might break someone else.

No, she said.

How come? It seems it might have.

He spoke so quietly.

She looked deep into his eyes and said, Harold St. Hilaire told me once that no matter what, you can not refuse one thing in your life or your life will be ruined. He said the demons you swallow give you their power.

What did the men say when they found out you were a woman? he whispered.

They hated me, especially Harold St. Hilaire. I didn't blame them—I wasn't who I said I was.

But they had benefited, he said.

Spiritual advice from a woman is second best, she whispered.

He could easily imagine this: the same words from a man's mouth would carry more weight. He didn't know why this was true, but it seemed it was.

You weren't exactly a woman, he finally said.

She pulled back to look at him.

What was I? she asked.

But he didn't have an answer.

He drew her into his arms again and felt the small, fine bones of her spine beneath his fingers.

You brought William Heathens that skull—you must have forgiven him.

She touched her lips to his throat. I would rather my burden than his, she whispered.

He caught her face between his hands and looked deeply into her pale green eyes.

You were a better man than I, he said.

She stared into his eyes and said nothing.

She moved slowly out of his arms and sat up and began to pull off her black boots.

Let me do it, he said.

Quietly, with minimal effort, he dropped to his knees on the floor and took her right foot into his hands and pulled the black boot slowly and carefully from her foot. She wore no socks, he noticed. He took off her left boot and noticed for the first time the branded O on her heel. He touched his lips to it. Oscar Lourde, he thought.

He pushed her pant leg up over her knee, and when he began to run his tongue up her smooth, white shin, their eyes caught. Her eyes flashed heat, and he detected the dare he'd seen a few days ago, but he didn't want to make love. He wanted something else from her, something he doubted she'd ever given. He wanted to touch her, just that, to touch her like she'd first touched Luther Wolfe, like she'd touched him.

He gently pushed her back on the bed, and instead of crawling on top of her, he knelt quietly beside her as she had knelt beside him last night in the desert. Their eyes caught again, and he knew she understood what he wanted.

Carefully he reached for the zipper on her pants, and when she made no movement to stop him, he pulled it down and slipped the pants down her pale, muscled body, where they dropped to the floor. He looked at her breasts underneath her T-shirt. He couldn't get it out of his mind—the idea of her unbinding them and flinging that elastic band across her unmade bed of white cotton. He imagined her breasts, warm and unbound, as she fell backward into the whiteness.

When did you finally unbind yourself? he said quietly.

Two weeks ago, she said.

He gently took hold of her T-shirt and pulled it over her head.

Why then and not before? he asked.

He watched her breasts rise and fall in the white satin cups of her bra.

I was finally ready, she said.

He delicately touched the swell of her breasts, and then reached underneath and unhooked her bra. Their eyes caught again as he pulled the straps of her bra over her arms and dropped it to the floor.

He touched his lips to the tender white skin of her breasts, then slipped her from her underwear and looked down at her. This is what she'd seen when she'd first unbound herself, he thought. A woman.

You are beautiful, he said.

She didn't say anything, not thank you, not anything. She didn't smile either. She just stared at him, and he stared back. When he looked down at her naked body, it excited him, her long legs, her round, white breasts. He realized how very honored he felt to be the first to receive her body after it had been bound for so long. But when his lips touched her thigh, fear came to him. What if he wasn't enough? He glanced at her again, and her eyes said, Do it well. He kissed her then, her whole body, as gently as he'd ever kissed anything or anyone. He wanted to please her. He wanted to welcome her back. He wanted to end the way he'd been before he'd gotten on this train. He wanted to start another way. He wanted desperately to be someone else.

He kissed her delicately, her sides, her chest, her arms, her neck, then he opened her legs and kissed inside. The whole time she watched him, and when he was done, he crawled up next to her, and she held him in her arms.

She hugged him close to her, and he thought how she seemed both man and woman, like some incomprehensible but tremendous combination. When he saw himself in his mind's eye being held by a naked woman while he was fully clothed, lying in a beautiful room on a train amid white cotton sheets and red velvet drapes, while the train descended the mountains, he thought it was one of the few perfect moments of his life.

What are we now? he asked her quietly. Are we still a mixed-up man and a ridiculous woman on a train?

No, we're a clothed man and a naked woman on a train, she said.

He thought then about the woman he'd left and their children, one a year old, the other only one month, and he was glad she didn't know. He remembered how he'd felt out in the desert, how he'd been choked with guilt for what he'd done. He had realized then that he hadn't broken past anything; his guilt was the proof. Yes, he had thought, take all the cruel, dark, bastard impulses and deny them, and then watch them all turn inside, driving

themselves like spikes into the souls of every poor fucking bastard who ever believed for a minute they could be vanquished.

He remembered having opened his mouth and having howled
FUCK as loud as he could, feeling the pleasure of the anger in
his throat, and how afterwards a wave of relief had swept him,
and suddenly he had felt elated about what he'd done, all of it—
climbing on a train, telling the woman in the motel that he was
Oscar Lourde, leaving his life in ruins. He had relished the idea
of the broken dishes, the heaved chairs, the overturned table, their
screams. There had been a certain gratifying pleasure in having
inflicted the suffering, rather than in turning it against himself.
He had even stopped in the road to savor it.

He remembered standing there wondering, was this freedom?
Had he made it happen? Had he broken beyond all that had
bound him? And his heart had pounded, and he thought, perhaps
he'd done it. But when he had tried to see what lay beyond the
narrow lines of thought he'd always had, what other ideas there
were, what other thoughts, wanting desperately to have them, to
think them, to imagine what had never before been imagined,
nothing had come to his mind. There had only been the desert and
his heart, which had pounded in dread.

He had wondered then, what if he kept going? What if he
followed his darkest impulses, all of them? What would he have
then? And he had seen destruction, nothing but destruction, and
he had wondered, was there nothing else? Was there only guilt
or destruction?

It was then that he had heard his own voice in his throat, a
sob, and in the intolerable silence that had followed he had discerned his own unbearable smallness, the limits of his own mind,
of his own reason, and he had understood how utterly imprisoned he was by them. He had felt his chest tighten, the asthma
attack coming on swiftly. It had felt serious, the constriction, so
severe he feared he might pass out. He had gasped for air and
had pulled the inhaler from his pocket and breathed in as deeply
as his lungs allowed. He had closed his eyes then and had struggled to wait for it to work, struggled not to panic and make it
worse. The panic he had had as a boy had been unbearable. He
had wondered if it was the desert, if it was the air out there, if it

was the fact that there were no boundaries, nothing to contain or confine him, as if the desert were creeping up on all sides of him and stealing inside.

He had stood there, his head pounding, as if the desert might hand him something, and then, with nothing left to do, he had turned and headed back to her.

The memory of this disturbed him, and he reached out now and traced her mouth with his finger.

Was this story true? he asked quietly.

She turned to him and smiled.

Was it?

What do you think? she said.

I want to believe it's true, he said, but I don't know.

She smiled.

So she wouldn't tell him, he thought. He would be left to wonder, along with everything else. What if it were all just a metaphor, her story? he thought. The knife scars, the O on her heel, gotten elsewhere, incorporated, imported into her story to give it some validity, some proof. Perhaps she was not Hemy Lourde, but had another name. Perhaps something like this had happened to her, but only in its essence, not the same details, but some others. Would this alter the truth of it in any way?

She sat up, and he watched her put her long arms through the straps of her bra and hook it in back with deft fingers. She then pushed her legs into her black pants and pulled her white T-shirt over her head.

She lay down next to him and turned to him and said, Now, can we talk about nothing, like I like?

All right, he said.

But while they made things up, like what they would do if this happened or if that happened, or the way it should have been or the way they meant it to have been, he found himself wondering what she would do now. While her hands motioned up and down when she talked, and she made sound effects and spoke in accents, he couldn't stop thinking how her life lay in ruins behind her. Then, in the midst of their random, floating topics, he heard his voice, inserted like a knife.

What are you going to do now?

I don't know, she said.

You must have some idea, he said.

I don't, she answered. Not yet. Do you?

No, he said.

They went back to talking about nothing, like she liked, and while he watched her hands moving as she talked, as if they were a shadow of her words, he found himself wondering what it meant to change the course of history. A question came to him— whether or not she had altered the course of his life. Though he didn't like to admit it, he thought that she had, yet he couldn't say exactly how. Even so, it made him sad at the same time—it seemed such a small thing. He wanted her life to have a larger consequence than merely changing the course of his life. Yet could something so small as altering the course of his life constitute changing the course of history? He thought of that, of how she might have altered something in him which might cause him to do something, which might in turn alter the course of another history, of a person or an event. It seemed so difficult and time-consuming, so tedious, mundane, especially when she had spoken of greatness.

He didn't know how it happened, but he fell asleep, and when he woke up, it was light out already. He saw that she was on her knees, packing her suitcase.

They just announced that we'll be in Los Angeles in fifteen minutes, she said.

He quickly glanced out the window and saw the brown, bloated mountains of southern California. He felt a panic rise inside of him. He sat up and put his feet on the floor.

What are you going to do when we get to L.A.? he said.

I want to see the ocean, she said.

Why? he asked.

I am impressed by its indifference, she said. By its ceaselessness. How it is beautiful and yet cruel at the same time.

Can I come with you?

No, she said.

It was the first time she had said no to his coming with her, and it wounded him, especially now.

Why not?

I want to be alone now.

Why now?

Just because, she said. That's all.

She looked over at him.

You will be all right, she said.

She went back to her packing, and he felt the sting of tears in his eyes, but he forbade them.

Will I ever see you again? he said.

I don't know, she said. How could I know?

Will you go back to New York?

Yes, she said. Zellie is there.

Good, he said.

Why? she said. Do you live in New York?

Yes, I do.

But she didn't ask him where, and he suspected she didn't want to know, as if knowing would somehow bind her to him, and he sensed she was not interested in being bound to him, or to anyone.

When she was finished packing her suitcase, she sat down next to him and pressed his hand between hers.

I shall never forget you, she said.

Spare me, he said.

He looked away quickly, over his shoulder, out the window. The palm trees looked so incongruous to him—so willowy and full of cheer.

She touched her lips to his neck, and though he wanted himself to remain aloof, he wrapped his arms around her instead and pulled her tightly to his chest, where he breathed in the scent of her hair, of her skin.

Why did you tell me your story? he whispered.

As an offering, she said.

An offering to whom? he said.

But she only smiled, and he knew she would never say.

He couldn't help but wonder again why this experience had awaited him on the train and not some other. Why a woman on a train who had lived as a man, and not a murderer or an adulteress or an ordinary man? He wondered if something in the psyche had the power to order circumstances, to bring about a certain collision, and then look purely random? Had he and the woman on the train been drawn to one another by something inexplicable? Drawn to one another because of the stories of their bodies? He thought of what she had written: the hesitancy of the mind to relinquish the story of the body's greatest suffering. The thought of it stabbed him. He hated to think that one day he would have to let up the story of his body's greatest suffering. He feared he was even less equal to truth than she.

He took her face into his hands and searched her eyes.

Did you learn to love like a man? he said.

I don't know, she said. Does it seem so?

But he could no longer articulate his thoughts. There was so little time left, and he didn't know how to spend it, what to do with it, how to make the most of it. He finally pulled her to him and held on to her, and she held him back, and all the while the train kept moving, pulling towards Los Angeles, inexorably, it felt, as though nothing could stop it.

He wondered what he would do when she left, but he didn't yet know. He imagined himself alone in some Los Angeles hotel, sitting on the floor, his back up against a wall, stripped down to the waist. He wondered if he would watch his breath, like Lausy Hayes or Leopold Harry, asking for a fate. He didn't know, but somehow he liked the idea that she would stretch out on a cool wooden floor somewhere, her pale, determined body yearning for her fate.

It disturbed him now, the idea of Bo's words being reinterpreted. Instead of *You have a great fate. You will change the course of history,* it would be *I know what happened to you, your fate is going to be strange. I wish I could change the course of your history.* It simply wasn't grand or eloquent, and he wanted to believe that despite everything, there was something grand, something eloquent.

Do you think you still have a great fate? he said. He knew it was ridiculous, but he had to ask.

She looked at him and smiled.

Will you change the course of history?

She tipped her head back and laughed with great abandon, richly and abundantly, in that way he'd come to love.

No, really, he said. I want to know.

But she said nothing, and the train began to slow down on the outskirts of Los Angeles.

Just tell me one more thing, he whispered.

She kissed his mouth and said, All right then. The story is over.

She took ahold of his hand, and he knew it was true, that within moments she would be gone, that he would be left with his own breath and beating heart, with his own story.

·A NOTE ON THE TYPE·

The typeface used in this book is a version of Palatino, originally designed in 1950 by Hermann Zapf (b. 1918), one of the most prolific contemporary type designers, who has also created Melior and Optima. Palatino was first used to set the introduction of a book of Zapf's hand lettering, in an edition of eighty copies on Japan paper handbound by his wife, Gudrun von Hesse; the book sold out quickly and Zapf's name was made. (Remarkably, the lettering had actually been done when the self-taught calligrapher was only twenty-one.) Intended mainly for "display" (title pages, headings), Palatino owes its appearance both to calligraphy and the requirements of the cheap German paper at the time—perhaps why it is also one of the best-looking fonts on low-end computer printers. It was soon used to set text, however, causing Zapf to redraw its more elaborate letters.